A
STATE
OF
FEAR

Jo

GIBSON SQUARE

This edition first published in 2017 in the UK by

Gibson Square

UK Tel: +44 (0)20 7096 1100
US Tel: +1 646 216 9813

rights@gibsonsquare.com
www.gibsonsquare.com

ISBN   9781783340743
eISBN   9781908096357

*Papers used by Gibson Square are natural, recyclable products made from wood grown in
sustainable forests; inks used are vegetable based. Manufacturing conforms to ISO 14001,
and is accredited to FSC and PEFC chain of custody schemes. Colour-printing is through
a certified CarbonNeutral® company that offsets its CO2 emissions.*

Printed by CPI in the UK.

1

Julie was never at ease in the City. Each time she came there seemed more cameras, today she saw police dogs, and Finsbury Circus was the closest to the centre she could park. Keeping their guard up, she supposed, even if the Olympic games had passed off safely. Walking back to her meeting she resolved to get away quickly. It wasn't just the security. Everything made her feel that she didn't belong, as if the buildings themselves looked down at her loftily, like dumb men flush with cash.

It was because of two men that she had come, neither of them stupid, though both a source of trouble in her life. First there was Martin, her husband of six years, from whom she had separated; the second was her father, Duncan, whose advice not to marry Martin had proved so galling. Now Duncan was acting nobly: refraining from reminding her of his warnings, he had put her in touch with his City solicitors to discuss a divorce. Entering their marble-clad premises she was grateful for his eagerness to foot the bill.

The meeting went better than expected. Instead of a dried-up lawman, she found herself talking to a woman her own age, confiding about Martin in a way she'd done with no one else. Not that there was any mystery about how they'd got to where they were. She was an able, professional woman who had fallen for a male of childlike insouciance.

She was drawn to his playfulness, he relied on her rigour. The illusion had been to think that a balance would establish itself over time, but it hadn't happened. Insouciance had turned to drunkenness, and instead of him loosening her self-constraints in the way she half-wanted, she'd felt herself hardening at his fecklessness.

Only alcohol, no drugs? the solicitor enquired, making her notes, her eyes in neutral. Only the vodka, Julie replied. Once she'd asked him why, and he told her: he'd done drugs early because he'd had the money, and got over them early too, after some bad experiences. There could be advantages to being a spoiled youth.

Martin wasn't a bad man. He didn't tell lies, he made things up, then convinced himself they were true. A child might sober him, she had thought, but she'd been wrong there too; Jackie turned out to be another responsibility for him to escape. Now their trial separation was coming to an end she had decided to make it permanent. The solicitor did not seek to dissuade her.

A nervy wind had sprung up, and she began hurrying. Her route back to the car took her along Threadneedle Street, past the Bank of England. A starchily-dressed woman her own age emerged from its vast bronze doors as she went by. Accosted by an American in blazer and slacks holding out a map, the woman pointed up at the façade in an expert manner; an economist, Julie guessed.

That was what her father had wanted Julie to be; one reason she became a doctor. Did she too look the part? She glanced down at herself: pink shirt, dark trouser suit and ankle-length boots were on the prim side, and older than her thirty-four years. Though that was for the solicitor: proof that she was not the guilty party.

On an island across the road from the Bank a silver-haired black man holding a white cross bigger than himself was encamped with a couple of others. So much for all the security. Amber alert, the papers said, and here were people demonstrating yards from the Bank. In the solicitor's waiting room she'd read an Evening Standard piece about them. Demonstrations outside the Bank had been recently banned, so the question was whether a silent reminder of Our Lord outside a temple of Mammon constituted a demonstration. The law concluded that it didn't, so the men with their cross had stayed.

She walked faster. She was late, her car might be ticketed, school would be out and Jackie would be waiting. On the corner of Old Broad Street she caught sight of the Gherkin. It was the first time she'd seen it and for a moment she slowed to stare. It was then that, with a languorous growl, the bomb exploded.

*

Normal time ceased, then resumed, seconds later, more slowly. She had spun round at the blast. Smoke was advancing on her like a flood, rising and cresting at second, third, then fifth storey level. The billows carried fragments of cars or windows like debris in a surging wave.

She plunged into Old Broad Street, and ran. She turned to look as the smoke surged past the corner. Seeing it veer towards her, as if giving chase, she tore on at panic speed. At the junction with London Wall she slowed and bent double, winded.

Between intakes of air, she thought: something at the Bank. She waited for someone who might have seen more than her, but no one came. Was she the last to get away? There could be dead and injured, people needing help. She walked back, professionally calm, in the direction of the cloud.

Sirens were sounding. A police van raced along the road behind her. It slowed as it passed and a policeman opened the window an inch.

'Where you going?'

'The Bank.'

'Turn around, go back.'

He pointed towards Finsbury Circus.

'I'm a doctor.'

'We have specialists. Later you can help. Right now you'd better help yourself. Get the hell under cover!'

'Specialists? For what?'

Past the driver, in the rear of the van, she caught a glimpse of policemen struggling into polyethylene jumpsuits and respirators. The turquoise suits seemed designed to alarm. Given leave to look to herself she ran back towards Finsbury Circus, to her car.

More police vans, one of them announcing:

'A radioactive explosion has occurred in the vicinity of the Bank of England. Pedestrians should stay calm and take cover immediately, anywhere they can. Breathe through a folded handkerchief till you can find shelter.'

Radiation? Jackie would be waiting for her at her school, near Aldgate. Waiting uncovered, in the school's rooftop garden. Exposed to the air, five floors up.

The streets were emptying fast, people who'd begun pouring from shops and offices rushing back in as they heard the announcement. Should she try getting to Jackie – or take cover? *Pull on your own oxygen mask before trying to help your child.* The airline safety briefing had always seemed sensible, but there'd been no briefing for this, and her child came first. She ran on as fast as she could. Roads were being cordoned off, people turned away, she'd never make it to her car, to the school.

She turned right, into Camomile Street. Another police van, its driver signalling to her brusquely to get under cover. She looked round. Ahead, a short parade of shops: a cleaners, a beautician, a chemist. Four-storied houses in dirty brick with an end-of-lease look to them, amidst proud new buildings. The chemist seemed the most obvious refuge, and she dashed for the entrance. The doorway was jammed, the last people on the street piling in, then yelling to close the door. The cleaners too was full: a dozen startled faces in the window, an assistant in the process of bolting the door. Julie threw herself into the entrance to the Marusak Beauty Salon, shoving the door as it was closing.

'No more room ! There is pub on corner!'

A blonded woman of fifty was putting her weight to the door to keep her out. Julie was stronger and struggled in.

'Why you have to –'

'– the police told us to take cover.'

'But there is pub. It is me Mrs Marusak, this my shop. I not allow –'

Julie brushed past.

It was a small salon, four hairdressers' chairs back to back. Five people filled the space, none of them customers it seemed. The beautician sat on a high stool at a counter, her loose white coat open on a frank display of leg. An indolent-looking creature, unlikely to be proficient in the list of services behind her: Nail extensions, Eye-lash perm, Basic Bikini, G-String Bikini, Stress relief massage, Detox scrub. With no idea what was going on, the girl scowled at this unglamorous irruption of people.

Besides Julie there was the elderly American she'd seen outside the Bank. Then a lean man of forty carrying a newly cleaned suit, an older, spivish-looking fellow with a dated, thin moustache, and an Asian girl dressed in garishly Western clothes: a high tank top exposing an enviably flat stomach, and a denim skirt worn low on her hips. Lavishly applied lipstick and diamante clips in her hair jarred with pallid, distraught features.

Reluctant to sit, for some minutes the refugees from the streets stood in the narrow alley between the empty chairs. Meanwhile Mrs Marusak – a pulpy, over-powdered face atop a stalwart body – blustered about, swearing and shouting orders. She was finishing bolting the door top and bottom when there was a commotion outside.

Forced from the road by a police car, a van had crashed into a lamppost. They watched as a policeman in anti-radiation gear sprang out, wrenched the van door open and, yanking out the driver – a boy in overalls – marched him to the beautician's and banged at the glass.

'We full!' Mrs Marusak shrieked.

The policeman went on banging.

'Open the bloody door!'

Spitting obscenities – it sounded like *yebjena maty* – Mrs Marusak complied, and the police pushed their catch inside. Black and muscular, the boy was red-eyed and desperate-looking. At the same moment a road worker in a yellow jacket appeared from nowhere, jostled past the policeman, and slipped in as well.

'Silly fuckers, I was all right in the van', the boy was shouting. 'Why they pull me out?'

Mrs Marusak finished re-bolting the door and turned to her

charges, all still standing.

'Sit down, sit down, you stand up I cannot move.'

Julie took a place, indicating to the American that he should take another. The Asian girl hesitated over a beautician's chair.

'There is chair, sit in it! You think I charge for sitting?'

Seeing it vacant the black boy limped towards the fourth chair – he'd banged his leg in the crash – and slumped into it. A mistake.

'You dirty clothes on my chair! And where I sit?'

He got up, wincing, and found a ledge to squat on, next to the road worker. Mrs Marusak stayed standing.

Everyone except the Asian girl was on their mobiles, each with a finger in an ear against the sirens and blaring announcements in the street. In the salon itself there was silence: the lines were jammed, no one was getting through. At a signal from Mrs Marusak the girl behind the counter, less dozy by now, hid the phone.

After hanging on for some minutes in mute determination the people in the chairs gave up and confronted themselves in the mirror, dead mobiles in hand. To escape the fear on their faces one by one they swivelled round, only to see it confirmed in others' eyes.

*

To Julie the anxious faces were reminiscent of her surgery. Should she announce she was a doctor? It went against her training and her instincts, but she decided not to. The delivery boy looked bad, so did the American, but what could she do? Telling them would excite expectations of more than she could deliver. Someone had written, she recalled from nowhere, that the English were the world's nurse, but for now the world would have to do without her: nurse was having trouble biting back her own misery. Fearful for herself – she seemed to have been on the streets an age after the explosion – she was terrified for Jackie.

How wide would the radiation spread? How long would she have spent in the playground, before taking cover? She'd have been the last to go in, stubborn as her mother. Come inside, it's dangerous. What is? Radiation, you can't see it. But I want to see it, so where is it? How can it be dangerous if you can't see it?

She thought back to the accident and emergency manual she'd skimmed during training. Ebola outbreaks, chemical spills and yes, something about the risk of radiation incidents. RDD – radiation dispersal device – the name came back now. Otherwise all she could remember was that children would be most at risk. She pictured Jackie's thin body and pellucid skin, no barrier against the cancer-inducing rays.

The room was still quiet.

Julie said, 'Is there a television?'

Mrs Marusak began raising a prohibiting arm but the beautician had already gone to the back room, returning with a portable set.

A woman announcer was confirming that the explosion at the entrance to the Bank had been a dirty bomb. There'd been a number of instant deaths, the bombers included. An unknown but larger number would be injured through radiation. She began reading off symptoms: vomiting, nausea, diarrhoea – the words came strangely from the smartly coiffured announcer, sterile and secure in her glass box.

Watching the screen the Asian girl began sobbing. The road worker shouted at her: 'shut it, darlin', and listen.'

The Metropolitan Police are advising people sheltering in covered premises to stay where they are until evacuation can be arranged. Rescue personnel cannot be exposed to unnecessary risk, so this may take time. Priority will be given to those who were nearest the explosion, and who show the most severe symptoms.

A wan smile, meant to be encouraging, did nothing to soothe feelings in the salon, as they decoded what the announcer was saying: that if you felt nothing much for four hours or longer you could be OK, but if you vomited or your bowels melted within an hour, you were dead.

After the list of symptoms came the first-aid measures – a briefer section. All anyone worried about contamination could do, the announcer seemed to be telling them, pitying again, was to take off the outer layer of their clothing, and shower.

People in the salon studied their clothes, as if expecting to see a layer of lethal dust they could brush away. Then heads turned to Mrs Marusak. A collective imperative this time.

Her chubby arms spread in helplessness:

'When we have accident in Chernobyl in my country people have no shower, or when they shower it not help. Anyway you want shower it is there.' She indicated the back room. 'In bathroom.' She gestured to the beautician, 'Anya, give me towels.'

The girl took a pile from a cupboard and handed them to her. Tight-mouthed, Mrs Marusak began counting them out, with a disapproving eye on the road worker, the delivery boy and the Asian girl.

'Maybe some people need wash anyway,' she observed, standing back from the roadworker as she delivered his towel.

'Any more showers upstairs?'

Julie pointed to a door at the rear of the back room.

'No, upstairs not ours.'

'There must be another bathroom up there. This is an emergency.'

'We not go upstairs.'

Julie went to the door, tried it. It was locked. Before she could say anything Mrs Marusak, agitated, shouted across:

'No key. No key. Cannot go upstairs.'

With a last wrench at the handle – it was locked firmly – Julie gave up.

'Ladies first,' said the elderly American, gesturing to Julie and the Asian girl with his spectral smile.

'We'll be quick,' Julie promised.

Hurrying out of her top clothes in the small room she signalled to the Asian to go into the bathroom first. The girl went in, snapped the lock shut.

'Don't lock the door,' Julie instructed mechanically from outside. A pause, and the lock clicked back.

'And don't use any conditioner. It'll glue in the radiation. Radiation sticks to hair, and yours is long.'

The detail from the manual had sprung to mind, unbidden.

Again she dialled Jackie's school. This time she got through. There was an automated answer:

We are sorry we cannot respond to individual enquiries. All the children are now inside the premises and parents will be informed when it is safe for them to be evacuated.

Now inside? Only now? Oh God.

In the other room, with a glance at Mrs Marusak, the road worker and the boy stripped off their outer clothes and wrapped themselves in towels. In their socks and underwear they formed a pocket of rank air in the scented salon. The boy's strong build made his nervily defiant look all the stranger, the offence-seeking eyes at odds with the muscled body.

The workman, a stocky figure topped with a sheaf of reddish hair, rolled his jacket and trousers into a bundle and held it out. He was signalling 'where do I put these?', but to Mrs Marusak it was an order to take them. Up went the interdicting arms, as she backed away.

'In bin!' The workman made for a plastic bin. 'Not here, *durak*, the big bin, at back. All nuclear clothes,' she called out so everyone could hear, 'in metal bin at back.' The worker moved towards it. Mme Marusak barred his way. 'Women in there first. When it your turn.' The worker obeyed, holding his bundle away from his body, tentatively. Observing all this, the black boy did the same.

The man holding the cleaned suit had placed it on a peg, stroking it into position so it hung neatly. (He turned out to be a banker, and French). In a matter-of-fact way he took off his jacket and trousers and, his towel round his waist, waited. The American, still in his chair, did nothing. His reddening face looked resigned.

The Asian girl had been in the bathroom a few minutes when Mrs Marusak stormed into the back room and banged the door.

'What you doing?' she shouted, opening it as she spoke. The girl, naked under the shower in the bath, turned to face her. In the instant before she could cover herself Mrs Marusak surveyed the neat breasts and cambered hips. As the girl bent to reach for the towel her eyes ran to her buttocks.

'You take long time. You hurry,' she said after a silence.

'Too much foreigners,' she whispered to Julie, closing the bathroom door. To distinguish those she had in mind from herself she passed a flattened palm across her face as she spoke. 'That is how English have terrorists. Too much foreigners.'

It was another few minutes before the girl came out. Her make-up was gone, her towel stretched carefully from throat to calf. A smaller towel she'd found in the bathroom covered her head like a shawl. Mrs Marusak hurried over and pulled it off.

'Two towels, why you need two towels? Aiya! What she do?'

The girl's hair had been cut short, hacked away with scissors she'd found in a cupboard. Without it her face looked young and pure, like a choirboy's. Now the shawl was off Julie could see a patch of flesh on her neck striated with blood, as if by cat scratches. Mrs Marusak smirked and whispered:

'Maybe she punish herself? Is their religion, no?'

'The loofah. She's scrubbed too hard with the loofah. Do you have Savlon or something?'

Anya brought ointment. Julie applied it over the brown, superfine skin. The girl veered from her touch, but thanked her.

'What's your name?'

'My name? ... Safia.'

'Scrubbing yourself till you bleed won't help wash it off, Safia. Radiation can get into cuts and abrasions. Just soap and water.'

Julie took her turn in the shower, followed by the road worker, the delivery boy, the Frenchman. The spivish man with the moustache next to Anya hadn't moved. When Julie looked in his direction – she'd begun playing nurse despite herself – he shook his head. He hadn't been in the street, Anya explained in cracked English. Nobody except

Julie seemed interested.

The American insisted on showering last. When he'd finished he came back to the salon in his shirt and trousers, with no towel. Mrs Marusak remonstrated, respectfully:

'No nuclear in here, please Sir. Trousers are nuclear. You take off trousers.'

'If you insist.'

The American smiled, went to the back room, returned with his towel round his waist, and sat.

Everyone stood or sat in towels, the women covered to the neck, the men in their vests. Safia's hand strayed to her hacked-off hair. Julie's shortish locks hung lank over her brow. Mrs Marusak surveyed her.

'You want Anya do your hair?'

'No,' said Julie. 'It doesn't matter.'

Safia did not receive the offer.

Everyone stared at the television.

'So what's your advice to people trapped in offices or shops?' the announcer was asking a police spokesman.

'If you're within a mile radius of the explosion you should keep the doors and windows closed. If you have very sick people and you can't get through on the emergency number put a sign in the window, and an ambulance will pick them up. Only the very sick please.'

Julie glanced round. The boy looked worse, and getting jumpy. With a defiant expression he took out a cigarette, lit it and began to smoke.

Mrs Marusak glared.

'What's your problem?' the boy shouted across at her. 'We're sittin' 'ere fuckin' dyin' of cancer and you're worried about a bit of smoke!'

Mrs Marusak found no reply. Testing her face and seeing her hesitate, the road worker pulled out his packet and lit up as well.

*

It was three quarters of an hour since the explosion. The TV had said it would be an hour before they knew. People began sitting abnormally still, glancing down at themselves from time to time, as if monitoring their innards.

Someone in overalls, giant gloves and a visor passed the window. No one remarked on him: it seemed natural, what you would expect, a fictional image turned to fact. Then there were more, a whole troop of them. The rescuers didn't stop at the salon.

The TV was showing a map of the area affected, with concentric waves pulsing from the Bank. Julie examined it for the school, her eyes searching for something she did not want to find. If it had been hit they'd have singled it out for mention, a primary school... The longer they didn't the greater the chances...

But it was there, inside the danger zone, just, within the one mile band. Halifax Street Junior. Would it get that far? A lot would depend on wind direction...

'A plume of radioactivity is believed to have drifted eastwards…'

Eastwards towards the school... She tried her mobile again. The same recorded message, this time with an addition: 'We shall shortly be evacuated. The police have assured us we are a priority.'

'… Now back to Michelle in the studio…', a TV voice soothed.

Michelle's lips had a kind of frozen chirpiness, to buck people up, but again it came out wrong. She looked as though she was straining not to smile.

'It's almost exactly an hour since the explosion, and reports of the first radiation casualties are coming in…'

The smallest tremor of excitement heightened her voice, as if it were a prize draw or a boxing countdown.

'Emergency ambulance crews in protective suits are in operation. I apologise for the lack of pictures. This is for the safety of our crews. But viewers in the City area have sent these mobile photos in. I apologise for the quality...'

Hazy shots showed police and ambulances calling at an office building.

It was past the hour now, in their relief people had begun talking to one another, and as time went on the place began settling into a pattern, like a drawing room. The American was submitting to Mrs Marusak's attentions, the workman exchanging curses against Muslims with the boy (murderin' fuckin' bastards), extra loud for the benefit of Safia, who was sitting next to Julie, sobbing. Julie turned to them:

'How about keeping your voices down? And watching your language?'

'Sorry Miss.' The workman smirked. 'Didn't realise you was a Muslim-lover.'

The man with the moustache was chatting to Anya in Russian, as if passing the time of day. Talking to him Anya crossed and re-crossed her legs a lot.

Running low on amiabilities to exchange with Mrs Marusak, the American turned to Julie. His eyes were glassy now, his talk feverish. She half-heard him saying:

'Got a son at Morgan Stanley. Out of town today, cancelled on me at the last moment, the Lord be praised! I came early to have a look at the Bank of England, the Royal Exchange and the – Lordy, my memory! What's the other one?'

'Mansion House?'

'That's it, the Mansion House. All that history in a few square yards! Never seen the Bank till today. Can you believe it? Been coming here all these years and never got there.'

Julie signified that this was remarkable.

'First I couldn't find it – there's no brass plate. I had to stop a girl coming out – mousy thing she was, but I guess she's good at math. When I asked why there was no plaque she said 'Everyone knows it's the Bank. We don't have to advertise.'

'The interesting thing is'– Julie's eyes swivelled to the TV – 'is that modesty? Or kind of uppity?'

It was as if he were making conversation while sheltering from the rain. He was sweating now, Julie noticed, red and sweating.

'In America we'd have a sign the size of a house, in neon: '1694 this place goes back to, and don't anyone forget it!' Now if I was to meet that girl again, know what I'd say? I'd say well young lady, the Bank of England's sure got itself advertised now!'

The fellow smiled, alone. Julie went on trying to listen. Keeping a sick old American contented as he waited to discover his fate was a way of not thinking about Jackie. Therapy for them both.

All the while she was keeping an eye on Safia. The girl didn't look ill – no redness or fevered eyes – but seemed crushed and afraid. When her sobbing became more audible Julie took her hand. The girl half-withdrew it, then left it in hers. The hand was trembling.

'Try to stay calm. We're lucky to have found somewhere to shelter. With a bit of luck we'll be fine.' It was all she found to say. What else could she? 'You work round here?'

'I was looking for work.' The girl paused. 'And who are you?' she added, with caution rather than curiosity.

'I'm a doctor, Safia, my surgery's not far from here.' She leant closer: 'I work with many Muslim women.'

She felt the hand stiffen, then relax. Under probing the girl explained that she was frightened of her family's reaction when they found out she'd been alone in the City. She was an only child, she added, and her parents were strict.

The Frenchman, erect in his chair next to the beautician, had not spoken a word. When not working on his Blackberry he sat silent and aloof, glancing only occasionally at the television. The American turned to him:

'You visiting too?'

'I work here. I am a banker, from France. I just came out to get a suit from the cleaners before it closed.'

Soft and pale and with delicate glasses, he seemed frail-looking in his towel and singlet, and vulnerable in his socks.

'So you live here?' the American pursued.

'I lived 'ere.'

'You won't stay?'

'What do you think?'

M. Denizet, it emerged in their conversation, was one of the generation of Frenchmen who'd come to London a decade previously.

'At first it was fine. Then the recession. That was bad enough, but we stayed. But this… No, you cannot live with this.'

He seemed to be readying himself for his return as he spoke, getting more French by the minute. His lips were permanently sardonic, his right hand perpetually throwing something invisible over his shoulder. A gesture of abandon.

'The cleaners is next door. I just come out. I was exposed' – his lips became French again – 'for twenty seconds. Then I come in 'ere because in there was already full. Maybe the wave not reach me, I will recover. But this country…' The country, he indicated, would follow his mouth, downwards.

He waved his Blackberry.

'The Footsie is collapsing. 53 per cent down so far. Surreal! 'Alf your wealth gone in an hour! I 'ave never seen figures like that. Worse than when Lehman Brothers went down, much, much worse.'

Nobody reacting to his stock market summary, the Frenchman went quiet.

Julie's mind had gone back to Jackie. Suddenly her eyes swivelled to the TV.

'News is coming in of an explosion in the financial district of New York. Over to Steve Hardcastle, our American correspondent.'

'Thank you Michelle.' The gravitas of Hardcastle's tone was out of sync with his excited eyes. 'First reports suggest this was a dirty bomb that didn't come off. That is to say one where the explosion worked but failed to trigger the nuclear device. The police are talking about several dozen casualties from the blast – it could be more. It's morning here and it may have caught people on the way to work.'

'Tell us about what the authorities are saying, Steve.'

'Well Michelle, what they're saying is that the atrocity was evidently timed to coincide with the one in London. There's speculation that a simultaneous dirty bombing was meant to be the highlight of Al Qaeda's response to the killing of Bin Laden. As you know there've been a number of revenge attacks around the world, but this seems to have been the big one. It looks like the Americans may have been spared the dirty part, but –' shouting now to make himself heard above the sirens, the reporter jerked his head towards the smoke and flames in the background – 'the explosion alone has wreaked havoc in the heart of the financial district.'

'Presumably the Americans are as terrified as us.'

'Indeed. Though in a way it's not entirely unexpected.'

'How's that?'

'Because we know that terrorists have cased the New York Stock Exchange, the World Bank and the IMF in the past. The Bank of England would fit naturally into the pattern of economic targets. Assuming of course this was an Islamist attack.'

'Which of course we can't', Michelle interrupted, tight-mouthed. 'Thank you Steve.'

The room listened in silence. It was broken by the American.

'Which of course we can't…' With a grim smile he mimicked the announcer. 'Oh yes we can. Who else would it be?' He sighed. 'Jesus, Bin Laden, back from the deep.'

The workman shot him a puzzled look.

'What you sayin'?'

'I'm saying they buried him at sea, didn't they? Left him on the ocean bed like a dead monster, so as to be finished with him once and for all. But he's back, isn't he? Back from the deep. With a vengeance.'

'Should 'ave thought about vengeance before you did 'im in,' the workman shot back. 'Was always goin' to be a comeback, wasn't there, and now we got it. The Yanks take 'im out and the Brits get nuked. Brilliant.'

More than an hour and a half had passed and the nervous, broken conversations were draining away. The delivery boy sat on his ledge, silent now and strangely stiff. A smell around him was getting stronger. Guessing the problem, when the road worker moved away

Julie took his place.

'How did you come to be in the area?'

'On a delivery, wasn't I, round the corner from the Bank. Ran like a fucking rabbit back to the van, but I got a dose all right.'

'How do you know?'

'I could feel it.'

'But it's not like smoke you know.'

''Ow do you know what I feel?'

'Well of course I don't.'

She said it quietly, to win confidence, building up to her big line.

'You're sure you don't want to go to the lavatory?'

'I'm not a fucking baby!'

The boy was sitting rigidly now, his hands gripping his ledge. The smell from him had become a stench.

'You must go to the lavatory,' she whispered.

'Who are you to tell me –'

'– I'm a doctor. What's your name?'

'Kingman,' the boy forced out.

'Well Kingman, I'm the only doctor here and I'm trying to do what's best for you.'

He hung on for a minute more, finishing his cigarette. Then stubbed it against the wall, slid from the ledge and covered the ten paces to the back room in small steps, pulling up his towel between his legs as he walked, like a giant nappy.

Grimacing, Mrs Marusak sprayed perfume where he'd been sitting, looked around, then squirted it everywhere, with fiercely triggered finger and downturned mouth. The workman had turned off the ventilation, as the TV had instructed, to reduce the inflow of contaminated air, and by the time she'd finished the atmosphere in the salon, a mixture of scent and faeces, seemed sicklier than before.

From the toilet they could hear the boy sobbing.

'We get him out,' Mrs Marusak announced. 'He will spread nuclear. He is priority.'

Julie asked for paper, pen and Selotape, wrote out a notice and stuck it in the window: VERY SICK BOY HERE.

Talk was at an end, everyone staring at the television. There were pictures now, including shots of the street they could see through the salon windows. Images of people like themselves, staring from shops and offices across the poisoned emptiness. Picking out close-ups – a child swaddled in a towel, as if readied for bed, a floppy-haired young banker, heroically bare-chested – the cameramen had been unable to resist a brunette gazing from a display window. Her towel had slipped from a shoulder, making her alluring in her distress, like a tart in an Amsterdam street.

The boy still hadn't come back from the lavatory when the American got up and strode shakily to the bathroom. The noise of the television helped disguise his retchings. Minutes later he returned, one hand holding up his towel, the other wiping his lips with a handkerchief.

'Maybe just nerves.' A compassionate Mrs Marusak. 'They say some people sick with nerves.'

'No, I was closer,' the American said in an all-things-considered voice, standing at the door, looking out. 'A deal closer than you.' He nodded at Julie. 'I saw you running, way ahead of me. My age, you can't scuttle along like that. I got here quicker by a back street. I didn't get hit by anything, but I felt a kind of burning. Burning needles.'

There was no room for them to shrink away as he passed them to resume his seat. Once there, instead of sitting down he stood, thought a moment, then turned to Mrs Marusak.

'Well thanks for the shelter. It was worth a try. I don't think there's much point me hanging on here. With due respect to you all, if I'm in trouble I'd like to be with my wife. We're staying in a place just north of Finsbury Circus, so I can walk it. Good luck.' He did his best to smile. 'Pity about the Bank. 1694…'

Shaking his head the American went to the backroom and returned carrying his trousers, his shirt, his jacket. Walking to the door he unbolted it, slipped out swiftly, shook his trousers in the entrance then eased them on under his towel, like an old man on the beach.

Then his shirt and jacket and, with no appearance of hurry, walked off along the street, out of view.

He was gone before Julie realised what was happening. She ought to have stopped him, she thought, or at least tried.

'You see what he did with clothes?' Mrs Marusak was close to tears. 'He didn't want to shake nuclear at us. A gentleman. But what if it only nerves? He get second dose.'

'He's old.' The road worker, Steve, shrugged. 'Eighty if he's a day. If I was that age I'd have done the same.'

An ambulance screamed past as he spoke.

'Maybe they pick him up?' Mrs Marusak said.

*

People's mobiles had begun ringing, and soon only Safia and Julie hadn't had a call. Then Martin rang.

It was five months since she'd seen him. Time and the rancour of their last meeting had left a wariness, even now.

'How's Jackie?'

'Still at school.'

'It's outside the limit, right?'

'No it's in. Just in.'

'Oh no! Oh Jesus! But maybe she was inside?'

No point in reminding him about the roof garden. Julie had moved to the East End after their split, and he'd been to collect her from school only once. He wouldn't remember.

'I tried to drive there,' Martin continued, 'soon as I heard, but I couldn't get through. What's happening? Are you there?'

'No.'

'You're on your way?'

'I'm in the City.'

'The City? Why? Where?'

'Taking cover in a shop about a quarter of a mile from the Bank.'

'You didn't –'

'– we'll find out when they come to get us.'

'Oh God, Julie, oh God. What the hell were you doing in the City?'

Seeing a solicitor, to discuss a divorce, she decided not to answer. Because I'd thought long and hard and concluded that the trial separation I'd agreed to – conditional on you weaning yourself off the bottle, you'll remember – wasn't working. Because you weren't adult enough to do it. I would have gone for a cheaper lawyer but my father said he'd pay. And we deserve the best, don't we? Break up in style. Money matters because after four months here it was obvious that though the primary school's OK – just – letting Jackie go to a secondary in the area is out of the question.

At the one I'd had lined up when I came there've been three knifings in as many months. One of them rushed from the pavement straight into my practice, a fifteen-year-old gushing blood. So it has to be private. I'd begun saving every penny to avoid the humiliation of going to Duncan for cash, after telling him he was hopelessly prejudiced about state education and that the schools round here were fine.

And all this because I can no longer rely on you for anything, absolutely nothing. So that's how I've come to be where I am. Don't feel guilty.

She said: 'I had to go to a solicitors.'

'What for?'

His voice was fearful.

'How important do you think these things are, Martin, in the present situation? Anyway I can't talk here. I'll ring when I get out.'

'Keep me informed about Jackie.'

'Where are you?'

'At home. Kensington. I'm supposed to be on the road to Birmingham. Assignment for Mark Pelling, at the paper. Has this hunch there could be a nasty reaction up there, more than in the South. Looks like I'll be running up and down for some time, keeping an eye. Maybe I shouldn't go? Is there something I can do for you? Or Jackie?'

She had difficulty thinking of him as a journalist, rooting out facts. He'd fancied himself an actor, but it hadn't worked. He had the imagination – a surplus of that – though not the discipline. It was thanks to a contact of his father's that he'd found a niche in one of the dailies, where travel pieces and features proved an outlet for his fantasy.

'An assignment? Well you'd best go ahead. We're stuck here for God knows how long, but we're safe. And the school's being evacuated.'

'But you say you may have got a dose.'

'I'll be fine. I just can't talk. I'll ring. There are people I'm helping to look after, I've got to go now.'

She rang off. A rescue squad was passing. Mrs Marusak banged the window, pointed to the notice. One of them looked, hesitated, stopped, called ahead to his mates. She stood at the door, shouting through:

'We have sick boy, very sick. He has – ' she pointed to her backside '– in less than hour.'

Minutes later a small ambulance pulled up. A paramedic got out and signalled that they weren't coming in, that the patient should be passed out. The ambulance backed onto the curb, so the doors faced the salon entrance.

Kingman, whimpering now, stood at the door clutching his soiled towel. He didn't say goodbye; nobody except the road worker and Julie said goodbye to him. Julie held his arm and wished him luck.

In the instant the salon and ambulance doors were open Safia made a rush from the back of the room, pushed a rescuer aside and scrambled into the ambulance after Kingman.

'The fuck she doin''? he screamed from inside. 'Get that cunt out of here!'

Disregarding her flapping towel and naked legs the paramedics, brawny fellows, lifted her from the ambulance, thrust her back into the salon and rammed the door closed. Safia lay inside, shrieking and flailing till Mrs Marusak subdued her with an almighty backhand smack.

'When I young I work in Ukraine prison', she announced to the room with satisfaction. 'They teach us to do this.'

Safia was on the floor, half-stunned, her back to the door and the towel rucked to her waist, exposing delicate thighs in largish knickers. With her mad hair she looked crazed.

'Prostitute in my salon!' Mrs Marusak pointed at her crotch. Safia covered up. 'You not priority case, but you are afraid, no? Muslim make bombs and Muslims are afraid. Is good you are afraid!'

Safia sobbed loudly. Julie knelt down and held her.

'I just wanted a check-up,' she said when she had calmed.

'We all want check-ups, darlin'.' Steve, who had eyed her frankly when she was sprawled on the floor, looked away as he spoke. 'But we don't all rush the ambulance, do we? We wait our turn. That's how we do things in this country. Time you learned.'

'I want to go to the bathroom.'

Julie helped her there.

'Do you feel…?' She pointed to Safia's stomach.

'No, just normal.' The woman indicated the toilet. 'Leave me here.'

'Wait.'

Before letting her close the door Julie ripped the plugs from the bath and, in an afterthought, from the hand-basin. A bit of basic training that had come in useful.

'I'm coming in in two minutes,' she announced.

She stood in the doorway between the two rooms, waiting. One ear was trained to the bathroom for sounds of vomiting, the other to the shop front. The street was quiet again – they must have picked up the urgent cases – and the TV louder in the silence. Experts were rationalising, debating.

Probably a three-layered device, one of them was saying. Thermite – an incendiary material – on the outside, Semtex or TNT in the middle, and a quantity of isotope at the centre. Cesium-137, cobalt-60 or strontium-90, someone else chipped in. Of which strontium would be the nastiest, right?, a presenter interjected. Certainly, another scientist confirmed, oh Lord yes! So how would it work? the presenter asked. Well the radioactive stuff would turn to vapour and the thermite would be on fire and carry it into the atmosphere. And then the cancers. Though if the isotope wasn't triggered by the explosion you'd just get dead and wounded people. Which is what seems to have happened in New York?, the presenter said. Correct, the scientist nodded.

Yet another expert – the show seemed scrambled together – was brought in on a screen. He disagreed with the first. The impact of dirty bombs had been exaggerated, he insisted, the number of cancers after the Chernobyl disaster far less than thought. But you're overlooking the density of population and the wind, the first scientist shot back. The wind changed everything. And if it didn't cause horrific effects why would Al Qaeda do it? Fear, the sceptic interjected. Fear of anything nuclear. And we should avoid doing their job by talking it up.

At the words Al Qaeda the presenter looked mortified, but held her peace.

Julia listened, numbly. The exchange seemed schoolboyish, nerdy. There they were, imprisoned in their evil-smelling salon and desperate for diagnosis, while scientists squabbled about what might be killing them and how likely they were to die as they waited.

She rapped on the bathroom door.

'I'm coming in.'

'It's alright, I've finished.'

Safia came out. Composed again, she'd re-ordered her towel, dried her tears and tidied what was left of her hair.

On television an expert, scarcely troubling to mask his excitement, was saying that he'd just heard that it was Strontium 90. Not that anyone should be surprised. Medical treatments, nuclear power station waste – providing you knew where to look it wasn't as if it was hard to get hold of. So the most surprising thing about the attack, he concluded, smiling almost, was that it hadn't happened before.

*

An hour and twenty minutes later two ambulances drew up outside the window. A grudging cheer in the salon was cut short when the ambulance men began to evacuate the cleaners. About fifteen came out, all in towels, some of them holding plastic-wrapped clothes on hangers, as though determined they at least would be spared contamination.

Mrs Marusak banged the window, to no avail. In keeping with their space suits the rescuers were in robot mode, and no one so much as turned in her direction. After loading up at the cleaners they drove off.

'They may be leaving us till later because they've got our two sickest people,' Julie warned the three remaining. She was sounding officious, but officiousness, she was finding, helped keep her steady.

She was right. It was twenty minutes before they came. During that time nothing was said. People seemed locked into themselves, listless. The Frenchman and Steve sat opposite one another, making no pretence of having anything to communicate, while Anya chattered to her spiv softly, both of them smoking. Safia sat alone.

Seeing they were in for another wait Mrs Marusak plunged into a chair, summoned Anya and gave instructions. Anya put a cape round her and began massaging her face.

'Stress release massage', Mrs Marusak explained, articulating each syllable. 'In City women need. Now I need too.'

'Fifteen or thirty minutes?' Anya asked, sulkily.

'You do till I tell you to stop, stupid girl.' She half-turned to Julie. 'Maybe you like massage before go?' she offered through Anya's coaxing hands. 'A present.'

'Not me thanks. But maybe Safia?'

Encouraged by Mrs Marusak's frown Safia shook her head, declining an offer that hadn't been made.

To Anya's relief, after a few minutes Mrs Marusak struggled her head free:

'Enough. You don't do right.'

Hoisting her superb frame back onto her high stool, Anya rolled her eyes and filched another cigarette from her man friend.

When at last an ambulance came for them Mrs Marusak was cheery with farewells.

'Free pedicure for everyone who was here!' she called from her chair. 'If toenails not fall out.' No one responded. Uncertainty was a stranger to her face, but for a second it was there. 'English humour – no?'

Julia let the others get in the ambulance before her. Waiting by the door she glanced at the television, in time to see Michelle announce:

'Breaking news from America. Come in Steve Hardcastle.'

'Thank you Michelle. It seems scarcely credible but people close to the FBI are saying they've got the cell behind the explosion, a mere couple of hours after it happened. It was a group they'd been monitoring, I'm told. It seems one of them panicked when the nuclear element failed, and used a mobile. You won't like this bit Michelle, but I'm hearing they've found material at their base for another bomb. It looks like they were lining up a second strike. So nothing for our comfort there, I'm afraid.'

'Indeed not. Thank you Steve.'

2

Amer the Syrian craned towards the mirror, razor raised. Then lowered it to stare into the glass, turning this way and that to inspect himself one last time. The mirror showed an aquiline profile, to which a short, jutting beard gave an even sterner aspect, yet in the eyes there was a soft regret. He stroked the blade over the black, soaped hair several times, tenderly, before slicing in.

'The devil!'

A drop of blood ran over a cheek into the sink, to be absorbed by the sludgy remains of Turkish coffee.

'Amer, lemme help.'

Interrupting his press-ups Jayson levered himself to his feet.

'I am not an idiot. I can cut my own beard.'

'No one's sayin' you can't, brother.'

His offer refused, Jayson, from Trinidad and in his low twenties, got back down on his face in the corner, alongside his makeshift bed. Twenty-four done, seventy-six to go. It was days since they'd left the basement room and his lean torso, exposed by a grey-white singlet, was in need of exercise.

Amer went slowly with the razor, blinking and wincing, but by the time the press-ups were done the beard was off. As the Syrian stood drying his face Jayson sat on the floor against the bed, recovering. He stared ahead of himself, his nostrils crimped in distaste. It was the smell. The back of the room overlooked a dank concrete area enclosing a drain with a fractured cover. The stench of their morning excrement, disguised for a moment by the reek of coffee, infiltrated the barred window.

He looked up at Amer.

'You got cuts all over, brother. Should have let me do it. I used to shave people.'

'You were a barber?'

'No. I shaved people in prison.'

Amer stopped drying his face.

'They didn't tell me you'd been in prison. They said you'd been an electrician. They said you'd been in trouble, but not that you'd been in prison.'

Jayson said nothing. There were other things the Syrian didn't know. About his dead-beat father and pretty, Mexican mother, who when the father left them the day before his ninth birthday paid the bills the easiest way she could. Or the accident at the boxing club seven years later. Till then he'd been doing well, a nifty kid, a bit undersized but they were building him up, grooming him for professional fights.

Then the accident. He'd been sparring, fooling around really with an older kid, no headgear. He was dancing about, teasing the heavier fellow, scoring, and when it was over the bigger kid lost his cool. Just came at him when his guard was down and landed him one on the side of the head.

For a week he was concussed. When they let him out of hospital he said he was fine, wanted to get back to his training, to his career in the ring, but they told him no chance. And they were right. Physically he seemed undiminished but his reflexes had lost some of their speed. Not just that but he'd become generally a little slow. He could read things, learn things, do things, like the electronics course he'd completed in jail. In everything he did he was thorough, but slow.

'So you were in prison. What was it for?'

Jayson shook his head:

'I don't wanna talk about it, brother, I wanna forget. But Allah must have wanted me to be there, 'cos it was in prison I converted. And if my sins are forgiven and my life is one of piousness and righteousness, like they told me, and my heart is clean like a child born from its mother's womb, it's OK not to think 'bout it no more, ain't it? I don't have to confess nothin', like the infidels with their Pope.'

'You speak truly, brother. Though I would prefer to have known.

The conversion I knew about, but not the prison.'

He threw down the blood-spotted towel.

'There. You wouldn't recognize me, would you?'

Jayson studied the beardless Syrian. The truth was that he would: the face he saw was the same one as before, hairless. With his assertive jaw and nervily alert features he just looked like Amer, shaved. And he'd made a poor job of it.

Without a word he got up, went to the lavatory, came back with a length of toilet paper and began sticking bits to the Syrian's cheek, his chin, his neck. Amer thrust out his face as he did it, holding his body back. The Trinidadian was sweaty after his press-ups, but it wasn't that. In keeping his distance Amer had other reasons.

'Today we have to get out,' he announced through tight lips as Jayson worked, 'we can't go on cowering here like dogs forever.'

Finished, Jayson stepped back.

'You can't go out like this, brother. People will look.'

A smile almost broke through his dulled features. It was three years since he'd touched the heroin he'd begun dealing when his mother's earning power faded with her looks. The stuff that had got him a stretch in Port of Spain. After coming to London he'd found a young and rounded Somali wife, and it was Ayan who had kept him clean. But religion had taken over where the drugs left off, so that his face still had the trance-like insensibility of his injecting days. The disconnect between the lithe, strong body and the half-stupefied face was strange.

His ministrations completed, Jayson prowled the room.

'Hour or two and the cuts will dry. You're right, we gotta get out. Time I checked the equipment.'

At his words Amer turned his paper-stippled face sharply in his direction. A hand went to his mouth, the other jabbing at the ceiling.

'How many times have I told you not to speak of it?'

Jayson slumped onto his bed, cowed, as if expecting to be hit, but with the Syrian it was verbal. In a flush of courage he said:

'You talks about it, sometimes, brother. You're not patient with me. You oughta be nicer. Being nice to people is like an act of worship, Mohamed reckoned.'

'If I am impatient,' Amer said, 'it is to see Paradise.'

'Me too, brother.'

A table and two hard chairs were all that furnished the room, other than the makeshift beds. The Syrian had gone back to his and was squatting, cross-legged, head-down, writing in a notebook. A dozen of them were stacked against the wall, all in blue, with the crest of the Institute of Foreign Languages of a Midlands town stamped in black on the front.

Committing plans and maps to paper was not advisable, but he couldn't help it. Writing things down was like conversing with himself in clear, logical sentences, and Amer was fond of his written voice, liked seeing what he had to say. As for the notebooks falling into the wrong hands, he was happy to risk it: if the two of them were discovered the plan couldn't go ahead, and if they weren't and it did his writings would be a historical record. Like a great general's campaign plans, to be pondered and admired.

The paper he wrote on was lined, and Amer liked that too: it helped make his writing, manically neat already, more meticulous still. His grammar too was perfect, though his style a little turgid. At that moment he was writing under a sketched map:

Were the explosion to take place at the intersection, the result in terms of victims would be commensurately greater, calculations indicate, and hence more desirable.

The truth was that the tall man in drab and dirty Western clothes with toilet tissue stuck to his face saw himself as a person of refinement. His father was a rich Damascus lawyer, though also a drunk and a womaniser who mistreated his pious wife, which was why his God-fearing son turned against him.

The break came when Amer returned one evening to find his father beating her, this time with a strap. Their fight was little more than a clinch, but it was the end between them. Packed off to university in Cairo he took a course in religious studies, but here too there were problems. Too much dogma, his tutor sighed, too little sense of nuance. And you, you are no true Muslim, with your secret drinking and fornicating, was Amer's unvoiced reply.

His studies went badly, but there was compensation. Jamila was a student at the same university, one of the few who dressed correctly, and before long Amer became her boyfriend, if that is the word. She felt safe with this angular, austere young man who looked at her with fixated eyes, but never touched her. The trouble this time was that Amer's personality had congealed in his teens, whereas sweet-faced, long-lashed Jamila was developing, fast, and by their second term drinking mint-tea while he gazed at her with a kind of watchful worship was not enough.

Sensing that she was clearing a space between them he made no attempt to persuade her into seeing him more; he was too proud for that. And how could he? The pious clothes were on the way out, and when she took to wearing jeans and her long dark hair fell to her waist, wantonly, the slope of the hips he had only guessed at was displayed to the world.

And not just the Middle Eastern world. There were westerners at the university, and one day he saw her on a restaurant terrace with a Canadian, drinking wine. The discovery that she had taken the road to hell gave him an acid pleasure. In Jamila he had witnessed the degeneration of a woman who might have made him a pious wife, not just into a whore, but a whore of the infidels. It was Allah who had done this, given him the best lesson he would learn at the university, and in the bitterness of his heart he was grateful.

But it didn't help his studies, and his mediocre degree put an end to his academic aspirations. It was during this vacuum in his life that he fell in with a group he met at a mosque, and now all questions of work and marriage were forgotten. Instead of the doctorate he'd hankered after he was offered a more purposeful course of study, in the hills of Waziristan.

His jihad training proved to him what he had long suspected: that when it came to anything practical he was less than adequate. For the planning of atrocities, on the other hand, he showed genius. Theoretical-minded he may have been, but the Professor (as they'd nicknamed him in Pakistan) did the business, and his promotion was not long in coming. After service in Iraq and Yemen he was selected for despatch to the UK, with the necessary papers, and ordered to prepare himself for a great task, one so important that he could not be told what it was, or who his brothers in the cell were to be.

His mission meanwhile was to bed himself in. Teaching English to Arabic-speaking immigrants in a Midlands town was the best job he could find. It left him feeling demeaned – his true place was at a university, he felt – though at the institute his profile was lower.

*

He worked and he prayed, and he waited. More than a year passed and he heard nothing. He was content to be a sleeper, but the sleep seemed long. Could he join the jihad against the infidel Assad in his native land?, a message he passed to his superiors pleaded. No he could not, the reply came: he was to stay where he was. He was beginning to get restive when one summer evening, in matter-of-fact fashion, it happened.

On his walk home from the Institute to his flat he was joined by two Pakistanis in their mid-to-late twenties. Falling into step in a quiet street the older one addressed him, softly:

'Mind if we join you, Professor?'

Amer started: in the town nobody called him that. Without waiting for a reply the man introduced himself and his friend as Umair and Tariq: 'We are brothers,' he smiled faintly, 'in both senses.'

The casualness of the approach alarmed him. He wasn't sure he liked the look of the pair, with their slovenly jeans and tea-shirts and Mancunian accents; people had accents in the town but he didn't like that either: accents lacked purity. Yet in minutes the two of them began gaining his confidence, by the simple means of telling him who he was: his mother's name and address, the dates of his Pakistan training, examples of his Yemeni and Iraqi exploits. Their refusal of his invitation to take tea at his flat – for professional reasons, they said – was also a positive sign.

Instead they fixed to meet the next day at a café in a Muslim quarter, where they talked politics: Afghanistan, the Arab Spring so-called, prospects in Syria and Egypt. The day after that it was for a walk in a park, and it was there, against a background of squealing kids and footballing youths that everything was explained.

They too were sleepers, they said, but they'd been given a task to complete while they waited: the import and concealment of a bomb – two bombs, in fact. When that had been accomplished and the weapons were safely in store there had been another wait: this time for the most suitable moment to explode them. And finally, after the death of Osama, God bless his memory, instructions had come.

The weapons, put together abroad, had taken time and trouble to import because they were dirty bombs. And the twin strike, they told a silent and electrified Amer, was to be now. The first, Umair explained, deadpan, was to be on the Bank. There followed a farcical moment. A bank in the town?, Amer asked, puzzled. No, Umair went on, still unsmiling: the Bank of England.

Momentous, was all they'd told him when he'd enquired about the nature of his task before they'd sent him to Britain, and he'd never forgotten the word. In the time he'd been here he'd thought a lot about what the target might turn out to be. An airport, a power station, Whitehall, a military camp – the possibilities were endless. But the Bank of England? Too momentous, surely, to be true.

The Syrian's suspicions returned. Was this some set-up? The fact that they knew his name and background proved nothing: if his identity had been compromised they could have got them from the CIA, or MI5. As Umair continued to sketch out the tactics for the attack he stayed silent, watched him closely.

'And the second strike?' he said, still scouring his face.

The target for the second, Umair continued coolly, was to be decided after an assessment of the impact of the first. With the country's finances still shaky, the guiding principle must be to inflict the largest possible economic damage. In addition to maximising the number of dead and injured, naturally.

As he spoke nothing in Umair's features betrayed anything to cause concern. Amer's doubts waned.

'The ambition is great, brother,' the Syrian said when he'd finished. 'A wondrous gift to Osama's memory.'

The brothers would make the first strike, Umair announced, decisive as ever. Then the Syrian, together with a technical assistant he would shortly meet, would execute the second.

The path they had taken wound close to the football pitch. As Amer walked on, head down to mask his excitement, a ball came bouncing off the field towards him. Instead of catching and returning it, the Syrian, surprised and alarmed, stepped aside and let it pass. The ball rolled on for some distance into some bushes. Wearily a boy jogged past them to retrieve it.

'Paki cunt,' he muttered at Amer on the way back to the field.

Wincing inwardly (and not only at 'cunt') Amer walked on.

'Radiation dispersal devices I have of course read about,' he explained. 'On the other hand I am not a scientist, and unfamiliar with the precise effects of the technology on the target in question.'

Maybe he didn't care for Amer's donnish manner, his way of speaking like a newspaper editorial, but Umair frowned.

'I'm not clear what you're saying, brother.'

'I mean the numbers dead.'

Umair shrugged.

'Who can say?'

'It's not like other bombs,' Tariq came in. The younger of the brothers, he seemed the more spontaneous. 'And of course no one's tried it yet. It's not so much the people who're killed outright, it's the ones who get contaminated, die of cancer and things. So you get two waves, Inshallah. Plus the psychological effect.'

'Of that I am aware,' the Syrian said, 'but how many?'

Umair took over.

'Hundreds, perhaps. A thousand if we're lucky. Depends how close we get, and how many people are around. Impossible to predict. With the cancers and things it takes time for people to die. Our equipment is large, so who knows, it could be thousands in all. God willing, the twin strikes could be greater than the twin towers.'

For a minute Amer stayed silent. He did it because he had nothing to say at that moment, also as a mark of status. A year or two older than Umair, he didn't want to appear too easily impressed. And he was beginning to think Umair's manner presumptuous.

Yet these were passing thoughts. A man of God to the point of yearning to be in His presence, the Syrian's heart was soaring. At last it was to come, the death he lived for! There'd been no lack of opportunities before but nothing on this scale, nothing he had rushed to embrace, nothing to justify his personal martyrdom. Here was a feat worthy of his immolation, and his name would be forever attached to that of Bin Laden.

'I have met Osama,' he said quietly, 'during my training. He came to the camp, a lightning visit, and I spoke with him. For several minutes we spoke. We talked about bombing methods and he mentioned the possibility of using nuclear one day. Imagine his joy in heaven.'

'It will be great.' Tariq looked impressed

'And now I shall avenge him,' the Syrian added.

'We will all avenge him,' Umair corrected.

'And the material?' Amer asked. 'It is ready?'

'As I said, it's in the country.'

Umair frowned as Tariq added:

'Came in as stone artefacts, statues and things, to account for the weight. You know, lead-lined crates and stuff. A cell in Liverpool. It wasn't from Pakistan – too tricky. We got it –'

'No need to weary Amer with details,' Umair stopped him. 'Let's just say it came from brave fighters...'

It was a week later, in London, that they introduced the Syrian to his number two: Jayson the convert. Along with Tariq, a computer specialist, he'd been trained to handle the equipment. Not to meddle with it – Jayson wasn't up to that, Tariq hinted – just handle it.

Better if Tariq had been his technical partner, Amer thought after an evening with the tongue-tied, blank-looking Caribbean. And better to die at the Bank, surely the more prestigious target, whatever the next one turned out to be. As it was his operation risked being a mere follow-up mission, a second order event.

The idea preyed on him and for a day or two he'd been tempted to question the arrangement, ask on whose authority the division of the groups had been handed down. In the end he refrained: complaining about orders would have been a breach of discipline, so he let it go. It was how Allah wanted it, and there was a logic.

Umair and Tariq had been allocated the Bank, he could only assume, not because of any superiority (how could their experience be greater than his?), but because they were British-born brothers, a natural pair. There was another reason to accept things as they were. To take the lead on the second strike would be to see their mission through to completion, so in that sense he was senior to Umair. And if the brothers failed and he succeeded, his achievement would stand alone.

Meanwhile he would have to make do with the convert. The boy had advantages – his physical strength, his ready acceptance of his subordinate status. Though in other ways, as the Syrian discovered while he lived with him, there was clearly something wanting. After days locked up together it could be trying.

*

Looking for ways to please, Jayson pointed to a portable radio:

'Number's still growing, said this morning. This goes on it could soon be up there in the big hundreds. Count in the ones who're gonna die anyway 'an it might be more. Said they was running out of hospital places. Think what it'll be when –'

Glancing up from his textbook the Syrian held a finger aloft, shushing.

'I would be glad if you would not interrupt me while I am working. But you are right. A wonder of the world, brother, though it is a shame about New York. 34 only. We must not fail as they did.' He looked at his watch. 'Come, let us thank Him and ask for His help and protection.'

Kneeling on the floor, each to his improvised mat – strips of carpet torn from the stair of the abandoned house – they prostrated themselves in prayer.

3

The first Tony Underwood saw of the holiday camp was from a mile down the coast. 'Fabulous seafront position', the Internet advertisement had said, and so it was: hundreds of mobile homes set on a cliff-top overlooking a beach on a stretch of the Norfolk coast a mile or two north of Cromer. Must be a thousand or more evacuees packed in there, he thought. Quite a change from the East End of London.

He eased back his speed. It wasn't fear of being caught – round here the police had disappeared from the roads – just that it was only a half-hour run to the camp from his office in Norwich and lack of traffic was making him early. The container trucks that used to smash along the roads were a rarity now that everything coming into Lowestoft or Great Yarmouth was crawled over with Geiger counters, creating huge delays. Then there were the cancelled holidays, the spurt in the cost of petrol, the halt to construction – everything was conspiring to slow the country to walking pace. It wasn't something you could say out loud – the nation's sense of irony was not what it had been – but the slower rhythm of life this last month or so had its upsides.

Rabbits and foxes scampering across the almost empty road brought to mind something he'd read about the aftermath of the Chernobyl disaster: how left to itself the untilled land had become like a nature reserve, tempting back wolves and boar. If the Bank bomb was just the first of many, he mused, would it get like that here? Wild life overrunning the streets of London, Manchester, Birmingham?

With time on his hands before his meeting he stopped in Sheringham, a short distance along the coast. He'd visited the seaside town before, one weekend that Spring, after his posting to the

Norwich outpost, and been unimpressed: he was fond of old-fashioned resorts but this one had been windy and deserted. Now, at the height of the holiday season, little seemed to have changed: the run-down air, the chilling weather, a population that appeared to consist of elderly retirees in plastic parkas.

That was the view from the car park. In the town centre, things had changed. Ambling along the narrow street that led to the seafront he came across improbable scenes. Outside a shop window, a knot of women in hijabs pointing at exotic items – fudge, rock, carrot cake – and filling the street with excited tongues and gestures. A few steps further a group of black girls, their shorts as ill-suited to the climate as to their generous hips, were whooping happily from store to store and buying nothing. To avoid them, and the Somalis stalking along the pavements, local folk took to the centre of the road, kept their heads down and scuttled past.

On the seafront, there was more. The grey-haired town, so apt to lament its lack of young folk, had got itself a teenage generation overnight – though not the one it might have chosen. Teenage Caribbeans, hoods up in the breeze, had commandeered the seats on the terrace outside the Seaview hotel, shouting and laughing and cursing above the blare of a boom-box. Opposite, in a pub car park, a rival band of Pakistanis lounged and smouldered.

The inside of the pub beckoned, and Tony entered.

'Quiet day,' he said, ordering his beer in the empty bar.

'Every day's quiet now we got that lot.'

The barman hoiked his head towards the youngsters. Like the town itself he had a despondent air, and it didn't take much to get him talking.

'And they're just the latest menace. Place doesn't know what's hit it, last few years. First we get swamped with City folk, so no one local can afford to buy. Next we get the recession, and now this. OK, it's an emergency, they've got to go somewhere, but where was the consultation? First we knew was when every chippie and plumber from here to Norwich was crawling over the holiday camp. New bathrooms, new kitchens, verandas painted up, brand new medical centre – all very smart and respectable. Can't say the same about the inmates. To say it's not what we expected…'

'And what did you expect?'

The barman looked uncomfortable.

'Day after they did the Bank the M11 from London was crawling with over-loaded Volvos and BMW estates. Weekend mob became permanent residents overnight. Anything to get the hell out of London. They was the refugees we expected. No one wanted to say it but locally there was a feeling the bomb would give us a lift. Bring money in.' His grin was acid, as a hand swept the empty bar. 'We were wrong, weren't we?

'Talk about high feelings. Council chappie came down from Norwich to address a public meeting. Says all the stuff about East Enders with uninhabitable houses and a long-term cancer risk and the need to play our part. See what he can do 'bout some extra police he says, but no promises 'cos they've all been sent to Manchester or Birmingham or wherever.

"Any questions?' he says when he's finished, and there's silence. No one's going to say what they're thinking, and what every last bugger in that hall is thinking is that we live up here to escape these lunatics, now they're sending them after us! Then one old boy pipes up: 'If we're going to be crawling with Muslim bombers we don't want police, we want soldiers. Armed!"

'So how's it been?'

'Where do you start?' The barkeeper grimaced. 'Remember the days when the Mods and Rockers used to go to the seaside for their dust-ups? Brighton, wasn't it? Well Sheringham's got like that. 'Cept it's knives and drugs. And race. Mixed communities they call them, don't they? Well here they're mixing it with each other. Ones who rubbed along in London don't get along here, not after what happened, with the Sikhs and the Caribbeans saying it was the Muslims who've given their kids cancer.'

'So there's trouble.'

'Total bloody mayhem from day one. Caribbeans versus Somalis, Sikhs versus the Pakistanis and the Bangladeshis, and the white trash versus the lot. Had one good effect though. Local yobs have gone to ground. Don't know what's hit's them either.'

It was getting towards midday and a few customers were drifting in. A stooped, scowling fellow came up to the bar and waited, tapping the counter with his money.

'That's him,' the barman whispered, winking. 'The old boy at the meeting.'

'Let me guess what you're talking about,' the man said after ordering his pint, gesturing towards the noise of the ghetto blaster. 'Wanna know what they are, the lot of 'em?'

'I think you told me,' the barman smirked. 'But you can tell the gentleman.'

Turning to Tony the fellow said:

'Radio-active waste, in't they?'

*

And on it went. Tony left them to it, content to be dropped from the conversation. Alone on his stool further along the bar, shoulders bent a fraction as if to deflect attention, he was the sort of man your eyes would pass over. For him bars of every sort had been a way of life. Not that he was a lush – in his work you learned to pace your drinking. Keeping watch over some nervy-looking corporal in civvies offering his services to a Soviet intelligence man in symmetrically knotted tie and winkle-picker shoes, or sitting as close as was wise to a clutch of IRA men, Guinness in hand and a mike under your lapel, you needed your wits about you.

The thing was to become part of the background, and Tony had no trouble doing that. Sixtyish and conventionally suited he had a face you were unlikely to remember, if you noticed it at all. Once it could have been good-looking, intelligent too; now the tired eyes and taciturn mouth left an impression of blunted sharpness. It would have been easy to make himself younger, yet nothing about his clothes or the way he combed his ever sparser hair suggested that he cared. The truth was that ageing into anonymity suited Tony, as much as his profession.

That and sitting in bars. It was in a bar – a discreet one, near the river in Chelsea – that he'd met Manci. He'd been waiting for a Soviet Embassy man to turn up for drinks with his journalist contact. The man was a double agent as it happened, though an amateur whom Tony had spent many an hour licking into shape. To not much purpose, it seemed. Whenever the door swung open the journalist, all wired-up and ready, would feel inside his coat in a way he'd been specifically instructed not to. As time passed and there was no sign of the Russian the fellow was getting twitchy, shooting Tony glances every few minutes saying he's not going to show is he, how about we call it off?

The poor man nearly fell out of his chair when in came Manci, looked around, walked up to Tony, bent to murmur a question, smiled and sat next to him. After trying to make sense of this for a moment the journalist downed his drink, got up and left.

What Manci had asked, with an accent, was could she share his table? There were spaces elsewhere, but she didn't look like a prostitute, he'd given up on the Russian and in a what-the-hell moment he said yes. Normally foreign girls with raven hair and burning looks did not angle for his company, and Tony had a secret yen for exotic-looking women. It was part of his simplicity.

What happened next tested his reserves of anonymity. Glad to have found him, she said after ordering herself a drink, Safronov told her he'd be there. This was Konstantin Safronov, First Secretary for Cultural Affairs and the intelligence man Tony had been expecting. Should he get up, he thought, and get out? But that would be to confirm who he was and why he was there. His response was to take a long draught of his beer and stare away: if he could hold out till he'd finished she might give up first and move off.

The Russian must have rumbled the journalist. Sending a pretty woman to accost him was cheeky, but then it was a time when the KGB was at its cockiest. And more cheek was to come. While Tony sat in silence ('I don't expect you to say anything'), downing his glass as fast as he reasonably could, Manci talked on.

She'd been instructed to tell him, she said, that she was a Hungarian student who'd been offered money to sleep with him, and that she was telling him because after the '56 invasion of her country she had always detested the Russians. Safronov's idea, she explained, was that she would befriend him on this basis, then hook him just the same.

Tony stared away.

'Well it's true I'm Hungarian – my name is Manci – and I did take money from them to report gossip, because I was broke. But when it came to this… I just couldn't work for them. Not like that. So there, I've carried out my instructions,' she said sweetly, and with her lovely dark smile. 'I'm a real student, by the way, a postgraduate in architecture.'

For the first time Tony looked back at her, considering. It was a dizzying situation, capable of infinite regression. At what point could he be sure it was Manci talking, and not Safronov? Obviously never. So the answer to this delectable woman was clear enough: all very interesting but she'd got the wrong person, and would she excuse him?

He couldn't bring himself to say it. Something in her eyes… The matter needed investigation, he told himself, because the eyes were compelling and he wanted to believe her. Which would mean keeping in touch.

'I hear what you say.' He edged up from his seat. 'Now would you excuse me?'

He ran some checks and she was who she claimed: a student from Budapest. Out of prudence he reported to superiors. Inevitably the instruction came back to treble-cross Safronov and recruit her, but for once Tony did not do as he was told. With Manci his dutifulness had met its limits, and out of consideration for her safety he scarcely attempted to turn her.

To keep Safronov sweet she'd told him she was seeing him, but that he was showing little enthusiasm for getting her into bed. Was he gay, the Russian had asked? Should they put a young man on the case? All this she told Tony, amidst delicious laughter. At the sound of it a lightness of heart came over him he had never felt.

A few months, and it was over. Tiring of the game, and suspecting her commitment, Safronov arranged for Manci to be forced back home by her Embassy, on pain of 'measures' against her parents. At their last meeting, in a bar in Richmond, she cried. Nervous about being compromised by the woman with whom he was undoubtedly in love, till then he had behaved more than correctly. His kiss when they parted was the only thing that happened between them. The pressure of her lips on his hesitant mouth he had not forgotten.

His marriage to Jean came eight months later. Jean the tall, cool-mannered optician and his on/off girlfriend of long-standing. The 'off' times due to his fear that she attracted the more introverted side of his character, which at that stage of his life he'd still had hopes of transcending.

On Manci it was some twenty years before he learned the truth. It came when, trawling through documents released after the fall of communism, a colleague with a sense of humour slipped him a copy of a Hungarian Intelligence Service report of the time. The true reason Manci had been ordered home, it suggested, was because she'd fallen for him for real.

He was 51 when this happened, about the time he discovered that his daughter had become a drug addict. Under the double blow his taciturn nature became more marked. His work wasn't affected; his increased reticence, together with the premature stoop he began to develop, as if shrinking from himself, had advantages, professionally speaking. 'No one will ever know if Tony's on his tail,' an FBI man he'd worked with said of him. 'The guy's invisible. When Tony comes into a room it's like someone just went out.'

When the Cold War ended and they transferred him to the anti-terrorist beat, Tony's heart sank. It stayed down during the years he spent chasing Islamists in Manchester, Bradford, Bolton. He perked up when they parked him in Norwich, one of the new security service centres in the provinces, no doubt in anticipation of retirement. In the absence of much in the way of a Muslim population, let alone extremists, they'd put him onto illicit movements along the coast, and till now it had been a quiet life.

There'd been a three-month spell of Olympic duties in London, and that was it. Being out of the anti-terrorist business felt good. He'd had enough of snooping around mosques and bookstores, of pep talks from his bosses about not alienating the moderates, of worrying about how much of a racist he was or wasn't. And he'd seen more than enough of the militants, their fearful zealotry and incomprehensible hatreds, the whole deformed creed. When the Bank bomb had gone off his first thought had been, thank God he was no longer in that line of business. Now, out in the English countryside, Islamism had come back to him.

4

'Why wait for trouble to start?' Martin asked the soldier. 'Why not surround the pub?'

'Soldiers, surround a pub?'

'If you know it's their base of operations and they're acting against the law – riot and affray, isn't it? – why not?'

The soldier grinned. Big teeth and a lithe body made him look skeletally tough.

'If you sealed 'em in think how pissed they'd get. Then you would get trouble.'

'You from Afghanistan?'

The soldier flashed the insignia on his arm, not happy to talk. Then said anyway:

'Queen's Royal Lancers'.

'Of course. I was out there.'

'You don't say.'

The soldier rested his rifle on the barricade. At this point it took the form of a wrecked lorry, *Alhura Builders, Quality and Reliability* inscribed on the side. It had come to rest at a handy angle, its smashed offside window pointing along a broad road, giving him a good sight of troubled terrain. Behind was the railway bridge Tony had crossed after showing his journalist's pass to the soldier guarding the other side.

'So what were you doing?' the soldier enquired, tentatively.

'Correspondent.'

'Kabul?'

'Helmand.'

'No joke. So was I.'

As if to inspect his fitness for the task the soldier gave Martin an appraising look. What he saw was a near forty-year-old who was beginning to look a little pulpy around the midriff, though not in bad shape overall. Blondish locks were a rejuvenating frame for a still handsome face that was beginning to look a little pulpy too.

'How do you feel about running down our boys over there?'

Politics. The soldier looked wary again.

'Oh come on. Off the record, what do you think? Smart move, wasn't it? Gets the boys home, takes the load off the police, and best of all we can go on saying we never surrender to terrorism while giving them one of the main things they wanted.'

'That's what you think,' the soldier said, looking canny. 'I said nothing, did I?' He let a moment pass. 'Not that I don't get your drift. When your house is on fire you drop everything and take care of it, right?'

The soldier coughed as he spoke. The burning the night before had been real here, and there was smoke in the air. Two hundred yards from them a mosque had been firebombed. The interior was burnt out, though its dome had settled to the ground, strangely intact and jaunty-looking, like a bowler hat at a rakish angle.

'Got us out quick all right. Berlin fucking airlift in reverse. Whole regiment home in six days flat, minus three quarters of our kit. Not that you need much here.'

Martin pointed to his semi-automatic assault rifle.

'Not the sort of thing you expect to see on British streets. Used it yet?'

'You're joking,' the soldier grinned. 'SA-80. It'd probably jam. 'Designed by the incompetent, issued by the uncaring, carried by the unfortunate,' is what they say.' He looked serious. 'Will I use it? Depends how bad it gets. If things get totally out of order – which is what that bastard over there wants – who's to say?'

He gestured over the railway bridge. A skinny man in glasses and a beret was standing outside the Wheatsheaf pub, surveying the Muslim quarter through binoculars.

'It's him in charge round here. Acts up all military. Napoleon of the London Road they call him.'

Martin studied the man, then stared round. Up here was not his territory; for him it might just as well have been Helmand. For two days he'd nosed about, talking, getting a feel, scribbling notes for his piece. Part of them read:

Before the bomb Muslims and poor whites cohabited peaceably, if only because the streets where they lived were too neatly separated for friction to occur. The railway's the barrier. A kind of respectful alienation, satisfactory to all sides.

That was before. Respect has gone now, so there's only the alienation. The day after the bombing the footbridge over the railway was closed and guarded by police. The same evening a bunch of whites began trampling the fence and crossing the rails to get to the Muslim quarter. A couple of dozen drunks at first, but when the Americans pulled the plug on the car plant it was hundreds every night. Of the 1,200 who lost their jobs a third were Muslims. At least they've got something to occupy them: defending their streets from nightly attack by former workmates.

The bomb's changed everything, people tell me, and you can feel it. Smouldering grudges have come roaringly alight, and the tribalism is depressing. Working alongside their white colleagues for years, playing football together and being orderly heads of families has not spared Muslims having their mosques petrol-bombed or their homes and shops torched.

The Government says using soldiers pulled out of Afghanistan to keep the two sides apart is sensible, since the Afghan veterans are more ethnically aware. Muslims I've talked to don't seem grateful: they feel they're getting the Taliban treatment.

Surveying the desolate townscape he cast up a despairing hand.

'Not your scene is it?'

The soldier followed Martin's gaze. Disused factories, a century old housing stock, cheap new structures, walled up pubs and churches.

'I've seen better parts of Kandahar. Could use a good shelling, this place.'

'So how bad do you think it'll get?'

The soldier reflected.

'Any other country you'd have had a hundred dead. Round 'ere it's been three killed, twenty wounded and two silly buggers burned to death by their own incendiary bomb.'

He indicated a wrecked four-by-four a hundred metres away. The silly buggers, it turned out, had wanted to propel a jeep loaded with petrol cans into the mosque. It exploded while they were trying to fix the steering. The mosque had gone up anyway, a day later.

'All this chaos and just the five dead,' the soldier mused. 'What's that say about us?'

He waited for Martin's reply. He was a thoughtful, patient soldier.

'You tell me,' Martin said.

'Well it's one of two things, ain't it? Either we'll come through like we come through everything, because we never lose our cool.'

The 'or' seemed a long time coming.

'Or?'

'Or we've lost the fucking will to defend ourselves. Could be putting their second strike together under our noses, for all we know. The old one-two.' He indicated the Muslim streets. 'Who's going in there to find out, 'cept that lot.' He jerked a thumb towards the Wheatsheaf, then looked at his watch. 'In an hour and a half prompt they'll be over here making trouble. They get across the fence further up. Bugger-all we can do about it. One man down there is all we've got.'

After a bit of unspecific reminiscing about his experiences in Helmand, and a promise of a drink if they met off-duty, Martin crossed back over the bridge.

*

One advantage of an alcohol-clear mind was that he was getting more work done. A disadvantage was that it forced him to be more honest with himself. Why had he said all that about Helmand? The fellow would have talked anyway. It just came out. Mythomania Julie had called it, in their final scene.

For Martin, final scenes were proliferating. There'd been another a week ago, with his editor. Mark Pelling called him to his office as soon as he arrived. A small man with a sharp face and clipped manner, he stabbed a finger at a chair but remained standing. He seemed to want to get something over with, fast.

'You've been turning in good stuff,' he began, looking him in the eye for the time it took to say it, then smartly away.

'The stuff we were allowed to print, that is.'

Whining about censorship. His first mistake. Mark was in with ministers and a big supporter of the emergency powers.

'The piece from Bolton was noticed. Model of responsible journalism the Home Secretary told me.'

After you'd eviscerated it, Martin thought. To read the piece as it had come out anyone would have thought that the seething town, where street after street was barricaded, was a model of race relations.

'Glad someone liked it.'

'I'll be honest, the fact that you've been doing good work is a problem.'

Oh Jesus.

'A problem because it makes it more difficult to tell you I'm going to have to let you go.'

Small as he was Mark was a great pacer, as if trying to lengthen himself by his strides. He set out round his room.

'I don't have to tell you why. The ads are down two thirds and the Internet's where people are getting the news we can't print. All I'm hoping for at present is for the paper to survive.'

Mark was speeding up. Martin followed him with his eyes, trying to fix him to the spot.

'If it's the booze I swear…'

He looked strained as he spoke, strained in the way people who have come off drink only recently sometimes do.

'If it was I'd have told you. Martin, don't force me to explain. It's tough because of me and your father, but choices have to be made. There are people here with families…'

'I have one too.'

'Well I know and I'm sorry about you and Julie.'

No Julie, no work, no travel – and no drink. Anticipating the vacant hours Martin felt himself trembling.

'I'll work for half.'

'Martin, how can I –'

'– no expenses.'

'You're making this –'

'– OK, I know, I'm sorry. I'm talking rubbish. Put it down to'– he shrugged – 'panic. When do you need me out?'

'A month. Meanwhile I want you to go on covering the Midlands, if you would.'

'I'm planning to be up there anyway, as it happens. For a magazine.'

'I'm glad you've got a second string.' You wouldn't say that if you knew what they paid, Martin didn't say. 'I really meant it when I said –'

'– kind of you, Mark.'

The editor's office was a glass box on an open-plan floor. Remembering that his face and gestures were a theatre of mime for a hundred colleagues, Martin got up, made an inane joke, laughed at it, and left the office.

*

There were a couple of hours to go before the action, and with local colour for his piece to spare his instinct was to do nothing. It was a de-motivating sort of place, the edge of some inky blob on a Midlands map, one of those suburbs you only read about in crime reports, whose location you can never remember and that induce a pointless pity when you see them.

The streets he walked were almost empty now. The few passers-by seemed beaten people, obese women overflowing with helpless flesh, haggard men with tight, resentful faces. The shops were full of cheap goods and empty of customers. The only thriving business seemed to be a pawnbrokers, its bright façade advertising loans, cheque-cashing, pay day advances (*Too much month, not enough money?*)

The road he turned into was pocked with newly-vacant premises, though *Bargain Booze* was still in business, its window piled high with cut-price six-packs and Johnny Walker. Next door a steel grill protected the windows of *Farooq Travels*, where a poster showed a pretty, head-scarved young woman on a pilgrimage. Before, people had accepted the incongruity of the neighbouring shops; now the woman in the poster was giving a blow-job. The same graffitist's hand had crossed out Travels and scrawled Terrorist Tours.

Over the road was the Wheatsheaf pub. Martin crossed towards it – then veered at the last moment to a café a few shops along.

Inside he hesitated. Bare walls, plain wooden chairs, empty tables. What was this? It began to make sense when from an improvised sound-system he heard soft, religious rock. A whey-faced girl of eighteen took his order for coffee. As he waited he saw a sign next to the counter:

We pray every day before serving. If you want us to pray for you, write your name and tell us your problem. We do not ask for addresses.'

He paid the girl, then said:

'Pray for me, would you?'

'We will Sir, if you want.'

A hand gloved in plastic gave him his change like alms. She took out a note-book with a cross on the cover and looked up in expectation.

'My name's Martin and my problem is that I'm a mythomaniac.'

'Myth –' The girl began writing, then hesitated.

'– o-maniac. It's a real word.' He gave a resigned smile. 'It must be because it's what my wife calls me. It means someone who can't stop himself, well, elaborating on the truth.'

The girl wrote it down.

'My second problem'– the girl had begun closing the book – 'is that I'm a drunk. When I've finished this coffee – and it smells very good, thank you – I'm going next door, to the Wheatsheaf.'

He watched as she re-opened the book, turned the full stop into a comma, and added '– and a drunk.'

A Londoner's ignorance: he had strayed into a revivalist café. It wasn't alone, the whole area seemed overburdened with the reclaimers of souls of all denominations: Baptists and New Life Wesleyans, the Church of God and Prophecy, the Church of the Five Precious Wounds. Spiritual reawakening?, Martin had jotted in his notebook. Or a rallying of Christianity's ragged armies?

*

The Wheatsheaf drummed with music and percussive talk, and like most pubs now it was dense with smoke: the ban had lapsed overnight, just like that, and no-one thought it wise to do anything about it. The pub itself was one of those Edwardian structures that had turned drinking halls into palaces, but its more opulent days were over. Amongst the fruit machines, ATMs and plasterboard partitions, all that remained were the forty-foot bar and the insignia on coloured glass above it: Champagne, Madeira, West Indian Rhum, Foreign Cigars.

The place was filling rapidly. Men of all ages were drinking with a purposeful air, their hairless or close-shorn skulls glowing waxenly in the half-light. The troubles, Martin told himself, looking round. Belfast in the troubles. The frothing pints and murderous jokes, himself drinking and joshing with the hard men, the sound of shots in the near distance. The image evaporated in a second. Martin had never been to Northern Ireland, had never seen a riot or a shooting in his life.

'Soda water with a bit of lemon.'

The barman, a twenty-year-old with mean lips and a crimped face, a record of God knows what deprivations, didn't move.

'You what?'

'Pint of Stella.'

Three weeks two days was a good run, better than the last. And if these weren't exceptional times… Plus no one here was going to talk to a Londoner nursing a glass of soda water.

He glanced at the TV above the bar. The eight o'clock news. The sound was off but he didn't need it, knew what to expect. An announcer sombrely explaining that the police were no nearer to capturing the bombers' accomplices. A security analyst weightily opining what everyone knew: that unless there was progress soon there was little to prevent them doing it again. A Muslim scholar insisting that anyone guilty of such an atrocity would be an apostate to Islam, while finding words to imply that Muslims were almost certainly not involved. And last, so routine they'd been relegated to the end of the bulletin, shots of the latest disturbance.

'Turn it up!'

Before taking his money the barman touched a switch and the sound of rioting filled the pub. A mob was attacking a Muslim area of Bristol. Conversation stopped while the entire pub cheered on the rioters and jeered the Muslims, the soldiers and mounted police attempting to protect them. A close-up: a thuggish group had cornered a young kid in a galabiyya. Seeing it was over he stopped trying to fend them off with pitifully feeble gestures and went down, his hands over his head.

'Kick 'is face in!'

'Burn the bastards,' the barman shrieked, abstractedly handing Martin his change.

He took his beer and looked for a quiet corner, but when the TV was turned down as the news finished the excitement around him rose. *Bristol boys know what they're fuckin' doin'. That'll be a few more gone to meet Mohamed…*

He needed to phone Julie. He ought to have done it in the quiet of the café, the hubbub here might tell her where he was. Finding an empty seat near the end of the bar he took a long drink, then dialled her number.

'Where the hell are you?' Her voice was neutral. 'It sounds like a riot.'

'Not yet. In an hour or so. I'm in a place near Birmingham, and they're gearing up for trouble. So what did they say?'

'Who?'

'The experts. You've seen them, haven't you?'

A chilled, sardonic laugh.

'Ah yes. I'm not used to this tender care and attention.'

'Julie, don't.'

'I'm OK.'

'No Julie. What did they say?'

'What they said before. That I exhibited traits that were inconsistent with the usual symptoms of autonomic arousal to radiation.'

'For Christ's sake –'

'– in other words that I'm not faking.'

'Faking? They must be idiots.'

'Actually they're right. People do go mildly crazy. You know how many people came forward for examination in the Litvinenko case?'

'No. Tell me.'

She knew things, Julie. It could be annoying.

'More than 3,000. 200 were followed up, and a couple of dozen referred to clinics for possible exposure.'

'Which tells us that people are naturally terrified of something they can't see.'

'I've been mugging it up – there's not much else to do in the evenings. It's one of those areas where you get the feeling the experts are in the dark. The UN are still arguing about how many people got cancer after Chernobyl, as against how many would have got it anyway. But there's some good data, especially on the psychological side. Even if they're told they've nothing to worry about people drink more, smoke more, have more sex, use drugs, become depressed…'

'Can you hang up your stethoscope for a moment? I'm just asking how you and Jackie are doing. For a start, where are you?'

'Norfolk. I left a message on your phone to tell you, so you could forward anything.'

'Sorry, I've been on the road. Where in Norfolk?'

'A holiday camp, near Sheringham. Top of a windy cliff.'

'Not my idea of a holiday. Why not stay in my parents' cottage? I'm sure they –'

'– I don't want to sit it out in a cottage. I want Jackie's condition to be monitored, and my own. And we're not holidaying. It's an evacuee camp. They've set up a medical centre and I'm doing a crash course in early diagnosis, so I can help out.'

'Christ almighty, sounds like the war. How long will you be there?'

'We can't go back to the house or the practice till the area's been decontaminated.'

'Which will be?'

'Anyone's guess. They got the spread of radiation wrong by 100 per cent, so who knows? Six months, a year…'

'A year!'

'Martin, don't you read the papers? You need sandblasting and acid to get the stuff out of bricks and stone. You have to take up roads. Trees have to come down, topsoil has to be carted away…'

'You're not well. I don't want you breaking your health looking after everyone except yourself.'

'You're sounding very proprietorial all at once,' she said, a bit sharply.

'And who are these evacuees? Eastenders? I don't want Jackie –'

'– I know what you're going to say, and you sound like my father. We've managed in Aldgate, so we'll get along here. The great thing is she and I are in the same place. They say that because it began late in both of us there's a good chance the vomiting will die away. And it has, more or less.'

'Bloody hell, you didn't tell me about any vomiting.'

'We got a dose Martin, we both got a dose, but we're far from the worst cases. We have what they call mild-acute syndrome.'

'And what the hell does that mean?'

'That on an 0 to 10 scale we're at the lower end. Somewhere between minimally depressed white blood count and more impressive symptoms.'

'Like what?'

'Like immunodysfunction, infectious complications, haemorrhage, sepsis anaemia, impaired wound healing. Want any more?'

'That'll do.'

'At least we escaped the gastric lavage and phosphate soda enemas. I must have run faster than I thought. And they got Jackie in from the roof garden fairly smartly, thank God.'

'It would be nice to see you.'

'You're lucky you can't. I've lost a stone and a half.'

'And Jackie?'

'When I kiss her we're like skeletons knocking together.'

'Tell her she has all my love.'

'Mmm.'

'So when will they let me see you?'

'It's not they, Martin.'

'Well when?'

A pause.

'Not yet.'

'When then?'

'When I've had a chance to think.'

5

Tony joined the queue of vehicles outside the camp entrance. Ahead of him a low-loader delivering medical equipment – A GIFT FROM THE AMERICAN PEOPLE was inscribed in large letters on the side – was strenuously inspected. The MI5 man in the car behind was equally painstakingly checked, vehicle and all. And all the while inmates of the camp, the younger ones the kind of customers the locals in Sheringham had crossed the road to avoid, moved freely in and out.

The woman who checked his papers directed him to the administrative offices, a clapboard building rigged up by the army in little more than a week. His first meeting was with one of the camp doctors, and by now he was late. She hadn't waited: a piece of paper pinned to the door announced 'Dr Julia Opie (GP and tests)'. Another said 'Sorry, back soon'. He knocked anyway, waited, then went for a stroll round the camp.

Next to the offices were the medical facilities – the former reception centre for the camp with clapboard sections added on. A hundred yards away stood a vast, dark green Army tent: an improvised sign over the door read 'Multi-faith Worship Centre'. The holiday homes themselves, some thirty feet long by eight wide, were scattered over several grassy acres. To avoid looking like caravans, verandas had been appended and honeysuckle grown by the doors to mask the calor gas cylinders.

A few steps further into the camp a wild profusion of music hit him. The day had brightened, doors were open, and from almost every porch came the sound of Indian sitars, chanting voices or – its beat imperious above the others – hip-hop. A brief stroll revealed that the camp had divided itself along racial lines. Veils were confined to one area, turbans to another, black folk to a third.

Only a dozen or so homes were occupied by whites. On the

veranda of one a group of youngsters were sprawled, drinking beer. A few paces on he came across an artificial fishing pool. It had attracted no anglers but was host to a sprinkling of bottles, plastic cups, cigarette packets and a semi-submerged supermarket trolley.

Home from home, Tony thought derisively. But then these kids could be sick, some of them facing cancers or leukaemia... Walking back he stopped to look them over for the signs he'd read about, but saw nothing: no missing tufts of hair, no violet skin or wounds to their upper bodies. The lads on the veranda looked normal, suntanned – and in good spirits.

'What you starin' at?', one of them called out.

'Fuckin' perv is what 'ee is,' another shouted. 'Ere, 'ave a good look.'

The bare-chested boy got up and, holding his beer can like a champagne flute, between two fingers, minced towards him. The group erupted. Tony walked on.

This was no colony of lepers, he told himself, so no need to worry about contamination. Exposure to radiation outside the body does not make that person radioactive, the guidance issued to officers interviewing victims had insisted. Even lethally exposed patients are no hazard. If you say so, Tony thought, scanning a passing Indian couple, the woman with what looked like burns to her face. If you say so.

Through a window of the medical centre he saw a line of old folk waiting to be examined. A number of the men were robed and bearded, the women mostly in black. The patience and quietude written on their faces seemed at once noble and eerie. Eastern faith and occidental technology, Tony reflected morosely, had finally come together.

*

At the offices he found Dr Opie's door open and Julie at her desk. Strange how closely she tallied with what he'd expected: youngish, in control, not noticeably impressed by an MI5 visitor – though better-looking than he'd imagined. It was a prettiness that revealed itself not in her smile – she hadn't smiled yet – but gradually, as it broke through the professionalism of her manner. As she stretched to shake his hand her coat opened on a slim – perhaps excessively slim – figure. Remembering that she'd had a dose of radiation herself, he began:

'So you're doctor and patient.'

'I volunteered. The alternative was to sit and worry about my daughter.'

'Your daughter's here?'

'Like me, for the duration.'

'Is there a school?'

'The school's provided.'

'And how is it?'

'Fine.'

It wasn't. Local charities had done their bit to help, but there'd been opposition. Pleading unspecific health risks, parents in the area had opposed a plan to cram the camp children into prefabricated extensions of the town's primary and secondary schools. The greatest separation possible was what they wanted, and what they'd got. A group of barns on the side of the town nearest to the camp was hurriedly converted into classrooms, with junior and secondary pupils lumped together.

Alarmed after seeing the way some of the tougher boys behaved, Julie had bought her daughter a mobile, just in case. Jackie was proud and thrilled, and like all phones belonging to the primary kids it was gone within a week. Then mysteriously returned to her coat pocket, a few days later.

'How did you allocate the homes, as a matter of interest?'

'Randomly, pretty much.'

Julie looked discomfited.

'And did they stick to them?'

'Well, no.'

'Ethnic redistribution, I imagine.'

'They naturally want to group themselves with former neighbours.'

'I understand. And I don't suppose that Sikhs and Caribbeans are too happy to be corralled with Muslims at a time like this.'

'Why do you say that?'

He looked back at her, puzzled. He was used to certain things being understood, to not having to spell them out.

'Because we know from the people they picked up in New York that this was exactly what it seemed: a memorial to Osama. And in Britain Sikhs and Caribbeans are high on the list of victims.'

'So are Muslims.'

'You must have worked with a lot of them,' said Tony, nudging the conversation sideways.

'Many.'

And the experience has made me fiercely resistant to casual critics of Islam, she could have added. With Julie this was more than a question of fashion; she was too much her own woman for that. But this same independence of spirit could lead her to be intolerant of the innocent perceptions of common folk. For all her experience of living in tough areas there were things about life in the raw that she did not want herself to know.

Seeing her eyes glinting Tony stopped. For him anything touching the Muslim religion was a pain. It wasn't so much prejudice – for an atheist all churches had their unappealing aspects. The pain was because the whole business made him ask questions about himself that he'd rather not.

'Muslims were the main victims,' Julie repeated. 'The camp's full of them.'

'I know. It's one of the reasons I'm here. Whoever did it underestimated the dispersal effects. They went for the financial system, but overdid it. Hence the East End victims.'

The security service man's pride in his knowledge was evident, and for the first time Julie smiled.

'I sorry, you know all this, the numbers you have here. Though I suppose you must come across a lot of malingerers.'

'There's sixty thousand evacuees all told, ten thousand in Norfolk and about a thousand in this camp. There's probably nothing wrong with fifty percent or more, but try telling them. You even get a kind of auction of symptoms. People imagining new ones every day, desperate for attention.'

'Interesting, but I've got us off the point. We're following through with everyone evacuated from the immediate area of the Bank. Which includes a number of your residents.'

'In case they were involved?'

'Or saw something before taking cover. I don't have to repeat what happened...'

'No, you don't.'

Julie knew what everyone knew. That the bomb had been carried in a white Ford Transit van. That it had slowed in front of the Bank, then swerved towards it before wedging itself between the bronze doors, and exploding. That the dismembered parts of two South Asians, both unidentifiable, had been recovered, and that the dead men's presumed accomplices were still at large.

'There's a photo of the only one of the bombers whose features may be readable. Provided you have a strong stomach.'

'You've got it?' Julie asked instantly.

He reached into his brief case, found the envelope with the photo, took it out and held it up to her, tentatively, as if ready at any moment to withdraw it. With a tug Julie took it from his hand.

The head had been blown off at the neck, and the upper, left side of the face shredded. A pulpy remnant of nose and half a mouth were all that remained to help identification. Julie looked at the photo for a long moment, longer than necessary it seemed to him, so long that he reached out and took it back.

'Sorry, it was just a chance. There's no reason... Though who knows, if they were from your area...'

'It means nothing to me.'

'Of course.'

'Isn't this police work, rather than for the security service?'

The question touched Tony on the raw. The truth was yes, and for an MI5 man of 37 years standing the tasks he'd been allotted were demeaning. But there you were. Well before the bomb the security services' Norwich outpost had shown itself to be not just redundant but generously staffed.

'Well,' he looked up, smiling. 'There's a fine line. Normally some of it might be coppers' work, but these are abnormal times, so no one's sticking to protocol. I'm not going to try to cover everyone, door to door. Just the ones we know were nearest the explosion.'

'Which means the sickest.'

'I suppose it does, but let's get on.'

He fished out another photo, a blown-up CCTV shot, and passed it to her. It was the outside of the Bank before the explosion. She studied it. Everything seemed as she remembered, nothing more.

'Anything there?'

'I wonder what happened to him.'

She pointed to the profile of a black man, half cut off at the picture's edge.

'You saw him?'

'In passing, yes.'

'Any idea who he was?'

'A demonstrator. There were three of them picketing the Bank with a cross.'

'A cross?' A commonplace enough fellow to fancy himself a man of imagination, Tony raised a brow. 'Maybe he was a look-out. Couldn't ask for a better disguise.'

'He was Caribbean,' Julie said flatly. 'A religious freak if you ask me.'

'Richard Reid, the shoe bomber, was Caribbean. And it's freaks we're dealing with, Dr Opie. We also have pictures of people arriving at the salon. Spillover from a CCTV outside a Barclays. Take a look at these, could you?'

He produced stills from his briefcase, and picked one out:

'Here's you. Very collected in the circumstances, if I may say so, but let's do it in order. First in was this woman.' He showed another photo. 'She's Asian, right? Pakistani?'

'Yes, Safia. What happened to her I wonder?'

'I was going to ask. Was she local?'

'She didn't say. She was so frightened, poor girl, being abused by everyone.'

'Everyone?'

'Mrs Marusak, the owner.'

'Just her?'

'And Kingman.'

'Him?'

Tony showed her the picture of the black delivery boy being forced by the police into the beautician's.

'That's him, Kingman Waters. He's here.'

'I know. He's on my list of visits.'

'I'm his doctor. Two things you should know about Kingman,' she said quickly. 'He's a very sick boy, and a changed character.'

'He has a minor conviction, I'm sure you know. So it's a change for the better I would hope. I thought people with radiation sickness sort of gave up on life, went to the devil.'

'With Kingman it's the opposite.'

'A tribute to your reforming influence.'

'I don't preach at my patients, Mr Underwood.'

Tony indicated that this was fine by him. He spread out the other CCTV shots like a deck of cards.

'Anything of significance here you think?'

'Let me see… The Frenchman, the American, the road worker, no. Then there was this moustachioed fellow, the Chechen. You don't have him.'

'Chechen?' Tony held out a staying hand. 'How do you know?'

'Because I dabbled in Russian once. Enough to learn the Russian for idiot: *durak*. Mrs Marusak didn't say a lot to him – she seemed to despise him – but when she spoke to him it was in Russian. I heard her call him a Chechen idiot – *Cheshnyi durak.*'

'How did he like that?'

'He laughed.'

'Did they know each other?'

'I couldn't say. All I know is that he was there when I arrived.'

Tony was as close as he came to getting excited. He knew something about Chechens. It was in the late 1970s. A brace of them were travelling the country, claiming to be buying high tech goods, and so they were: metal pressing gear, new dyeing technologies – but also military items under embargo. One of them was an aviation technician, the other a GRU military intelligence man operating from the trade delegation. Their main job on the trip was to collect American night-vision equipment from a bent arms dealer in Manchester.

The business was to be done in the men's room of a public bar in Salford. Tony was an uninvited guest, and when the police roared in he burst from his cubicle. He still remembered the weight of the £20,000 in fivers he confiscated from the GRU man's coat lining while the fellow shrieked it was an outrage, he had diplomatic status.

Comic, really. Except that Tony turned out to have been a little precipitous from the legal viewpoint. The GRU man did have diplomatic cover, and the crooked dealer got off because technically the cash had never been handed over. An unfortunate business, and an uncharacteristic excess of zeal on Tony's part, brought on by the Chechens' intolerable cockiness. Together with the Manci business it was one of the reasons he had got stuck on the promotion ladder.

But that was then. In truth all he knew about Chechens was that they'd been kicked around by history and got themselves a reputation as seriously wild people. And from what he'd seen, they were. He'd never seen anyone drink like Chechens, drive like Chechens, or scream like them when you ripped the linings out of their fancy overcoats and relieved them of £20,000.

From the briefing notes they'd sent from Thames House since the bomb, now he'd learnt something else.

'Chechens are the only people who've done this before,' he said. 'The communists had a radioactive waste dump there. When the war with Russia started terrorists got hold of a canister of Cesium-137, mixed it with dynamite, left it in a park near Moscow and said they were going to turn the city into an uninhabitable desert. A bit over-dramatic. In the end they didn't detonate it, it was just to show what they could do.'

'I read about it,' Julie said, coolly. 'I just don't see why Chechens should bomb the Bank of England.'

Tony let pass what he hoped would be a weighty silence, as if there were things he wasn't at liberty to discuss. Then said:

'I'm not saying they're the bombers. But we know Chechens have been trafficking nuclear materials. Maybe for resale to Al Qaeda.'

'Know – or suspect?'

'Sort of mixture. Bin Laden said it was a religious duty to acquire chemical, biological and nuclear weapons. Can't get clearer than that. And the FBI are looking at a possible Chechen trail for the stuff they picked up when they uncovered the cell. Anyway, the Chechen in the salon. Did you hear anything else between him and Mrs Marusak?'

'No, that was all.'

'You didn't get his name?'

'No.'

'How did he behave?'

'Ignored everyone. Flirted with Anya, the beautician.'

'Is she Russian?'

'She spoke it. A glamour puss.'

'So I gather.'

Tony was looking knowing. From his briefcase he took another folder, selected a photo from an envelope and laid it before Julie, who frowned.

'What's this?'

'The puss.'

The Russian girl was naked, with a man.

'So what –'

'— let me tell you something that may amuse you. When the police went to check that all the occupants had been evacuated they found the property abandoned. Front door not even locked. They broke down an inside door to get upstairs.'

'Mrs Marusak said it was a separate flat, with no access.'

'She would. Couldn't have respectable City gents marching in and out through a beautician's. The upstairs was a brothel, with its own entrance at the back. Nicely done, apparently, all silk drapes and satins. Fancy end of the market.'

After taking this in, Julie said:

'You mean there were people – girls – up there when it happened?'

'To judge from the footage the police got, the place was in full swing. It's all there on film. Mrs Marusak must have been security conscious. All brothels are. Got out too quick to unload the cameras. Left us with a historical record of the moment.'

'Pompei,' said Julie wryly.

Tony got there after a moment.

'Oh I see, yes. Ruins of Pompei. Still at it when the roof fell in. They had customers all right, two of them, and... Well I won't trouble you with their reactions. I have to say it had its comic aspects.'

Tony risked a smile.

'Can't say I'm tremendously amused, the number of people I treat with Aids, prostitutes most of them. Seems in character though, for Mrs Marusak. Have you met her?'

'Not yet.'

'A Gorgon. And I can guess where she got the girls.'

'Illegals, I imagine.' He tapped his file of photos. 'Seems to have been a multicultural service. Maybe your friend Safia was one of them?'

'I doubt it,' Julie said quickly, before thinking back. 'Prostitute' Mrs Marusak had called her when she'd tried to break out into the ambulance. Her clothes looked the part all right, though not for an upmarket brothel.

'That's not her at all. She was just a terrified woman.'

'Pity. We could forget about her if she was a whore.'

Julie glanced at her watch.

'And to think none of this would have happened if the Americans hadn't shot Bin Laden. It was asking for it.'

There seemed no future in pursuing that. Tony let it pass, but Julie went on:

'What are the chances of us stopping another bomb, if there is one? Like the one they apparently planned in America? I say apparently because'– she shrugged – 'with Americans you never know. Maybe it's all a myth.'

'You want the official assessment? Or mine?'

'Yours.'

'Worst thing is the element of chance. Few years back some bored customs official in Uzbekistan thought he'd have a look at some heavy containers leaving the country. Heavy because it turned out they were lined with lead. Which didn't stop them releasing radiation when they tested them.

'The stuff was being shipped to Quetta, Pakistan. Bit where all the Taleban trouble is. Transport documents said it was metal, turned out to be the only true thing about it. It was strontium-90, same as they used on The Bank. Soft and silvery it is, apparently, turns yellow when you cut it. Creepy stuff.'

'Well I did ask.'

She wanted him out now. She looked tired and strained. It struck him that she'd said nothing about herself and the problems of life in the camp. One of those uncomplaining women, he sensed, whose purpose was not to invite the condescension disguised as caring that men were all too ready to deploy. That much he knew about women, and about himself. Which did not prevent Tony from giving her a pat on the arm as he left, unconsciously, as if to say well done young woman. Or from reflecting, at an even less conscious level, that the reason he'd enjoyed their conversation despite their disagreements was that in the liveliness and intelligence of her deep brown eyes there was something of Manci.

The low structure, little more than a 5x10 foot concrete box, stood in a deserted alley, between huts with smashed windows and garages with gaping doors. One of those items of street furniture at which no one so much as glances, it could have been anything: a fuel bunker, a defunct telephone installation, a municipal storage site housing God knew what.

Walking past in the half-dark, Amer stopped and looked round before rapping on the door, hard, so as to be audible through the steel. Walking on swiftly he turned into a side-street, checked again, saw no-one – the street was deep inside a derelict industrial estate – and waited.

The door in the alley opened and Jayson emerged, crouching. Grazing his head against the rusted frame, he cursed softly. After stuffing his monitoring equipment into the pockets of his blouson he re-locked the door and joined Amer round the corner in the empty street.

'It's all right?'

The Syrian, fretful as ever, looked anxious.

'Fine. I checked. Same as we left it.'

'No leaks?'

'None I saw.'

'And the reading?'

'Normal.'

'Allah be praised! And outside, in the alley? The reading there?'

'You said to test the equipment. Outside I didn't check.'

'But the rays do not respect walls. It is from outside that someone might detect it. Go back and do it.'

'I don't think –'

'– do it, brother.'

Amer was gone another three or four minutes. He came back and they walked on.

'So?'

'Bit higher than what it was, but not much over the, you know, limit.'

'How much?'

'35 rems.'

'Which means?'

'100 to 200 rems is when you get light radiation poisoning. 10 per cent fatality after 30 days, is what they taught me.'

'Do not talk to me about rems, and never mind what they taught you. What I am asking is, can anyone detect it?'

'Course you could pick it up if you was looking, I'm not sayin' you couldn't. But who's gonna come to a place like this with his Geiger and stuff? Nobody here, is there? Even the police don't come round this area no more, don't dare, says in the paper.' He pointed to a local freesheet in his pocket. 'So how they gonna –'

'– and will it remain stable, till we need it?'

'Depends when, brother.'

'I mean…' The Syrian was getting exasperated. 'I mean till the moment.'

'Yeah, safe till then. Safe till the moment. I mean that's if we're talking'– he stopped, his face as insentient as ever, 'like days. Yeah so it's safe till then I reckon.'

'I asked if it's safe. You tell me it is. That is all I need.'

They walked on, Amer quickening the pace, Jayson a step behind.

'So when we get the van?'

'The next thing,' Amer said, without turning, 'is not a van, it is a target. Then a van. The aim, brother, precedes the means.'

'I'm with yer. You tell me when an' I'll get one. Be cheaper than the one they used. People ain't buyin' nothin', is they, so down goes the price. Good time to pick up a motor. An' it don't need to be as big as last time, the Transit.'

'Why's that?'

The Syrian was fretful again.

"Cos ours is less than half.'

'Ours is smaller?'

'Yeah, bit.'

'Why is it smaller? Why less than half? When did it get smaller? It was supposed to be divided equally. Those were my instructions. Not so difficult, is it, to divide things by half?'

Jayson began looking confused.

'It wasn't me did it, it was Tariq.'

There was a silence.

'For themselves,' Amer said, tightly, 'they took the biggest half.'

'I said to 'im it was bigger, the one he took, I told 'im. But Tariq said Umair said they needed more 'cos the Bank was all stone and stuff –'

'– and if ours should be in stone?' The Syrian was silent again, then: 'The biggest half, the most glory. And you gave it them…'

'Umair –'

'– do not speak to me of Umair.'

They walked on along the darkened street, past a disused factory. All at once Jayson grabbed the Syrian's arm and pushed him through the door of the gatekeeper's lodge. Inside he forced down his head. Allowing himself to be manhandled, Amer crouched inside the lodge, rigid, speechless.

'See that van?' Jayson breathed. 'That torchlight?'

To peer out of a side window Amer raised his head an inch or two, and saw it. Two hundred yards along the street a van had stopped. Someone had got out and was shining a light at a gate.

'Gotta wait till it goes.'

Amer's head shot down again, quickly.

They waited, heard the van start up, stop again, start, stop again – nearer this time. Minutes later it was in front of the lodge. Jayson pulled Amer lower, waited for the engine to cut. It didn't. While it ran on a beam played over the factory's gates, its windows, then the lodge. Hitting the space above their heads it lingered a few seconds over a

Playboy cut-out sellotaped to the wall behind a desk. Then the van revved, and was off.

When it turned from the road Jayson indicated it was OK, they could come out. Amer stayed where he was.

'Why go out? They know we're round here! They're looking for us!'

'It's nothing, brother. Ain't even the police. Security van. Seen it around before. Checks the factories once in a while. Makes sure the gates is closed, people not dumpin' stuff or strippin' lead and copper is all they do.'

'They don't check the garages?'

'They didn't turn in there, did they? Watched 'em and they didn't turn in. Went the other way. The garages, they's a ruin, brother, wide open, nothin' there. It's why the box is good.'

Jayson was proud of his concrete box. It was him who'd found it. With his experience of being on the run with drugs to stash he had a nose for hideaways. Though not the stinking basement, that was Amer, and while he'd never dared say so he thought he could have done better.

A minute or two later they came out and walked on, the Syrian's head twitching right and left with every step.

Jayson said:

'Can I ask a question, brother?'

'You may.'

'Maybe we should go somewhere else? Outta that basement. I mean if it's not gonna be today or tomorrow we can't sorta settle in somewhere, we gotta keep movin', right? That room, we been there ever since, an' the smell in there, smell like that ain't good for you. Makes me think of...' Not wanting to talk about prison he petered out, then added: 'Course I'm not suggestin' we move jus' 'cos of the stink. All depends how long you was thinkin' before we –'

'– we shall see. Maybe it would be good if you found somewhere else for a while. By yourself. Maybe it's less safe to be together.'

'What you sayin', brother?'

All the time Amer was walking a step ahead, talking over his shoulder. Jayson had noticed this tendency to keep space between them. He didn't resent it – didn't dare – though he didn't like it. Now he caught up.

'I think we should stay together, brother.'

When strong fingers grasped his arm Amer shook them off, and strode on.

'I don't feel well,' he said. 'My throat. Something not right there. When I don't feel well I prefer to be alone.'

'What you got?'

'I feel something here.' A hand went to his beardless upper neck. 'Maybe it's you. Maybe you've given me something. You've been so close to it, and today, today you were close again.'

Relieved, the Trinidadian almost smiled.

'Don't be afraid, brother.'

'I am not afraid. I just don't want to get sick. To be unable –'

'– it can't happen, brother! No way! Allah won't allow it! How he let you fall sick when you're doin' His work? An' whatever you got it ain't radiation, I'm tellin' you. You don't catch it just from being with someone, is what they taught me. It's not like, I dunno, the 'flu or somethin'.'

'I am not saying it's only you. Maybe I got it when it happened. We thought we'd be all right a mile away, didn't we? It was Umair who said we'd be alright, that it was the place we should wait. But the wind. He didn't know the wind would take it so far. And we were in that café, all that time. It was open at the front, remember?'

'Moment of glory is what I remember, brother, on the TV in that café. Know what I was thinkin'? I was thinkin', they showed all them pictures of Osama after they got him, didn't they, lookin' at the TV in 'is 'ouse. Let's see how they like lookin' at this, was what I was thinkin'. Took 'em a while to get those pictures, of the dead people and people hidin' in those shops and stuff. But when they came… And us sittin' in that café, knowin'… Sweet memories, brother…'

'But it was only a mile away.'

'Mile an' a half more likely, where we was, so don't worry. And that wind, you can't knock it, it was Allah! Was the wind that did the damage, the TV said.' Jayson's spaced-out face brightened as much as it ever did. 'If you's worried you could have a check-up. Plenty of people doin' it, heard on the radio. People who thought they was too close, and they wasn't. Don't take no time it says in those adverts tellin' people to check themselves out. Put your heart at ease, brother.'

'A check-up. You think I should have a check-up. In a hospital, where they ask you for papers now. And if I've got it, they will ask me how? Where had I been, what was my address, what had I been doing? In hospitals they have security people, watching.' He sighed and said. 'Sometimes you say things, brother…'

They walked on, Amer leading, till they'd left the estate behind and were in sight of a row of shops. At a bus stop, the Syrian stopped.

'You will get a bus here.'

'Why? Where?'

'I need to be alone. To preserve my health. To think, to plan.'

'What'll I do?'

'You can visit your wife for a few days. Otherwise she will worry, tell relatives you've gone missing, maybe the police. Women will say anything when they're worried, neurotic. You will go to her, now, tonight. Get a bus. Here.'

Feeling in his pocket, he handed him some notes, at arm's length.

'In a week you will come. No, in five days. If my throat – if I feel weak – we have to be ready. I will think, I will decide. We may have to go quickly.'

7

Feeling low after his phone call to Julie – images of Jackie, swollen-eyed and sickly, had lodged in his mind – Martin bought a second pint. It was darkening outside, and excitement filled the bar. At a neighbouring table three men had their heads together. The one doing the talking turned to him.

'Ain't seen you 'ere before. New recruit reportin' for duty, are we? Wanna change them clothes, mate. Mohamed-bashing 'as its pleasures but it ain't worth ruining a nice suit of clothes.'

'Hi. My name's Martin.'

He held out a hand. The man shook it.

'And what would you be doing up here, Martin?'

'Seeing what's happening, analysing the situation. I'm a journalist.'

'Right. So you're not doin' anything.'

'Sorry?'

The man leant closer:

'I 'eard you on the phone. Wasn't listening, just 'eard. Got a casualty in the family?'

'My wife and daughter weren't far from the explosion. They may have got a dose. They're under observation.'

The man stared in mock bewilderment:

'Pardon me, son, but I'm not sure I get you. How old's your daughter?'

'Six.'

'Pretty girl is she?'

'Lovely.'

'And your wife?'

'We're separated actually.'

'Not the point. Your daughter and 'er mother 'ave a fair chance of getting's cancers 'cos of what these cave-dwelling bastards 'ave done and you sit there tellin' me you're analysing the situation.'

The two others at his table had turned away. He banged for their attention:

'Listen to this, lads. You lot lost your jobs, but that's nothing. Martin 'ere's got a six year old daughter who got hit. And all 'ee's gonna do is analyse the situation.' He put an imaginary monocle to his eye. 'Don't panic, chaps. Just sit back and take it, what?'

Martin got his beer and stood up. The man held his arm.

'OK, I take that back. Least you've come 'ere. We 'aven't 'ad that many journalists. In fact we 'aven't 'ad none.' To his companions' amusement he sat up straight, as if on his best behaviour. 'Well go on then, ask me somethin'. Interview me.'

'I will if you tell me your name.'

Martin sat back down.

'Boney 'ee's called,' the man next to him guffawed. 'Fuckin' Napoleon 'ee is.'

Martin recognised the man in the beret with the binoculars he'd seen from the other side of the railway bridge. Close up he bore a resemblance to James Joyce: small glasses, a concave face, an intellectual manner out of sync with the earthier types around him.

'Yeah, give Boney an interview,' the man continued. He had a brawny body and a round but unkindly face. 'Ask 'im 'bout 'is grand strategy. Tell you what mine is. Give the fuckers one back. Only a small one, mind you, see 'ow they like it.'

'Tell you what, Eddy,' the first man said in a considered voice. 'Why don't you shut the fuck up? The gentleman from the press is tryin' to conduct an interview. With me.'

'Fire ahead,' said Eddy, 'fire ahead. We're listenin'.'

Martin took a recorder from his bag, then put it back; in the din it would be hopeless. He scrabbled notebook and pen together.

'So your name is?'

'Billy Furlow.'

'Do you think it's wise,' he began, 'to take it out on Muslims who had nothing to do with the bombing? I mean aren't you only going to make it easier for them to claim they're being persecuted, surrounded, to all intents and purposes interned? I mean making them into victims?'

Eddy gestured at the TV, grinning.

'Talks like 'em, dunnee?'

'That's 'cos 'ee is one.' Billy said it equably, as if Martin weren't present. 'One of the Jeremies. Fuckin' country can be zinging with radioactivity and the Jeremies will be in their studios doin' in-depth interviews with their Muslim scholars, so-called.' He looked Martin up and down, then said. 'Lemme ask you a question, Martin my lad. What do you know about this area? You a Londoner?'

'I'm from Manchester.'

'Don't sound like it.'

Martin gave a smile.

'You get a scholarship to Manchester Grammar, you go to Cambridge, and after fifteen years living and working in London, you don't.'

He said it in a raw Mancunian accent. He was good at accents – one of his university acting skills – and Billy and his boys laughed loudly, fooled and charmed.

Martin was from Surrey. He'd been to Millfield school as a boarder, without benefit of scholarship, which hadn't mattered because his father was big in the insurance industry. After a middling performance at A level, due to what a master called his congenital lack of application, he'd gone on to Edinburgh University, where he'd got a third in the history of art, due this time to his dalliance with the theatre.

Scholarship boys were not given a sports car for their twenty-first birthday, or an annual allowance of £25,000. None of this stopped Martin affirming his meritocratic credentials crisply and with conviction. While he spoke them he meant every word. As a self-made man, he even felt a shot of pride.

'You don't sound too local yourselves,' he countered. 'Up from the South?'

'We's mixed,' Eddy grunted, 'but we's British.'

There was a silence. Then the short, blond man on Billy's right, quiet so far, said suddenly:

'I was at the plant, thirteen years. The ones we 'ad there was no bother. 'Ad one in the paint shop with me, never said nothin' about Afghanistan or whatever. Then I saw 'im on a Sunday, in the park with 'is wife and kids. Couldn't believe it. You work with a feller every day of the week, no problem, nice as you like, and his wife goes round in a tent with slits for eyes.

'"This is my wife, Sana', he says, and I'm wanting to say, 'Well pleased to meet you Sana, how 'bout you comin' out of your tent so we can say hello.' He paused and looked down at the table. 'Kids seemed alright though. Behaved themselves better than ours'.

'Never felt the same 'bout 'im after that. Gives you the 'eebie-jeebies. Like seein' 'em bangin' their 'eads on the ground in mosques. You start thinking, well if they can do that, what else could they do?' He looked round, as if expecting an answer. 'Now we know. I read in the paper someone sayin' it was God's judgement. Depends if it's our God or theirs, dunnit? Well I'm a working man and a father and I don't accept the judgement.'

'Phil's new to the cause,' Billy explained, 'rallied to the standard.'

'But aren't your tactics destructive?' Martin asked.

'We got constructive suggestions all right.' Thrusting three fingers in the air, Billy ticked them off. 'One, stick to your own territory, for your own good. Two, sell up for what you can get in the national fuckin' depression you've driven us into. Three, fuck off home. Safe conduit far as the airports and the docks. Anyone left after six months is interned. Then we can rebuild the country. No point tryin' now. If the Stock Exchange comes back from zero and they start taking on labour, all they gotta do is let loose with their second strike like the one the FBI says they was plannin', time and place of their choosin'. And down we go again.'

He paused, pointing at the pen in Martin's motionless hand:

'Didn't see you taking that down. Where's your recorder? We've no objection to being recorded, have we guys?'

The guys indicated that they hadn't.

'It's too noisy. Anyway they wouldn't publish it. Too incendiary.'

'That's because we're feelin' a little incendiary. Right lads?'

Eddy's guffaw got him coughing, made him stub out his cigarette.

'You gotta do something,' he said when he could speak, his brow wrinkling with menace to come. 'Mustn't take the law into your own 'ands is what you lot say. Well it's not in anyone else's is it?'

Martin opened his mouth on some judicious sentiment. It was as far as he got:

'Say one word about race and I'll bop yer.' Eddy leant forward, meaning it. 'Racist to stop your children being slaughtered or malformed or whatever, which is worse? What about racism, racism –'

He dried and looked to Billy for help:

'Inverted,' said Billy.

'Yeah, inverted.'

'Well said Eddy lad.' Billy looked at Martin, full on. 'So there you go Martin. Time to choose sides. You with us or with the Jeremies?'

'I've got a job to do –'

'– more'n we 'ave,' Phil interjected.

'– and I've come up here to do it.'

'Good on you son,' Billy said. 'Provided you does it properly. Tell your paper we're doin' everyone a favour keeping the place safe from the Mohameds. Wallin' 'em off, 'emmin' 'em in. With a raid or two to show who's boss.'

'But incursions onto their side of the line will just provoke them.'

Billy looked at his comrades, smiling.

'Swallowed the lot, 'asn't 'ee? 'Ook, line and sinker for seconds.' His head came closer. 'It's a war situation and we got a right to patrol our country. You 'ave to 'ave the right to piss on your own territory.'

'So what do you have in mind?'

Billy sat back, drink in hand.

'Thing is to 'ave a strategy. What Napoleon said was –'

'–'ere we go.' Eddy smiled, though with respect, urging Martin to listen.

'– ignore my friends. It was Boney who said the thing is to get behind 'em, go for their supplies, as well as doing your frontal assault. Plus you 'ave to undermine their will to fight. Boney said it but so did Sun Tze the Chinaman. Which in the Muslim case means takin' out their jihad propaganda.'

'Or as they would see it, attacking their religion.'

'If it's an attackin' religion itself, where's the harm in that?'

'Of course they'd say that Christianity –'

'– pardon the interruption, Martin, but you Jeremies wear big boots and I can 'ear you comin'. You're gonna say Christianity was an attackin' religion in its time – 'cos its time's over in this country, tell you that for nothin'. Capitulated, 'asn't it? No more cheeks to turn. Anyway you're talkin' hundreds of years ago, I'm talking bloody now!'

Billy banged the table, shivering the beer.

'So you're going to mount patrols.'

'Patrols and SOE.'

'Special operations,' Eddy explained.

'I understand,' said Martin. 'What exactly?'

Billy ran his tongue round his mouth and smiled:

'If you're not allowed to report it, why would you want to know?'

'Come on, what have you got in mind?'

'Could be anything. A mosque. Some hell-raising imam's house.'

'Not a private house. Or a mosque.'

'You think mosques ain't fair game? That's where you're wrong, Martin my boy, 'cos you 'aven't done your 'omework. They don't worship buildings like we do with our churches. Sunni Muslims that is. That's why they demolish thousand-year-old places in Mecca. So they got no reason to get into a state if they 'appen to burn down, 'ave they?'

The three of them put their heads together, excluding Martin, lowering their voices in the din to a pitch Martin couldn't hear.

'Looks like the grocers then,' Eddy said.

Billy glared round.

'I'll be the judge of that. Not sayin' it won't be, mind you. Legit target I would say. Back room full of inflammatory literature, could go up any time.'

He turned to Phil.

'Jawar's grocery. Know where it is? Corner of Keighly street. We done it before but we'll do it again. You all right with that?'

'Yeah, I'm fine.'

Phil nodded several times too many, convincing himself, it seemed.

They came out of their conclave.

'Right then,' Billy said, standing up. 'Off we go. Take two – with feelin'!' He looked down at Martin. 'An' our war correspondent's comin' along. Embedded with the troops, right?'

*

Falling at the first hurdle, Martin floundered astride the fence separating the railway from the street, six feet from the ground. Wire spikes needled his flesh, wetting his trousers with blood. It was painful.

Billy, Phil and Eddy had gone over before him and stood on the other side, the last two laughing themselves silly.

'Shut up, cunts,' Billy said, 'and get him down.'

Martin allowed himself to be disentangled and lifted over. The humiliation was the greater since, younger than the others by a decade and thinking himself in shape after his latest bout of abstinence, he'd tried taking the fence in a single, scrabbling leap.

The four of them stood by the side of the track. A freight train was approaching, sluggishly. While the others waited for it to pass, with a kind of concentrated nimbleness – there were points – Martin picked his way across the tracks, close enough for the looming engine to catch him in its glare.

'Silly bugger,' Billy said when they joined him on the other side.

Martin shrugged, manfully, though the second fence he took slowly.

A lone soldier guarded an alley leading to the street beyond. Martin crouched after landing, looked round warily. The others stood up and walked on, chatting, towards the alley and the soldier, whose back was towards them. The man must have heard them coming, but moments before they caught up with him he reached for a breast pocket, took out a cigarette and turned sideways to light it, crooking his arm as if to avoid the breeze. His fag alight, and the four of them in the alley, he turned towards the railway and took long, contented puffs.

'Local lad,' Billy explained in response to Martin's lifted brows.

'From Afghanistan?'

'Nah, from barracks. The Afghan boys are more trouble. All that 'earts and minds stuff got to 'em. Sapped their patriotism. Our friend 'ere does 'is job according to 'is conscience in the service of 'is country. Got an impossible task, 'asn't 'ee? There to stop us going in and the Mohameds from coming after us. Patriot can't face two ways at once, can he?'

Halfway along the alley Billy stepped into a patch of undergrowth. Parting a clump of bushes, he emerged with what looked like a swatch of reddish sticks. Brandishing them briefly, he thrust them at his mates. As they took them Martin saw what they were: lengths of rusted steel, concrete reinforcement rods, most likely. Two, he noted, were bent.

Billy held one out to Martin, who shook his head.

'Jumps over the track in the face of an oncoming train then faces the enemy unarmed. Go on like that and you'll get yourself a dead man's medal.'

The three of them stowed the steel lengths in their clothes, then walked on stiffly.

'You're going to walk round a Muslim area with those?' Martin asked.

'Gotta right to go where we like. An' it's not walking, it's a patrol. If anyone tries to stop us'– he pointed to his side –'we got a right to self-defence.'

'And if no one does? You might as well walk along Oxford Street.'

'Less we take a stand, another few years and Oxford Street'll be same as 'ere,' Eddy grunted.

'Too right!'

Turning towards him Billy did the pointing thing Martin had noticed in the pub. A politician in his own mind, like the professionals Billy made contact with his men through the magic finger, making them glow in his orbit. The evening was to see a lot more pointing.

From the alley they emerged into a near-silent street. Everywhere there were relics of incursions before the area was sealed. Billy pointed at Shaz Hairdressers, a burnt-out barbers' shop, its multicoloured pole now a charred stub.

'Now who could've done that? Must have 'ad a thing about them and their beards. Personally I got no objection to fuzz on a religious man. I mean what about Jesus Christ for Christ's sake?'

Eddy laughed and looked at Martin as if to say, you can't beat him.

'Least 'ee 'ad the decency to keep it trimmed,' Phil threw in. Sensing the flatness of the joke, he looked as if he wished he hadn't made it.

There were more people on the street. Passers-by skirted the trio as they strode on three abreast, Martin in their wake, then looked back in derision. Closer to the centre more places were open and more late-night shoppers appeared. Billy picked up his step to a near-marching pace, head thrown back, accentuating the mismatch between his fragile glasses and bonily assertive head.

'Government says it don't allow no no-go areas, but show me a policeman 'ere,' he threw over his shoulder to Martin. 'Or a journalist.'

More people were watching them, some shooting hostile glances. Nervous now, Martin was on the lookout for side-roads into which to disappear, but Billy marched on. At a signal from him the three of them had fallen into single file, patrol-like, Billy striding along in a patriotic trance, Eddy looking around with menace, Phil slouching, and Martin, head down, bringing up the rear.

Teenagers in galabiyyas began trotting alongside.

'Off to war then?' one shouted.

'Fucking Dad's army,' another called out.

Ignoring them Billy marched on. A thin-faced youngster on a bike, nose bent to the handlebars, headed straight for him, forcing him to dodge at the last moment, then swerved and cut between Eddy and Phil.

'Paki bastard,' Eddy yelled, reaching for his bar, but Billy signalled to let it be. The boy rode off, laughing and doing wheelies.

They had reached the main shopping area. The numbers stopping and staring were building up. All that stood between them and a lynching, Martin began to fear, was incredulity at their appearance. Suddenly Billy's pace slackened: two hundred yards ahead a group of young men had cohered and begun moving in their direction, gathering recruits as they went.

The four of them wheeled into a side-street, Billy in the lead, broke formation and began running. The street veered sharply left so they were going back on their tracks, parallel with the main road, towards the railway.

Sensing where they were heading, keen to get away and swifter than the others, now Martin was in the lead. In the street of silent, dismal houses, an abandoned corner shop caught his eye as he ran by. The words 'Jawar' and 'Food' in Jawar Food Store were scorched and blackened, the side and ground floor windows boarded up, an awning ripped and sagging over emptied stalls.

Hearing the others' steps slow behind him he glanced round. For a few seconds Billy and Eddy huddled at the door of the darkened shop, while Phil hung back. Then the three of them sprinted on, faster.

'What was that about?' Martin panted when they caught up.

Eddy dried a watery nose with the back of his hand.

'Jus' leaving a message.'

'Right!' Billy's finger was in action as he ran. 'A peaceful fuckin' message!'

Minutes later the street rejoined the main road and, through the alley, the railway. Before turning the corner Martin searched the darkness behind him. Two points of light met his gaze: a small but gathering blaze at the door of the shop, and an electric light in a room above. Smoke from the door had reached the window, and as it scudded across the glass he thought he glimpsed a human figure.

'There's someone in there,' he called out to Billy. 'We better go back.'

'Fuckin' jokin'. He'll get out.'

'Did last time,' Eddy puffed. 'Fuckin' Houdinis they are.'

They reached their crossing point on the railway. Seeing them coming the soldier turned towards the line, busy with another cigarette.

'Wanna watch those lungs o' yours, Pete my lad,' Billy murmured to his back as he passed. 'You'll 'ave to go to 'ospital but you won't get in 'cos they're full up with woggies.'

Stowing the steel bars in the bushes before crossing the track, they walked to the Wheatsheaf, cleaned up in the toilets, and found a table. Martin bought a round.

'Here's to a successful sortie behind the lines,' Billy announced and raised his glass. Martin didn't. Billy blinked at him. 'You're buying and you're not drinking? Disowning your compatriots?'

Martin said: 'Why did you have to firebomb the place? You'd forced it to close anyway.'

Billy looked at the others, forehead ridged in disbelief.

'Anyone see me firebombing anythin'?' He looked inquisitorially at Phil and Eddy. 'You two done any firebombin'?'

Phil, uncomfortable, looked away. Eddy held out his freshly-washed hands in innocence.

'So it was spontaneous combustion,' Martin said tightly – and got the political finger.

'Absolutely! Straight from the 'ills they are. Never could look after their electrics.'

Martin didn't laugh.

'Someone could get hurt.'

'And so? Be an act of God, won't it?' Billy joined his hands as if in prayer. 'Place was a propaganda centre, 'cording to our intelligence. Jihadi literature. Glorified nuking the country. No God worth 'is salt's gonna stand for that.'

'Have you read any of it?'

'Read any? It's in fuckin' Urdu and Arabic.'

'So how –'

'– look,' said Billy. 'What proof you got that it was them that did the Bank?'

'None, so far as I'm aware. Except perhaps the New York –'

'– but we know they did, don't we? Fuckin' know it!'

'Well it seems probable, maybe.'

'Maybe probable!' Billy put down his glass, his eyes alight. 'An' maybe it was the Jewboys done it, same as the Mohameds said they done the Twin Towers. Or probably the Governor's a closet Muslim and did it 'imself. There's times when you 'ave to skip the maybes and the probablies, Martin my son, an' fuckin' do somethin'.'

The others banged the table, cheering.

'One more thing.' Billy lowered his voice. 'Just so's the position's clear. I don't mind you reportin' any of that. We're not ashamed of being patriots. Remember the French resistance, blowin' up the occupiers and suchlike, in the war? Well that's what we're about.' He smirked. 'You can quote me on that, but not from my mouth, right?'

'As you like,' Martin nodded. 'Background information, not for attribution.'

'Not for attribution! I like it! Least the Jeremies is good with words. Went to better schools than I did. We do what we do and it's not for attribution. We'll drink to that, right boys?'

8

In a corner of the restaurant a middle-aged couple shared a table. It was a description Mrs Marusak would have contested, hotly, though one her companion would have had a hard time disputing. Not that Sergei Pavlovich Dolgorukhov cared what people said: his physique – thick-set, flat-nosed, stolid-looking – seemed designed to resist any words thrown at him. Nor would he have felt offended to be told that the way he described himself – 'general trader'– was a charitable term for his usually fraudulent property deals, or that his mistress/business partner was here on forged papers. 'And how you prove?' he would have said, with a shrug of those beefy, back-off shoulders. And back off you would.

They gave their order and the wine waiter approached. After a survey Sergei jabbed a stubby finger at the list:

'Two bottle.'

'I'm sorry, Sir?'

'Give me two bottle. Of this.'

He jabbed again at the Chateau Liversan '82.

'Fine, Sir.'

The waiter returned with a bottle.

'Two. You bring one. I order two.'

'You want them together, Sir?'

'Of course together.' Sergei glanced at Mrs Marusak, as if alerting her to what was coming: 'You not read papers? People dying everywhere. Maybe you fall dead before we need second bottle!'

Laughing through his grimace, the man bowed away.

The joke was a necessary accompaniment to their drinking style. They always drank two bottles, three often, and Sergei was impatient when the first ran out and drinking time was lost while he ordered another. So the first two had to come together, to be opened at the same time and stay on the table within instant reach. And always the waiters got it wrong.

His usual quip was: 'Wine like women. One is nice, but two together better,' at which Mrs Marusak would touch his arm in reproof. At the one about people dying she merely smiled.

The restaurant was going through poor times, its grandiose dining room cavernous-looking for lack of customers. The only other couple were Russians too, the man a distant acquaintance of Sergei. On arriving he'd hailed him, a trifle sourly, after noting that his companion was an expensive-looking woman some twenty years younger than his own. Later yet another Russian couple were to arrive. The place used to be popular with Americans, but they'd been the first to desert London after the Bank. Terrified of cancers, the majority had scuttled off to Paris, New York, Geneva, Frankfurt – anywhere but here.

Sniffing the chance of windfall profits as property was sold at discounts, and even the rouble rose dramatically against the pound, the Russians proved more resilient. Carelessness about questions of health was a factor. Sergei had the nonchalance of a man whose country had lived through a nuclear mishap of its own ('A few people die and other people get sick,' he would shrug about Chernobyl. 'Plenty people left.'), and who'd smoked 40-60 a day since the age of seventeen.

For him the bomb was a god-sent opportunity to expand business. The one above the beautician's was gone, but he'd make up for it. The brothel had not been his idea. It began when Mrs Marusak overestimated her capacities for running a proftable beauty salon; for whoredom, on the other hand, she showed an indisputable talent. Her spell as a prison warder proved an ideal apprenticeship, and not just when it came to handling troublesome staff: in managing her girls she was efficient, in selecting them she showed genius. How it happened was this.

At the prison rookies were assigned a large proportion of night shifts. With her plumply lascivious figure, screaming blond hair and frankly semaphoring eyes she was unused to spending her nights alone, and it was to while away the tedium, rather than by innate preference, that she allowed herself be drawn into liaisons with her female charges.

What began through no fault of her own – a debauched kid offering fingered comforts, a pretty slut looking for favours – before long became a perk. The favours involved a blind eye to the screws of powder circulating ever more widely in the years when communism foundered and prison discipline collapsed. Though unlike the addicts Mrs Marusak could take her midnight douceurs or leave them, and drop them she did after she was dismissed from the service for complicity in the drug trade.

Her interest in good-looking girls was not however over, and turned to good account. To launder the cash she'd put aside in affluent times she trained as a beautician. The course was run by Anatoli Stepanko, one of the new race of Eastern entrepreneurs, and a handsome devil. It was of course a cover. His real business was the export of Ukrainian beauties westwards, by means of Internet advertisements on the lines of *Never married lady with blue eyes and chestnut hair. Your neighbours will envy you.* Such were the beginnings of what was destined to become a roaring career: with profits from his trafficking venture to legitimise and political ambitions to pay for, he was later to be big in the industrial cleaning business.

An affair with Anatoli led the ex-warder to involvement in his scams. Her job was to select from the hundreds offering themselves for work abroad as maids, waitresses or nannies the ones most likely to appeal to Western tastes; it was not to inquire into their moral conduct once they were in London, Dubai or Miami, or how they earned the cash to repay the funds invested in their language tuition, their travel costs and bogus papers. The prettier the girl the faster the return on Anatoli's outlay, he quickly discovered, and it was here that Mrs Marusak scored high.

When Anatoli took up with a younger woman Sergei the Russian was the next step up. A native of the Donbass region, she had nothing against Russia – to her it was a second homeland – though when she re-routed her affections towards him it was because of his foreign contacts: Sergei was a small-time banker with links in London and she was keen to travel. So when he transferred his operations there he brought Mrs Marusak with him, by means of a British passport that cost him 150,000 roubles, some £3,000 pounds.

He wasn't allowed to call her Anichka – too much of the peasant about it. What she did like being called was Mme Marusak, the nickname Sergei had come up with in its place, the rascally fellow.

A restless woman determined on her own career, it was her idea to open a beauty parlour in the City with Sergei's money. A rash move, it turned out: her training fell short of Western standards and her idea of customer relations had too much of the prison warder about it. It was when the flat above the Marusak Beauty Salon became vacant that she had her brainwave. Rather than close down, why not snap up the lease and expand into a more rewarding branch of the beauty business?

Getting the girls into the country was no problem, with her experience with Anatoli, but the device she hit on – an international school of cosmetics – was her own. The Marusak Beauty Academy consisted of a top floor room in Camden Town, its teaching staff herself, its degrees validated courtesy of a Ukrainian lady of Mrs Marusak's acquaintance with a husband in the education business.

A few Internet adverts and the girls flooded in. The guarantee of a job on graduation at £1,500 a week minimum was a draw, and illusions about the nature of the work non-existent. With a little help from Sergei – not that it was needed, but he enjoyed the work – the crème de la crème was selected, and after perfunctory training reported to Mrs Marusak's salon, for duties they understood would alternate between the ground and top floors. Eight to ten girls worked a roster, two of them trimming nails or massaging faces and the like downstairs, the rest working above their heads at what they were good at.

£80 a time they scored. Exorbitant, Sergei grumbled, given they were paid for their beauty work, but when it came to her girls Mrs Marusak was not without a certain solidarity: £1,500 a week she'd promised, three tricks a day was about average, so £80 it remained. The charge to the customer being £500 Sergei got a fair return on his money, and there was a bonus: the product of the security cameras he insisted should be installed in every room. On these, as a man of business, he did due diligence.

*

Tonight Mrs Marusak was entertaining him with less appetising fare: yet more memories of the day of the bombing. After the story of the self-sacrificing American, the memory of whose four-buttoned blazer brought a tear to her eye, she was detailing once again the appalling behaviour of the delivery boy.

'I saw his photo in the paper, in hospital. Nasty black boy. And the smell! He died I suppose, one of the first.'

Sergei glanced at her abruptly.

'And you Madame Marusak, you're sure you have nothing?'

'Afraid of contamination, are you?'

Her fingers crept up his arm, spider-like. Sergei watched them, unsmiling. Since the explosion he hadn't touched her. He'd seen the articles about how radiation wasn't Aids, and people who'd got a dose were safe partners whose human needs and feelings should be respected. But he didn't believe it.

'Maybe you need a check-up? You'll have one, won't you, *golubchik*? Privately, just for me?'

Sergei touched her hand so tentatively it looked gentle. She sighed, then with girlish submission, nodded:

'If you insist, sweetheart.'

Talk of what to do about the brothel led him to his favourite theme: the future of the City.

'Remember how they used to boast about London as if it was the centre of the world? Now it's payback time for the Brits. And the

Americans. The terrorists got it wrong this time but they can hit them again, you watch, whenever they like. Shall I tell you where the future is?'

'Tell me, sweetie.'

'Russia. All that oil and gas in the Arctic, like we've been keeping it in storage! They'll be begging for it! Remember what people used to say about Moscow? The Third Rome, and there won't be a fourth. Well that's what we're going to see.' He paused. 'And China, of course there will be China.'

Mrs Marusak sniffed disgustedly.

'*Limonchiki*. Little lemons. Just looking at them sours my stomach.' She shivered. 'I never kept one in my salon, no one ever asked for one, not even Chinese. Why would a Chinese want a Chinese woman? They have nothing here'– she indicated her own un-Chinese buttocks. 'Nothing.'

'Nothing to slap and beat at all!' Sergei said, and got his fingers rapped.

'But of course you're right,' she sighed, 'there's no future here, not long term there isn't. It's too small, and they're all terrified, because there's too many foreigners. Now they're saying it was a mistake to kill Bin Laden. Terrified of killing the people killing them! But short-term there are things. You see what the papers are saying? That people have more sex when they're contaminated.'

'How come?'

'Because they're afraid of running out of time. Even when there's nothing wrong with them they do it more, because they're secretly convinced there is.'

Sergei smirked.

'Packing in the fucks while they can!'

So there'd be greater demand, she explained, whatever happened. They'd have to give the City a miss, so she'd been thinking about the suburbs, of a string of beauty parlours in the suburbs. Staffing would be a business now immigration was tighter. On the other hand there were plenty of ethnics around, and there could scarcely be a better time to recruit:

'Stores closing, restaurants folding, pubs shutting down. Think of the waitresses and bar girls and shop assistants out there looking for work!'

Which set her off again about Safia.

'Remember the girl I told you about? Pakistani or whatever? I could get onto her for a start. You know I have an eye, my pigeon, and I could see the potential. I took a look at her in the shower and her figure was good all right, very good.' A hand sculpted the air, briefly. 'Smarten her up, I thought, and this one could do some work for us.'

'But where will she be?'

'I got her address. Took it from her bag when she wasn't looking. She's a stubborn girl, mind you. She'll say no at first, but you don't dress like her unless you're ready to open your legs. Maybe I'll ring her when we get a new place. After what's happened there'll be plenty of people who fantasize about fucking a Muslim woman!'

'Maybe you, Mme Marusak, maybe you fantasize about her, the way you talk.'

Leaning, she grazed his ear, whispering:

'Maybe you want me to. So I can tell you about it.'

'Anyway it won't be me,' Sergei said with finality.

'Of course not you! You have your little *Ukrainka*, pravda?' She gave him an air kiss. 'By the way, did I tell you, there was another Muslim there. At least I suppose he was Muslim. A Chechen.'

'Chechen!' Sergei stiffened. 'What the hell was a Chechen doing there? He came to escape the bomb?'

'No, he was already there. For a girl. I said to use the entrance at the back, but he's an impudent devil, a smart-arse, he does what he likes. He saw Anya through the glass, so in he comes. Said he liked the window display.'

'What Chechens like is screwing Russians. I know, I fought the bastards. I've seen what's left of a man after they've finished with him. Head gone, balls off, like he'd been attacked by a pack of animals.

Capable of anything those savages.' He thought. 'Maybe they were behind the bombing?'

'Sergei, what are you saying? Why should Chechens –'

'– because they're lying, filthy scum. Maybe one of their Al Qaeda friends paid them?'

He was getting upset. To calm him she reached across and rested a hand on his. It was the one that was about to sign the bill he'd been studying. Examining it again, his brow wrinkled.

'Look at this! £288! They're laughing at us! The British sense of humour! They're going to have to cut their expectations. They'll be colonials themselves soon, the way they're going. Any Brit you want will work for peanuts as it is. If there's another bomb – imagine!'

'And us, my pigeon? What about us?'

'Maybe we'll sit things out in Moscow for a while. It's hard getting more deals done while they're cleaning things up, and I don't want to put too much money in just yet. Have to see whether the Bank was the end or the beginning. The thing is to make sure we can get back when the time's right.'

He paid the bill, the waiter asked for their coats to be fetched, and watched them walk off into the night. What held his attention was that the stumpy middle-aged figures were holding hands. He called the cloakroom girl, a Brazilian, to the door to take a look.

'How about that?' He pointed after them. 'Will you hold hands with your fat old husband when you're sixty?'

'Russians...' The girl shook her head, half indifferent, half-admiring. 'So sentimental.'

9

Amer was feeling better. The tingling in his throat must have been imagination. Conscious of his tendency to hypochondria the Syrian was feeling guilty. The idea that he could be taken ill at this moment was an insult to his God. And Allah might interpret his fears for himself as weakness of purpose, an excuse to delay the Day of Glory.

It was getting on for ten, he was tired but too restless for sleep, his head full of plans and stratagems. Putting his notebook aside he switched on the TV Jayson had rigged up at the bottom of his bed, and settled back. As always he felt a twinge of conscience about watching television, though he was obliged to, he assured himself, for operational reasons.

The truth was he enjoyed it, especially without Jayson. The boy would make an effort to follow the reports and discussions, staring at the screen from his bed with his arms around his knees, but within minutes his face would shed the last remnant of comprehension. His body would subside by degrees till he slipped backwards onto the coat that served as a pillow, and off he'd go like a child, his hands together beneath his head, as if praying even in sleep.

For Amer the news bulletins and debates were a nightly treat. Before going to sleep he would spend an hour channel-hopping for bomb-related items. The hapless ministers with their sombre warnings, the crowded hospitals, medical discussions about the prospects for radiation victims – all this the Syrian watched nightly from his bed in beatific contentment.

Politicians snapping at one another about their impotence in the face of the attacks he contemplated with a quiet smile, though Muslim spokesmen reduced him to rage: 'Son of a whore, living abortion, filthy abomination!' he would howl from his bed at some imam pleading for peace, or murmuring reservations about the massacre of innocents. Then he would calm himself, switch off and lie there on his raggedy bed in the stinking room, serene in his secret power. Power to strike where he willed at a time of his choosing, power to impose righteousness on the world.

Once, when he switched on, it was a report of a huge gathering of Muslims at Wembley stadium to denounce terrorism. A capacity crowd, eighty-six thousand from across the country, a speckled sea of taqiyas, kaffiyas, niqabs and hijabs and burkas roaring approval when speaker after speaker, scholar after scholar, proclaimed that violence and intolerance had nothing to do with Islam. His eyes alert for bare-headed women he scanned the crowds closely. And yes, there they were, thousands of them, shameless Jamilas every one, may God curse her name!

The climax came when different religious leaders – Muslims, Christians, Hindus, Sikhs and Rabbis – Rabbis! – came together in prayer. The sight of the taqiyahs and turbans and bishops' mitres, promiscuously mixed, mesmerized him with horror. And when the mullah spoke in Arabic to denounce jihad, that was it.

Grabbing a shoe from beside the bed he hurled it at the set with all his force. The steel tip on the heel must have caught the screen, there was a bang, then the whole thing began gushing smoke. A sign, a prophecy? Or a remonstrance? Fearful of what he'd unleashed the Syrian shrank back in his bed in awe, then leapt to the sink, filled a bottle with water and poured it on the set.

The smoke stopped, but there was a flash and the lights went out. For over an hour he lay in the dark room coughing, his eyes smarting, not daring to open the back door to let in air. When Jayson returned he let out the smoke and fixed the fuse. Next day Amer said he needed another TV, instantly, that evening, couldn't take his plans forward without it, and Jayson was straight onto it. The same day he located a replacement set for £50. He was good at finding bargains.

Amer was careful to plan his viewing. Tonight it was to be a programme on the economy, at ten thirty. What interested him especially was the state of consumer confidence, and the rise that had

been reported in the number of people daring to go out into the
streets to shop. That, and weather forecasts for the coming days.

*

Outside the basement entrance at the front of the house, Jayson
hesitated, then reached a hand through the grill to knock at the
scabbed black door. It was the first time he'd used the security code
and he did it tentatively, with application. One-two-three. A pause.
Then one-two. Five knocks in all, that much he remembered.

The door beyond the grill stayed shut. From inside, silence. No
light showed, but then it never did, he'd sealed the front window with
a sheet of hardboard.

Above him someone passed on the pavement – a rarity in this area.
Flattening himself against the wall he watched the receding figure: an
elderly woman in a burka, black against the blackness of night, using
the uninhabited street as a short cut.

After she'd gone he tried again. One-two. A pause – about the
pause he was sure – then one-two-three. He waited. A minute later the
door opened a chink, an eye looked out. Then the Syrian unlocked the
grill and let him in.

'You knocked twice, I heard you. The first time was wrong.'

'I know brother, I'm sorry, I forgot.'

'Allah help you.' Amer sighed. 'Allah help us both, if you're going
to forget everything.'

Entering, Jayson put a hand over his mouth and nose. It was a
warm evening and after the fragrance of Ayan's flat the stench of
drains seemed worse. While Amer lay back on his bed he began telling
him about his visit. A waste of breath: it was ten o'clock and the
Syrian wasn't listening. Switching the TV back on while the boy spoke
he began watching the news. Jayson shut up.

Amer smiled through the first two items: a Defence Minister
confirming that the last of the British troops would be leaving
Afghanistan within a week. Are they being pulled out as a gesture to

the bombers, because the government is afraid of a second strike? the interviewer asked. Not at all, the minister replied. The reason they're coming home is to beef up security here. The interviewer pressed on: Well of course it could be a combination of the two, couldn't it? Irritated, the minister snapped back: It could, but it isn't. Next, a wan-looking Prime Minister speaking at yet another rememberance service, this one for Muslim victims of the Bristol riots.

Next came the programme on the economy. When the presenter spoke of a rash of sales in West End stores he leant forward, eyes alight, keen to miss nothing.

Massive sell-offs by a series of chain stores are giving rise to disputes with the Home Office. Following several incidents in which fighting broke out amongst crowds of bargain-seeking customers, the police claim that sales like these were becoming a threat to public order and security, and violate the ban on large gatherings. Our correspondent takes up the story.

Previously confined to poorer parts of the capital, the correspondent explained, one-price shops were springing up in high streets across the countrry, as chain stores off-loaded stock or were forced into liquidation. Everything-for-£5, £10 or £20 sell-offs were bringing in the crowds.

The reporter was standing in front of an Oxford Street store, its windows festooned with monster signs: EVERYTHING FOR A TENNER! Close-ups showed wildly foraging hands churning coats, underwear, shoes or dresses into a tumbling mass. Outside hordes of customers waited, spilling over the pavements and into the street, while ranks of police, hopelessly outnumbered, fought to man the entrance. As the correspondent spoke a fight broke out behind him, and the police surged forward to break it up.

'That's crazy, real crazy.' Jayson stared raptly at the screen. 'Like pigs at a trough they are. Got no spiritual life.'

'Shut up, Jayson.'

Scrabbling around for the zapper Amer turned up the sound. The reporter was saying:

'Such was the scene this morning the instant the store opened for business. The police say that if this goes on they will have to call for army reinforcements. For its part the government claim that banning the sales would play the terrorists' game by shutting down the economy. Now back to the studio.'

'People like that –' Jayson began.

'Shush!'

Amer's eyes were still fixed on the set. He watched till the programme ended, and switched off.

Jayson began to undress, then stopped and said:

'I was thinkin', brother. You know what you said about laptops?'

'No mobile phones, no laptops, is what I said. Osama was strict about it.'

'Didn't stop them from –', Jayson began, then stopped. 'I know, brother, I know how you feel about it. Just that I was thinkin', Ayan, she got a laptop. It's in her name, her name before we was married. So you need to look something up, I dunno, a map or somethin'– no problem. When she's out workin' is what I mean.'

Amer thought before replying. A laptop at his disposition would be useful, no question. He'd thought about it, but it was impossible. Jayson had managed to tap into the electricity in the flat but there was no phone line that was active, and wifi could be detected.

There was another reason for his reluctance. For a private man, private to the point where the company of humans could be painful, the idea that when it was done they would take away his laptop, retrieve the hard drive and analyze everything he had viewed, like they had with Osama, caused him a secret horror.

In any case a laptop wasn't essential. Anything pressing and he could go to an internet café. In that area the owners and users were Muslims to a man, but then how many of them were spies? Bought creatures forever whining on about their duty to help the authorities, show how British they were?

Though there was one owner, Hani the Iraqi, he sensed he could trust. Piously dressed and with a seemly wife who stood in her burka at the till, everything about him inspired confidence. Towards Hani he felt a spiritual affinity. Hani who showed no inquisitiveness about what he was looking up, Hani who made dry jokes about the bomb to certain of his customers – he'd heard him do it, seen them smile. And the atmosphere in that café the day after Osama's death he would never forget. Like a funeral without speeches.

No, with Hani he was fine. Going to Jayson's place would mean more travelling, and though Ayan worked at a B & Q checkout, who knew? She might come back unexpectedly. And at Jayson's there'd be a smell of women. Something he preferred to avoid.

'Jayson, that was a good idea, and I thank you for it, brother. But I have what I need.'

He left it there. About Hani he'd said nothing to him. There were a number of things the Syrian hadn't told Jayson.

He did his ablutions, prayed, switched off the light and got into bed. Jayson lay in his, having washed and prayed already. After lying a moment in the fetid silence the Syrian said:

'So you have been with your wife.'

'Five days, brother, like you said.'

'She is well?'

'I hope so, brother.'

'She's not well?'

'She thinks she's not.' A rustle as Jayson turned. 'Thinks she's pregnant.'

'Ah.'

'And she got problems.'

'What problems?'

'She won't say. She's, you know, sick in the mornings and all that, but she got other things, women's things. Not normal she said. Said she saw on television that radioactivity can be absorbed by the babies of pregnant women.'

'Ah, the tales women tell.'

In a small voice Jayson said:

'You was afraid, brother.'

'Me?'

Jayson hesitated, then went on:

''Bout contamination.'

'About what?'

Jayson had spoken so softly Amer hadn't heard.

'You was afraid yourself. Of getting it.'

'That was… nothing. I am well now. There's no reason for her to be afraid. Where is it you live again?'

'Leytonstone.'

'Nowhere near. Even with the wind.'

'But she was in Stepney on the day. Doctor's consultation or somethin'. Didn't say nothin' about it before, didn't want to worry me. An' if it's true about pregnant women…' He stopped, as if digesting what it meant. 'Be a pity for her to lose the child.'

'Of course it would be a pity. But if she does, that will be Allah's punishment.'

'Punishment, brother?'

'For tempting you at such a moment.'

'She don't know 'bout it. So how'd she know she's not to… tempt me?'

'Women are temptresses.'

More silence from Jayson's bed, then:

'Maybe was me tempted her. Maybe I gotta repent. So the child won't be punished.'

'No, it is women, always it is women, with their hair, their eyes, their smell. Remember the Sura, brother: Men are tempted by the lure of women. These are the enjoyments of this life. Far better to return to God.'

'I'll remember it, brother.' He went on, tentatively: 'You never wanted a wife? Or a child?'

'These are not things for us to discuss.' Amer spoke sharply. 'It is not the past we should be thinking about. You're sure Ayan is not pretending, about her child, and her health? To make you come home, make you falter? If she knows, if she suspects? Maybe she's pretending?'

'She don't know, I told you brother, I swear it. An' if she did she'd envy me my martyrdom. Ayan is a pious woman.'

It was as well that it was dark. For all his comatose expression Jayson lied badly. Even in the darkness he rubbed his nose as he spoke. It was true his year-old wife didn't know, true too that she was pious. As pious as she felt the need. She'd taken to the hijab at his insistence but she wouldn't do the niqab or the burka. Also she had pretty feet, liked shoes, asked him for money to buy them. And she was worried by his Koran-reading, his constant prayers. Of course you must follow Allah's teachings, she would say to him, but why do more than other people?

She was restless too about his long absences. His lie to her was that he'd landed a job helping to re-wire an old house in Sussex, a big job that paid good money for working flat out, weekends included, to get it done on time. So far his punctiliousness about giving her cash helped quell any misgivings. The money came, in fifties, from the Syrian.

'Though maybe the baby'll be fine,' Jayson went on, 'if number two goes well –'

'– shh brother, I have told you!'

'I mean if things is a big success, maybe Allah will relent, give her a healthy child. What do you think, brother?'

'It is possible. If you clear your mind for the task, and your martyrdom is sufficiently glorious and productive, I am convinced He will relent. God willing it will be even more than they did, even with less than half.'

His voice a dreamy whisper, he went on:

'If the numbers are the biggest the world has seen, if the leaders of the government are humiliated, on their knees on television, imploring us to stop, begging for our mercy, saying they will accept Sharia and the Caliphate, how could He not relent?'

'He couldn't, brother, no way.'

'So now you have three reasons to do it. For Islam, for your eternal life – and for your child.'

'For my child. A child of Mohamed.'

'But do not hanker after your wife. Remember you have left Ayan. Taken your leave. That is a reason I wanted you to see her. So you have taken leave of her and she is gone from your life. It is as if you were not married. That way you are ready, like me. Do not think about her.'

'It's hard not to, brother, so long as we're... sorta here.'

'We are here and not here. No longer of this earth, but not yet departed. We are,' Amer thought for a second, 'in limbo.'

'Didn't know there was a Muslim limbo.'

'Ah, but there is.' The Syrian's voice softened. 'The prophet Mohamed, peace be upon him, had an experience that was like limbo. What vulgar people call a near-death experience.'

Jayson settled in his bed, contentedly. It sounded as if Amer was embarking on a story, which he sometimes did, and he liked stories.

'Go on,' he said.

'It happened when he ascended to visit the seven heavens, in the company of the archangel Gabriel.'

'Why'd he do that, brother? I mean before he was dead?'

'Because his enemies said they would not believe his message unless he ascended to heaven and brought back a book.'

'So he went there, still alive?'

'No.' Amer frowned in the dark. 'He went in spirit, in the night. His body remained on earth, in his bed. That's what I am trying to tell you. He was neither here nor there. He was in limbo.'

'Got you, brother. Thing is, how'd he do it?'

'He was prepared for his visit one evening when he was asleep. His body was opened to purify his heart by taking away all traces of error and filling it with wisdom and belief. Then he ascended on a ladder of light to the seven heavens. The story tells us what to expect at the time of death. What it is like to be between life and eternity. Mohamed states that the ladder on which he ascended to heaven was the one to which the dying man looks when death approaches.'

Jayson had been listening, wide-eyed. Now he closed them, tightly.

'I see the ladder, brother. I see it.' His eyes opened. 'And the book? He got the book, right?'

'Naturally.'

'So his enemies, the unbelievers, the infidels, they were sorta gutted.'

'Exactly.'

'Great story.'

'It is a beautiful story. And it is true.'

A peacefulness descended on the room. If Amer lay awake for some time it was not because he'd heard something between a sob and a sniffle from Jayson's bed. He was reflecting on what he'd seen on television about the high street sales, and the weather forecast. Unsettled, it had said, with the possibility of strong winds to come.

When eventually he whispered towards Jayson, 'Tomorrow, you can look for a van, brother,' there was no response. Jayson was asleep, deep in a dream about a ladder of light to the sky.

10

The beach below the camp had little to recommend it for inclusion in the tourist trail. Here there were no painted huts or squealing bathers, and the sea itself, full of browns and greens yet somehow never blue, did not beckon. No shells or pebbles disturbed the shore's flat surface, nothing except the algae-draped breakwaters interrupting the monotone stretch of mud and sand.

The camp doctors encouraged the belief that sea air was good for the inmates' condition. The idea that irradiated skins could be blown clean by the wind and lungs purified by salt sea air was appealing, yet few seemed keen to take the cure. As a group they were not a beach-loving crowd, at least not this beach and not in this weather. The only visitors were the huddles of elderly whites who came down on the few sunny days to do what tradition required: spread a towel on damp sand, stow their sandwiches and thermoses, improvise their wind-breaks and hunch against the breeze.

The younger crowd found another use for the beach. The camp overlooked four breakwaters, a happy chance for the Nukies and the Bikeys, the main two gangs. Pakistanis, Somalis and Bangladeshis composed the first. The Bikeys – so named for the elaborately deformed handlebars on their machines – consisted of Caribbeans and Africans, with a handful of Sikhs and whites grudgingly admitted.

The division of the beach into proprietary zones had come about spontaneously. It was understood that the most northerly space between the breakwaters was reserved for the Nukies, the most southerly for the Bikeys, while the old folk served as the buffer in-between. It took a day of rare heat to coax the youngsters into the water, and the gangs had little reason to make the trek to the beach, except to assert ownership of their slice of shore.

To do this they would lug their bikes down the path, so the wheels could trace great looping signs and signatures in the flat wet sand. By the time they'd finished, each crew seeking to out-do the other in the size and swagger of its vast cursive sweeps, from the cliff-top the beach resembled a wall of graffiti.

*

Today the rival insignia had once again been washed smooth by the tides. Instead parallel footsteps indented the sand and mud. The two walkers were Julie and Safia. It was a day or two after Safia had come to the camp, and thinking she looked run-down Julie had taken her out for some fresh sea air and exercise.

The way the girl had arrived had been irregular. The hospital she'd gone to after her evacuation from the salon had administered the usual tests, and found nothing. Insisting she was at risk, she was tested again, with the same result. And when she claimed she was suffering worsening symptoms, displaying reddened skin on her shoulders that doctors instantly saw was the result of the scrubbing Julie had warned against, she was marked down as one of those who had suffered mental trauma and whose contamination fantasies would take time to dispel.

The hospital was close to Julie's surgery, and the psychiatrist who examined her, Sheila Lomax, a professional friend. So when Safia gave Julie as her doctor, asked where she was and insisted she wanted to go on being treated by her, Sheila rang Julie, and after some hesitation it was fixed.

The hesitation was because of Safia's fib. The reasons Julie relented were the memory of her being abused in the salon, and because Sheila told her that the girl was estranged from her parents and had nowhere to go. Bending the rules, she arranged for her to be admitted to the camp, on the grounds that she was a former patient in need of 'further investigation and recuperation.'

The moment they were alone in Julie's office, Safia, dressed in a hijab whose blackness accentuated her pale gaunt face, was tearful in her gratitude:

'It's so beautiful here, if only I can stay, I will recover.' She dabbed her cheeks and looked up. 'Forgive me please for saying I was your patient.'

'You're not living with your family, Sheila Lomax tells me,' Julie probed.

'No, they're in Pakistan.'

'So where have you been staying?'

'After the hospital I moved in with a friend, in Hackney. A small flat with her husband. It's in a block with a lot of Muslims – Bangladeshis mostly – so it's not too bad.'

'I see you've gone back to the hijab,' Julie was saying on their walk. 'Quite a change from what you were wearing before. You feel happier in it?'

'It's what I normally wear.'

'But not in the City.'

'That was to look for a job. I was afraid –'

'– I know, I understand.'

How often she found herself saying 'I understand' to Muslim women. It troubled her sometimes. Her protective instincts were in reaction to the treatment some of them endured, a lot of it, she knew, from Muslim men. Hence her refrain: 'I know, I understand.' What troubled her was when she felt that understanding was turning into a form of condoning.

Their walk seemed to have perked Safia up. Suddenly expansive, she began talking about clothes.

'When I was younger I wore Western dress once, secretly, to a party. The other girls were a bit older, and they went into a station toilet to change back into Muslim clothes to go home. I was too scared to go in. One of my sisters caught me coming back and threatened to burn what I was wearing – borrowed of course. It was lucky it was her. My eldest sister was stricter. She would have told my parents, and my father…'

'I can imagine,' said Julie.

'After that my other sister gave me a book about Islam and women. I read it because I thought it would be about sex…'

Julie liked her smile.

'And was it?'

'No it wasn't, but I was interested. I had so many mixed-up thoughts. I was attracted to the life some of my schoolfriends lived, but I also hated it. And I was afraid, of everything. Of my father, my elder sister, my girlfriends, afraid of them and of feeling I wanted to be like them. That book calmed me. Islam began to seem so practical. There is a rule and a lesson for every side of a woman's life.

'People talk about submission but it isn't that. Being humble makes you stronger. Islam is not against sexual attraction, I began to understand, it's just that it's saved up for marriage and for the home. It helps bring peace, not just to yourself but for everyone.'

She stopped on the sand, as if to check what Julie made of this. Julie nodded, and said nothing. The girl had a stranded look, there on the deserted Norfolk beach in her bleak clothes. Her hesitant expression and ever-changing eyes, she realised at that moment, were those of an unformed personality. She was obviously lonely, talking to her like this, as if she were a teenage friend. What she was hearing seemed to her girlishly pious, a phase that ought to be over in a woman of twenty. Talk of sisters surprised her; she remembered her saying she was an only child, but then it had been in the hubbub of the salon, so perhaps she'd misheard.

Safia went on, earnestly:

'The book said the hijab wasn't demeaning. It gives women confidence, because it means they're beautiful and need hiding. So far from showing that men despise women, the hijab makes them feel good towards them.'

Why was she coming out with all this? Was she trying to convince herself? But then so long as it soothed and calmed her, what did it matter?

'Covering myself gave me pride,' Safia continued, 'and I needed some pride because my elder sister and my father lowered my view of myself.'

'Isn't that a bit contradictory? I mean saying you need the pride the hijab gives you because you father takes your pride away – partly by forcing you to wear it?'

Safia thought, then smiled: 'You see how confused I was.'

'Am,' Julie thought to herself. 'Am'.

The camp was almost out of view, it was getting windy and darker and Julie proposed they should turn back. It was also time to tell Safia about Tony Underwood.

'You'll find there are a lot of officials here,' she began. 'Doctors, administrators, psychiatrists doing research on the after-effects of the bombing. And sometimes we have the police. Someone from the security services is coming to interview people who were in the area before the bomb exploded.'

As expected, Safia was apprehensive.

'But you were with me. We didn't see anything, did we?'

'It's routine. He's been here several times, and he's interviewed me too. Don't be anxious.'

She was a little anxious herself, at the thought of Tony Underwood being officious with the girl. When he'd rung to say he'd be coming she'd told him about Safia turning up unexpectedly, but tried to get him to leave her off his list.

'She'll be no help at all. I can account for her. She was with me at the beautician's, all the time.'

'Which is why I have to see her. Things come out, unexpected things. We'd never have known about the Chechen if I hadn't seen you.'

'She's in a fragile state. Family problems on top of everything else.'

'Most people I'm seeing are in some sort of state. That's why they're there.'

'You're not doing this just because she's a Muslim I hope.'

'Absolutely not. On the other hand,' he added drily, 'Muslims are not excluded from the investigation.'

On the beach, Safia still seemed troubled.

'What's he like, the security man? What will he ask?'

'He's fine, but you'll find him a bit old-fashioned about Muslims.'

'Like the police?'

'Well he is a sort of policeman. Just tell him you didn't see anything. You're sure you didn't?'

Safia reflected, head down.

'No,' she announced. 'But then I was too frightened to have noticed.'

Her voice, plaintive and resigned, irritated Julie suddenly. She knew that tone well, and for all her pity for her patients, it could annoy her: some of them she suspected of playing up to stereotypes of helpless women. It made her want to tell them to stop this fatalistic nonsense, and brace up.

They were nearing the path up to the camp, slithering over a breakwater, when a posse of Bikey boys rode into view. Preoccupied with tracing their name swiftly in the drying sand, to begin with they'd taken no notice of the two women. At the sight of them crossing the breakwater, they broke off from their swoops and whirls and rode towards them.

Safia looked at Julie, questioningly. Julie frowned. The boys were not her patients. They didn't look too friendly. Safia's hijab, Julie thought, must have drawn them.

Reaching the women they began circling them, slowly, silently, round and round, forcing them to stop, motionless, trapped. Safia took Julie's arm and the girl pressed close. And so it went on for several minutes, there in the centre of the beach: the languorous swish of waves, the keening gulls, the sand and the circling boys. Finally, with an air of frozen calm, Julie took out her mobile, dialled and spoke softly, head down:

'… Hi Kingman. Dr Opie. A bunch of your boys are on the beach trying to intimidate a Muslim woman. Out of order, wouldn't you say? Call them off, could you?'

Seconds later one of the boys' phones rang. He drew it from his jerkin, his bike wobbling as he rode on, listening. Putting it back he shouted to Julie:

'Sorry lady. It's not you, it's just that she –' he pointed resentfully at Safia – 'she's on our patch.'

He hitched his head towards the cliff-top as a signal to the others, and off they rode, whooping.

Safia looked at her in awe.

'You can get them to go away!'

'I know their leader. Remember the delivery boy they took away from the beauty salon? The sick one?'

'The black one who called me things?'

'That's the one, Kingman. He's twenty-two but I'm not sure he'll see thirty. Meanwhile he's improved his behaviour – relatively speaking. You'll see him, in the camp. And when you do don't be afraid.'

It would be too much to say that a realisation of his mortality had driven Kingman, whose van-driving job was his first since his release on parole from a drugs charge, to re-think his style of life; his leadership of the Bikeys hardly suggested a reformed character. Yet it was true what she'd told Tony Underwood: without preaching, somehow she'd got to him. It was Kingman, she'd learned from Jackie's headmistress, who had made sure the girl's mobile was returned to her by the boy who'd pinched it, when he realised she was Julie's daughter.

11

Amer sat in the front seat of the green van with *McCullough's Gardening Services* emblazoned in yellow on the side. Sat there upright and alert while Jayson did it. On lookout, the Syrian said he was. The truth was that he stayed in his seat because he couldn't face the sight of the transfer of the bomb from bunker to van.

With heart-stopping matter-of-factness Jayson had shown him how he'd do it: the trolley, the winch, the cushion of foam rubber where, once inside, it would rest on the van floor. For the Syrian that was enough. Staying to watch the thing dangling from the winch's hook as it swung from trolley to van was not for him.

He felt calmer where he was, in his front seat, muttering prayers, his eyes shut against the emptiness of the alley that the moon filled with suggestive shadows. To close out the sound of the trundling trolley and the squeal of the rusted winch, the prayers grew louder. Louder still when a thud reached him through the plywood partition and the rear of the van sank on its springs, groaning, and he was jerked upwards in his seat.

'What in God's name –'

'– no probs.' Jayson's whisper came through the partition. 'Came down a mite soon, on the edge. Winch's a bit weak, is all.'

Amer sat, frozen. His seat levelled. Then a second, lesser thud as Jayson let down his load a little more gently on the rear springs. Then:

''Kay, got it.'

He closed and barred the van doors, locked the bunker, did a three point turn in the narrow alley, and drove off.

'Is there something wrong? Why did that happen?'

'Like I said, brother, it's the winch. Plus the suspension's not too good. £2,800, you don't get much. Gardening van, they probably overloaded it with soil and stuff. Done the springs in.'

'I said to get something reliable. Can we rely on it?'

Jayson forebore to remind him that it was Amer, miserly as ever, who'd insisted that £3,000 for a van doomed to be blown to bits in a few days' time was the limit.

'Sure. Nothin' broken. Didn't come down too hard. Do the job, you's not to worry. Anyways Allah'd never allow that thing to go up in a Muslim neighbourhood, would He?'

It was just after 2 am. There was nothing on the roads, but the trip to the lock-up garage north of Shepherds Bush where they were headed lasted well over an hour. On Amer's instructions Jayson took it easy, sticking to the side roads the Syrian had marked out on a map he'd downloaded at Hani's café. The bendy route meant a lot of cornering – a detail Amer had overlooked – and when they took one a bit sharply, and a sound like a shifting load reached them from the back, the Syrian turned to Jayson with a mute beseeching look. It didn't happen again.

The garage they were making for, one of a row of six, was in an uninhabited spot south of Willesden, a no-man's land between the railway line and Scrubs Lane. A desolate stretch of dead land bordered with wire fences, it was the least frequented location within quick and easy reach of West London. Jayson had done good work scouting the area, pinpointing the vacant garage and renting it for a month. He'd tried for a week, like Amer said, because it was all they'd need, but the deal was a month or nothing.

The £90 rent he paid in cash to the Albanian with whom he'd done the deal, a fly-looking fellow who worked at a nearby petrol station and had a key. He was good that way, Jayson, picking up contacts when they were needed. Perhaps it was his simplicity. People trusted him.

The plan was for the Syrian to stay with the van overnight while Jayson did his stuff in Kensington. Once he'd inspected the garage, however, Amer was reluctant. Looking at the improvised bedding Jayson had brought for him and spread out on the floor, then at the van, its rear end sagging under its load, he wavered.

'I'll never sleep on that. And lying there all night, so close to it…

I won't stay here. I'll go somewhere, till the time.'

'Like where, brother?'

'I don't know. An all-night café perhaps.'

'Nowhere like that round 'ere. An' I know those joints, brother. Not good places. Police go round 'em, pickin' folk up. I know it ain't much,' he indicated the blankets spread over the three foot, oil-bespattered concrete space between wall and van, 'but it's safer, brother. Safer for the task.'

After helping the Syrian install himself he set out for Kensington High Street, on foot. A fast walker, he loped along in his air-soled trainers, keeping as far as possible from the sodium lights yellowing the empty streets. By 4.15 a.m. he'd covered the four miles to the High Street, and taken his place in the queue that had already begun forming outside the store. Settling himself on the pavement with his sandwich and flask of coffee, he counted the bargain-hunters camped beneath the darkened windows. Two to three hundred, he reckoned. And this was only the beginning.

When Amer told him the morning before that today was to be the Day of Glory, all he'd said was 'Aye, brother.' After the Syrian sketched out his tactics, he thought some more, then said:

'Only thing is, why I need be at the store? I ain't sayin' I don't wanna be there, ain't sayin' I'm afraid or anythin', I jus' wanna know why?'

The Syrian didn't encourage questions, but this was no normal day. To ensure the boy understood the logic of what he was doing he'd taken him through his reasoning, step by step.

The reason to spend all those hours waiting before the store opened, he explained, was to be sure they were in control of events. Being there right from the beginning meant he could check on the build-up of customers through the day. Then report to him the optimum moment. Because timing, Amer went on patiently, was crucial. That had been their brothers' only mistake at the Bank, Allah grant them rest: timing. Their knowledge of conditions on the ground in the final approach had been faulty, and it had cost them lives.

'Imagine they'd done it in the middle of the lunch hour,' the Syrian went on, his dead eyes suddenly alight, 'instead of after two o'clock, when a lot of people must have been back at their desks. They could have killed 500, a thousand, not to speak of the casualties, the contaminations. Had it not been for the wind – a stroke of good fortune, remember that Jayson, nothing more – the result would have been next to nothing: a couple of hundred at the most. That is why we must have the best possible timing, as well as the wind. The weather forecast I have attended to. It is for you to calculate the timing.'

'You's right, brother,' Jayson had nodded, his screwed-up brow serene again.

So there he was at the store, waiting, counting. He ought to have brought a coat, he began thinking around dawn, it was chillier than he'd expected, squatting on the pavement in his jeans and jersey amidst the sharpening breeze and drizzle. But it was right he should be there. It was like Amer said: Allah wanted him to be one of the first inside, to control the situation. As dawn brightened into morning he sat totting up the growing throng. Remembering the huge crowds in Oxford Street on the TV programme he'd seen with Amer, he wondered how many thousand it could reach by midday.

He scanned the people around him. Black folk, a lot of them, maybe a third he reckoned. Must have come from across London. Some of the women with crosses around their necks, others dressed like whores with low-cut blouses and jumpers, even in the chill. Come to get even more shameless clothes, cheap. Clothes to show off their legs and breasts while they sat around pubs, drinking.

Ayan never did that, never. Though he wished she'd wear a niqab going out, or best of all the burka, to disguise her round young body. What would Amer think if he met her? He'd made her promise his child would dress properly if she was a girl, soon as she was old enough, even though he wouldn't be there. Then he could look down on her happily, watch her grow.

Half past six. A guy in a sleeping bag next to him woke up, unpacked his breakfast, began eating, wanted to strike up a conversation. Pakistani by the look of him, though in his bracelets and cocky hat he might just as well have been an infidel. A girly boy, it seemed to Jayson.

He'd driven in all the way from Luton, the man explained without being asked, but it was worth it, they'd be amongst the first inside.

Jayson said nothing.

'You from London?'

'Nah.'

Jayson turned away.

It was no strain keeping himself to himself. Who the people round him were was not his business, though of course he knew: infidels and apostates, all of them, otherwise they wouldn't be here. Get what they deserved. And infidels who die unbelievers shall incur the curse of God.

Later he turned down the girly boy's offer of coffee, though he'd finished his own flask, it was still cold and the coffee was steaming, hotter than his. Smelled better too. The way he'd dismissed the offer put the fellow off all right, he could see it. After that, not a word, which was all right with Jayson. He had to forget these people, concentrate on his waiting, his counting, and how he was going to make the judgement. Assess the optimum moment, when the crowd had reached its peak, and how he'd give the signal.

Amer said to check the phone booth on the High Street was working, and he'd done it; it wasn't vandalized, there was a tone, it was fine. And he'd given him the change for the call. Pound coins, three of them, in case one failed. They did that sometimes, so much counterfeit stuff around nowadays. He felt for the coins in his pocket – one, two, three – and was comforted. Stupid to reach the Day of Glory and not have change for the call.

Even if one was phoney there'd be one to spare. One he could use to ring Ayan, maybe, to say goodbye. Amer wouldn't like that, but then he'd never know. And it wouldn't be like he was talking to her as a wife. No risk of that, because he was in limbo. Which didn't mean he shouldn't talk to her at all. It must be all right reaching out to her, one last time, from limbo. Just so Ayan could tell him the baby was OK, like Amer said it would if he showed strength in their task. And now would be the time to ring. It was seven o'clock but she'd be up early, with her morning sickness.

'Mate, can you keep my place a minute?'

The girly boy looked back, unaccommodating, and said nothing.

'I gotta sick child, gotta check she's gettin' better.'

The boy indicated that he could go.

The phone booth was a couple of hundred yards along the street, past the Tube station. He put in his pound and dialled the landline number. Ayan took her time to answer. As he waited a police van arrived near the crowd outside the store. Policemen were getting out, weary-looking, stretching.

Ayan answered, weary-sounding too.

'Hello? Who is it?'

'Who do you think?'

'Jayson. You phoned.' She sounded grumpy. 'Well, that's something.'

'To say hello. See how you doin'.'

'You on the job already? How's it going? When do I get to see you?'

'Don't worry, we gonna meet, before long. You all right?'

'Same as I was. I'd be better if you were here.'

'How's the baby? Any more tests?'

'I went to the hospital for one. Consultant said it's all right.'

'So no bad effects or anything?'

'Radiation you mean? Couldn't find anything, they said. And I wasn't to confuse being sick 'cos of the baby with people vomiting because they've got it. Lotta mothers do that, he said.'

'So Allah's taking care of you. Taking care of you both, so you can stop worryin'.'

'If you was here I wouldn't worry.'

'Jus' wanted you to know I'll be with you soon. And the child. Always. Forever, Inshallah.'

'That's wonderful, Jayson. And you'll bring some cash, right? 'Cos they're talking about putting me on part-time at B & Q.'

People were pouring from the Tube and hurrying along the pavement, more of them every minute, streaming towards the store to join the queue. He'd better get back counting.

'Gotta go now. Do my work.' Jayson's voice was a flat whisper. 'Love to you both.'

He put down the receiver and went back to the queue. The boy had another go at chatting, asked about his child.

'It fine.'

Jayson turned away. Now more than ever he wanted to be left alone in the morning chill, shivering with cold but also exultation. The child would be OK, Ayan OK. Amer was right. A big one, really big, a thousand or more dead, and they'd both be fine.

*

The Syrian walked and walked, slowly, heels dragging, shuffling at times, along Scrubs Lane. A few hundred yards up one side of the road, wait for a gap in the traffic, cross, then back in the opposite direction. And so on, for several hours.

He was going nowhere, though with a purpose: walking so he could stay near the phone, the one on the deserted stretch of pavement in the booth no one used, so as to hear when it rang. Jayson said to buy a mobile, just for this one last call, but Amer had said no: mobiles were out even today, the last day, the Day of Glory. Look what happened in New York: a single impetuous call, and they'd got them. He was allergic to mobiles, even pay-as-you-go, no contract. There could still be someone listening even though nothing was said. In fact a call from a phone booth to a mobile where nothing was said would be all the more suspicious.

Though his own plan was not so good, he was starting to think.

What he'd forgotten were the lorries. Each time he passed the phone he strained for the sound of the bell from the door he'd wedged open a little, with a stick. But what about when he walked away from it, or crossed the road? Desperate not to miss the call above the roar of the hellish traffic, he was having to stay closer than he wanted. Walk up and down the same short stretch of pavement, without crossing the road. Which could look strange.

He was tempted to wait inside, in the warm, shut the door and be done with it. But no: standing there for hours he'd be too conspicuous. Somebody might see him waiting without phoning, think he was acting oddly, and report him. People were paranoid nowadays.

Then there was his appearance. That too he'd got wrong. Industrial estates lined the lane and people round here were dressed in workmen's clothes. A tall, lean Syrian with a grey-white complexion and a raincoat flapping in the breeze didn't fit. After an hour of it he began to feel stupid, undignified, pacing up and down aimlessly, like some down-and-out. But it was the only way. Timing was of the essence, essential for the numbers, to do more than Umair had done.

Then it came. At two twenty-five it came, while he was within earshot, thanks be to Allah. He resisted an impulse to dash inside, grab the receiver, ask for an estimate of the numbers. There could be no question of answering. That was the plan, the ringing phone would be enough. Thirty seconds exactly Jayson was supposed to let it ring, and he did. He stood there checking his watch, savouring the sound. To his tense, straining ears it seemed to ring extra loud, joyously, like a muezzin's call, a summons!

Hurrying back along the lane to the track that led to the garage he felt himself treading air, aloft on a cloud of serenity. His journey was about to begin, his final journey! Then the hold-ups. Whole minutes lost getting the van from the track onto the road. Traffic piling past and no one with the courtesy to let him out. Then the infernal, never-ending drive along Scrubs Lane towards town, inching along in the wake of the lorries and containers spewing from every entrance to every industrial estate.

With this he hadn't reckoned. Time was passing, the optimum moment in danger of slipping away. He could see it in his mind: the bargains gone, the crowds thinning, people leaving the store, a hundred lives lost to him every minute. Infidels escaping Allah's wrath, the wrath that would explode from the van the moment his finger willed it. His impatience for their extinction, and for his own, tormented him every inch of the way.

And him who hated driving, avoided it whenever he could. On those endless rides from Syria into Iraq, back and forth, Yemen to Saudi Arabia, or Peshawar to the tribal territories, always he'd managed to be a passenger. They'd found it arrogant of him to insist on being driven, teased him about it. Here, Professor, take a turn at the wheel a moment, can you, while I have a rest? Knowing that Amer the white-handed intellectual never would. I would gladly do it, he would respond, solemnly, but Allah never meant me to drive, it is not in my destiny, He has other tasks for me.

Then the clutch, the clutch Jayson had to replace when he'd bought the van cheap. The new one so sharp and springy that the least easing of his foot and the thing shot forward. What if he ran into the back of someone and – Allah forbid! – the police came, wanted to search the van. Forced him to send it up, pointlessly, in this wasteland, with a mere scattering of deaths.

Ten more minutes and he still hadn't reached the flyover with the turn to Kensington. He began losing his cool, mouthing curses at other drivers, glowering at them through the window, throwing up his hands, drawing attention. Then he stalled the engine. The clutch… It was a moment before it would re-start, and a queue built up behind, everyone hooting. Swinging out to pass the stationary van a burly fellow in a lorry leant from his cab window and shouted:

'Where d'ya get yer licence, sunshine? Fuckin' Kabul?'

So gross was the insult it took a moment to register. An Afghan! They took him for an Afghan! Imbeciles! Ignorant imbeciles!

Then the leak, the radiation leak. Something beyond the plywood partition leaking, he was sure of it, could sense it in his throat. Or was it his imagination again – his weakness? Though that didn't mean there wasn't a leak, brought on by all this jerky starting and stopping.

Over half an hour, just to get to the end of the lane and onto the flyover. Then more jams, more wasted minutes – road works this time, on the approach road to Shepherds Bush roundabout – before he finally reached Jayson.

Their rendezvous point was in Royal Crescent, opposite the Kensington Hilton. Selected because the smart white houses were the sort of place a gardening van might well pause to pick up a labourer. And labourers was what they were, both of them. God's labourers, about to terminate their work on earth.

12

It was half-past twelve and Martin, up since six, was at work in the spare room of his Kensington mews house. The account of his Midlands adventure was needed by the end of the day. Not for Mark Pelling, whose paper had gone under a week after he'd given Martin his notice, but for Freddie du Sautoy. Freddie was a university friend who ran a magazine, also on the blink as censorship bit and the Internet took over. For that reason he was keen for something hot in the next issue, holding back publication for Martin's copy. Hence the six o'clock start.

It was a tricky piece to write. In addition to Freddie and his readers there were three audiences to satisfy. First there was Julie, who'd known Freddie at university too (had there been something between them? He'd never been sure), and though disapproving of its politics, read his magazine. Then the censor: raids into Muslim areas by riotous whites were frowned on. And with himself a witness to a firebombing there were also the police to keep in mind. Not to speak of Billy.

Trickiest of all was whether he could portray the corner shop as a centre for subversion. The answer, he suspected, wasn't one that would commend itself to Freddie's right-of-centre magazine, or to Billy. So he wrote:

> With the flames engulfing the store went the proof that the shop had been a centre of jihadist propaganda. All I can say is that one of the fugitive figures disappearing along the street was toting plastic bags containing perhaps – who is to say? – what might well have been books and magazines.

For this he had no evidence – though with the smoke, how could he? In any event it made good copy, one of those things he could imagine so clearly it might just as well have happened. Julie would dismiss talk of jihadi literature and subversion as overblown, she always did, but then he'd been there and she hadn't.

What he didn't mention, tried not to think about, was the outline of the figure in the upper window as the flames mounted.

*

It was when he took a break to listen to the three o'clock news that he heard the announcement of the deaths by arson of the old man and the boy, the first item. The boy had been five, the old man his grandfather. They must have held it back for fear of the consequences on the streets, but now it was out. For an instant he hadn't registered what the announcer was saying – she gave no place, simply the Midlands. Then, when the truth came to him, for a long moment there was a cold blank space where his fear should have been.

An instinct to ring Billy Furlow lasted ten seconds, a decision to contact the police scarcely five. Deleting his article with a numbed finger he went to the Internet for instructions on how to wipe the hard disk clean. It turned out to be a complex process, on which his mind refused to focus.

His mobile rang.

'Martin?'

'Yes.'

'Billy here.'

Silence.

'You there Martin?'

'Yes, I'm here.'

'Good, 'cos I got a message for you. I'm summarising, mind you, but what the person I'm speaking on behalf of said I was to pass on was this. Say you had a friend who through no fault of 'is own – an accident, a one in a million accident – was to find 'imself involved in an unfortunate death. You wouldn't see it like the law sees it, would you Martin? 'Cos you know the feller and 'ave broken bread with 'im and can vouch for 'is good character as well as it bein' an accident, 'cos it turns out you was there.

'Now what 'appens if your mate doesn't help you out? Well the person on whose behalf I'm speaking stops being your friend, don't he Martin? Might even turn unfriendly.'

Silence.

'You still there?'

'I am,' Martin said firmly, which was an effort.

'Well it would 'elp if you was to give some fuckin' sign of life. What the message I am deliverin' is saying is you don't rat on people caught up in accidents that is not of their makin'. What my friend says you are in a position to confirm – not that there'll be any need will there Martin? – is that there was no means of knowing there was someone in that shop.

'My friend ain't sayin' nothin's 'appened, 'ee's not tellin' a lie. Pity about the kid, course it is. And it's a pity about the hundreds of British kids who stand the risk of dyin' an early death. For example your daughter – what's 'er name again?'

Silence.

'I'm asking her fuckin' name!'

'Betsy,' Martin said quietly.

'Well it's a pity about Betsy too. On the other 'and helps you keep a sense of proportion, don't it? So my friend's made 'is position clear, an' I don't 'ave to tell you 'ee is not alone. There's a lot of people up here who feel strongly about these things Martin my son, and one accident's enough, wouldn't you say?'

Silence.

'Will you open your fuckin' trap? What I'm sayin' is that we are in a war with these people and in war civilian casualties is inevitable. Always assumin' the casualty was a civilian and not a soldier of Islam, which we 'ave reason to suspect he was. In which case he 'ad no business exposin' 'is grandson to the risks of conflict, did 'ee?'

A silence.

'I hear what you say,' Martin replied, and hung up.

He stared at his computer. Instructions about cleaning the disk were beyond him now. What he needed was... He went to the kitchen. Nothing there, of course there was nothing. Then out of the house and towards Kensington High Street.

At the door he stood back to let a line of uniforms pass. The soldiers were from a Territorial Army base at the end of his mews, a large building with proud signs on the gate: Field Hospital (Volunteers), 256 City of London. Till the bombing the place had seemed under-used, half-deserted. Now it was a buzzing barracks, as TA men were repatriated from around the world to hold the fort at home. A day or two's training and they were out on patrol, equipped with night sticks, to help keep order on the streets.

Waiting till the column had passed – there was something admirable about their dutifully stony faces – Martin fell in behind them.

Again the High Street was a mutinous roar of stagnant cars. It happened whenever one of the high street stores sold up, and today it was the biggest. Giant adverts, loud-speakers and pavement stalls with gaily striped canopies – if it weren't for the police ringing the store it would have been a festive sight, but with the crowds reaching their peak things had started to look ugly. As they approached the store the TAs marching ahead of him broke into a trot.

The store was packed, and yet a thousand people – more perhaps – were still thrusting and fighting to get in, or pushing for a space before the stalls outside. Trouble had been expected: a police helicopter had arrived, swooping and buzzing low, and as well as the police half a dozen troops were strung out along the storefront, armed, more for show than anything. Which must be why the TA had been called in, with their night sticks. As they approached the crowd surged. Running ahead of the column for a closer look Martin came across a surreal sight.

Two women had fought their way to a stall and grabbed a hold of a dress. As he watched one punched the other's face, bloodying it with a ring. A soldier was trying to drag them apart when with a crazed shriek the ring-wielding woman made a grab for his rifle, and when the soldier, a tall fellow, held it above his head the woman kicked him, viciously, in the balls. The man doubled and clattered to the ground. The woman summoned her boyfriend, a shaven-haired bruiser, and the two of them went to work to wrest the gun from the sprawling soldier.

Seeing him go down Martin pushed towards him; the throng threw him back. Pressed towards the kerb he mounted a car's bumper, scrabbled up the back and onto the roof. From here he could see the soldier still tussling with the woman and the wild-eyed man, the woman pulling at the barrel and the man with a grip of the stock.

Why am I doing this? Martin had time to reflect, surveying the faces turning up to him as he crouched for take-off. For the same reason that moron is trying to snatch a soldier's rifle. Nothing matters in the way it did, so why not?

The damage to the moron when Martin landed owed as much to his having the nous to keep his toes up and heels down as to the accuracy of his leap. Catching him under the ribs as the bruiser swivelled to land him a punch, the heels winded the man terminally. The soldier yanked back his rifle. His attacker lay coiled on the ground. Fighting a path through the crowd the TAs arrived in time to pick up the floored man and pacify the demented woman, who had somehow retrieved the bloodied dress.

Martin too was bloodied, from a flying fist that had caught his nose. Clamping a handkerchief to his face he pushed off through the crowd as best he could.

A TA man stopped him.

'Need any help?'

'I'm fine thanks.'

And he was. Fine in the way a schoolboy is fine after a fight where he gained a showy wound. Fine because the panic that had gripped him after Billy's call had been replaced by more agreeable feelings. His one regret was that Julie hadn't been there to see.

'Sure you're OK?' The TA man was persistent. 'You don't look nice.'

'I'll manage. All I need is somewhere to wash up.' He gestured across the street towards the Prince of Wales pub. 'Maybe more.'

'Bit early for me,' the TA man grinned, 'But you've earned it.'

13

With a last hoot from behind – afraid of disturbing his load Amer had slowed almost to a stop then swung to the centre of the road before turning left – the van crawled into Royal Crescent. Jayson was there, waiting, but the Syrian drove past before stopping. He'd failed to recognise him. Rather than reverse – he didn't like reversing – he waited till he caught up. Amer shifted across, Jayson got into the driver's seat, and they drove off.

'You have a new coat,' the Syrian observed.

'Yeah. Got in in the sale. Spotted it soon as I walked in. A tenner it was. Bargain at double the price.'

'Whatever possessed you,' the Syrian asked, quietly and with genuine interest, 'to buy a coat you will never need?'

''Course I won't need it, brother,' Jayson agreed, equable as ever, 'just that I thought it'd be good cover. Saw a couple of store detectives hangin' round, soon as they let us in, so I wanna look like I'm takin' an interest in the sales, don't I? Buy somethin'. Plus I come out lookin' different to what I did goin' in, right?, 'Cos they got these cameras.'

Sensing the Syrian's displeasure, he added:

'Tell you what, brother, it's the optimum moment all right. Place is swarmin'. A madhouse! Plus they got stalls on the pavement, people outside as well as in! Must be a thousand of 'em, brother, round them stalls, out there in the open, like a street market or somethin'!' He glanced at him, sideways. 'Askin' for it, ain't they? An' it's comin' brother, ain't it?'

Numbers. The Syrian almost smiled.

'You counted? That's not just an estimation?'

'I counted, best I could. Could hardly get out the store.'

They had turned off the road to Notting Hill and were heading south towards the High Street, along Melbury Road, adjacent to Holland Park. A residential street, it was mined every few hundred yards with sleeping policemen of the most abrupt kind. Spotting the first one coming the Syrian tensed:

'Gently, for Allah's sake!'

'Don't worry, I got it brother.'

Easing over the hump, the van slowed almost to stopping point. Then picked up speed, cautiously. At the next one, it slowed again.

'We're losing time,' the Syrian fretted. 'Why on earth did we take this road?'

Approaching the third, Jayson speeded up.

'Slower!' Amer gestured behind their seats. 'The springs! You mustn't shake it!'

Jayson slowed.

The Syrian settled back in his seat, calmed himself. On his lap lay a black cable. It led from his seat to the back of the van, through the partition. At his end of it, held so it pointed away from him towards the engine, was a pump action switch.

'There you go,' Jayson said, crawling over the next one. 'Slow as I can. Hey!' He braked, gently. 'There's a post box. Said I was to remind you to post the videos. You want I post them, brother?'

The package on the dashboard was addressed to The Press Association, 295, Vauxhall Bridge Road, London. The writing – black ink, printed capitals, precise – was Amer's. After he'd handed it to him the previous night Jayson felt through the paper, surreptitiously. Two DVDs he was looking for, one for each, the way they'd made them. His fingers sensed two, and he was pleased. What Jayson didn't know was that one was blank.

As the van dawdled a car hooted behind them before swinging out and overtaking on the wrong side of the road.

'No, not here,' Amer rasped. 'In the High Street we will do it. It is wider, and there is a post office there. Here we are holding up traffic, drawing attention.'

They drove on till they were almost at the junction. The Syrian, breathing deeply, was re-adjusting the cable on his lap, positioning it exactly right. Seeing him fidgeting Jayson said:

'Careful with that, brother. Don't want no accidents.'

'Turn left!'

The Syrian had difficulty taking in air, his voice faint and taut. Eager for the moment, and forgetting they'd have to stop to post the DVDs, he turned the switch ninety degrees right, his thumb still not touching, but ready.

In a flat voice he began mumbling prayers:

'We hasten eagerly towards You and we fear Your punishment and hope for Your Mercy as your severe punishment is surely to be meted out to the unbelievers. The infid – '

Amer broke off.

'You're in the wrong lane! I said turn left!'

'I can't! Look at them, brother!'

They had reached the junction. Jayson had stayed centre lane because the left-turn into Kensington High Street was blocked. A police car was slewed across the street, an officer lounging against its door, taking the sun, his gun at a relaxed angle. After the squalls and the drizzle the weather was turning. Against expectations, it was a beautiful day.

Halfway into the inside lane Jayson stopped the van, staring dumbly. The officer, pointing southwards, was waving them on. Jayson glanced at Amer.

'Wan' me to take it through?'

'Can you?'

'Could try gettin' past, but it jammed further along, brother, before the store. Look, you can see.'

Erect and irresolute in his seat, Amer looked. From a hundred yards on, in both directions, the High Street was an immobile mass of cars. Hooting behind the van made up his mind. That and the helicopter that had begun circling above the intersection, droning ever more loudly, so low now it seemed to be buzzing the van.

The Syrian signalled Jayson to do what the officer was instructing them – drive on, south, across the High Street and on towards the Cromwell Road.

The van moved on.

'Turn left. Now!' Amer shouted, a hundred yards down.

'Where, brother?'

'Anywhere!' the Syrian shrieked. 'So we can get round to the High Street!'

Jayson drove on, in spurts, looking for somewhere to turn into. There was nowhere. Police cars had blocked the side streets all the way to the Cromwell Road. Reaching it, they stopped at traffic lights.

'No way round, brother. They've sealed the area. Can't get to the store.'

'Park up!'

'Can't do it, brother.'

'Find somewhere!'

'Ain't nowhere. All yellow lines. We try, they might stop and search. The 'copter, it still there, it'll be watchin', brother.'

Amer looked at him, agitated and annoyed. What angered him most was Jayson's unnerving calm.

'Know what I think?' Jayson said.

'What?'

'Allah, He's tellin' us somethin'. Look!'

He pointed to a small flag he'd fixed to the front of the van: his wind gauge. He was pleased with his St George's flag, had bought it at a garage, £1.50. When Amer picked him up it was still fluttering cheerfully. Now it was limp.

'The wind's gone. We gotta have wind, reach more infidels. So it's a sign He's givin' us,' Jayson said, driving on. 'A sign Allah wants it somewhere else. An' maybe not today. Different place, different time. I hear Him saying not today, brother, the time ain't right, is what I'm hearin' Him sayin'.'

'Drive back, and don't talk.' The Syrian moved the cable on his lap, gingerly, so the switch turned away. 'I have to think.'

They drove on southwards, along the Earls Court Road, Jayson mumbling the incantation the Syrian had begun, as if echoing a tune from the radio, his monotone just audible above the rackety engine:

'We hasten eagerly towards You yeah, an' we fear Your punishment and hope for Your Mercy. Yeah and Your severe punishment is surely to be meted out to the unbelievers.'

14

More trouble for Tony, this time an alert at Great Yarmouth. A container on a ship from Karachi with 'light industrial goods' on the manifest had tested positive for radiation. Security service systems went red, with good reason: Karachi was the centre of operations of D-company, a criminal syndicate suspected of links to the 2008 Al Qaeda attack on Mumbai.

Emergency routines had gone into operation. The Pakistani captain and crew were detained, reinforcements rushed in from the Midlands, and roads in and out of the port blocked. As alarm grew Tony was pulled in to join a surveillance team tailing a Pakistani. A local businessman, he was assumed to be the shore contact. The ship's captain had made a call to his mobile the day before docking, contents unknown, due to a computer snarl-up in the monitoring of ship-to-shore calls.

For forty-eight hours Tony and the team trailed him deep into the night: the businessman, a lumbering fellow with a limp and a military-looking moustache, had a habit of walking close to the docks at two or three in the morning. Waiting no doubt for a signal to come aboard. One he would never get now the captain's mobile had been seized.

As the feeling grew that finally they could be onto something big more operatives arrived from London. Tony was caught up in the excitement. Stalking the Pakistani and struggling against fatigue, he remembered the discovery by the Uzbek customs officials. Already he could see the lead-lined boxes of Strontium-90. The soft, silvery, death-inducing metal that turned yellow when you cut it.

When the container was ransacked and the ship with it the radiation boys finally tracked down the source of the emissions. It wasn't Strontium-90, it was Cobalt-60, a more common substance frequently used, one of the boys explained, in medical labs and for food irradiation. A large quantity in a bomb would be dangerous all right, no question, but there was scant fear of that. Because the radiation aboard the vessel was coming from a shipment of metal buttons. Buttons of the kind used in operating machines, or lift panels.

A check with the manufacturers explained what had happened. The container had been transhipped to Karachi from the port of Chittagong, a ship-breaking centre specialising in derelict hulls from the Soviet navy. The raw material for the buttons was scrap metal, it turned out, in all probability from redundant nuclear-powered submarines. Everything was thereupon stood down, Tony included. Embarrassing if it had been public, but then the censors ensured that it wasn't.

It hadn't all been wasted effort. Under interrogation the captain revealed that his Pakistani friend ashore, a former naval officer settled in Britain, was indeed in the smuggling business. His phone-call had been to alert him to the imminent arrival of thirty thousand Camel Lights picked up in Aden and discovered, when the nuclear teams had searched the ship, stashed behind the bath in the captain's cabin.

As for the old sailor's night-walking, it turned out he was a chronic insomniac, a condition brought on by a lingering pain from a wound he'd received in the Indo-Pakistani war of 1971, which he sought to relieve by walking the streets in the early hours, in places where he could have the sea in his nostrils.

*

I'm too old for this business, Tony was telling himself by the time the button farce was over, but there seemed no respite from pointless, exhausting missions. Behind with his programme of interviews, and under pressure for faster returns, after a brief night's sleep, he drove directly from Great Yarmouth to the camp.

By the time he got to Safia it was late afternoon. Before he'd been obliged to spend hours in the Caribbean sector. More wasted time. None of the lads he talked to turned out to be Islamics, though some of them were Bikeys, which meant listening with a respectful air to vociferous opinions on all things Muslim ('Dey just not like you and me, man'). Nor was there any shortage of suggestions as to whom, in the gowned and veiled sector of the camp, the security services would be well advised to give the third degree.

Next on the list was Steve Roundell, the road worker from the salon. Feet up on his veranda table, a beer at his side, Steve was in hearty mood. Having dived from a truck straight into the beautician's, and been shielded by his thick yellow plastic jacket, he seemed in excellent health. 'Radiant health by the look of you,' Tony found the energy to joke.

On the salon all he had to say was that he was sorry for the remarks he'd made about Safia:

"Eat of the moment was all it was. I mean we thought we was goin' to die. Tell you what though, she looked better in what she was wearin' there than she does in that crow outfit she goes about in 'ere. Nice pair of legs on 'er when you can see 'em.'

Tony did his best to get away, but Steve got talkative. Turning his contrition about Safia into an act of largesse, he described how he'd gone to her camp home to make his apology personally, and how grateful Safia had been.

'Soon as Kingman told me she was in the camp I went round and we was on 'er veranda and I ask if she minds me smokin' and she says go ahead, so I offer her one, you know, as a joke like, and blow me she takes it. Gives you a funny feelin' watching one of 'em smoke in that thing they wear, 'specially when you've seen their knickers. Like a sexy nun.'

Later he saw Kingman, who'd been unavailable in the morning due to an appointment at the medical centre, with Julie. As part of his Bikey gear he was wearing low-slung pants, so low he seemed to wade in them when he moved. For Tony the knowledge that the boy was ill took the edge off the aura of toughness he seemed anxious to project.

As expected he had nothing to offer on the explosion. He was keener to relate how he too had said sorry to Safia, and again she was said to have been mightily grateful. Tiring of the refrain, Tony brought things to a close by saying:

'Glad to hear it. I'd be even more impressed if you used your influence to stop the Bikeys baiting Muslims altogther. I get complaints about it each time I come. Why not just wind them up?'

Kingman seemed genuinely puzzled:

'Wind up the crew? What we supposed to do round 'ere, middle of nowhere? It's a game is all it is.'

His brow wrinkled with the effort to convince himself of his sincerity.

'Knives, a game? Who are you kidding? Not yourself I hope.'

'You the police, or what?' Kingman was getting fretful, hostile. 'You can't tie me up with no knifings. Ask Miss Opie.'

Tony let it go. Why bother? Knives weren't his job; dirty bombings were. Remembering Julie's claim that Kingman was on the road to salvation, and disinclined to tangle with her if he complained, to smooth things over he did what he'd forgotten to do when he'd first come in: asked after the boy's health.

'Well you're goin' from day to day, ain't yer? First they said I'd be alright, not to worry. Now they's talkin' 'bout a bone marrow transplant. Want me to sign this letter.' Poking about in the chaos of his home he produced an NHS letter and read with effort: *It is a com-plex and con-tro-versial pro-cedure wiv a success rate that's by no means gua-ran-teed*. Know what they mean 'bout signin' your life away now, man. Suppose I better.'

Wishing him the best with the operation, Tony left. Lucky Julie hadn't witnessed his performance. He may not be MI5's biggest hot shot, but he'd make an even worse social worker.

*

As a non-priority case, Safia was obliged to share a mobile home with another inmate, a devout Muslim grandmother. Tony arrived early. For once it was warm and the door half-open. Climbing the steps he knocked, waited, peered inside.

Some of the evacuees trashed their homes within a week. This one was immaculate, an old-fashioned, house-proud Asian woman's world: neat, colourful with the old lady's patterned table covers and knick-knacks, and filled with spicy aromas. The television was on, with no sound.

Hesitant about entering he strolled about outside, waiting. The beach was nearby, and ambling towards the fence at the cliff edge he glanced back at the home's veranda. On it was a young woman: Safia he assumed. She was sitting with her back to him, her head inclined and the cowl of her headdress stretched forwards. It wasn't the right position, and yet it occurred to him she might be praying. Till he saw an arm move impulsively to her mouth and smoke spiral over her head. Hearing his step on the path she turned. She was puffing, urgently, on a cigarette.

Their eyes met. She made to stub it out under the metal table.

'Don't worry,' he called up, fishing a packet of cigarillos from his pocket and brandishing it as he approached, like a badge. 'Maybe I'll join you.'

As he climbed the steps she stood up. She was holding her cigarette tip down, between thumb and two fingers, as if it was nothing to do with her.

Tony introduced himself, sat down and lit up. For a long moment nothing was said between the incongruous couple. A snapshot would have shown a white, tired-eyed male wearing an equally exhausted suit, and a woman in a hijab a third his age, both of them staring from the veranda at a featureless sea, silently smoking. Age, sex, race, religion – nothing except their mingling fumes and shared guilt linked these people.

'A minority vice.' He grinned, awkwardly, then made things worse. 'I didn't think Muslim girls – I mean women –'

'– I don't really. At school I used to do it as a dare. Then I stopped. And then when it happened I had one or two. You won't tell Dr Opie, will you?'

'Of course I won't. And you're not the only one. These are stressful times. Lots of people have taken it up again, especially now they don't enforce the ban.'

He gestured backwards, to the house.

'Watch the news do you?'

'Sometimes, but it's all so bad, so tragic.'

'Unless we get their friends, and quickly, it could get worse. There'll be camps like this across the country.'

At his solemn tone the girl nodded.

'Of course I understand why you need to talk to me.' Safia became firm suddenly. 'We must catch these people.'

A line of concern etched itself on her forehead as she spoke. It looked out of place on the smooth skin.

A last puff and she stubbed her cigarette under the table. He watched what she would do with the butt; she held it, tightly, in a fist.

'I won't take a lot of time. Dr Opie will have explained what I'm about. If you could just tell me –'

'– of course.'

She began speaking, rapidly. She was explaining how she'd been looking for a job before the bomb exploded when Tony stopped her, looking puzzled.

'Excuse me asking, it's just interest really, about Muslim customs. But if you were looking for a job in the City wouldn't it be more normal to wear what you're wearing now? I mean, to make a good impression? Because you'd be looking for something in Muslim banks, wouldn't you?

'I was reading about it in the paper. The way Muslims are

developing usury-free mortgages and all that, to cater for Islamic customers. It's quite a big movement, what with the Middle East and all. Did you know Christians used to be against usury too? Interesting isn't it?'

'What is usury?'

Tony stared a moment.

'Well, you'd have to know about that if you worked with Muslims in the City. It means charging interest, which Muslim banks don't like I gather. For good reason if you ask me. Did better in the recession than ours did, but that's by the by. So there you were in Western clothes...'

'In the City they wear different clothes,' Safia said as if explaining to a child. 'So you're right, I might have worn a hijab.'

There followed a shorter version of what she'd said to Julia about how people got it wrong about the hijab, how it wasn't demeaning. Tony pondered this, took out a pad and made a note. Catching her following his movements, he looked up.

'So you didn't go to the salon for beauty treatment. I don't know, eyelash-lengthening or something.'

Tony smiled at his own knowing.

'You think my lashes –'.

A hand went to her brow.

'– absolutely not. I mean –' He was floundering. 'They're fine, couldn't be nicer. Sorry, I was being frivolous.'

It must have been like this in conversation with ladies in Victorian times, he thought. Tiny jokes, little naughtinesses. Charming in its way.

'That's all right.'

Safia came near to a smile, and looked pretty. Especially the long lashes, now he looked. A pity about the wan face and nun's outfit.

'So you were passing the beautician's. And this was when –'

A shattering boom echoed round the mobile home, which shook. Then another. Tony got to his feet and made to go inside. Safia stayed seated.

'Don't worry,' she said calmly, holding up a hand to stop him, 'it's the boys.'

He went inside and looked from the window. The white kids he'd seen drinking were playing football, using the side of the mobile home as a goal. Tony made for the front door.

'Don't,' Safia called from the veranda. 'They do it on purpose, to annoy us.'

'That's why I'm going to stop them.'

'It'll be worse when you've gone if you do. They call us terrorists.' She shrugged. 'There's nothing we can do.'

'You're sure you wouldn't like me –'

'– sure. It's better to do nothing.'

All this submission.

'All right,' he sat down. 'If you say so. Now where were we?'

Short-term memory lapses, irritability with feckless youth, tiredness in the afternoons. Jesus he was aging.

'You were asking whether I went for beauty treatment,' Safia said, with a half-smile.

'Oh yes. And you didn't see anything unusual on the streets.'

'Nothing I remember.'

Another ball bounced off the side of the home. Tony had a headache. It felt as if it had hit his temple.

'Well I think that covers it.'

Tony excused himself, and stood up to leave. Safia looked surprised.

'You don't want to hear what happened inside the salon?'

'Not unless you speak Russian.'

'I don't,' Safia said, looking mystified.

'Sorry, it's a joke.

'Ah,' Safia said. 'I just hoped I could help.'

'Oh you have, you have. The more people we can eliminate –'

He stopped himself. Now he was even talking like a flat-foot.

'So I'm eliminated?'

Safia smiled, fully for the first time.

'Absolutely,' Tony said.

He was half way down the veranda steps before he remembered.

'Actually –' He heaved himself back up. 'There's one thing you could do for me if you wouldn't mind. There's a photo I'd like you to glance at.'

'Of course.'

'It's not terribly pleasant…'

He opened his briefcase and began easing the picture of the dead bomber he'd shown to Julie from its envelope. Seeing the severed head and lacerated face in stark daylight, its empty eye socket staring at him as he slid it out, he began stuffing it back.

'On second thoughts I'm not sure –'

'– no, show me. I want to help.'

Before he could stop her she took the envelope from him, pulled the picture out. After a single glance she thrust it into his hands and, fingers clamped to her mouth, rushed into the mobile home. Putting his photo away Tony heard the sound of retching. That wasn't clever, he told himself, walking off. But she did insist.

*

He'd lined up more interviews to finish the day but decided to call them off. It wasn't only fatigue, he had to get away from the camp. Sick of the pointless work, he was sick of the whole place as well. The word had got round about who he was and people had begun pointing him out as he passed. There goes our security service man, he could hear them saying, our MI5 copper on his beat.

Then there were the whispers in his ear. A Caribbean swearing blind he'd seen Somalis buying a carload of hydrogen peroxide in a DIY store, for a bomb. Loading it onto a trolley they were, like it were crates of beer or something. I mean I know they don't drink… A hijabbed woman assuring him that a black man was a terrorist pretending to be a Muslim. I saw him the other day in the tent, praying. A wild-looking man, all that hair, maybe not right in the head. You know how the blacks get after smoking their drugs?

A Bangladeshi confided that black nurses in the medical unit were poisoning Asian babies. A white woman with bruised eyes was convinced a Pakistani doctor was injecting our kids with God knows what, Mr Underwood, just 'cos we're white, Lennie had this terrible rash, it's wrong what they're doing Mr Underwood, in our own country. Come and look Mr Underwood, come and look. I heard one of them say it was our fault, we shouldn't have done Osama, I swear it Mr Underwood…

Instead of heading back to the office he drove away from the coast, randomly, into the fraying autumnal countryside. A few miles along a sign pointed to a church. Norfolk churches were Jean's thing: she visited them with a conservation group at weekends, forever trying to get him to come along, but he made excuses. The sudden bulk and splendour of this one made him stop the car.

He ambled round the path in search of the entrance. It was locked. A notice said visitors could obtain the key at the post office in the next village. He drove on a mile. The postmistress, a small bundle of a woman with a tight line for a mouth, surveyed him with a mistrustful air before handing him the key and apologising for keeping it locked.

'There've been so many burglaries. What with the thieves from Norwich going after the country houses, now that camp at Sheringham.' She looked at him, testingly, before going on. 'Not the sort to care about churches are they? Our churches I mean. They tell me they've started burning them down, but they don't put it in the papers. Maybe ours will go up next. Who's to stop them, now we've got no police…'

He drove back to the church. Dutiful even in solitude, he read the guide provided, paced the chancel, contributed a fiver to the church's upkeep. Then moped about the graveyard in the premature twilight of what had become an overcast day, peering at headstones with half-obliterated names, relishing the isolation, the mournful air. His career was an unmarked tombstone, his marriage lichen-covered, the country a sepulchre teeming with anguished spirits… And they said religion was a solace.

He sat on a bench and smoked a cheroot. The more Jean moaned about his absences the less inclined he was to hurry home. I know about national security, but what about my security, living on my own when you're away, with all these robberies and muggings? While he'd been in Great Yarmouth there'd been a robbery two doors away, she'd told him on her mobile.

'Four o'clock in the afternoon, can you imagine? And the beating the man gave her! I saw them taking her away, she was in a shocking state. Gratuitous the policeman said, he hadn't even taken much. That's the worrying part. Maybe it was you they were after, and got the wrong address? You must be a target.'

'Be good to think I'm that important. And Norwich isn't Manchester. It was probably some druggie. Maybe we should upgrade the alarm?'

'How am I supposed to sit behind an alarm all day, when you're not there?'

The Manchester incident had been kept from the press, but she knew about it. Reluctance to send the police on raids into Muslim areas meant security service people were going in under cover, to check out suspect premises. Not long ago an MI5 man had been caught and shot. Drug dealers, probably, but who knew?

He hadn't told Jean, but she'd picked it up on the Internet, of which she'd become an addict. The rumours and suppressed stories she read there, most of them overblown, were making her nervy and depressed. Her growing neurosis was not what he'd expected of her, and a disappointment to him. After all she was an educated woman, a scientist before taking up her career as an optician.

Then there was Debbie, his daughter. Drugs took you out of yourself, people said. Well they took you out of your family too. A matter of personal choice, they said, and it had been Debbie's at university. Private specialists, rehab, he'd tried everything, and there was nothing else he could do, except forget. For years he'd done his best not to think of her, mentally to disown her, and it hadn't worked. Worst of all was the sadness he felt when she'd had her child.

He'd been working on the IRA at the time. A summons to Belfast had taken him there the day of the birth, so he hadn't been at the hospital. He made it to the christening (Jean had insisted on one, Debbie was indifferent) but almost wished he hadn't. Apart from themselves and their daughter they were alone in church. The child howled and Debbie scarcely bothered to soothe it, as if to say there you are, that's what you get, it was you who insisted. Sensing the un-celebratory atmosphere the priest seemed in a hurry. Tony couldn't wait to get away either.

He looked at the squalling, rusty-faced, furious-looking thing in his sulking daughter's arms. That's it, he was thinking, the end of my line and we don't even know whose it is. They'd never met the boyfriend, and whoever it was he was no longer around. Now here they were, in church, not for a marriage but a christening. An infant nobody wanted being solemnly inducted into a creed its own mother cared nothing about. Or himself, her father, come to that. Like his presence at the baptizing of a child he could never love, the whole thing seemed a heartless formality.

Later he'd had an attack of guilt. But how had this come about? At a bitter moment in Debbie's downward spiral Jean had blamed it on him: that's what you get, she'd said, with an absent father. Yes he'd replied, you're right, it's true. Absent for most of her childhood, working twelve hour days, weekends, recalled from holidays sometimes, in the service of his country.

Though what sort of a country was it, he reflected now, where marriage, christenings and parents themselves had become formalities? Things you could take or leave, in which few believed. And now God himself had become absent from the nation's affairs.

It was only just five but a thirst was coming on. It happened a lot lately, and if he'd had a bottle with him he'd have drunk it.

Maybe he should keep one by him, the way things were going, to help him through the day. Jean was starting to watch his drinking as closely as she watched his cigarillos ('do it if you have to, just not in the house, they stink up the furniture'). Though if he kept it in his official car she wouldn't know. He could stow it in the compartment they'd installed after the Manchester business, alongside the revolver issued to operatives doing fieldwork on the emergency. Something else he'd hidden from Jean.

15

'Styled on a donkey-jacket, brother. What do you think? Fits a treat, don't it?'

Taking off his new coat, Jayson was holding it up. It was his first remark after they'd got back to the basement. The Syrian didn't look, said nothing. After his night on the garage floor and the dramas of the day he was trembling with exhaustion, near collapse. They hadn't dared transfer the bomb back to the concrete box in daylight, which meant driving around with it till dark, doing their best to keep it under cover: sitting in car parks, stopping under bridges. And all the time Amer fretting silently at the thought of it dangling again from the faulty winch.

The Syrian need never have worried. Edging into the alley just after eleven, they stopped. Some hoodlum in a woolly hat was backing what looked like a truckload of loot into a garage a dozen yards from their box. Switching off their lights, they watched as he closed makeshift doors and disappeared inside. Taken up residence, obviously, so that was the end of the concrete box.

All the way back to Scrubs Lane Amer worried away about security. Parking the van in the garage for a few days was one thing; leaving it longer – a week or more, who knew? – something else. Did Jayson's Albanian still work at the petrol station? So shiftless and unreliable, these immigrants. Was he Muslim – and what kind? Might he have a duplicate key, and who rented the other garages? Questions to which Jayson's perky reply – that the way to be sure was to fill up at the garage on the way back and have a chat to the fellow – seemed less than serious.

It was one in the morning by the time they got back to the basement, the security of the van compromised, Amer feeling ill, the Day of Glory a fiasco. And Jayson asks his opinion on his cut-price coat.

*

Shame and remorse were Amer's feelings in the days that followed.
Planning at the Bank had been more thorough: at least Umair had got
his van to the target. In their case, not even that.

The inquest in his mind was long and thorough. The first
conclusion he came to was that it was Jayson's fault. He ought to have
warned him about the traffic – though how? He couldn't have done
it by phone, and by the time they'd met up in Royal Crescent it was
too late. Nor could Jayson have known that a riot would break out
minutes after he'd left the store, so serious they'd closed the road.

And the boy had done well enough on their escape, he had to
admit. Shown the presence of mind to get the van under cover in a
petrol station, and go through the motions of fiddling with the engine
till the helicopter gave up circling the area. In many ways Jayson was
a child, certainly, but he was a child of Allah.

No, the Kensington plan had been his alone. The beauty of the
symmetrical strikes – first the financial district, then the commercial
system – had overwhelmed him, come to him in the night like a
revelation, a God-given chance to annihilate a street packed with
gluttonous infidel swine. He had pictured the scene in his mind: the
wrecked store and smashed bodies, the High Street a slaughterhouse,
heathen blood flowing along gutters into sewers. And the survivors
wishing they'd died, as they waited for their deformities to develop.

His failure was a humiliation before Allah, atonement was in order,
and in the aftermath of that terrible day his time was given over to
prayer and fasting. Amer's health did not suffer – in a strange way he
seemed to thrive on it, his appetite was never large, and gauntness
suited him – though not his Trinidadian brother. The Syrian could live
on the food of fervour, but soon Jayson began to look weak and ill.
His stomach contracted painfully when he ate nothing, the room full
of the stench of his diarrhoea when he did.

After a week of it the time came to call a halt. Any more would be displeasing to Allah, Amer explained, for it was specifically forbidden, the rules of fasting said, to risk damaging the faster's health. All the more when good health was so vital to bring to a conclusion their stupendous task.

The thing to do, the Syrian had decided, was to see the Kensington failure as a test run, and learn the lessons. Especially about traffic. Nobody wrote about road conditions in the press any more – the subject fell under censorship rules, he saw why now – though online it was all there. A couple of hours at Hani's told him what he needed, and what he read was a story that gladdened his pious heart.

After the Bank the centre of London had emptied. In their panic people spent a minimum of time in the open, and bus services and the Tube were closed. When cars were back on the streets it was clear this was no return to normal, because the rules of the road had fallen apart. Traffic lights were ignored, speed limits and congestion charging a joke, and crashes had gone unrecorded as ton-up boys from across London used the near-empty streets as race tracks, steaming along Park Lane or the Cromwell Road or Kensington Gore at ninety an hour, with no police in pursuit.

That was stage one. After that motorists had returned with a vengeance. Forced back to work after weeks of paralysis people had taken the government's message to heart: that you were better off in an enclosed space, anywhere but in the open. The Tube and the buses were back, but no one trusted them. Which was why to this day the streets of central London were a sea of cars.

There were lessons here, operational lessons for when and where the Day of Glory would finally come about. After his week of penance, followed by another of planning and reflection, Amer was convinced he'd learned them.

16

Maybe there was a God, Tony thought. The day after his churchyard lament brought relief in the unexpected form of Mrs Marusak. He'd tried to locate her before – apart from Anya and the Chechen she was the only one in the salon unaccounted for – but given up. The last he heard she'd joined the tide of Eastern Europeans – bankers, plumbers, call-girls – pulling out of the country in the weeks since the explosion. Knowing that her City pleasure-house would be discovered she would get out of the country sharpish, and that would be the end of her, he'd reckoned.

But no. The woman had a thick hide, it seemed. Now she'd turned up in Moscow. A letter to 'the English service of security', c/o the British Embassy, claimed she had something to tell. Or *fact of signification on bomb* as the letter put it. The MI5 man in the Embassy who was declared to the Russians had rung her up, offered to see her, but it wasn't enough. No no, she'd said, it was too important, she absolutely had to see 'London person.'

As the officer investigating the evacuees from her salon Thames House forwarded the letter to him. Was it worth him going to Moscow to see what the lady had to say, they asked? Tony reflected. Nothing he'd heard suggested she was anything more than a brothel-keeper. On the other hand there was the presence of a Chechen in the salon…

For all his Cold War service – or because of it – Tony had never set foot in Russia. A spell away from the camp was enticing – and from the country. A sortie from what a newspaper columnist had described as 'this doom-infected island' beckoned.

*

Heathrow was half-deserted, many of its shops and cafes closed for the duration, including the boutique where Tony had looked forward to stocking up on tax-free cigarillos. His hope that he might be spared exhaustive passport checks and whole-body scans for everyone going in or out was another disappointment: he showed his security service pass but the lady was inclined to make checks before accepting its validity ('it's a new instruction, Sir'), so in the end he submitted.

Nor had anyone thought to give him a decent seat on a decent airline – his junior rank, he supposed. The four-hour economy flight on an Aeroflot plane proved a poor introduction to Russia. Things got worse. Insufficiently senior to merit an Embassy car he was left to the mercies of a Russian hire firm to pick him up. The driver – the first person he met on Russian soil – greeted him with a grunt, left him to carry his baggage, played idiot music at top volume and drove like a lunatic in pelting rain.

Sightseeing from the back seat as well as he could through the torrent, Tony discovered a Russia that was a caricature of the one he'd expected. On the airport road hideous showrooms for Volvos and BMWs helped screen out Soviet-era housing estates of equally monstrous size. In Moscow itself the frowning buildings, gaudy lights and highways with traffic like charging tanks were the reverse of welcoming.

On the hotel the MI5 moneymen had been more generous. Five star and self-consciously classy, at first sight it looked as if it had left the Soviet era behind, yet somehow it retained a lugubrious, gangsterish air. Hit or miss sophistication in the would-be swanky bar included sour-looking waiters in gilded waistcoats, and grand cru wines upturned in a row, like spirits, the quicker to dispense a shot of white or red.

It was here he was due to meet Mrs Marusak, for tea at five. To select a spot favourable to his recording he made a point of arriving early, though not early enough. Drinking had begun, and with it a rising clamour of shouts and laughter. The place was almost full, so the best he could manage was a table uncomfortably close to a group of Russian businessmen and British engineers, Tyne-siders by the sound of them, exchanging obscene toasts. What looked like a bodyguard, complete with earpiece and over-emphatic breast pocket, sat lumpenly by.

Liaison with Moscow had been re-established after the break due to the Litvinenko affair. The Russians had come up with an instant visa, worried no doubt that what could be done in New York and London could be repeated in Moscow. It seemed unlikely that his meeting would go unmonitored, however, and he checked the bar to see who would be performing the task. The youngish fellow in the blue suit who sat down two tables away, looking resolutely the other way, seemed a promising candidate. The possibility increased when he was served a beer, swiftly and without asking.

In rising spirits – it felt good to get away – he had an urge to go over and introduce himself to the fellow, a rookie by the looks of things. Maybe give him a tip or two, such as the advantages to someone in his line of business of going through the formality of ordering his drinks before they were delivered.

For himself, tea didn't seem right in a place like this; after all it was lunchtime by his watch, he told himself, failing to notice that he was reasoning like an alcoholic. He ordered a double whisky, not too much soda, and downed it before Mrs Marusak arrived. Which was quite a moment. From people he'd talked to in the camp he'd formed a pretty full picture ('a right bloody bitch', according to the road-worker, 'fuckin' ball-breaker, man', in Kingman's words), but the reality was something.

She arrived late and greeted him loudly, over-dressed for the occasion in a kind of silver lamé blouse, whose tightness against her breasts troubled him for un-erotic reasons. The pressure of metal on flesh produced a chain-mail effect, like something from a Wagnerian heroine, or a blonded Boadicea.

'It is first time I meet English police,' she said, setting herself into her chair as daintily as her bulk allowed.

'I am not a policeman,' Tony corrected. 'I work for the British security service. I've come to talk about your letter, which we were grateful to receive.'

'It is good you come. I no want talk to Embassy bureaucrat. Here we speak person with person.'

The smile from lips over-painted at the edges pained him.

He called a waiter, enquired what she wanted. She didn't hesitate: 'Cointreau cocktail.'

The waiter asked what it was. In astonished tones she told him, finishing in English:

'Large one.'

Tony ordered a second whisky, double.

A silence followed as Mrs Marusak's eyes searched the bar. She seemed especially interested in four girls in tank-tops and designer jeans at a table a few feet away. The moment he'd entered Tony had taken in the hotel whores. What struck him was how demure they looked, drinking tea and chatting discreetly, minding their business, with no attempt to advertize their presence. To pass the time one of them, a brunette of about thirty, was knitting.

A fair slice of his working life had been spent idling away the hours by watching every type of girl on the game, and he thought he'd seen everything. But a pretty young woman, in jeans, knitting? This was new, and he found himself darting glances. The movements of her arms, bare to the shoulder, seemed restful and domestic, giving the woman a kind of erotic innocence.

Their drinks came and were ceremoniously served. Mrs Marusak made the fellow wait while she tested hers, then shrugged and gave a reluctant 'is OK.'

By now Tony was relaxed. Toasting her with a faintly collusive smile, he took a gulp of his whisky, lit a cheroot, puffed out smoke contentedly and said:

'We know about the brothel.'

'Brothel?' She nodded to the collective of whores. 'Brothel here, in hotel?'

'No. In London. Above your salon.'

Mrs Marusak assumed an affronted air.

'You are right. I suspect there was brothel upstairs. Men come and go all day, by back entrance. And some come into my salon by mistake. People see and they think, what is this? Not good for my business.'

'Mrs Marusak, you have a lease on the upstairs flat. Plus you forgot to empty the cameras.'

'Sorry.'

She gave a twee smile, as if he'd accused her of failing to flush the toilets.

'We were in such hurry. A catastrophe –'

'– I don't think you understand what I am saying. There are pictures of the girls working downstairs for women, and the same girls doing different things upstairs for men.'

A hand went to her breast, as if in shock. Tony was a patient interrogator when he chose, but now he chose not to be.

'Please don't do that. We have pictures of you upstairs, taking money. Pictures of –'

Mrs Marusak, wide-eyed, interrupted:

'– maybe fucking against the law in Britain? Where is harm? Men in City work hard, need relax. It is men who need, always they need.' She had put her drink down to give full rein to her gestures, the air in front of her a storm of hands. 'Is better than dirty bomb!'

'I'm just telling you that we know.'

'I think you want to talk about nuclear. Otherwise why I come?'

A hand went down her side, as if to collect up her skirt. Jesus, he thought, I've overdone it, she's going to go. He had a stab at a disarming smile:

'I'm sorry. I thought you wouldn't mind if I sort of cleared the air. So we can talk frankly and straightforwardly.'

She leant forward.

'Never mind fucking, I come to talk about bomb. Muslims, they are terrible, do anything. And who is worst? You think Pakistani worst, or Arab person. But there is most worst.'

'And who is that?'

'Chechen.'

'I've heard they can be nasty.'

Mrs Marusak leant further:

'There was Chechen in salon.'

'I know.'

Deflated, she sat back.

'How you know?'

'You called him a stupid Chechen. Tell me about him. Where did he go afterwards?'

'How I know? He not radiated, he not go to hospital. He just go away.'

'You think his behaviour was suspicious?'

'Yes of course suspicious. He is Chechen. Only Chechen make dirty bomb before, because Chechen dirty people. This Chechen say he is businessman, and use our girls. But how we know? Maybe he only use for, how you say, *krysha*, roof…'

'Cover?'

'Yes, like cover.'

'You're well informed.'

'My husband tell me. He fought in war, know about Chechen. So I tell you. To help. Because I have Chechen customer.'

'Why was he suspicious?'

The hands stormed again.

'Why I need prove Chechens thieves and murderers? Ask my husband, ask anyone,' she gestured round the bar. 'And how can be proof when everything blow up?'

This was going nowhere. He ordered more drinks. Looking round the bar while they waited his eyes came to rest on the knitting woman. They must have rested too long.

'You like girls?' Mrs Marusak leant forward, speaking softly, imitating discretion. 'Here very expensive. Maybe I can arrange, cheaper.'

'You're very kind, but not just now, thank you all the same.'

His irony may or may not have struck home. Perhaps she hadn't heard. A football match was showing on the television. The Russian for soccer fans, Tony had learned from the Aeroflot magazine on his flight, was 'sufferers', and the TV commentator seemed to be suffering badly. At the same moment in a room nearby a Gypsy violin had struck up at a private function, in high-pitched counterpoint to the football cheers and belly laughter in the bar.

Bosoms exploding against the metallic blouse, her Cointreau almost beneath his nose, again she leant towards him:

'I tell you name of Chechen. Then he give you name of bombers. And you let me come back, when nuclear gone. OK? Come back and no trouble about girls.'

Half-hearing and scarcely listening, Tony nodded. The whiskies had begun toning him up, toning up the world. How long since he'd been free to switch off and smoke, drink and look at beautiful women in a swank hotel? He was afloat above the conversation, Mrs Marusak and her blather forgotten.

Next time he looked she was delving into her vast handbag. Terrible to think what a whoremonger might have occasion to keep in there. Finding a pen and paper, with exaggerated precautions she was writing a name on a scrap of paper. Folding it, she slipped it into his hand.

'So this is deal.'

Tony took the name, glanced at it, stowed it in a pocket.

'Deal? We'll see about that. Let's forget about Chechens for a moment. What else do you remember about the people in your salon?'

'Only other Muslim was Safia. I not race person, Mr Underwood, but she dress terrible.' As if banishing the memory she closed her eyes. 'Terrible Mr Underwood, like first time in Western clothes. Hair terrible, nails terrible, too much hair where it shouldn't be, men don't like –'

'– how do you know?'

'What about?'

'The, er, hair where it shouldn't be.'

'I saw in shower. She asked me to help in shower, to scrub off nuclear.'

'I thought Muslim women were very modest. Even with other women.'

A shrug.

'Maybe because she afraid.'

In the growing din around them Tony was losing the thread, insofar as there was one. For something to say he went on:

'So what you're saying is she looked a mess and had come in to fix her hair?'

An explosion in the bar. Someone must have scored. Mrs Marusak began denying something, loudly, though not loud enough for him to hear. The fiery gestures, the querulous tones were beginning to weary him. His eyes sought solace in the round arms and mechanical movements of the knitting whore.

He wanted to be done with the Marusak woman. On the other hand he wouldn't mind a last drink. While she gabbled on inaudibly he signalled to the waiter, lit a final cheroot.

'And then?' he said, absently.

'She was frightened, the bomb go off and frighten her.'

'Well it would, wouldn't it?'

To speed things to a close he made the mistake of thanking her for her help.

'Of course I help, so you help me, OK Mr Underwood? You tell passport friends so no trouble when I come to London. For me or my husband. Or partner I maybe say. He come back when it over and help build up City. Many Russians spend money, help business.'

Finishing her drink she put it down, crossed her legs, settled back in her chair and sought to look – there was no other word – winsome.

'You sure you not like girl?'

Tony smiled and shook his head.

'Maybe for you older is better? And cheaper.'

Till that moment he'd done his best not to look at her. From incredulity now he did, and saw the meaning in her eye. A former madam had caught him ogling a girl in a bar and was offering her blowsy, superannuated self as a cut-price version. The low point, surely, of a lowering few months.

'What I need is a little sleep. We'll be in touch.'

It was said with such finality that she got the message. With some help from the table she got up and they said goodbye.

When she'd gone he turned to look for his blue-suited shadow. The man had gone, defeated by the racket he guessed, like himself. Finishing his drink he paid, went to the lift, fumbled for his electronic card, slotted it in, pressed his floor number.

The doors closed. Nothing happened. A second later they opened and the woman with the knitting stepped in, smiled, and pressed the 'close door' button.

17

The sound of a grill closing. Amer woke, stabbed a hand beneath his pillow, sprang up, stared round in the dark. Nothing. Pulling the curtain aside he peered up into the half-light of the garden. Scuffed white trainers beneath a pair of jean-clad calves met his gaze. Jayson? He glanced at his bed: empty. He looked back at the garden. The legs were planted apart amongst the weeds and brambles as if he'd gone out there to piss. Unlikely. To see his face and body he crouched lower, craned up his head – and there he was: Jayson amongst the brambles, holding a mobile to his ear.

As he watched the boy rang off and, secreting the phone in his blouson, climbed down the stone steps to the area, locked the grill over the door, and came back into the room.

Amer was waiting, in his underwear, his Makarov revolver in one hand, the other outstretched.

'Give it to me.'

'What?'

'The mobile. Give it to me. I told you, strictly no phones.'

'I can't give it you, brother, it's not mine, it's Ayan's. She lent it me, when I went round.'

'I repeat,' the Syrian said, 'no phones. Not even ones you've borrowed.'

'I thought you meant we wasn't to use one for – you know – stuff, brother.'

'Never. I have told you, never. You saw what happened with our brothers in New York.'

'It's only for Ayan, just her.'

'Why do you need to phone her?'

'Because she keeps askin' why I can't. What I gonna say? I told her my mobile wasn't workin' and she said here, take mine. Said she gotta be in touch, to ring her in the mornings when I can. I was careful to use her landline, brother.'

'I said no phones. That means landlines as well as mobiles. And I explained you had already taken leave of your wife. So why call her?'

'But she ain't well. Says she wakes up every day, worse. An' it's not just the sickness.'

The conversation with his wife had been difficult. She'd taken the promises to be with her soon and forever literally, assuming it meant the re-wiring job was almost done. Soothing and cajoling her into accepting more delay, explaining that another job had come up in the same area, had made it a long call. And there was a money problem. She'd been off work for a week, she said, now they'd put her on half-time, so she was low on cash.

For a moment Amer and Jayson faced each other. The Makarov wasn't levelled, but nor had Amer put it down. Remembering it was in his hand he stuffed it back under his pillow, and began pulling on his trousers. Buckling his belt, he looked stony.

Jayson waited till he'd turned his back before adding:

'Other thing is, she needs some cash.'

The Syrian glanced round, even less happy.

'A month ago I gave you £600 for her. Is it gone? What does the woman spend it on? Clothes, is it? If so she can earn it herself. She's working, isn't she?'

'Sort of, brother. But they've put her on part-time at the checkout. People not buyin' stuff no more. I don't want her sittin' round worryin'. Thinkin' things, or gettin' onto the social security. Said she wants to sign on for housing benefit but I said no way. Don't want anyone signin' things, brother. Names, addresses. Then they come round checkin' and askin' what I do...'

He was still addressing the Syrian's back. As he'd spoken his eyes had gone, fleetingly, to the garden. It was there that the Syrian kept his money: buried against the left-hand wall, a foot down, in a green plastic bag sealed in a tin box. Eighteen thousand, it looked like. There were Euros and dollars too, about £25,000 in all.

Amer hadn't told him. He knew the cash was there because he'd seen him in the garden in rubber gloves at daybreak one morning, a time when he must have thought Jayson, a long sleeper, wasn't awake. It was the day he'd given him the £600.

While Amer was at the Internet café he'd dug it up, had a look. Not – Allah forbid! – to touch it, just check how much there was. He knew what it was to need money, knew too well, what it was to be on the run and not to eat. And if the Syrian went out one day and didn't come back and they were onto him too he'd need ready cash to give Ayan, and get away. That much Jayson had thought through.

'No housing benefit. Absolutely not. How much is the rent?'

'£170 a week.'

'Tomorrow I will give you another £600.'

That's not going to last long, now she's on half-pay, Jayson wanted to say. And what happens when I'm not here, and she can't work, with the baby? All that ready cash lying out there – why not make it £1,000, or £5,000? No point letting all that money go to waste, or be dug up by the police. A new pair of shoes could help console Ayan when he was gone. Allah was merciful, he would understand.

'Your wife seems very extravagant', the Syrian grumbled. 'Tell her she must be more frugal.'

'I will brother, I will.'

After they'd prayed he made them breakfast. The Syrian was silent, then sighed.

'It is unfortunate to be married at such a time.'

'You never married?'

Peeved about the money, Jayson was bold enough to put the question a second time.

'I had a fiancée,' Amer said, 'but I renounced her.'

'Why'd you do that, brother? She do you wrong?'

'Certainly not!' The Syrian's face was angry.'How would I have a fiancée who would misbehave?'

'So why'd you leave her?'

'To be ready.'

Jayson looked mournful. Was Amer saying he wasn't ready?

They ate breakfast. The Syrian went to the bathroom and came back, still sombre. To cheer him Jayson said:

'You heard what they sayin' 'bout the Chechens? Rumours sayin' they helped?'

'I know, I saw on television. And so?'

'I dunno. It's sorta – interesting. I mean if it's true that –'

'– these are questions we do not ask. The Chechens are brave fighters. That is all we need to know.'

'They is brother, they is.'

He went to the window.

'Nice day out there. Kinda warm and fresh. Be nice to be out.'

His voice was wistful, a whimper almost, like a dog begging for a run.

'I don't want you in the garden. Ever. Someone might see. Someone opposite.'

'Isn't no one opposite. I never seen anyone. Houses boarded up, empty.'

'How do you know? People think this one's empty, don't they?'

''Suppose that's true, brother.'

The Syrian contemplated Jayson's back: his dejected stance, his listless shoulders.

'You must have patience. It will not be long. The last touches. And this time, no mistakes. No traffic.'

Jayson turned, more alert.

'So what's the plan, brother?'

A silence, then Amer said:

'The plan is that it will be soon. Then we shall have our wish. *And their faces that day shall be shining and radiant.*

'*Shinin' and radiant,*' the Trinidadian intoned softly. 'And the plan?'

'The day before, I will tell you.'

'But I gotta be ready. In my head. And if it's that near, my wife –'

'– how many times must I tell you? You have said goodbye to Ayan.'

'Well I see that, brother. It's just that she said to me on the phone –'

'– I don't need to hear what she said. I'd like to hear what you said. What you said on the open line.'

'It was nothing, really. Ayan, she did the talking, it was about her going to the hospital and things she gotta get. It's why she needs the money, an'–'

'– all right, enough.'

Jayson was crestfallen.

'OK, I'll try stayin' in limbo. Like you said.'

For a few minutes he stood at the window, silent, while Amer settled down with his notebooks.

'Thing is, if it's soon, I got check-ups to do. On the van and stuff. You said you wanted it painted, that the green colour was, like –'

'– compromised, was what I said. That you may do. You may go there – but briefly. I don't want any risks. Absolutely no risks.'

'Aye, brother. So what colour?'

'The colour? What does it matter? Make it blue, blue will do. Just paint it, and change the plates.'

'The plates I got, ready.' Jayson pointed to a corner. To Amer, he still looked down. With the day approaching he should be in better shape.

'And do not fret about your wife, your former wife. Remember how she will be when she hears.'

'Shinin' and radiant,' Jayson chanted, his face a little brighter. 'I feel the day comin'. Gonna be soon, brother, my heart is tellin' me.'

'I have said: the day before I will tell you.'

*

It was the following evening before Amer said anything more. As always for serious talking the Syrian insisted on an evening walk in the park.

'So where's it to be, brother?' Jayson asked as they took a shadowy path beneath anaemic lamps.

'Bristol,' Amer breathed.

'You don't wanna try London again? Why's that, brother? Is it 'cos Tariq and Umair done it?'

'No, not that at all. It is because Bristol is better,' the Syrian was quietly emphatic, 'in every respect. The traffic is better. Climatologically it is better. It is the Bristol Channel, the wind roars up the Bristol Channel. Tomorrow and the next few days, west or southwest 3 or 4, increasing 5 or 6, the Internet said. Force 6 is strong. 6 would disperse it widely.'

'Good choice, brother. Wind comes from the sea, don't it, where Osama's hidin' out, so it comes from him. So where 'bouts in Bristol?'

'A shopping centre,' Amer said softly. '300 shops.'

'You know it?'

'I have been there. I had friends in Bristol, some time ago... So yes, I know the area.'

'That's great, brother. Although...' His brow lined with doubt, for a few moments he walked on, unsure whether to give voice to it. At last he said:

'I remember Umair sayin' maybe we should do a shopping centre, but Tariq said –'

'– I know what Tariq said, but Tariq was wrong. I will tell you something about Tariq. Before his martyrdom he said goodbye to me. I asked if he had ever been to the City, he said he had, once, an errand for his father, and that he was worried. It wasn't just bankers there, he said, there were women and children and some faithful, working in Muslim banks.

'Was I sure it was right with Allah, he asked me? And you know what I said? I said yes it was, a thousand times yes, he must not think such thoughts, it would paralyse his will. And he was strengthened by what I said, and he did it.'

'Sure, brother, he did it.'

Unsure whether his words had struck home, the Syrian tried to read the motionless face,

'Imagine he hadn't,' he went on. 'Think of Allah's punishment for Tariq if he had weakened! The joys he would have foregone! In Paradise rivers flow, and the fruits are perpetual and plenty. Such is the end for those who keep their duty. And for those whose faith shrivels and dies at the thought of the sacrifice of a handful of people, men and women of sin, probably, and so few He would scarcely notice, what would be their punishment? Imagine we don't do it, and sow terror in their hearts, a terminal terror this time because they will see no end to it, till they desist from their unbelief and accept the Caliphate!'

'Aye, brother! The Caliphat!'

'Caliphate.'

'Aye, Caliphate.'

'Anywhere we go there will be Muslims. But how many are loyal to the faith? You see what happened in the East End, when the bomb reached them? Instead of greeting the cleansing fire, welcoming martyrdom and glorying in their injuries, how many people of the faith said it was wrong to kill? These are not Muslims, they are apostates. They pray once a week but they are apostates!'

'Apostates is what they are, brother!'

'And apostasy is treason, and for treason people are killed everywhere. In the Hadith it is written. You remember?'

'I haven't read it, brother. Or maybe I don't remember. I can't remember everything. I'll try to learn, do my best to remember.'

'It is late, brother, too late. To finish what you have not read we would have to delay forever. Take my word, I know, I have studied!'

Jayson walked on, his agitation showing in his step.

'I never said I's against stores or supermarkets or shopping centres or whatever. Gotta have the numbers, brother. An' those shoppin' centres is all glass so it'll break and the radiation'll get in and they'll be like roasted in hellfire.'

'So why did you hesitate?'

Jayson's face allowed a trace of puzzlement at himself.

'It's just that when I used to go to his mosque the imam there said —'

'– I know what that imam said. You have told me before. That is why I told you not to listen.'

'It's hard not to listen, brother, when you're there and he says it.'

'That imam was working for the security services. I have seen his house, his car.'

Jayson was silent. The imam was the father of a Caribbean friend, and fellow convert. He'd been proud to know a Caribbean imam, and found it hard to believe he was working for the security services.

'P'rhaps he's just got a wrong understanding of jihad.'

'No understanding. He has no understanding.'

'Aye, brother,' Jayson shrugged. 'None at all.'

'Good.' Amer turned back on the path, towards the park gate. 'So that is the plan. A shopping centre in a windy city, to spread our gift generously. But we need an exact moment.'

'The optimum moment,' Jayson nodded, 'An' the optimum day.'

'Precisely. So I want you to go there and find out three things. The first, when it is most crowded. The second, the traffic. And third, how close we can get.'

'I'll do that brother, I'll go there, whenever you say.'

'Tomorrow. You will go tomorrow. Then we shall be ready.'

They were almost back at the house when Jayson said.

'There's a Muslim area in Bristol, brother, right? 'Cos there's all these riots.'

'Correct.'

'So what if there's a force 6 or whatever on the day and it blows it into the Muslim quarter, like it did in London?'

To contain himself Amer drew a breath.

'We have discussed that, a moment ago. Just as we cannot choose between one shopper and another, a mother and a child –'

'– but what...'

Seeing Amer's face tauten into anger, he hesitated. In the Kensington store there'd been no children, he was thinking. In a shopping centre there would be.

'But what if it's like Ayan, goin' shoppin' with the money you gave her, with her unborn child? What if it was her? We'd be killin' a Muslim that's not born so it couldn't have any sin, an'–'

The Syrian cut him off:

'I don't like your way of thinking, brother. It is not stable. It keeps slipping back. I told you, these are the kind of thoughts that paralyse your will. And if your will to serve Allah is paralysed, you are not a true convert.'

They were in front of the basement door, Amer reaching for his key. Jayson turned to him, blinking in the dark, fearful.

'Don't say that, brother! How can you doubt my faith, my conversion! I've done my trainin', I'm ready for martyrdom! I testified before God! *La illah illah Allah. Muhammad rasoolu Allah.* You see? Even in Arabic I remember! There is no God but Allah, and Mohamed is his messenger.'

'No true God,' the Syrian corrected testily, opening the door. 'And prophet is better than messenger.'

18

At the entrance to the school a new notice, signed Sheringham Town Council, had been erected: SHERINGHAM WELCOMES EVACUEE CHILDREN. Outside the gates sixteen-year-olds in full city gear stood about smoking, the boys joshing and jabbing one another, the girls with their shrieking voices and violent colours.

Seeing Jackie emerge Martin stepped forward eagerly, though with trepidation.

'You can kiss me,' she said, proffering a cheek. 'It isn't contaminous.'

To hide his dampening eyes he pressed his lips to her face so long that she jerked away. On the walk to the car he scrutinised her for signs of sickness – over-bright eyes, a feverish complexion, he wasn't sure what – but she looked well enough, if a little thin.

'You didn't come and see me after the explosion,' she said matter-of-factly.

'I did try,' Martin said, loathing his smile.

'Did mummy say you couldn't?'

'Not at all, of course not.'

'Well I caught some radiation,' Jackie said, pointing to her throat. 'It wasn't my fault. I was just in the school garden, breathing.'

'Of course it's not your fault.'

'Everyone here has some, even mummy. But I haven't got as much as Amel.' She pointed to a tiny dark girl with large eyes, whose mother was leading her out of the gate. 'She's Pakistani you know. She was my best friend in London. Mummy looks after her. Her mummy says my mummy's an angel. Do you think she is?'

'I do, yes.'

'She's quite a strict angel isn't she?' Jackie said with a conspiratorial grin.

'Only when she has to be,' Martin said, closing the car door.

*

When agreeing to let him come Julie had asked Martin to pick Jackie up from school the day he arrived. It was because she had a meeting, and there was no one else. Louise, the calm and grave Jamaican who usually fetched her, had died suddenly. A cleaner at the Mansion House, she'd clocked off from her seven a.m. shift at two-thirty, exactly the wrong moment. The meeting was with the camp administrator, to seek permission for Safia to stay on as Jackie's new nanny. It was granted.

Later she was taking Martin to eat at the hotel in Sheringham on the sea front. It didn't promise to be much of an evening, each was thinking. On the legal side Julie had put everything on hold. The drama of the last months and Jackie's illness had distanced her from her own problems. Now the idea of giving him another chance was beginning to seem less like an act of weakness.

He'd found ways to convey that he was drinking less, but he needed her help, it was obvious. He too was a kind of patient, she reflected, for whom it would be unethical to abandon hope. A man to whom she was bound by a kind of marital Hippocratic oath: above all, do no harm. And if she abandoned him now, she might.

Was this the way things had been in wartime, she wondered? Would there be more human solidarity in the face of an endlessly insecure future? It would be good to believe it, though scientifically the answer was no. Every study she'd read about the impact of the bomb suggested that fear of disease and an early death would do little to improve people's behaviour. On the contrary, it would be a goad to selfishness, to cynicism, nihilism and the neglect of future generations.

There were signs of it in the camp, visiting psychiatrists reported.

An increase in intolerance and incivility, and family arguments, violent sometimes. Of insubordination by children, even amongst Muslims, and of late night prowlings between the holiday homes as people engaged in petty thefts or casual affairs.

It was good she could protect Safia from any of this, had her safely under her wing. As Jackie switched her affections from poor Louise the girl was cheering up. Most comforting for Julie was her punctiliousness in making sure Jackie took her medicines at the right times while she was at work. Louise, as her illness advanced, had become forgetful.

Her only concern about Safia was her excess of zeal. She treated the child too much like an invalid, pandering to her whims in a way the more matter-of-fact Louise had never done. Though maybe it was understandable: a case of her seeking to give Jackie the childhood she had never had.

Watching her help with homework, her fears about her reading and writing levels were resolved. For all her limited education she turned out to read perfectly well, and write clearly in a small, studied hand. The years she'd spent at school had been well used. By recommending books for her to read, Julie hoped to raise her aspirations.

'I'd love to be a doctor,' Safia volunteered one day. 'Like you.'

'Nothing's impossible,' Julie replied, without thinking.

*

Martin had no intimation that a second chance might be in the offing, because Julie was determined that he shouldn't: if he knew the way her mind was working he might relax, and slip backwards. In thinking this way the danger she overlooked was that her failure to show confidence in him might have the same effect. All the more since he was coming to Sheringham with the memory of a phone call from Freddie du Sautoy hot in his ears:

'You were there for Christ's sake! Told me you'd got a scoop. That you'd seen the goings-on in the place where the old guy and the boy were burned. Said you'd done the piece and were on the verge of sending it through. And here was I holding up the mag.

'Maybe you'd just thought you'd done it, done a great job of convincing yourself you'd done it, because I'll give you this Martin, you're a plausible fellow, especially to yourself. 'One day you'll be able to explain', you say. But I won't be interested in your explanations Martin because the way things look, by then I'll have fuck-all to edit.

'I don't know how Julie put up with it. Feel free to tell her she has my commiserations. Maybe she's all that kept you going, and now you're losing her there's nothing left.'

To round off a bad few days there'd been a message from Billy Furlow on his phone that morning:

'Hi Martin. Seemed a good moment for one of our little discussions, but you're not there, at least no one's answerin'. So it looks like another of our one-way chats.

'Don't see nothin' by you in the press these days. Not that I'm complainin' 'bout your golden silence. On the other hand I saw what I presume to be your lady wife doin' a number in a BBC documentary about evacuees. Bit too nice to the Mohameds for my taste, but she's a handsome woman Martin, and if I were you I'd stick with 'er. I mean there'll always be a need for doctors, way we're going, even if the journos lose their jobs.

'I'm ringin' from the car, off to Bristol, see how they do things there. Fuckin' brilliant those lads. See their latest stunt? Took a bulldozer round a Paki estate and smashed up every car they could find. TV showed this Paki whinin' about insurance not paying up for riots. What a joke that is. As if they was insured!

'Eddy drives me on my travels, so I can get some readin' done. I'm into Citizens by Simon Schama, read it have you? The French Revolution it's about, and it got me thinkin'. Say what you like and they killed a lot of people, no two ways, all those drownins and toppins, but after it was over the French revolution stood for somethin'.

'Time for a spot of revolution here, wouldn't you say? Then the military can prepare the country for a return to democracy which let's face it we lost a long time ago. Think it over, maybe you'd be in a position to give it a push. On a non-attributable basis, eh Martin? I don't think I'm givin' anything away when I say I'm in contact with a few people in the ranks and higher. People that might surprise you. People who want to do a bit more than sit back and wait for the second one.

'Yes there's a lot 'appenin' out there Martin. Meanwhile I respectfully suggest you keep that golden silence of yours fourteen fuckin' carat.'

*

A group of Bikeys were lolling on the benches in front of the hotel restaurant as Martin and Julie approached. Rap hammered from a portable radio and the smell of marijuana overlaid the fresh sea air. Across the road, by the pub, some Nukies hovered. As always the crews had been ignoring each other, till a Somali, a skinny boy of sixteen, found a way of provoking the Caribbeans' attention.

From time to time gulls fluttered onto the sea wall to parade along it, and one alighted now. Scooping up gravel from the car park the Somali began tossing it towards the bird, not to hit it but to make it bob along as the stones sprayed the wall beneath it. Get it right – and the boy had clearly practised – and the bird would progress in a series of comical hops along the wall.

The trouble came when it continued its parade on a length of wall belonging to the rival gang. With his fourth, deft throw the boy hit the wall a foot or two into alien space.

A Caribbean lad stiffened. Looks were exchanged. In a tone of false surprise the Somali boy shouted across, 'what?' It took the sight of Julie coming along the road to cool things off.

A boy of twenty or so in dreadlocks under a new leather cap raised a hand as Julie passed:

'Hi Miss Opie.'

'Hi Kingman. Love the new style.'

She indicated his tall, coloured cap. The look seemed to her dated, but then Kingman was an amateur in the world of gangland fashionistas. The Bikey leader for lack of a rival, and from respect for the gravity of his illness, the boy was putting on style. Any style.

'Yeah, well you gotta move on, ain't ya? Sorry about that hassle on the beach.'

'Never mind. You stopped it.'

'It was Ricky and 'is boys.' He indicated the youngest at the table. Julie recognised the menacing jaw and nervy eyes. 'Tough man, Ricky. Long as he's got 'is boys wiv 'im, coupla ladies don't scare 'im at all.' Ricky shifted on his bench, head down over his cigarette. 'Tell 'im he go on like that and you'll get 'is medic to cut off 'is pills. Let 'im get cancer.'

'Gonna get it anyhow, way he smokes,' a second boy laughed.

'We'll give him another chance,' Julie threw back, and they walked on. Kingman came up behind them.

'Weren't me last night Miss Opie. You gotta know that. New boy got pissed up.'

'Glad to hear it,' Julie said, 'but not about your new friend. What am I supposed to tell the police if they ask?'

'Ain't none round 'ere. An' you could say it was 'is med'cine made 'im do it.'

'I doubt it,' she sighed, and he went back to his mates.

'You seem to be respected,' Martin laughed, 'where it matters. Who was that?'

'Kingman. He leads the Bikey crew. The Muslims were the Sea-squad at first. Not too clever either. Then the Bikeys started calling them the Nukies, and the name stuck. Sad thing is they don't mind.'

They took their table in the resturant, where the low ceiling seemed to compress the food-stained air. A pair of disoriented-looking tourists glanced at the gangs through a window. Opposite was a table of camp administrators, at whom Julie nodded.

She ordered a gin and tonic, Martin a soda water; when it came their eyes converged on it, unsmiling. With thoughts of an article, Martin came back to the gangs, asking what Kingman had been saying.

'There was a fight last night,' she told him. 'A Bangladeshi kid knifed, not too serious but nobody arrested. It's that he was talking about. But they're not all bad. Just that they're out of it in London, and doubly deracinated here. On top of that there's their health.'

'They look strong enough.'

'Looks can be deceptive in this field.'

I hope that means you're in better shape than you seem, he wanted to say. She'd taken off her shawl in the stuffy room and her bare arms looked frighteningly thin. It wasn't just for her that he was afraid: a frail Julie frightened him for them both. A loss of strength in her, he sensed, would be a loss to himself.

'And what about you? Isn't it dangerous up there?'

'It's not so bad, a bit like hospital: up to a point they have to behave. It's when they get outside that they go for each other.'

'How bad is Kingman, health-wise?'

'Bad. But if his treatment works he could come through, and surprise us. If he does it'll tell us something about what can be achieved in some of the worst circumstances you can imagine. Medically and morally.'

'Not the sort of person,' Martin was picking his words, 'you would normally look to as a symbol of hope.'

'You think I'm romanticising don't you? Because he's Caribbean.'

Normally he would have protested absolutely not. Now, there seemed no point.

'I suspect you are a bit.'

'You didn't see him in that salon, when he was sure he was going to die. The rage was imposing. Now he's been told he could survive a bone marrow transplant. It's as if it's the first time in his life he's been given a chance.'

He hesitated, then said:

'And us? Our problems look a bit trivial now, don't they? Which means they could be overcome. Doesn't it?'

The waitress spared Julie the difficulty of replying. When they'd ordered he said:

'Before you ask, I can't say it's been much of a time for me since we last spoke. You know the paper went down, of course.

'I heard.'

'I was lucky. I'd been up and down to the Midlands and Freddie du Sautoy's magazine wanted some pieces. So I went back up a week ago –'

'– wasn't that when they burned that boy and his grandfather?'

He'd planned to tell her, sworn to himself he would. Now he wavered. As he'd spoken about himself a hope-against-hope expression had come into her eyes, one he knew well. Now all he had to tell her was that he'd got mixed up with a bunch of racists and was terrified of going to the police. Before he could dream up some fable, the truth came out:

'Yes it was,' he said. 'It happened while I was there, but it's rather worse than that. I was with the people who did it. And it's got me into a heap of trouble.'

That took care of the hope-against-hope expression; by the time he'd finished she was shaking her head, speechless.

'Sometimes I think you ought to have done what you really wanted, and gone on in the acting business. Being at arm's length from reality would have made you happier. You look so desperate when you're telling the truth.'

His attempt at a smile was cut short when she added in a matter-of-fact tone.

'So you've been to the police.'

'I was thinking maybe I ought –'

'– two dead people, and you haven't been!'

'It was at a distance. There was smoke. I couldn't swear...'

'You haven't been!'

'You think I should?'

'It's not what I think. It's what you feel.'

Helpless, he said: 'I don't think they'd have done it if they'd known about the boy.'

'Oh for Christ's sake! And it's not just the boy. It's given a new twist to the whole race-riot thing. Don't you listen to the news?'

'So you think I should ignore the threats, be a witness.'

'How can you hesitate? Do they know where you live?'

'No. All they've got is the mobile.'

'Change it.' Again, she shook her head. 'Well I'm sorry but I'm staggered.'

'Julie, I'm going to the police. Of course I was going to go.'

He spoke resolutely, and he meant it. If only because he could see from her eyes that if he didn't go he would lose her once and for all.

19

'We must make new videos,' Amer announced when Jayson returned from Bristol, 'while we have time.'

'Old ones no good?' Jayson's brow furrowed, as it often did. 'I thought they was good, brother. Still, lucky we never posted 'em.'

'You have forgotten. In the last ones we talked about Kensington High Street. So we can't use them.'

When Amer was being patient he had a habit of looking at the floor and closing his eyes, as if to switch off from what he was hearing and reboot his mind. He did it now.

'One of the things we have learned from our trial run is that we shouldn't mention specific places. The videos must be up to date, without specific places. You understand?'

'Only a trial run was it brother? Seemed like the real thing to me.'

'Never mind that. Do you understand?'

Jayson signified that he did.

'Also,' Amer continued, 'we made them in a hurry. The quality wasn't good. We'll look at one again, you will see.'

Amer undid the package they hadn't posted and selected the CD with his name in red felt pencil, to distinguish it from the blank he'd surrepticiously inserted. While Jayson put it on he lay back on his bed, a leg on the floor, in his viewing position, and watched as he came up on the screen. Usually he wore Western clothes. For the video he'd put on a smart new Arabian jubba over a dishdash. Bought for the occasion, at a cost of £130, he'd found it on the Internet at Hani's, who'd agreed to take delivery on his behalf.

The recording had been the first and only time he'd worn the resplendent coat. Seeing himself in it again gave him a jolt of pleasure. The new jacket conferred distinction, he felt, lived up to the advertisement description:

Traditional collar, the buttons hidden in front panel reaching down to the waist for ease of salat, the five daily prayers. Sometimes referred to as an Imam's coat, it is worn by clerics in Middle Eastern countries. Includes shoulder pads and satin lining.

Torn between charcoal and navy blue he'd been tempted to take the blue, as more suited to his light colouring, though in the end he'd gone for charcoal. The dark material looked more menacing as, skull-capped, square-shouldered, bearded, resolute, severe, a finger jabbing towards the viewer he intoned:

'This is the second act of punishment for the arrogant British. There will be more, in Britain and other countries. Allah wills it, and for the chastisement of the infidel no weapon is out of bounds. The people suffered in Kensington High Street as Muslims suffer every day in the West's crusades against Islam...'

The Syrian was studying his image. Despite a glint of satisfaction over the jacket, his face was critical.

'What do you think?', he asked half way through.

'It's great,' said Jayson.

'It is a pity about the beard.'

'Yeah, it look sorta right, with that jacket. Like Osama, he looked good, in his cape and all, with 'is beard. Suppose you could grow another one. Or just, you know, some stubble.'

Amer did not trouble himself to decline.

'And the light,' he said. 'The light is bad.'

'Was a cloudy stretch, wasn't it? And it's not great down 'ere is it, best of days. Think I could make it better, rig up some lamps and stuff.'

To improve the light in the video Amer had been sitting close to the window. Jayson froze a frame and studied it.

'An' look,' he said, leaning in, pointing. 'You can see a bit of the garden. Top left corner. An' the bottom of the 'ouse behind, in the distance. Wanna get rid of that. Don't want the police usin' it to find where we was.'

'And why would that matter?' the Syrian asked, in a resigned voice.

'They will trace the van, they will trace everything. But when the first and second strikes are completed, and our task is done, why will it matter?'

'It won't,' Jayson said, cheerily almost, 'Will it? Anyways we gotta re-do it. Means I gotta get the equipment again.'

'From different people.'

'Why's that, brother? North End Road feller was alright, wasn't he? Muslim shop, did me a good price. £60 a day, stand included.'

'Different people, I said, because borrowing it twice in a matter of months could be suspicious. And a better camera, I will pay for a better camera. I don't want them looking grainy, like this one, dark and grainy. I want vivid colours, like those advertisements you see. These pictures will go round the world. In Syria, the Middle East, in Pakistan, Afghanistan…'

'And Trinidad,' Jason said. 'I remember seein' the 7/7 Tube videos in Port o' Spain. We was rejoicin', my brothers and me, listnin' to the martyrs. But the guards, they didn't like it. Confiscated the TV for a month.' His eyes shone, briefly. 'Think of them guards watchin' me.'

'And for America,' Amer said, 'they must be perfect. In America they will only look at things if the image is high quality.'

'Is it 'cos of the quality we never put out Umair's videos, brother? I thought we was goin' to put 'em out for 'em.'

The Syrian was silent.

'Umair was lookin' forward to 'is video goin'out, Tariq said. An' he looked good in it, didn't 'ee? 'Is clothes and stuff, way he talked. Sort of hard, make the infidels shit their pants.'

The Syrian winced.

'I did not put it out because it was not well done.'

'Technically, like? We still got 'em, maybe I could make 'em better? Lighten 'em up. Then we could put 'em out with ours, together.'

'Technically is not what I mean. Their videos were not good. Umair had a firm voice, but Tariq didn't. His voice was not manly, and since they were brothers that hesitant voice would disgrace Umair also. Umair's video was not so good either. He blinked. Perhaps it was

in anger, but he blinked. Several times.' He stopped, then said. 'And
no, there can be no question of improving them and putting them out
together.'

As the Syrian spoke Jayson's face came as close as it ever did to
puzzlement.

*

A sunny morning, yet the basement curtains were tightly drawn. To
help keep out the last slits of light Jayson's new coat was strung across
the window, together with some sheets. The beds were piled in a
corner, the table and chairs stacked in another. In their place three
black umbrellas trapped a lighted space. At its centre, against a blank
wall, beyond the sink piled with the remains of breakfast, irradiated
with light and resplendent in his jubba, sat the Syrian.

He'd been sitting there some time, the time it took Jayson to master
the new video machine. An up-to-date model, it was semi-professional
and more complex than the last. While he consulted the instruction
book, re-positioned the umbrellas and adjusted this and that Amer was
growing restive, shifting position and trying not to screw up his eyes
in the dazzling lights.

Finally it was ready, and the Syrian recorded his martyr's piece.

'Seems OK, brother,' Jayson said, playing the video back. 'Here,
have a look.'

Amer looked, considered, shook his head.

'I am blinking, like Umair. And screwing up my eyes. You are
blinding me with those lamps of yours, brother.'

'I didn't see no blinkin'. It's fantastic.'

'Do it again,' the Syrian ordered, and Jayson did.

'Too soft, my voice is too soft,' Amer decided this time.

'You wanna do it again?' Jayson's eyes widened.

'Osama did his videos many times to get them right.'

The third try resulted in a louder, more irascible Amer. Yet at the
same time he looked serene, gazing into the camera with just the right

balance of anger and contempt.

Jayson displayed the take:

'That all right?'

'Perfect,' the Syrian said, and put a hand on Jayson's shoulder. 'That is fine work, brother. I shall commend you for it in my prayers.'

Perhaps it was the still blazing lights, but at his words Jayson's eyes seemed to mist.

'Thanks, brother. Gettin' the hang is all.'

No question of the Syrian reciprocating when it came to his own video, and Jayson didn't ask. While the Trinidadian pre-set the camera Amer took a seat on the far side of the sink. Seeing him in a good mood, Jayson said:

'Mind if we open the door a bit while I do mine? It's hot in here. The lights...'

Graciously, the Syrian nodded. Jayson unlocked the back door, leaving the grill closed. For a moment he pressed his face to it, breathing deeply as he looked up at the sunny garden. The area stank of drains, as always, but it was air.

Still in his jeans and sweat shirt, he took the Syrian's place against the blank wall. Without hesitation he recited the martyr's farewell he'd done on their first recording. A compilation of quotations he'd got by heart and could reproduce at will, he reeled it off with no attempt at expression, droning like a chant, and finishing: 'An' they deserve it 'cos of killin' Osama.'

For Jayson a single take proved enough. When they played it back Amer nodded.

'Your video is excellent, even better than the first. So now you can pack up the material and take it back. And close the door. I have some plans to perfect.'

'Heard someone on the radio say reason there was no video of Umair and Tariq was 'cos now they got a law against broadcasting 'em on the BBC and things', Jayson said, packing up his gear. 'That wouldn't be good, would it brother? If our videos weren't broadcast. Be good if they was broadcast on the BBC.'

'Of course they will be shown!' Amer said, dreamily almost. 'Under sharia law they will show them!'

''Course they will, brother!' Jayson said, folding his tripod. 'When we got sharia 'course they will.'

20

Back from Moscow, Tony had got down to transcribing his conversation with Mrs Marusak, and it was giving him trouble. One by one the Norwich outpost was being cannibalised, the Birmingham office had snaffled his secretary whilst he was away, so he had to do it himself. Disentangling her voice from the drunken yelps in the bar, the football commentator and the screechings of the Gipsy violinist wasn't easy.

Forgetting how the evening ended was another problem. A pitiable lapse in a man of his age and experience, in Moscow of all places. What in God's name had happened to his prudential instincts? Was it his daughter, his wife, his looming retirement and the country's future? Was he turning him into one of the 'nuclear nihilists' the press had begun writing about? Citizens of regular habits and unimpeachable morals who were going off the rails, failing to turn up for work, not paying taxes, taking up drugs or running off with their best friends' wives?

He was drinking more, no question. Two bottles of red a day now, dipping into spirits when he got a chance. He sensed in himself a what's-the-point lassitude he'd never felt before. Even Jean had noticed.

'I see they're talking about a new Cold War if it turns out to be Chechens,' she observed one day over the Sunday paper. 'Well I hope there is, for your sake. You seemed happier those days.'

After a quick smoke at the back door of the office, alongside one of the remaining secretaries, he got back down to the transcript.

Chechen… Screech of fiddle… Dirty bomb… Booming guffaw… For a long time he sat with his ear to the machine, endlessly replaying the same passage, cursing. Why bother? The Chechen stuff was bullshit. He hadn't even troubled to run the name she'd given him past Thames House. The bitch had made it up, anything to get a

British passport. Though why anyone should want one…

He cruised on till he got to the part about Safia. Laughter, chairs scraping, the violin, then his own voice:

'So you're saying she'd come to fix her hair?'

'No, not fix hair. I look at her when she come in and I say 'You want fix hair?'. And she look at me as if… I don't know, she don't know where she is. Then she say she just come to look round.'

'Cointreau cocktail. A large.'

'Scotch whisky please, not much soda… You were saying about her hair.'

'When she say she didn't want hair, I look at her and I think, she dressed like woman off the street. Maybe she know? Maybe she come for job upstairs? Then she frightened, the bomb go off and frighten her.'

'Well it would, wouldn't it?'

It was the part where he'd switched off, wasn't listening, his eyes on the knitting woman. Now the import of what the bitch was saying came to him. If it wasn't for her hair, for treatment, why had Safia come into the salon? For a job as a whore? Absurd. To escape radiation? But she was there before the bomb.

Feeling a little stupid, he checked the CCTV shots of people arriving at the salon. First in, Safia. He played it back. On the street she'd been walking swiftly, with agitated steps. Tripping a little in her tight skirt and high heels, her mobile glued to her ear, her eyes wide with fear. After looking around she'd swerved blindly, desperately, into the salon. That much was normal: others who'd followed her in had behaved much the same. But there was a difference: in her case the time of entry was 14:31 p.m. The time of the explosion (he double-checked): 14:39.

The thought that she'd dived into the salon with no apparent purpose minutes before the bomb exploded, while listening to her mobile in an agitated state, hit him like a brick.

Switching the recorder off he rang Safia. It took her a while to answer.

'Who is it?'

It was as if she was surprised to get a call.

'It's Tony Underwood. You remember? We spoke.'

'Yes, of course.'

'Could we have another word?'

An instant's silence.

'Whenever you like.'

'How about this afternoon? I could be there in an hour.'

'But it's half past three.'

'And so?'

'I need to pick up Jackie from school. I can't be late. Some of the older children steal from them. And her medicine... Perhaps tomorrow?'

'I'd prefer today. Maybe when you get back.'

'Today is difficult. I have to give Jackie her tea.'

'I'm afraid I must talk to you today. I have a question to ask.'

'At five. Come at five. No no, six, six is better. Not here, not to Dr Opie's flat,' she added quickly. 'To the holiday home, where you saw me last time.'

Just after five he set off along the traffic-free Norwich to Cromer road. He switched on the radio. As always the news spoke of little but the emergency:

> Following Muslim accusations of a cover-up by the army and police, there was more rioting last night in the Midland town where a grandfather and his grandson died in an arson attack. In a worrying turn of events the crowds went onto the offensive, breaking out of the Muslim area by storming a railway bridge to reach a police station. The soldier guarding the Muslim side was attacked and abducted after he fired into the air to warn them off. Reports say he has been badly beaten.
>
> On the international front the Russian government have denounced as malicious fabrications suggestions on British websites that Chechen nationals employed by Russian intelligence were involved in supplying radioactive materials to

terrorists. Such reports, the Russian Foreign Minister was quoted as saying, were part of a systematically hostile campaign which could not remain unanswered.

Chechens again. More bullshit. On the other hand anything the Russians denied bore looking into, and Thames House would be pushing for news of the Marusak interview. Maybe he should go back, have another crack at the transcription, file a quick report, give them the Chechen's name to keep them sweet... No, better wait till he got back. He was half way to the camp, he'd send something off that evening. First, Safia.

At six exactly he knocked at the door of the mobile home. No movement, no reply. He went round the back to check the veranda, see if she was out there having a smoke. There was no-one. He went back to wait at the front, stubbornly. Stubbornly because he didn't like the idea of going to Julie's flat to check if she was there, to be faced with her disapproval. And because he was angry with Safia for keeping him hanging around.

Six twenty, still no Safia. He rang Julie's flat. No answer. At the camp entrance he asked whether the woman on duty had seen her going out. Yes, she said. It was a half-day at school, Dr Opie had the afternoon off – 'she deserves it poor woman, the way she works'– and she'd driven out three hours ago with Jackie to see a film in Cromer. And Safia? Well, obviously she must have the afternoon off too. She'd taken a taxi at about four. She didn't know where.

The doors to the mobile homes were flimsy and it took him half a minute to break Safia's open. While he was searching every crack and crevice and finding nothing beyond a half-empty packet of Marlboro behind the oven, the ancient lady turned up. Tony apologised, claimed to have broken the lock by accident, but she appeared to accept his presence.

'She's gone to live with Dr Opie,' the woman said. 'She took her last things and her suitcase this afternoon. But she'll come and see me, she said she would. I feel a bit lonely, with those boys...'

'I'll make sure she does,' Tony promised.

A Muslim woman he wanted to question had done a bunk, he told the duty officer at the Norwich office on the phone. He needed to trace her, pronto. She knew nobody in the area and would probably get a train somewhere: London or the Midlands. Maybe the police could do their job for once, and pick her up. Fine, said the duty officer. And what would she be wearing?

Christ, his reflexes were slowing. He was about to say Muslim dress, then remembered her sexy clothes in the City.

'I'll be right with you. Hold the line.'

He went back and asked the gatekeeper.

'A hijab of course,' the woman, a camp inmate and a Muslim herself, shrugged. 'She always does.'

'A hijab,' Tony said into the phone.

'You what?'

The duty guy, a local, was a rookie.

'Muslim gear,' said Tony.

He rang Julie's mobile. The film must have finished, and she answered at once. When he explained what had happened she expressed disbelief, then annoyance:

'Maybe you were questioning her too aggressively. Safia's a fragile woman, and not quite, well –'

'– grown-up?'

'In a sense, yes.'

'So she might make things up?'

'Depends what you mean.'

'Has she ever made things up with you?'

A silence, then:

'Only about her family, I suspect.'

Trying not very hard to suppress his satisfaction at Julie's misplaced faith, Tony said:

'Well there you go. But they can be hard to read can't they? I mean they're different people with different lives.'

'Different doesn't mean worse or better.'

'We're allowed different views on that,' Tony said, sharply, 'and in

Safia's case it's beginning to look as if my view's better. Now what's this about her relatives?'

'She has parents.' Julie thought, then added: 'And maybe sisters.'

'Why maybe?'

'It's not clear.'

'Does she have sisters, brothers, or what?'

'Hard to be sure. You'll have to ask her.'

'And where do they live? Her parents I mean. Or her sisters. Or brothers.'

'She never really said.'

'Or never let on.'

'Mr Underwood, I fail to see where this is going.'

'Dr Opie, I need to ask her one question. A single important question. If she gets in touch, make sure to tell her to contact me. Urgently. You have my home number. And tell her there's no need to be frightened. Say you can vouch for me.'

'I already have. I hope I'm right.'

No point in alerting Thames House to the fact that she'd disappeared. She wasn't on their radar. Couldn't be, because he'd yet to file his interview with her.

At eight he went home to a morose dinner with Jean, and listened patiently to her gripes. Another robbery, they'd got the man this time, a druggie. Debbie had lost her job in the music distribution industry, so she'd need more help with the mortgage, the nursery payments. Wasn't it time he tried to have a talk with her? Otherwise what was there to stop her going back on the drugs?

He was nodding over a night-cap after Jean had gone to bed when the telephone rang. He'd maligned the police, he thought, they must have got her. Good lads.

It wasn't the police, it was Julie, and she'd found Safia herself. Tony congratulated her, extravagantly.

'It wasn't so very clever. It struck me she'd go to Cromer, because she wouldn't want to spend the little money she must have had on a taxi fare as far as Norwich. So I took Jackie to the station and there she was. Sitting in the café, in her hijab, drinking coffee. Not much of a terrorist, I would have thought.'

'Where was she off to?'

'I didn't ask. It didn't seem relevant. I just didn't want a young Muslim woman with next to no money wandering around the country on her own.'

'You might have enquired,' Tony sighed.

'I'm not a policeman.'

'Neither am I, Dr Opie, but there are things I need to know.'

'Actually it was the London train she was waiting for, or the connection, now I remember.'

'Did she resist the idea of coming back to the camp?'

'Sort of. The train came in while we were talking. It was a bit of a struggle to get her not to take it. In the end it was Jackie who stopped her.'

'How did she do that?'

'She said she couldn't go because there'd be no-one to remind her to take her pills. Safia cried at that, and said she'd come back.'

'So where are you all now?'

'On our way to my car.'

'Any sign of the police?'

'They got there when we were in the café, a whole gang of them. Safia was petrified. There was a bit of a discussion about whether they could detain her under the emergency.'

'You mean you prevented them taking her in.'

'I had a bit of a go at them, yes. And it turned out they had no real right. Didn't have the paperwork. We left it that she'd talk to you tomorrow. She asked if I could be there, I said I would be. I assume you have no objections?'

'None at all. Meanwhile don't let her go back to the mobile home.'

'How can I stop her?'

'I said don't let her. Make sure she stays at your flat. Tell her you're under instructions from the police. Which in a manner of speaking, you are. And keep a close eye on her.'

'I was planning to anyway. I don't know what you said but she's a frightened woman.'

*

Safia slept in the box room of the flat. The head of Julie's bed abutted the wall, and the sound of the girl's sobs through the thin partition was making it impossible to sleep. She'd been crying for an hour, in a half-stifled voice but on a penetratingly high note, like keening.

After getting Jackie to bed she'd intended to have a talk with her. Safia was reluctant, said she was too tired. Exhausted herself, she'd postponed it to the morning, but it would have to be now. A late night heart-to-heart, like the ones she'd had with her mother when her father had driven the pair of them to tears.

She knocked and went into the box room. There was just space for a chair next to Safia's bed. She sat there and turned the girl's head gently from the wall.

'Why did you run away?'

'I had to.'

'Is it something Mr Underwood said?'

'Yes.'

'Did he try to frighten you? Was he rude about Muslims?'

'No, no. He was polite – but I was frightened.'

'He said he wanted to ask you a single question. Do you know what it is?'

'I think so,' Safia said, quietly. 'I went away because I knew.'

'And what was it?'

Silence.

'Come on, tell me.'

Silence. This was becoming annoying. Julie's temperament was brisker than her mother's.

'Tell me what it was, Safia. If I'm going to help you I need to know, I'm not going to lie awake all night wondering. Tell me now.'

Silence again. Then, in a low voice:

'He wanted to ask me why I was in the beauty salon.'

'Is that all? That's absurd. You were there for the same reason as all of us.'

'But he knows I was there before.'

'Before the explosion?'

'Yes.'

'And were you?'

More tears, before she answered: 'Yes.'

Possibilities crowded Julie's mind: the girl had gone for cosmetic treatments, and felt religious guilt. Or something to do with the brothel. But that was nonsense, out of the question.

'So why don't you want to tell him?'

Safia sat up in bed. She had stopped crying, and before speaking dried her eyes.

'Because I knew there'd be an explosion.'

Julie put a hand on her shoulder.

'You mean you had a premonition – a feeling?'

'No. They told me.'

Julie had been leaning close. Now she edged back, her eyes assuming a clinical chill.

'You mustn't think things that did not happen,' she said evenly. 'How could you have known? Who told you?'

'My brother. One of them.'

'You have brothers? How many?'

Julie was sitting upright now. Safia turned eyes that seemed suddenly childlike towards her:

'Two. And they are dead, both of them.'

'Dead in the explosion?'

'Of course. Because my brothers did it. It's true that I'm a single child now.'

Julie's mind was in limbo. The girl was crazed – or it was true. Either way she must let her talk. She leant towards the blanched and fearful face.

'Tell me,' Julie said. 'Just tell me.'

21

'I went there by Tube.'

'Where?'

'The Bank of England.'

Julie said: 'Go on.'

'It was the first time I'd been in the City. I got lost coming out of the station – it has two exits – then I couldn't find the Bank. I was standing in front of it but I couldn't see it. It doesn't have a plaque. So I asked the newspaperman across the road. He was an old man, so nice. He showed me a guide they have for tourists that points to the different buildings. You know, like a sundial. I chatted to him and asked when it was busiest round there. He wasn't much help about that, he said it varied.

'I was sorry for him, because his stand was right opposite the doors of the Bank. He'd get such a shock, or a rocket might hit him.'

'Rocket?'

'My bothers told me it would be fireworks.'

Julie felt a stab of relief. Fantasy. An overwrought young woman. But with an air of concentration Safia hurried on.

'To make a show, to scare them. They even bought a box of rockets and crackers, to show me… A big box. I love fireworks and I remember thinking, what a waste, just to scare a few people.'

'Safia.' Julie stopped her. 'First you told me you were an only child. Then that you had sisters. Now you say two brothers.'

'But I had to hide it. Don't you see?' The childlike eyes widened, as if surprised it wasn't evident. 'If I said I had brothers people might think they were terrorists. What was I saying? Yes, the newspaperman. He was killed of course, like the man with the cross, demonstrating. I didn't tell my brothers he was there, they would have laughed. He seemed so sad, an old black man with a cross.'

'So it was your brothers who sent you?'

'Of course they sent me. To reconnoitre. Just do us a quick recce, Umair said, even you can do that. I didn't like the way he spoke but I laughed because it was a word Tariq and I used in a game when we were younger. Then I became afraid. Wouldn't we all be arrested? But they explained that it was the right thing to do, to protest about what was happening in Afghanistan and shooting Osama Bin Laden and, well, everything about Muslims.'

'And did you agree with them?'

'In a way I did I suppose. I didn't know much about it, but I didn't like the way people looked at me sometimes. The way they treated me at school. Sometimes they called me names, dirty this and that…'

She petered out.

'So what did you do in London?'

'The main thing they wanted was whether there were any police. Then about the traffic, and whether there were jams in front of the Bank. So as to let their fireworks off they said. And of course the time when there were the most people.'

'Why didn't they go themselves?'

'They said that if anyone saw them snooping around they'd be arrested, because the police hate young Muslim men.'

'And you did everything they wanted.'

Safia looked puzzled.

'They were my elder brothers…'

'All right. So you did it.'

'I wanted to impress them, and I didn't think I'd get caught. They were so careful about everything. Don't let the police catch you, they said, and wear Western clothes. I was amazed. Usually they were strict, and angry when they caught me without a niqab, especially Umair. But he said this time Allah would approve of me going bare-faced, because it was to frighten the Crusaders...

'They gave me some money to buy the clothes. I felt guilty in the high street, guilty and sinful because I was starting to enjoy going from shop to shop to find what I wanted.

'When I got them I wanted to try them on at home, see how they looked, get used to them, but Umair said we couldn't have them in the house. He gave them to his friends to hide. They must have been very religious, because they wouldn't have them in their place either. They would defile the house, they told Tariq. He said they buried them in a plastic bag in the back garden. He said if he'd known they were going to do that he could have buried them here. Anyway I had to wash them, they got dirty.

'Then there were the cosmetics. My brothers hid them somewhere too, wouldn't let me try them till the day.'

Attempting to take it all in, Julie stopped her.

'Wait. Who were these religious friends?'

'I never met them.'

'And their names, you know them?'

'No. They never told me.'

'What did your parents say while all this was happening?'

'They were in Pakistan, seeing relatives. Sorting out something they inherited, some little bit of land.'

Julie's face must have expressed scepticism.

'You don't think my mother and father were involved, do you? When they find out they will be... I can't think of a word. Their own sons...'

'I interrupted you,' Julie said, coldly now. 'What happened next?'

'Umair gave me the clothes and the make-up the day before. It took me time to put them on. Other girls do it in a few minutes, but I had no practice. Umair said I was taking too long getting ready, too long looking in the mirror, I would miss the train.

'I'd never made up before and I couldn't get it right, especially the lipstick. Umair said I looked like a prostitute, and I did, with my bright red mouth and cheap clothes. People must have thought so too. When I got lost in the station a man came up to me, a terrible man, he'd been following me, I think he was drunk. I wanted to tell a policeman – I saw one there – but of course I couldn't. In the end I just ran away.

'Tariq was nice to me – poor Tariq, he was younger, we used to play – but Umair always said I was stupid. So I thought I'd find out everything, even things they didn't ask. It was all on the guide the newspaperman showed me. I thought it might look suspicious if I copied everything down, so I memorised it.'

She chanted, in a schoolgirl voice, as if reciting a lesson:

'The Bank of England is the central bank of the United Kingdom. Sometimes known as the Old Lady of Threadneedle Street, the Bank was established on this site in 1734…'

'Safia'. Julie was sitting upright. The touch of girlish pride in her tone had upset her. 'You don't feel proud of what your brothers did to all those people, to the people in the camp, to Jackie… You didn't think your brothers were martyrs?'

A mistake. Safia collapsed onto the bed and turned away. It was several minutes before she would resume her story.

'You were saying about the buildings…'

'I shouldn't have bothered memorizing all that. It was a waste of effort. Umair wasn't interested. He said he didn't want a history lesson. They needed to know how big and strong the doors were, and how wide they were, open. And when was the busiest time of the day. Always they said that, the busiest time, so they could –' she paused – 'frighten the most people, especially bankers. I said I couldn't tell because I had only been there in the afternoon.

'Well go in the morning, Umair said. So I went again, and got the early train. This time I was there most of the day, till four o'clock. I began to get interested. So much history! You know how many statues there are in front of the Bank? Three. One for the First World War, one for an engineer who invented a way to tunnel underground that was used in the Tube. And one on a horse. Him I forget.'

'Wellington. He was a military hero.'

'Ah. Well he'll be gone now… I found out everything, and did some measurements. You know how long the front of the Bank is? 120 paces. It might have been be a bit less if I hadn't been wearing that tight skirt…'

Again that note of pride in having done what her brothers asked, and more.

'There didn't seem to be any policemen or security guards, so I thought, why not photograph things, on my mobile? I just stood there and photographed the door of the Bank. There were tourists taking photos all around, so why not? Maybe they have their own cameras to watch us, but in my Western clothes no one would recognise me. They were huge doors, made of metal, twenty foot high, and with a lion. I couldn't read what it said, it was in Latin or something. George –'

'– George the Second.'

'Yes. What interested them most was the size of the doors.'

'To wedge the van inside,' Julie said tightly.

'I suppose it was… Anyway I couldn't measure them, so I paced them. And of course I had the photos.'

'So where are they?'

'In my phone. It wasn't my normal one. They gave me two new ones: one for photos, one to talk, with a card. They said the police couldn't hear it and stop our… demonstration. But I threw it away after, just in case. I couldn't work the photo one properly, so I didn't give the pictures to Umair, in case they didn't come out. He would have said I was stupid. Luckily he forgot about them. He seemed so busy.'

'And where is it now? The one with the photos?'

'Here, I have it here.' She took it from her bag on the bedside table. 'I use it as my mobile now. I suppose they're still there, if they came out, I've never looked.'

Julie took the mobile, searched for photos. They were there. The Bank entrance, the metal doors with George II. Somehow she'd still been hoping, but here was proof. Disbelief, her last refuge, vanished.

She wanted to say to her 'It wasn't your fault', but nothing came. Instead she thought of the way Safia had spoiled Jackie, buying her sweets and silly plastic toys till Julie stopped her. And of her fanaticism over her taking her pills on time…

'On the day they said I must go to London and stay near the Bank with the mobile, so I could be a lookout, tell them what was happening from hour to hour. Whether the traffic was jammed in front of the Bank, whether any police were passing. We weren't talking openly, they'd given me a sort of code, where one thing stood for another. It was complicated but I did it.

'That part I liked, it was like a game. The idea was to make me sound like a mother, so children meant police and food meant people. So I was saying things like there doesn't seem to be much food around here. I was afraid of being arrested with my brothers when the fireworks went off, but I was excited, so excited I couldn't eat. I was starving but I couldn't eat.

'I was on the phone all the time. Tariq kept ringing – he said Umair was driving. Of course they had codes for names too. Umair was Gerry and Tariq was Frank. I said I thought they were coming by Tube, he said there'd been a change of plan. He sounded so tense, like in a trance. It was terrible, me standing there with people going past and my brother chanting things in my ear. Half past two they said…'

'– I know, Safia,' Julie said stonily. 'I was there. So was Jackie, waiting for me in the roof garden on top of her school. It was how she was caught in the open.'

Tears came again, but she went on:

'Half-past two, they said. It was ten minutes before. When I'd been reconnoitring I'd told them this would be the best time, the time with most people, but it must have been groups of tourists or something, because on the day it was windy and there didn't seem so many. The office people must have had their lunch and gone back to work.

'I rang to tell Tariq there weren't as many as I'd thought. I didn't want them to come, because by now I was afraid. Tariq's voice had frightened me, I'd never heard him speak like that. And I told him there were a lot of police – lots of children but no food. Which wasn't true, there weren't any police I could see.'

'So you tried to stop them.'

'Yes I did, I did. By not telling them things. But Tariq said they were coming. He was speaking in this strange voice, like a recording. With the code words it sounded even more weird.

'All he kept saying was get away from auntie – auntie was the Bank in code. There's no need for you to be there, for the love of Allah don't stay too close to auntie! He wasn't supposed to say 'Allah' but he did. Go somewhere else, indoors somewhere, make sure you go indoors, not on the street. Promise me Safia, not on the street! Go and have a coffee or something – but not outside. Or go to the Tube, yes down the Tube. Quickly, quickly.'

Her eyes ignited at the memory.

'Umair had told me to make sure I stayed at the Bank till they came, till the last moment. So I didn't know what to do, which brother to obey. I was confused. And when Tariq said I should go down the Tube I could hear them on the phone, arguing. Umair took the phone and said I should stay at the Bank. He didn't say auntie, he was so angry he forgot to use the code. Now I see of course. Umair wanted me to be a martyr. For my brothers and me to be martyrs together...'

There was a plangent note that Julie didn't care for.

'Do you wish you'd stayed with them?' Her tone was chilly. 'Been a martyr?'

'No, of course not. It was so wrong what they did. But at the time I just thought it would be fireworks, so I didn't know whether to go or stay. In the end I did what Tariq said, he loved me that one, I was sure of it. It was his picture Mr Underwood showed me. You can't imagine...'

She sobbed again.

'He showed you that?'

'He didn't want to, it was me. I thought it might be just a picture, a normal photo, I wanted to see him, I snatched it... It was Tariq who wanted me to go on with my education, to do the sixth form in Manchester with my uncle. It was Umair who told my parents I wasn't dressing properly, that I was learning dirty habits, and they should pull me out of school.'

'Never mind that, go on about the Bank,' Julie said crisply.

'It was five minutes before half past two, and I did what Tariq said, and walked away from the Bank. I didn't go to the Tube because I was afraid the drunk man would still be there. I ran up that street, Old something –'

'– Old Broad Street.'

'– that's right, that winding street. I got to the top and I was looking for a cafe and the phone rang again and it was Tariq. And he said why is your mobile working, why aren't you in the Tube? Listen to me, we're coming, we're minutes away, we're nearly there, wherever you are get off the street, instantly, this second!

'There wasn't a café. I was outside some shops. I couldn't go into the cleaners because I had nothing to collect. Or the chemists, because I didn't want to buy something I didn't want. Or the pub, obviously. So I went into the beauty salon. I was terrified, I could hardly speak. And that woman, that Mrs Marusak, you remember?'

'Yes I do.'

'That was the worst part. I thought I could just look at a brochure or something, pretending I wanted treatment, see what they did. There was a brochure but she wouldn't let me read it, wouldn't let me alone. She just kept asking what I wanted done. When I said I didn't want anything – it was a stupid thing to say, but it just came out – she gave me a strange look.

'Had I come for work, she said? I said maybe – I couldn't think what else to say. There was this notice saying they did nail trimming and things, so I asked how you trained for it, how much they paid, just to say something. I felt stupid, I could see that blond woman at the desk and the man she was with laughing at me. Mrs Marusak said we needed to have a talk, and took me into the back room.

'She closed the door and asked me, 'How did you hear?' I still couldn't say anything, it didn't make sense. 'Was it the advertisement, for the beauty course?' she said. So I said yes – what else could I say? And she was looking at me in a way women, well, don't. You know, looking at me like a man. Like she did later, when she came into the bathroom, because you'd told me not to lock the door…

'Anyway she said she could train me in the salon work in two weeks, then I could work upstairs. Up to £300 a day she said. It didn't make sense, so much money, so I said I wasn't sure, it depended what the work was. I would have to think about it, and ask my parents.

'Then she gave a sort of angry laugh. If I didn't want to work like the other girls why was I wasting her time? She got annoyed, and said terrible things.'

'Like what?'

'She said don't be stupid, are you trying to sell yourself as a virgin? Let's have a look at your figure. Take your clothes off, she said, and we'll see. I tried to get up and run out of the room but she got really angry and started pulling at my skirt, I thought she was mad.

'She was running a brothel upstairs,' Julia said tersely. 'She thought you wanted to work there.'

Safia's teary eyes bulged.

'That's incredible. But it makes sense now...'

'So then what?'

'I got away from her, back into the front room of the salon. But I was trapped. I looked at my watch and it was after half past two, after twenty-five to three. I thought maybe my brothers weren't coming, or the police had stopped them. Anyway I had to get out. I was going to leave when there was a huge bang, and I saw smoke over the buildings. And then the police vans, and the sirens, and the people coming in to get off the street. The American, the Frenchman, then you. At first I thought it was the fireworks, but... Well it was too loud and there was so much smoke, and the police announcements... Tariq said whatever happened I must stay inside, so I did. Now there were other people there, it felt safer.'

'So you didn't go out, and come back in?'

'No, I stayed inside. The noise and the smoke...'

'If you didn't go out then why did you scrub yourself in the shower, when you knew you couldn't have been contaminated? Why did you try to get out of the salon into the ambulance?'

'Because I'd seen the television. I realised what my brothers had done. I was afraid I was contaminated because they must have stored the bomb in the house. That I'd slept with it there, maybe for days, and the radiation would be on my skin.'

'But you had a check-up, at the hospital. And another one here. And you were all right. So why did you go on pretending you were sick?'

'I was devastated. There was nowhere to go, except here.'

'What about your friends in Hackney? The ones you said you stayed with?'

Safia looked blank.

'So that was a lie too.'

'I stayed at a hotel. It was awful but it was cheap, and I was running out of money. I couldn't go home because there'd be no one there, and the police might come. And I couldn't stay at a hostel because they'd ask for identification. Then the hospital told me you were here, and I wanted to come. In a way I was sick. Maybe I still am…'

'All this is about you,' Julie said icily. 'Many hundreds of people had been killed and maimed and many more were going to die, and you knew who'd done it. Why didn't you just go to the police and tell the truth?'

'I was frightened, terrified. And they were my brothers…'

Safia leant towards her. Julie didn't respond. The girl put an arm round Julie's rigid figure.

*

Leaving her in the box room Julie went onto the veranda to dial the home number Tony Underwood had given her. Halfway through she stopped, and cut the call. It was two in the morning. What could he do, what could anyone do at that hour? Safia would cry herself to sleep, then first thing tomorrow…

The night air – cold, clean, tangy with salt – cleared her brain. Safia had talked about others, others who would still be out there, her brothers' friends…

She dialled Tony a second time. It was a while before he answered. In a cool voice – cool because she was stunned by what she'd heard but determined to betray no emotion – she summarised what Safia had told her. As if delivering a preliminary diagnosis, she added that she did not believe the girl was imagining things, sick or delirious.

Tony's voice was sleepy, and a little slurred. He seemed slow to make connections. At first all he said was:

'So no Chechens.'

'I'm sorry?'

'Never mind. Congratulations. How did you make her talk?'

'It wasn't me. She was in a state. She knew the question you were going to ask and that she had no reply.'

'So she didn't turn herself in,' Tony corrected, briskly now. 'We caught her. Hold on a minute could you?'

Tony went silent.

'Mr Underwood?'

'I'm on another line. Hold on…'

A minute later he came back, and said tersely:

'Lock her in the flat and stay with her. Wake someone up to stand by to help if need be. A man preferably. The police will be round in fifteen minutes. I'll be half an hour.'

'Can't you let her sleep? Why not come tomorrow morning? She's exhausted.'

'My heart bleeds. You get more out of them when they're tired.'

'I see no need –'

'– sorry, I do. We're on our way. And if she's not there –'

'– she will be.'

'Stay with her at all times, even in the toilet. Especially in the toilet.'

'I know Mr Underwood, I'm a doctor.'

'Thank you Dr Opie. It's good I can rely on you.'

'One thing.'

'Yes?'

'I'm not entirely sure what she's –'

'– guilty of? Assuming she's telling the truth it would be

withholding information which might be relevant to the committal of an act of terrorism, at the very least. And that's assuming.'

'But if she didn't know…'

'We've only got her word for that, haven't we? And she's been lying to us for weeks. To you especially. Remind me, how many sisters and brothers was it?'

22

Tony left the City of Westminster Magistrates' Court through a gap they'd left in the line of troops circling the building. It was when he was forcing a path through a second barrier, of journalists and cameramen this time, that an urge came over him that he'd never felt before.

In all his years in the job he'd never spoken to a reporter, not even off the record, and never been tempted. Anonymity is its own reward, a tutor had said on his induction course, a phrase he'd never quite fathomed, but it stuck. Something else made him one of the few in his trade who continued to respect the agency's code of silence. It wasn't just that he might be caught, like a friend who'd tipped off a Sunday paper about a Russian defector and forfeited half his pension. It was something more complex, a mixture of fear and duty, a kind of loyal apprehension.

But that was his former life. Since the bomb – his behaviour in Moscow was an example – lifelong habits and assumptions were beginning to slip their moorings, and events were forcing him out of the shadows. That morning he'd had his first moment in court. Behind a screen, certainly, with his voice altered and a ban on publishing his name. But for someone who'd spent his entire life in obscurity it felt as if he was out there in the open, a public man.

Agent A, the press had called him in the lead-up to his appearance, the man who'd tracked down Safia and her brothers and the crucial witness. It was a snazzy title, and he felt good about it. Good about the things the press were saying about the anonymous, doggedly determined spook. A model for his profession whose meticulous investigations in an unglamorous provincial backwater had uncovered the cell behind the bombing, thereby diminishing the chances of a second attack. Good too about sitting in at the start of what looked like being the most dramatic trial in terrorist history, and what he'd done to bring it about. Good enough to stop worrying his head about somebody asking the dogged and meticulous spook why in hell's name he'd failed to spot earlier that Safia had gone into the salon before the bomb.

It was when he was making his way through the raucous throng of newsmen, a little miffed to be pushed about in the scrum, that the temptation hit him. How sweet to get in front of a camera and tell it like it was. Set their phony reality straight for once, instead of slinking away under their noses. All he had to do was turn around and announce to the their busy backs:

You're facing the wrong way, gentlemen. I'm your story. Agent A, the one who brought her in. You'll make up your own reality, as always, with its fantastical dramas and false mysteries, but if you're interested in the real, inside world, where things are more simple and straightforward, then I'm your man. So, gentlemen of the press, any questions?

Not that they'd be interested in the facts. Theirs was a world of feeling, and one thing they'd have certainly asked would be his feelings on seeing a vulnerable young woman accused of a monstrous crime. He'd have had an answer for that one: We don't deal in sentiment. Next question. He'd expected to register some emotion at the sight of her in the dock, and been surprised to find himself feeling nothing. Professional satisfaction, certainly, but that was all. Not a squeak of sympathy. For one thing he wasn't sure he swallowed her story. For another she'd been silent since her arrest – obdurate he would have said.

He knew this because he'd sat in on the interrogation conducted by the senior officer. The idea was that a familiar face might encourage her to open up, but it hadn't happened. Between them they'd tried everything to get her to elaborate on what she'd said in her late-night confession to Julie, with nil results. She had nothing to add, she insisted hour after hour, notably about her brothers' fundamentalist friends.

Then there was the way she'd behaved. He'd expected a broken, weeping woman, yet the Safia he'd found during those endless sessions seemed more self-possessed than before. It was her Muslim lawyer who'd changed her, he was sure of it. From the moment he saw them together he was convinced Safia had come under her spell. Bit of a bitch had been his first impression, not that he'd let it show. Seeing the stern-faced, black-robed figure enter the room he'd leapt to his feet, walked round the table and shaken her hand with as much geniality as he could muster.

He needn't have bothered. She seemed surprised at his outstretched hand, and no answering courtesies were forthcoming. He wouldn't have minded, except that she was clearly smart, to judge by her interventions. It was she, he sensed at once, who was going to make the prosecution's task difficult.

And he was right. The officer taking the lead was a tweed-jacketed smoothie, too smooth for Tony's tastes. Emboldened by his triumph, when Safia began stone-walling he found himself speaking up, giving vent to his feelings. The smoothie didn't like it, kept looking at him as if to say 'that's enough from you, Tony.' Not to speak of the lawyer.

She objected especially strongly when after an exasperating silence from the girl he found words to suggest that unless she told them everything she knew about her brothers' friends, and fast, she could find herself responsible for the hundreds who might die from a second bombing, and the thousands who could be condemned to a life of lingering sickness.

'Think of it in personal terms,' he said, glaring across at her. 'How long are you going to sit there saying nothing? How many Julies and Jackies are there to be, many of them Muslims perhaps, before you sharpen up your memory?'

That got through Safia's carapace all right, and brought on the tears. And so what? Unless they found her brothers' friends smartly there could be a lot more of those.

It wasn't the last time she would annoy him. It happened again, in the magistrate's court, when she chose to appear in a niqab rather than a hijab, at her lawyer's suggestion no doubt. He was glad when the magistrate, a quietly insistent fellow, ordered her to uncover herself forthwith to assist identification.

It was then that something discomforting happened. Safia's response was not simply to expose her face, as instructed: she removed her entire headdress, then stood there, erect, looking at the magistrate in what might have seemed a posture of defiance, were it not for the tears pouring down her pale, un-made-up face. The magistrate looked at his papers. Tony stared away.

Clear of the media mayhem round the court, he walked swiftly away. On a corner he stopped for an *Evening Standard*. The queue was fifty-strong. As he waited he found himself checking round to see if anyone was looking, had guessed he was the figure behind the screen. Strange how the celebrity thing can get a grip of you, he told himself, changes your outlook on the world in an instant, even when nobody knows who you are.

It was a special issue, too early to cover her court appearance, though they'd got her on the front page. The photo had caught her leaving prison that morning, and it wasn't flattering. The impression of fear in her eyes was the more striking because the eyes were all you could see. The picture was unfortunate in another way: the eyes looked not just frightened but – perhaps out of bewilderment at the cameras – a little stupid. Simplicity, arrogance, fear, then the courtroom tears – you never knew, he was coming to think, where you stood with this woman.

He watched as people got their papers, stared into the troubled eyes then turned to read the story there and then. A lot had already come out, he discovered when he got his copy: the Thames House newsroom boys, he guessed. Relieved to have progress to report the MI5 press machine had done little to censor the reports, and the account of Safia's capture was a full one, in which Agent A's prowess was once again lauded.

He liked that, though he didn't care for the description of him that followed: 'A previously unremarkable officer who before the dirty bomb had spent much of his career as a humble watcher, as footsloggers and surveillance men are known in the trade...'

After skimming the *Standard* he looked round at his fellow readers. What were they thinking? The faces seemed to betray a quiet elation (could it be over?), combined with a certain prurience at the involvement of a young woman. What seemed to be missing was any realisation that, trial or no trial, and whatever the verdict, there was still nothing to stop it happening again.

*

Agent A's personal feeling of elation returned as he hailed a taxi.

'Thames House, on the Embankment.'

The driver threw him a glance, but said nothing. If he asked whether he had the honour to have Agent A in his cab Tony had a non-committal laugh at the ready.

He felt cheery because he was en route to an audience with the agency's top brass. The Director General had expressed a wish to thank him personally, they'd told him, and his pleasure at the thought moderated only slightly when his mobile rang with a message that the DG had been summoned to brief the Prime Minister, and it was his deputy who would receive him.

The deputy he had never met, any more than the Director. He turned out to be a stick-like fifty-year-old with a quizzical, slightly pained expression, like a man who'd spent his life asking questions nobody could answer. With him at the table was a panel of underlings.

'This is a good day for the service and an especially good day for you,' the deputy began.

Tony nodded in gratitude, then dropped his head, worried that the nod might look too much like agreement.

'And to think we were thinking of closing the Norwich station.'

The deputy glanced as he spoke at his number two beside him. A woman of forty or so with square-set shoulders and impatient eyes, the deputy's deputy was reputed to be smarter than her boss, and after his job. Seeing her fail to smile at the mention of Norwich, and wary of office politics, Tony didn't smile either.

'A lot of people look down on the kind of meticulous interviewing you conducted in that camp as police work.'

'Yes, Sir.'

'Well you've proved them wrong this time.'

'Luck, Sir.'

'And what's your view of the girl?' the deputy pursued after a silence, almost for something to say.

'My view, Sir?'

'Yes. Of Safia.'

'How do you mean, Sir?'

'How deep is she in it?' His pained look relaxed enough to permit a thin smile. 'You're allowed a personal opinion between these four walls. Come on, Tony, tell us what you think.'

Tony reflected. Opinions he was not short of, but having them was not part of his work. What did they want him to say? Something he didn't believe, he suspected. He'd be retiring before the end of the year, so he might as well say something that he did.

'My view, Sir, is that I suspect she could have stopped it if she'd wanted.'

'I don't think many people out there believe that.'

Well I do, Tony thought. I know her better than any of you, you asked for my view, and that's it.

The deputy's deputy pursed her lips. For a moment he saw her as an older, less attractive version of Julie.

'What I mean, Sir, is that if she hadn't been such a submissive woman…'

Petering out, he tried not to look at the deputy's deputy.

'And what's your guess about the trial?'

We have an excellent case and I'm convinced the prosecution will succeed was the approved reply, Tony assumed. He said:

'I think she'll get off, Sir.'

'And why's that?'

'Public sentiment, Sir.'

'Meaning?'

'Her being a –'

The deputy helped out.

'– a personable young woman?'

'That's it, Sir.'

'Well I hope you're wrong. If she does it'll mean a lot of wasted effort, not least by yourself. The question is, can she stop the next one? Or rather will she, if she can? What's your hunch on that?'

'I wish I knew, Sir. I've worked on terrorist cases for nearly a decade but to be honest I find them – Muslims, Sir – a bit difficult to read.'

'In that case,' the deputy's deputy threw in, 'why are you so convinced she could have stopped it?'

Tony went blank.

'You find them inscrutable is what you mean, isn't it?' A brief smile played over her lips.

'Yes I do, to be honest. A bit like the Chinese.'

A silence. Tony had a feeling that he'd fallen into a hole. The half dozen faces around him seemed to be suggesting he pull himself out. Suddenly it felt less like a ceremony of felicitation, more like an inquisition.

'What I mean is that they're different. I'm not saying worse or better. Just – different.'

'Thank you Tony,' the deputy said quickly. 'And well done again.'

Leaving Thames House he felt a little sick. It had begun to rain, a thin, irritating spitting, and as he strode off into the wind and the wet he was overcome by an urge to get away. He would have liked nothing better than to ring Jean, tell her to throw some things in a suitcase, meet him at Heathrow and take off for a couple of weeks to Cyprus. To the little hotel with the palisaded restaurant on the beach where they went every year, where he could drink his wine over long meals in the Autumn sun and do nothing. And this year he'd have better grounds for resisting his wife's importuning to get off their backsides and see some of the mosques and minarets in the Turkish sector.

Out of the question. His reward for his coup was a transfer back to London, with immediate effect. A service flatlet had been put at his disposition in Earl's Court (an area that for some reason he'd always disliked) for the duration, and it was there that he headed now.

Jean's reaction was as expected. There would be problems there, but there was nothing to be done. He could hardly decline the offer to work on the team assembled to handle the Safia court case, and simultaneously step up the search for her brothers' friends.

*

That weekend he was up in Norwich to collect his things, and it was there that Julie rang him.

'It's disgraceful, the way the press have already condemned her. That spooky photo…'

'Niqabs look spooky, and nobody asked her to wear it. Except her lawyer, I suspect. Of course the red tops went berserk, what do you expect?' He paused, surprised to find himself defending the media. 'People want justice, Dr Opie. Your daughter deserves justice, wouldn't you say? Not to speak of yourself.'

It was the harshest tone he'd taken with her, and as always he was sorry. Before she could reply he went on:

'Maybe I shouldn't have said that. In fact I probably shouldn't be discussing it with you at all, now it's sub judice. You have a right to your views and you'll get your chance to say what you think in due course, give your impression of her character. And if there's anything you have to add to what you told me or the police –'

'– can I talk to her? Can I visit? Where are they holding her? What's the legal position?'

'High security and isolation, except for her family and lawyers, for 50 days.'

'I thought it had to be less than 28.'

'You're behind the game. Emergency legislation.'

'Isolated from her doctor?'

'I wasn't aware she was ill.'

'Ill or not, at the camp I was her doctor. Anyway it's imbecilic, preventing me from seeing her. Against natural justice, and the national interest. Maybe I could talk her into telling you more about the others, assuming she knows anything...'

'Leave it with me.' Tony sounded helpful, if unhopeful. 'The law was passed in a hurry. It wasn't designed for –'

'– the way human beings actually work.'

'If you say so Dr Opie, if you say so.'

'Oh and by the way.' It was Julie's turn to do some making up. 'I gather you're going to be at headquarters. Congratulations on your promotion.'

'Very kind, though that's not what it is. I'm too old for any of that. It's the same job, different place. More hours, same pay, is all it adds up to.'

Later Tony rang back. The idea that Julie might be able to get something out of the girl that others couldn't had caused wheels to turn. An area of discretion had been located in the legislation, he told her, under a mental health heading. The upshot was that Julie could be allowed an interview, without lawyers present, unless Safia insisted, and providing she agreed to be briefed and debriefed. And of course that Safia agreed to see her.

She did, and Julie turned up at two-thirty at Belmarsh prison the following day.

*

Her last meeting with the girl, when they'd taken her from the camp at half-past two in the morning, had been teary, and she arrived at the prison with her soothing instincts at the ready. They weren't needed. For the first time since she'd met her she found Safia calm and poised.

'How is your health holding up?'

'I'm fine. Why shouldn't I be?'

'Sorry, I had to ask. After all I'm your doctor. It's how I got to see you.'

And there, for a moment, the conversation stalled.

'I suppose you think they've sent me to talk to you.'

'Did they?' Safia seemed unconcerned.

'Actually it was my idea.'

'Thank you.'

'You do look well, considering.'

'Because I am free.'

'Free from?'

'My father, my brothers. All that… thing. And soon I'll be free from prison, my lawyer says. How is Jackie? She doesn't know, does she?'

For a moment anxiety was there again.

'Jackie's fine. I told her you were in hospital.'

'Thank you. But she'll see the TV, won't she?'

'I'll try and stop her. Safia, you should have told the police earlier.'

'It would have made no difference. How would it have changed things? How many times do I have to explain that I didn't know what they were going to do?'

'It could have made it easier to track down their accomplices.'

'If I don't know anything about them, how?'

'You must know something.'

'All I know is that there was a Syrian.'

'You didn't tell me that. You ought to have done. Are you sure? How do you know?'

'He came round to the house and I heard my brothers talking to him. They'd sent me upstairs, but I heard him. Afterwards I told Tariq. I said I'd heard his friend's voice and that he had a funny way of talking. Sort of too neat. Tariq laughed and said he was Syrian, and that was all.'

'What did you hear him say?'

'Oh, just a few words, I've forgotten. I didn't give it any thought.'

'You never saw him? A photo of him – anything.'

Safia half-smiled:

'Now you're sounding like the police.'

Her tone was confident, self-contained. It was not one Julie cared for. She seemed to have lost some of her authority over the girl. To her lawyer, she guessed. It was not a pleasant feeling.

'Safia, I want you to think every moment of the day about who your brothers' friends were. Maybe there's some detail you've forgotten? Promise me you will.'

Safia gave a sigh.

'Hours and hours we have talked about it. To jog my memory they even took me round the house. Except it's not a house any more. They've taken up the floors, demolished the garage, dug up the garden, taken the whole place apart, even my bedroom. But it's not important. Our family is apart, so what does it matter?'

For a moment the self-confidence was gone, replaced by the tone of plaintive resignation Julie so disliked. She had an impulse to tell her to be less egotistical, that she was at liberty to be fatalistic on behalf of herself, but not of others. And that it would have been nice to have an apology for the lies she'd told her.

'I tried to help you, and you've caused me a lot of trouble,' she said simply, preventing herself at the last moment from adding, and made me look stupid in Tony Underwood's eyes.

'I'm sorry, but my lawyer told me I mustn't say anything that –'

'– I know, I know,' Julie said wearily. 'Incriminate yourself.'

'The lawyer says I should –'

'– say what your conscience tells you, I hope,' Julie broke in, then bit her tongue. She shouldn't have interrupted. Tony had particularly asked her to probe what her lawyer was telling her.

'So what did she tell you?'

'She says that if I do what she says I won't go to prison.'

Safia seemed serene again. It was Julie who was troubled.

*

Tony debriefed her later that day. She hadn't liked her attitude, she told him, but put it down to her lawyer. And to hostile interrogations perhaps. But nothing the girl had said had changed her mind: she was convinced she'd known nothing.

'Still, there was one thing. She said one of her brothers' friends was a Syrian, with a comically precise speaking voice. Apparently – '

Tony stopped her.

'We know.'

'You bugged us?'

Julie looked annoyed.

'Monitored the conversation. Emergency rules. Anyway, it's no more than she's told us already, in our latest interrogation. It's all we've ever got from her, though it's something.'

'Well I'm sorry my visit turned out to be pointless.'

'Oh I wouldn't say that,' Tony said, patronisingly she thought. 'She's very attached to you. It's just that she didn't come up with anything new. At the very least that alone tells us –'

'– how can nothing tell you something?'

'Well it tells us that whether it's the truth she's telling us or a bunch of lies, at least she's being consistent.'

'Glad to be able to help,' Julie said. 'I'd better get back to the camp. I'll be of more use there.'

23

The doorbell in Martin's mews produced a clamorous jangle, over-loud for the tiny house, and although he was expecting callers, he started. He'd released the newly installed security bolt and chain in anticipation and, looking forward to his visitors, opened the front door with a flourish.

Two men – though not the ones he'd been expecting. It took a second to recognize Billy: a flat cap pulled low over his forehead had replaced the beret, making his face look more concave than ever, like an old man who'd lost his teeth. By his side stood fat Eddy, his moon face even stupider when he concentrated on making it glow with menace.

An impulse to thrust between them and out into the mews was swiftly thwarted: seeing him move towards them Eddy shot out an arm, flattening him against the wall to make room for his chief to pass. Billy strolled to the end of the short corridor and into the drawing room. Lingering at the door, Martin invited Eddy to follow. Eddy shook his head. He wasn't as dumb as that. Instead he signalled Tony to join Billy in the drawing room. From there he heard him bolt the door and re-fix the chain before coming in too.

The room was small and the pair of them seemed to fill it with their baleful presence. Billy looked round the cramped, fussily furnished space with distaste:

'Never been in one o' these. Fuckin' doll's 'ouse. Where they used to keep the coaches and the servants, didn't they? An' now they're worth a fortune. How come you can afford it, Martin, what with you not writing an' all?'

'I just rent it.'

'How much?'

'Nine hundred a week, furnished.'

'More'n our car lads earned when they 'ad a job. Overtime included. Now it's seven times their dole. Different world, eh Eddy?'

Eddy signified that it was, and began lighting up.

'You asked the gentleman whether you can smoke in 'is nine 'undred-a-week 'ouse?'

Eddy froze, lighter in hand.

'Go ahead', Martin said tightly, 'and take a seat.'

Eddy looked at a delicate Regency chair behind him, and chose the sofa. Billy sat alongside. A wall of Michelin men, Martin thought, in their grey parkas, metallic-coloured in the light. And he didn't like the look of Eddy's boots. The sort builders wore, the toes were metallic-looking too.

Billy stretched his legs.

'You 'ave an air of surprise, Martin my lad. Didn't think we knew your address, did you? If so I'm offended, 'cos it means you underestimate our contacts. The law, the press, phone companies – we got people where we need 'em. An army of volunteers marchin' to our tune. Got to the point where we 'ave to be choosy who we take on. Watch for the plants.

'And maybe you're wonderin' 'bout the reasons for our visit. Think of us like we're the bank, Martin, or the mortgage company, come round to see a customer who owes you. You play fair, you give due warning, offer to talk it over, ring 'im up, leave messages, but there's fuck-all answer. An' the debt's piling up. So you gotta call round, force yourself on 'is attention, let 'im know the gravity of the situation.'

'Debt?'

'A debt of loyalty is what you owe, isn't it Martin? And now there's a new twist in the story we've come to collect. Make sure we can rely on you payin' up. 'Cos now they got the girl, one way an' another we're beginnin' to feel a bit more 'eat in our direction. Right, Eddy?'

''Sright.'

'Never mind if there's another bomb out there, waitin' to rain cancer on the country, first things first. An' for them the first thing is to neutralize the nation's patriots, see we don't get in no one's way, complicate the situation. A situation the government an' its judges is doin' fuck all to control.'

'Fuckin' Safia woman'll get off, tell you that,' Eddy contributed through his smoke.

"Course she will,' Billy said. 'Want my analysis, Martin?'

Martin gave a frozen nod.

'It's psychology, ain't it? I read a book about it. We're captives, the lot of us, 'ostages in terrorist 'ands. An' when you're an 'ostage you don't do nothin' to annoy 'em. End up identifin' with 'em, like they was your protectors. And that's why the Safia woman'll walk free. Fuckin' terrorist, no two ways, in it with 'er brothers, chickened out at the last moment to save 'er skin.

'But they'll be too scared to convict 'er, won't they? 'Cos if they put 'er away for life – and life's what I mean – they'll let us 'ave it again. I can see it comin'. The papers'll be all over 'er, say she's an innocent woman, lovely girl who lost 'er brothers in tragic circumstances. So villains and victims end up on the same side. Stockholm syndrome, see? Why don't you write about that then, Martin?'

'Maybe I will. It's an angle.'

'There 'ee goes.' Billy smirked and shook his head. 'Can't 'elp it, you're one of 'em through and through, aren't you Martin? For you angles is all what matters, like you was playing a game. But it isn't a fuckin' angle, it's the truth.'

A lecture followed, on the evils of the press. Martin sat listening, hands between his knees. The attitude felt childlike, but there seemed nowhere else to hide his clenched fingers. Attending to Billy's rant as if engaged in normal conversation helped keep him calm.

The window gave out onto the mews. A man passed, then a car, slowly. His visitors, looking for his house? Though if they came now, what would happen?

Billy must have caught his anxious glance. Stopping abruptly he said to Eddy:

'Close the curtains. Another thing with these dolls' 'ouses, everyone peerin' in.'

Eddy drew the curtains, switched on the light. Now the room seemed even smaller, the two men closing in.

'Pardon me for askin',' Billy went on, 'but will you be offering refreshments?'

Martin sprang up.

'You'd like coffee?'

'Milk and two sugars for Eddy, black and strong for me. Don't wanna blow up 'is size.' His plastic arm squelched playfully into his neighbour's. 'Plus I 'ave to keep a clear 'ead.'

'For 'is books,' Eddy explained. 'I've never known a man read –'

'– shut up Eddy, and 'elp 'im make the coffee. Don't want 'im wanderin' off, forget 'ee's got guests.'

Eddy lumbered to his feet and followed Martin to the kitchen. When they returned Billy had lain back in the sofa, glasses on his nose, thumbing through the pages of a paperback. Reaching for his coffee, he took a sip.

'Very nice.'

'What's that you're reading?' Martin asked as matter-of-factly as he could manage, pained to see his cup tremble in his hand as he drank. 'Something on Napoleon?'

'*Citizens*, 'bout the French Revolution. Simon Schama. Foreigner's name if ever I 'eard one, but turns out it's all right. Told you I was into it didn't I, one of my messages.'

'Ah yes.'

'You read it?'

'No.'

'Well you wouldn't, would you, 'cos you're expensively educated. Which means they force you to read things you don't want to. Me, I gotta educate myself. I'm an auto–, auto– what's it again?'

'Autodidact?'

'That's it. Which means I read 'cos I want to, so as to learn things, so I end up readin' more than you 'ave. Anyway, a bit of business, if you don't mind.' He closed the book. 'Cops 'ave been onto Phil. Some Mohamed recognised 'im when we was doin' our patrol, guy who worked with 'im at the plant. And what does Phil tell 'em? Tells 'em 'ee was on 'is own, showing a journalist the sights. Said 'ee couldn't remember the fellow's name, but they might get it out of 'im. So I 'ave to know what 'appened to that article you wrote. 'Bout our accident.'

'Don't worry, I didn't publish.'

'I know that, course you didn't. What I want to know is, where is it? You rub it out? Dab 'and with the electronics are you? Never touch 'em myself, don't like the thought of all that recorded information.'

'I deleted it.'

'Sure it's not still in there somewhere, on the 'ard drive? Don't mean shit to me but that's where they pick things up, isn't it? The 'ard drive.'

'I did my best to make sure –'

'– when it comes to my personal security,' Billy said softly, 'your best is insufficient. I'm askin' a simple question. Can the article you wrote be traced on your computer or not?'

'I told you, I did my best –'

'– looks like we'll 'ave to consult a specialist. Where's your office?'

'Upstairs.'

'Eddy my boy, go and borrow the gentleman's computer from 'is office, if you would be so kind.'

Eddy thumped upstairs and came back with Martin's laptop.

'That all there is?'

'All what I could see.'

'That the one you done it on?'

'Yes,' said Martin.

'Good, we'll 'ave it.'

'Wait, I've got other stuff on there. Can I –'

'– I said we'll 'ave it. Now. And your mobile, while we're about it. One that took the messages you declined to answer. Rashly as it turned out, Martin, wouldn't you say?'

Martin took his phone from his pocket and handed it over.

Another car passed, slower than the last. Could it be them? Late afternoon was all they'd said. Be along as soon as they could make it.

'Well that's done then, time we was on our way.' Billy made to get up, then sat back. 'One more thing, I almost forgot. Eddy 'ere's got a message of 'is own to deliver, but you know what 'ee's like, man of few words. Won't take a minute.' He nodded at him. 'Give it 'im Ed.'

Eddy got up from the sofa. Taking the space between them in a single stride he stood over Martin's chair. His beer gut was a foot from his face, close enough for him to smell the warm, armpit stench from his open parka. Innocent of what was happening he was looking up at him questioningly, as if inviting him to speak, when Eddy brought his fist down.

It was a cack-handed punch – even punching Eddy tended to botch, he should have gone for him from underneath – but the fist hit flesh, caught Martin's forehead and the top of his nose. His hands went to his face and his head dropped, exposing his neck, as if offering it for a second blow. The offer was accepted: a chop from the edge of Eddy's hand and he toppled to the floor.

Eddy turned and looked at Billy, a brow raised, as if to ask: more? Sunk into the sofa, feet on the glass coffee table and his nose back in his book, Billy ignored him.

Taking this as a yes Eddy put a boot into Martin's groin.

Billy went on with his book.

'I'll eat your brains and shit in your scull,' he read out, chuckling. 'Marat that was, 'fore they did 'im in 'is bath. Good, eh? What I call command of language.'

Knees up to protect his aching balls, hands over his head, blood dribbling from his mouth where Eddy's downward blow had made him bite his tongue, Martin groaned. Billy put down his book.

'Noisy bastard, ain't 'ee? Why can't 'ee shut the fuck up and listen to somethin' for 'is edification. Thought you public schoolboys got used to a bit of roughin' up. Get on with it, Eddy boy, we 'aven't got all day.'

Eddy contemplated the writhing ball on the floor before him. There being nowhere else exposed, he kicked Martin in the ribs, twice.

Billy got up, pocketed his book.

'That'll do, all we got time for. An' you can stop whinin', Martin, it's not all bad. Think of it this way. You just cleared some of your debt, 'aven't you? Sorta made a down payment. And you've got Eddy's message loud and clear. Which is that one fuckin' word from you to anyone and there could be a lot more to pay.

'An' there'll always be somebody to collect, don't you forget it. 'Cos it isn't just you and me involved. It's like two armies, like you was plannin' a battle. You can go to the cops, take me out with a lightnin' strike. But then I got reinforcements, lots of 'em, an inexhaustible supply you might say. So when they see their leader carried bleedin' from the field what do they do? What they was trained for. They mount a counter-offensive. An' wherever you are, they'll get you.'

*

It was his visitors who found him, when the doorbell startled him back to consciousness and he crawled along the corridor to the door. Only in hospital, where he woke at four next morning after sedation, did he reflect on what had happened.

His own fault. He ought to have acted sooner, done what he'd promised Julie he would after their dinner in the Sheringham hotel. At the time he'd been resolved, absolutely determined, to go straight to the police. Then something had come up in the North. He needed the work, and it seemed better to go to the Metropolitan Police than out there in the sticks. Then came the announcement of Safia's arrest, a staggering event, and all it might mean for Julie...

One way and another it was a week before he'd screwed himself up to make his call to the police, that morning. Who'd said they'd send someone to take a statement just as soon as they could manage. Which turned out to be twenty minutes after Billy had gone.

Sod's Law of procrastination... If he'd done it a day sooner he wouldn't be here, one-eyed from his head bandage, a broken rib, feeling like shit. But then morally speaking shit was what he was. Was that why he hadn't even tried to fight back, just laid there and taken his punishment?

Alert suddenly, he craned up and looked round for a night nurse. Finally he saw one hurrying through the ward, and hailed her. She stopped, came to him, bent down:

'What you need?' She looked Vietnamese. 'Lavatory?'

'No,' he whispered, with his remnant tongue. 'Just something I have to know. You remember the Muslim boy who was killed, with his grandfather? Was there anything on last night's news…'

A cloud of unknowing passed over the woman's face.

'You get sleep. In the morning you better,' she said quickly, and hurried away.

His last thought before he dropped off was of how he would explain his delay to Julie. Though seeing the state of him, perhaps she'd be gracious enough not to ask.

*

Julie came at nine next morning. Frail-looking but purposeful as ever she strode along the ward towards him. His personal physician. And the sight of him, he was pleased to see, shook her a bit.

'Well, there's good news and there's better news,' she concluded after a brief examination. 'First, I've talked to the doctor, and he assures me you'll heal. Better, the police have picked them up. In Waterstones in Kensington High Street, would you believe.'

'Great news,' Martin whispered, shifting in his bed and grimacing piteously with the effort.

'What I don't understand is the time sequence. At first I thought someone had done you over after you'd told the police. It turns out it was before. Why did it take you so long to –'

'– I'll explain,' Martin lisped through the ice they'd insisted he hold in his mouth to help mend his tongue. 'when it's less painful to talk. Tell me more about this Safia thing. It's incredible.'

24

In the calm of a corridor in the Old Bailey, a sudden flurry. A woman wearing colours in flamboyant refutation of her age flew down on a group of people, her arms waving like some prehensile bird, as if to disperse them. To judge by the movements they made at her approach – a hasty step back, a revolving head searching for a line of escape – the four of them wanted nothing else.

'It is reunion!' Mrs Marusak proclaimed. 'Like at school. Only American friend not here. A gentleman, really. He died I read. And black boy. Very rude man. I remember smell.' A ringed finger waved the air from beneath her nose. 'Did he die?'

'He didn't, actually,' Julie said. 'He's coming along well. With luck he'll survive.'

Mrs Marusak spread her hands, indicating an open view on the matter.

'Well we'd better be off,' Julie said, loudly. 'We're not supposed to consort with other witnesses they tell me. Judges don't like it.'

'Consort?' Mrs Marusak looked suspicious. 'What is consort?'

'Meet.'

'So why you say consort? And why I can't consort friends from old days?' Indignation gave way to a kittenish smile. 'They think we make plot?'

Besides Julie there were the Frenchman, aloof as ever, Steve the road worker, pleased to be in the Bailey and in Sunday clothes, and a woman Mrs Marusak didn't know. After shaking hands with the others, she turned to her:

'And you?'

'I'm Anita Sampler,' the woman said. 'Dr Opie's lawyer.'

Julie didn't need a lawyer. The NHS had provided her with one, regardless, who seemed to her competent in her redundant way. Now she discovered urgent points of consultation with Ms

Sampler and began shepherding her to one side. Mrs Marusak was unwilling to let them go.

'You lucky to have lawyer.'

'Very lucky.' Julie turned back, looking solemn, yet with a hint of playfulness in her eyes. 'She specialises in women's rights. Things like woman smuggling.'

'Smuggle women? Why should smuggle woman?'

'To force them into prostitution, live off their earnings and get rid of them when they contract AIDS,' Julie explained. 'They're from Eastern Europe mostly. You must have heard about it.'

Mrs Marusak's moustache, powdered to prevent it contrasting too brutally with her blonded hair, began trembling. A fine precipitation of particles speckled the air.

'No, never heard.'

'Ah well you should. They're coming down hard on it, people are getting years in jail. Then they're thrown out of the country if they're foreigners, and banned from coming back. Ever. Right Ms Sampler?'

A bewildered Ms Sampler nodded.

Mrs Marusak shrugged.

'No one should be prostitute unless she want. It is men who should go to prison, eh?' She turned to the French banker. 'Especially French men. Everyone know about the French men.' Smiling, she put a hand on his arm. 'I mean joke.'

M. Denizet stared at the hand, looking pained. It had been a bad few months for him: transferring his family back to Paris, closing up the Holland Park house on which he'd lavished four years' bonuses, and for which he had still to find a buyer. And now the pain of giving evidence at Safia's trial, where a woman gross beyond belief had the insolence to lay hands on him.

'Vous m'excusez,' he bristled, continuing in his language, 'I think we have said everything we have to say to each other.' Freeing his arm M. Denizet moved resolutely away, proving once again that French is the perfect language in which to discontinue a conversation.

*

The prosecution lawyer was Sir Stuart Tisdale. A poor choice, Tony thought when he heard: the man had the reputation of a bully, and if anyone was going to drum up sympathy for Safia it was the bull-necked, hectoring Sir Stuart. He was a little nervous himself at the prospect of interrogation at his hands, but with Tony Sir Stuart was courtesy itself.

Coaxed along in unhurried fashion, Agent A told his story: his meeting with Safia at the camp, her nervous smoking, her evasion in reply to his questions, her revulsion at the horrendous photograph of her brother. He answered a query or two in a professional voice – flat, toneless – and that was it. All in all he was content with his performance, though glad when it was over.

Then it was the turn of Safia's lawyer. Now he was glad of his screen. Though they were invisible to him, the thought of the hostile eyes and accusatory finger he'd experienced during the prison interrogation sapped his confidence. Lucky no one out there could see the hands clutched in his lap and the anxiously inclined head. His apprehension was soon justified. The woman had a way of placing a question mark over his simplest statements. After asking him to confirm that he was a member of the security service, she came back:

'Thank you, Agent A, I'll take your word for it. No one here can verify it of course, because you are invisible to the court. 'Agent A' is an odd way to be obliged to address a witness, is it not, but then those are the arrangements we are obliged to accept. It doesn't say much for equality before the law, does it? My client has been obliged to reveal her face in defiance of her religion, but the rules for Agent A are different. We can't even see his eyes.'

And so it went on, as she picked him up on every detail.

'You say the defendant was smoking when you met.'

'That is correct.'

'Actually your expression was more loaded. You said 'smoking nervously', did you not?'

'I did, because she was.'

'Do you smoke yourself, Agent A?'

The question was so unexpected, he was silent.

'Don't worry,' the lawyer smirked, 'knowing whether or not you smoke won't imperil your cover.'

'Er, cigars, from time to time.'

'And have you ever watched yourself smoking? How do you smoke? Nervously? With the compulsive gestures many smokers appear to me to employ? Or are you seeking to imply that by the simple fact that my client had a cigarette in her hands when you saw her proved she had something to hide?'

'Not at all. It was the way –'

'– were you smoking when you met my client?'

'Just a small –'

'– the court has no interest in the size of your cigars, Agent A. That is a matter for yourself and your lungs. You met, I understand, in the afternoon. Was it after lunch? A post-prandial cigar, perhaps? Can you assure the court you hadn't been drinking too?'

'I may have had a glass, I don't remember.'

'Ah. A glass. And if you can't remember, it might have been two or three. Enough to put you in a combative mood perhaps. Have you considered the possibility that it was your bullying style that made her nervous? The authorities are liable to adopt a certain manner when dealing with Muslim citizens, are they not? Especially after a good lunch.'

'Objection,' Sir Stuart grunted.

'Sustained.'

'I think we have established an adequate picture of the relationship between you and the suspect, so let's move on. You showed her a photograph of her brother, I understand.'

'She took it from my hands.'

'But you intended to show it her, that is why you had it. Was that necessary? To show a young woman the mangled remains of a young man's face? Of course you didn't know at the time he was her brother, but was this not part of your intimidatory tactics?'

'No, not at all.'

'Did you show it to other people you interviewed?'

'To Dr Opie, yes.'

'She is a doctor, that is a different matter. But not to other people who'd been in the salon?'

'No.'

'But then they weren't Muslims were they, they were less suspect, so why distresss them? Were you trying to distress my client, Agent A, by showing her that picture? Force her perhaps into an admission of guilt? She smokes – so she's guilty. She's sickened when she sees the mangled face of her brother – guilty again. Always you seem intent on implying guilt. The fact that her brother was a suicide bomber proves nothing about my client, nothing at all.'

'I understand that. I was simply trying –'

'– trying a little too hard, I would say.'

He wasn't doing well. Behind the screen the hands went deeper into his lap, the head down further, like someone scenting a trap. He was waiting for the killer question. The one that could undermine his credibility: why it had taken a trip to Moscow, of all places, for him to discover the timing of the defendant's entry into the salon? And discover it from someone whose reputation was, to say the least, undesirable?

Miraculously it never came, perhaps because the lawyer was smart enough to avoid picking him up on something that could only point up the chief weakness in Safia's case.

When it was over he left the court, unseen, by a private entrance. After a drink at a nearby pub – the place was so packed with reporters it took longer than he'd planned – he hurried back, afraid of missing some of Safia's evidence. He made it just before she was called, and took his seat. He glanced nervously at his neighbours. The screen, the pub, now the official enclosure – it felt strange to be hidden one moment, exposed the next.

Against the hulking Sir Stuart she looked frail, though less frightened than he'd expected. With his nose for the media, the prosecutor began in a falsely genial style:

'It may be none of my business, young lady, but allow me to begin with a question that must be puzzling the court. I cannot be the only one who is intrigued by your change of headdress from one day to the next. Three days the court has been sitting, and on each of them I noted that you have appeared in a different guise.

'You began with a niqab, which you were required to remove. Next it was a hijab, today it is a scarf. What next? We are all keen to learn about different cultures, and perhaps there is some religious explanation for this dizzying change of court attire?'

'Objection.'

Safia's lawyer shot to her feet, livid.

'Sustained. No more questions about dress, if you please. Clothes – within reason – are the defendant's prerogative.'

'Understood, your honour. I merely hope the defendant is not about to change her story as frequently as her headgear.'

Everyone tittered, but not Tony. The changes were her lawyer's doing, he was sure of it. A cynical piece of theatre, one that had worked in the magistrate's court and he was afraid would work here. When the judge had insisted she remove her niqab the jury's first impression would have been of a nun-like Safia with wounded eyes. With the hijab, the pallid oval of her face, framed in black, had its pathos. Today, in her scarf, she looked prettier – though pretty in a fragile, vulnerable way.

Not the sort of face the court would want to see crumple in anguished tears, but after a few questions, Sir Stuart managed it.

'Have you ever met a victim of radiation? A young woman like yourself, perhaps, waiting to see how far their tumour or bone cancer will develop, wondering how much life may be left to them? Or a pregnant woman, say, terrified her unborn child may have been contaminated, and be born with some deformity?

'But you'd be indifferent to their suffering, I imagine. Because it is what you wanted, is it not, when you agreed to act as look-out for your brothers. And perhaps you would be content to see it happen again? What other explanation can there be for your refusal to reveal the identities of their associates?'

Another objection – again sustained – while Safia dabbed her eyes amongst courtroom murmurs.

'Tears,' Sir Stuart said when she'd dried them, 'would have been more use before than after, but let's get ahead. Tell me Safia, how do you feel about letting your brothers down?'

'I don't understand.'

'You were in a murderous pact with them, were you not, and you lost your nerve. Instead of dying with them at the Bank as had been agreed, you ran away. What sort of martyrdom is that? Tariq didn't tell you to take cover, and there is no proof that he did. You did it yourself, didn't you, without his bidding, at the last moment, to save your skin. Everything else is play-acting, a charade, is it not?'

Not too clever, Tony thought, scanning the jury's pitying faces.

'I don't understand anything you say,' Safia got out through her tears. 'I did not know what my brothers intended.'

'So you are asking the court to believe that you were one of your brothers' victims. A victim of their lies.'

More tears.

'I must ask you to compose yourself. These are grave matters.'

When it was her turn to face Sir Stuart, Julia's treatment was scarcely less brutal. After some opening exchanges the prosecutor said:

'Dr Opie, some of your remarks suggest you still believe the firework story. Is that the case?'

'I make no judgment, since I do not know all the facts. Any more than anyone else.'

'That is for others to decide,' the prosecutor replied, piqued.

'All I can say is that everything she told me was consistent with her behaviour in the salon. Why she was so distraught. Why she scrubbed herself so hard, why she was desperate for a check-up.'

'But Dr Opie, all those things would also be consistent with her being part of the plot from the beginning, then getting cold feet. She was desperate all right in that salon. Desperate to cover her traces. And not to suffer from the fall-out she had helped inflict on other people.'

Tony watched Julie, wincing. He knew who he wanted to win and had his views on her behaviour, but he didn't relish seeing her knocked about.

'How would you describe the girl's character?'

'Someone from a background of patriarchal repression can develop in ways that may not always be honest or pleasant. They can end up being,' she hesitated, 'quite manipulative.'

'Your relationship with her seems to have been a rather obvious example of that. Are you sure it wasn't you she was manipulating when you sheltered her in the camp? She told you lies, did she not? It was on the basis of a lie about her health that she got into the camp at all. A perfect hideout, she must have thought. And she hid there with your assistance. Looking at your professional record I am impressed by your expertise, Dr Opie, as much as by your wide experience. What puzzles me is that none of it appears to have helped you on this occasion.'

'In my work I meet many women who are duped or abused by their menfolk.'

'Perhaps what you're saying is that she's immature for her age? I called her a girl, but of course I musn't do that, she is a woman. Is she immature?'

'In some ways, yes. She was denied the education she needed.'

'But not so lacking in education that she couldn't pull the wool over your expert eyes. Have you considered the possibility that you yourself have been duped, Dr Opie? Duped by your own theories, maybe, by that business about patriarchal repression, which tries to persuade us that grown women have no responsibility for their actions. And duped by your own protective instincts towards such women.'

Julie didn't reply. For the first time she was looking strained.

Tony was pained for her, though content at the way things were going. As the lawyer continued to ridicule her credulity over the firework story, sentiment in the court had begun swinging against the girl, he could feel it.

*

It didn't last long. Later Mrs Marusak took the stand, and everything changed. It ought to have been quick and simple. For the prosecution she was there for a single reason: to confirm the CCTV evidence that Safia had entered the salon before the bomb exploded. Sir Stuart drew this from her in a brief exchange, with an old-world courtesy that had Mrs Marusak almost simpering.

'You will forgive me for troubling you with such matters, Mrs Marusak – and may I take this opportunity for thanking you for coming to testify all the way from Moscow – but could you confirm that the defendent did not come into your salon for treatment?'

'Yes. I mean, no. Not hair, not nails – nothing. I swear to it, Excellency, as God is judge, thank you.'

Then came Safia's lawyer. Suddenly Mrs Marusak's profession, her real business, unmentioned till now, became central to the trial, and the jury, the court, the media and the country were to love every salacious minute.

The lawyer's opening question set the tone.

'So, you have heard Agent A's evidence?'

'Yes.'

'And you can confirm what he told the court.'

'Is true.'

'Can you also confirm that your beauty salon was a façade, and that you are in fact a brothel-keeper, specialising in providing women from all cultural backgrounds for the gratification of City men?'

'Is dirty lie.'

'We shall be displaying evidence to prove it. Graphic evidence, Mrs Marusak – or perhaps I should call you madam?'

A Muslim lawyer in a hijab with a sense of humour. The court loved it.

'Can you also confirm that you attempted to recruit my client to work for you? That you did your best to inveigle a pure young girl into becoming a harlot? And that for your evil purposes you even tried to disrobe her?'

'I no inveigle. What is inveigle? I no understand, I need lawyer. Why I not have lawyer?'

'I am a lawyer, Mrs Marusak, and I believe you understand me perfectly well.'

And so on and on. For two whole days the safety of the realm was shuffled aside while the whore-mistress, her comprehension of the English tongue diminishing tactically by the minute, was hounded and harried without mercy about the details of her racket.

'What you say is nonsense lie. All beautician have men friend. They nice-looking girls. Not my business what girls do in rest time in upstairs flat.'

Clips from the cameras the police had recovered took care of that. At Sergei's insistence the filming had been thorough, and a selection was shown to the jury in a closed court. First came judiciously edited shots of a Chinese man and a black woman toiling naked on their flouncy bed. Then a close-up of Mrs Marusak entering the room to extract from the girl's hands the proceeds of her synthetic lusts.

Next they saw Anna and the Chechen sealing their acquaintanceship, a day before the bomb, in athletic embraces. Efforts had been made to locate them, so they could give evidence in person, the lawyer announced, but both had disappeared abroad. (It was the first and last time, Tony was glad to note, anyone mentioned the Chechen.)

The climax came with a film of Mrs Marusak's assault on Safia's virtue: a close-up of impetuous hands wrenching up her tank-top and pulling at her skirt in a single furious movement. Fearing perhaps that Safia's slutty clothes, such a contrast to her court attire, would play badly with the jury, the lawyer was careful to project the shot briefly.

Everyone stared at the screen in appalled silence. The lawyer herself watched tight-lipped, beaky profile erect. Modestly or under instructions, Safia stared at her lap.

'There is more,' the lawyer announced to the jury during a pause in the projection.

The judge shook his head.

'Enough! The jury are decent people. They will have seen sufficient to reach their conclusions.'

It was the end of the film show, but there was to be more from Safia. Now she took the stand to be pressed for every scurrilous detail: what Mrs Marusak had said about her pretending to be a virgin, her terror at her groping hands, her exact position when she'd ogled her in the bathroom, her feelings about the whole sordid episode...

Tony shifted unhappily in his seat. At first the exposure of Mrs Marusak seemed no more than a stunt, a diversion. Now it was clear the diversion was by no means pointless. The lawyer was succeeding in transforming the girl from suspect into victim before everyone's eyes, and Safia was playing her part wonderfully well. She might have been expected to wilt at the immodesty of the subject, yet she responded perfectly. The demure dip of her head as she stumbled out the facts, and use of terms like 'bosom' or 'lower back', affected the majority female jury visibly. And the theatre wasn't over.

'What next?' Sir Stuart had asked in his opening statement about her headgear. The answer came on the day of the judge's summing up. For this Safia appeared bare-headed. Not just that but her hair was cut drastically short, as short as it had been when she'd hacked it off in the bathroom of the salon, giving her the choirboy look. Was this sudden disregard of the tenets of her religion another example of a lawyer's cunning, or a whim by Safia herself? It scarcely mattered. What counted was the effect, and it was startling.

In his closing address Sir Stuart appealed to the jury, a little desperately, to avoid being carried away by the sexual side of things and focus on the clear and present danger of another bombing. The jury seemed less than awed. It was getting on for a year since the first bomb, there hadn't been a second, and there was no certainty there would be. All that was certain, Tony told himself as Sir Stuart rumbled on, was that Safia would get off.

And she did. Innocent on all counts, the jury decided, on the basis that the charge of withholding information relevant to a terrorist act, and of aiding and abetting that act, could not stand when the accused had no knowledge of what that act was going to be, and therefore what she was withholding or abetting.

Wasted months, wasted effort, a wasted end to his career. Tony did his best not to feel bitter, but he was. He'd sat through all the evidence and nothing he'd heard had changed his mind. Ruminating on what had happened he did his best to be honest with himself. Was it unconscious prejudice against Muslims? The difficulty of reading the minds of different people? Or a forty year accumulation of scepticism, maybe cynicism too? Either way it meant you could make mistakes, and looking back at his years in the anti-terrorist business there was one that haunted him, even now.

*

It happened several years earlier. Assigned to a branch specializing in the infiltration of Muslim organisations, he'd never felt at home in the role. Agent recruitment was not his forte. Many of the cases he'd worked on – pious family men with Christian mistresses and a drinking habit, petty criminals whose misdemeanors could be overlooked in return for services rendered – involved an element of blackmail, and from time to time he'd felt misgivings. Pressuring people he'd got to know personally into risky ventures, such as joining extremist groups, had forced him to toughen up, override his qualms.

It was how he'd weathered the case of Amir Hassan. A twenty-two year old teacher at a primary school in Liverpool, Hassan had joined a suspect group. Put under surveillance from the moment of his first meeting – a camera monitoring the annex to the Muslim bookstore where it was held caught him entering nervously – the first thing Tony discovered about him was that Amir was a homosexual with a double life.

His partner was Ahmed Ghazali, a senior education officer and a married man twenty years older than himself. A non-practicing Muslim, Ghazali had no adverse record, and it had been Tony's job to persuade him to talk Amir into reporting on the group. To avoid alarming the older man the message he left on his office phone was that a representative of the security services was conducting a review on how best to guard against radicalism in Muslim schools, a project in which Mr Ghazali's cooperation was invited. The rendezvous he specified was a café in Birkenhead.

It was a filthy day. Tony sat waiting in the café in a sweater, his wet parka over a chair by his side; Ghazali turned up in a smart striped suit, looking like a bank manager caught in the rain. Already ill at ease in the scruffy café, when Tony disclosed that the meeting concerned his boyfriend the poor man pretty much broke up before his eyes. It was quite a spectacle: the bank manager figure sitting there amongst the overalled laborers and mechanics with tears of fear forming in his eyes before a detached and unresponsive Tony.

He hadn't known of his boyfriend's involvement in the group. Appalled to hear of it, and protesting that he was a 'dear fellow, though naïve and impressionable, one of those teachers who never grew up,' Ghazali did his best to steady himself by talking his head off. It was not just for his 'dear wife' that he was afraid, he explained, the words tumbling out and a hand shaking. If Amir's sex life were to become public it would be a disaster for the boy as well as himself. His father (as Tony knew) was a businessman and one-time mayor, and it had been in the margins of a local government conclave on Muslim schools that Ghazali had met Amir.

On and on he talked, with piteous ingratiation and pleading eyes. Tony could have scotched his fears there and then, by explaining that there could be no question of threatening him or his boyfriend with disclosure. (The service had become very correct about these things in recent years.) But he said nothing, allowing Ghazali to assume that official blackmail was what it was all about. A lamentable trick, though one that spared Tony the discomfort of suggesting that he should find out from his partner what went on in the group. Ghazali was so afraid he volunteered to do it himself.

'I can't believe he's engaged in anything wrong, such a gentle boy. But if he is perhaps I could persuade him to tell me about it, and then leave?'

Well no, Tony said: if Ghazali could prevail on him to stay it would be a greater service to the nation. Then he could debrief Amir on each meeting, and dispatch a report to an address Tony would be happy to provide. The man's head was pumping vigorously and his eyes lightening before he'd finished. 'It will not be snitching, it will be for his own good,' he kept repeating, 'his own good.'

He must have had little trouble prevailing over his boyfriend ('I am like a father to him'), and within weeks reports began reaching Tony via the safe address. What struck him rather more than the content – Amir's accounts of the meetings seemed disappointingly tame – was that the English was excellent, the grammar punctilious, the handwriting superb. Not what you necessarily expected from an English teacher.

After five weeks the reports stopped. He rang Ghazali's office, to be told he was off sick; a nasty bug, his secretary said, he'd been a whole week out of the office. Tony left a message saying it would be good if they could meet when he was better. For reply a cutting from a local paper arrived about Amir's death by drowning: a suicide, the newspaper implied. He couldn't swim in troubled water, Ahmed had written underneath. Looking at the newspaper photo of the boyishly earnest face, Tony could believe it.\

At Thames House there was no post mortem, though Tony carried out his own. Amir's involvement in religious studies of the more fundamentalist kind had puzzled him from the start: fundamentalists, after all, were homophobic. But then according to Ghazali the boy felt guilty about his sexuality, so in some strange way joining the group must have been a kind of compensation for being gay, reconciling his contradictions, proving himself a true believer. On top of that must have been the agonies of betrayal, and in the end betraying his father as well as his religion must have proved too much.

Worried about Ghazali's state of mind, and to assure himself there was no risk of the story getting out, he met him again. The devastated man agreed with his analysis. Ill-looking still, he seemed too afraid for himself to think of revenge against MI5. Seeing his ravaged face and over-wide eyes across the table, and unhappy with his role in the affair, Tony felt sincere if limited pity.

He'd been instructed to offer him £3,000 for his services (and as an inducement to silence, Tony supposed), but it wasn't needed: the man seemed as overcome by fear of exposure as he was by his grief.

When, on the pavement outside the cafe, Ghazali mustered the courage to make his complaint, mild in the circumstances, about pressure from MI5 contributing to his lover's self-destruction, Tony had trouble resisting the temptation to hit back: and what the hell did a married man think he'd been doing playing around with someone twenty years younger than himself, 'one of those teachers who were always children, never grew up,' in the first place?

He'd wanted to leave it there, but his boss wouldn't let go. Convinced that the Muslim group had found out about Amir's homosexuality and tried to blackmail him into becoming a suicide bomber, rather than dropping the surveillance after Amir's death he insisted it be stepped up.

What came out was exactly as Amir had reported: anti-Semitic tirades, denunciations of British policy on Iraq and Afghanistan – and absolutely no hints of plotting. Solemn tributes by members of the group to their dead brother debunked the theory that that the boy might have been blackmailed, and taken his life when confronted with a choice between exposure and some murderous mission.

So there it was. A handful of low-level reports he had secured on noisy but innocuous meetings had cost a young teacher his life. Feeling none too proud of himself, he'd taken the next opportunity to move on from the infiltration business.

*

So no, he was no bigot, knew when he'd made mistakes, Tony assured himself. His judgement in the Hassan case had been tragically flawed, which meant he could be getting things wrong again now. But he didn't think so. For all her touching moments in the box there was something he distrusted. Something about her ingenuousness, about those remote and passive eyes that had spooked him a little ever since their first encounter. Not to speak of her ever-changing personality. Where other people had mood swings, she had swings of character.

Though why torment himself? What did his misgivings matter? It was the public that swayed things, and he monitored the backwash from the trial with growing incredulity. Almost no-one dissented from the judgment. Everywhere he saw sentimentalism, gullibility and a lack of rational thought even where their own security was concerned.

And these were his compatriots? It was as if Britain had become a foreign country, something completely detached from himself, the most English of men. A new, light-minded people whose whims and quirks and bouts of emotional incontinence drove everything in their lives. Never mind his trouble in understanding other cultures – he no longer understood his own.

How long would it take them to see the truth? That the trial had resolved nothing, that they were still at risk, that sexual rather than security considerations had swung the whole thing? Without the drama of the brothel business the jury would have found Safia's firework story impossible to accept. Rockets and jumping jacks, at the Bank of England? How could any girl be that naïve, people would have asked? And how could anyone live unsuspecting in a house where a terrorist outrage was being planned under her nose by her own brothers?

To that the public's answer appeared to be: well, a girl so innocent she couldn't dress herself in Western clothes without looking like a tart, and was a prey to every debauched person she encountered, from a drunken skirt-chaser on the Tube to a bisexual Ukrainian brothel-keeper. For them it was a case of beauty and the beast, and where there was a creature of Mrs Marusak's incomparable beastliness there had to be undefiled beauty in proportion.

*

The result of the trial became so predictable that its final days produced in Tony that lassitude of the spirit you get when the world around you takes a different view of reality from yourself. Accounts of the trial in the press didn't help. There was fun to be had from his humiliation at the hands of the Muslim lawyer ('B- for Agent A',), and a cartoon in a leftish paper touched him on the raw: behind his courtroom screen he appeared as a fat-faced, thuggish fellow in dark glasses, reclining in an armchair swilling champagne and chewing a fat cigar, a card saying 'MI5' tucked in his hat, and a bludgeon at his feet. The caption was *No Problem: She Confessed.*

By the end of it he was in more need than ever of a week or two in his Cyprus refuge, but the prospect was retreating to infinity. This was his mood when, slipping away from the court on the last day of the trial after hearing the chairman of the jury pronounce the 'not guilty' verdict in an almost gushing tone, with a tender glance at Safia, Mrs Marusak bustled up to him.

'Mr Underwood!'

Treating her call as a salutation, he nodded amiably in her direction and lengthened his stride. Hopeless. An outstretched arm intercepted him.

'What you going to say to me? That was terrible, terrible, never we have trial like that in my country. Islam lawyer is dirty woman. You see how she watch films? She has porno at home, you can see, no man so she needs porno. She make me say things, I have no translator.'

'You didn't ask for one.'

'How I know they treat me like I am bomber? Why you make me

come? My husband ask Russian lawyer who say I not have to come, so why I here? I come to help struggle with terror and tell about Chechen and about Safia and I come when you say will be no talk about my business and easier for me passport to come back later if I witness. Then that woman say terrible thing.'

She stopped, pursed her lips then continued, her voice slipping from peeved contralto to hissing bass:

'People say about me and prostitute, eh Mr Underwood? But what you say if I say about you?'

Her arms began moving. Tony looked down. She was agitating her hands, energetically, and for a second it seemed she was miming how she would like to wring his neck. With a cold feeling he saw that they were knitting motions.

'There'll be no problem about you coming back,' he said quietly. 'And no action.'

How he would ensure this Tony had little idea at that moment. Though from what he'd heard, there were ways.

'How you sure?'

'I'm working on it.'

'You work quick, because I need come back soon.'

This was no more than the truth. It was early days, the country was still in trauma, but Sergei and Mrs Marusak had an eye to the future. For them the trial had provided hope of a kind. Property values, for one thing. The feeling that there might be no second attack had given a boost to office prices, up 26 per cent from their catastrophic base. Having bought half a dozen suites in the City at a 50 per cent discount, on that score Sergei was a happy man.

There were also plans to be made for an expansion of his girlfriend's business. Their worry was that they could miss out on knock-down bargains for commercial premises in the suburbs, the site of their future operations, as prices rose.

It was one reason for her ready agreement to come over for the trial. The trip was a chance to nose around boarded-up retail premises in discreet corners of Wimbledon, Barnes, Lewisham, with flats adequate for her purposes vacant above. Wimbledon, she decided, she liked best: such nice big family houses, such respectable people.

'So we have deal?'

Mrs Marusak was still agitating her arms in suggestive fashion, though less furiously now.

'We have deal.' The knitting motions were upsetting him. To stop them he grasped her hand. 'I promise.'

25

'How well did you know her?'

Jayson looked back at the Syrian, dully. It was his turn to be patient with his brother. Amer had a thing about Safia, even before, something he'd picked up from Umair. Now he talked about nothing else. What Jayson couldn't know was that pictures the Syrian had seen in the papers, first in Muslim dress then bare-headed, brazen, evoked poisoned memories of Jamila. To him there even seemed a resemblance: the same age, that oval face, those long-lashed eyes… Enticements of the Devil!

Images till now consigned to the depths of his mind – of Jamila in her sweet, chaste days, then with her Canadian, their eyes embracing, their heads almost touching – re-surfaced. Jamila had sold herself to her rich indidel and Safia to the security services. Stupid of Umair to have involved her, even to reconnoitre. Always a mistake to trust a woman, even with the simplest tasks, because with them the simplest things turned complex. Whether she'd been lying or not in the trial he didn't know, hadn't been privy to her role in the attack. All he knew was that she'd betrayed her brothers.

When he wasn't raging against her to Jayson he was cursing in front of the television. He'd followed every bulletin, every day of the trial, and her release infuriated him more than a conviction would have done.

'An innocent victim. You hear that? A traitorous bitch is what she is!'

With his Bristol plans on hold he had little else to do with his time, and today he was at it again. For nearly an hour he'd stalked the basement muttering about Allah's desire for revenge, swearing that His wish was his servant's command. Jayson sat on his bed, giving every impression of listening, interspersing an 'Aye, brother' when it suited. Otherwise he kept quiet. It had worked for a while, but now the Syrian had turned on him. While Jayson stared up at him, nonplussed, Amer watched him keenly, his eyes flecked with red as he repeated:

'So how well?'

'Never met her, brother.'

'But you went to the house. You saw her.'

'Yeah, once I did. When I was collecting the clothes.'

'And how did you find her?'

'I dunno. Didn't think about her. Umair said she was a loose woman but he'd put her right. Got her out of school and things. Looked alright when I saw her. In a niqab she was.'

Jayson's slow-working mind was deadlocked, this time with reason. He was as indignant as Amer about the slut Safia. But how could the Syrian speak of punishing someone the papers said would remain under close surveillance? Had he known about Jamila the Syrian's talk of revenge would have made sense, but then Amer was not the confiding type.

He paced on, his fury made worse by their virtual incarceration since the girl's arrest. With Safia in their hands they'd be better informed, have stepped up the search. One reason he'd begun questioning Jayson about her was that he'd been to her house himself, to confer with her borthers. A mistake. He had no memory of seeing her, though if she'd been there she might have heard him.

It was why he'd never left the basement all these weeks, subsisting on a stockpile of food he kept in the fridge against an emergency such as this. Jayson was incarcerated too. The only time he'd let him out had been to check the equipment, pay the Albanian more rent, and restock with frozen food.

The weather was heavy, the basement stifling, and again the boy was looking ill, the result of the meagre rations and lack of air. Still Amer wouldn't allow the door or window open, not for a second. The Syrian himself was in a poor state. He needed someone to blame, someone who'd been as naïve as himself with Jamila. At first it had been Umair, now it was Jayson.

'So you liked her,' he went on, still striding about.

'No brother, I just said, I never met her, never talked to her. Just saw her.'

'And she liked you?'

'Brother, she didn't see me, far as I know. I walked in the door and through the hall to the kitchen and she was in a room and I saw her from the back.'

'You liked what you saw well enough to smell her clothes.'

'What you sayin', brother?'

'The clothes for Safia. Her slut's clothes. The ones you buried for them, in the garden.'

'Yeah, I remember.'

'You smelled them. I looked out of the window when you went to dig them up, and I saw you.'

'Musta been to make sure they wasn't damp.'

'You didn't do it that way, quickly. You did it for a long time. Smelled a woman's clothes.'

'They was new, she hadn't worn them.'

'That is not true. She had worn them, to try them on. Umair told me. A whole hour in front of the mirror. She lusted for them, Umair said, he could see it. The top, the skirt, they must have smelt of her, of her lust for them. The skirt especially.' The Syrian lent forward, his nose twitching.

'Was there underwear?'

'I don't think so. The top and skirt is all I remember.'

'And the skirt, did it smell?'

'If she'd worn it I suppose it must have.'

'Of what did it smell?'

'I dunno, brother. They was a bit dirty, but they wasn't damp. Maybe they smelled a bit, you know, of woman's soap or something...'

'I will tell you what they smelled of. They smelled of sin. And you sniffed at them, drew that sin into yourself, allowed it to inflame you.

Sniffed at the skirt of the sister of a martyr, a sister who failed him in her hour of trial. A sister who informed on him, put our enterprise in danger. Sniffed at them the way a dog sniffs another's rump. And what did you smell? You smelled treason, you smelled apostasy. And did you inhale them, with her lust? Have they contaminated you?'

Jayson drew back on his bed, the Syrian standing over him.

'Don't say it, brother, please don't say it!'

'The thought sickens me. You are not fit, not worthy –'

'– I'm fit, I'm worthy!'

'Unworthy to die a martyr. The smell in your nostrils will defile our enterprise.'

'I'll prove it, brother, show how worthy I am!'

When the Syrian turned his back Jayson went down on his stomach, reaching for his prayer mat. Hearing him the Syrian turned, put a foot on the other end of the mat and jerked it to him, out of reach.

'You are not worthy to pray! No expiation before Allah can be enough!'

Jayson crawled towards the mat, came close, reached out, but when he got a hand to it the Syrian stamped his foot on the other end, pulled it further away. So Jayson was forced to crawl on, head down, clutching for it, till with a look of contempt the Syrian kicked the dust-thick mat in his face.

Jayson took it, spread it out, removed his shoes and, wimpering, prepared to pray. Instead of kneeling in the required position he collapsed onto his belly, sobbing, his legs drumming the floor in frustration, like a child's.

The Syrian looked down at him, calmer now. Had the boy sniffed at her clothes, sexually? His memory of seeing him bringing them in was hazy, though what did it matter? If Jayson felt guilty, so much the better. Whatever the truth he musn't allow his anger to be deflected. It was Safia that mattered, and Allah's revenge. It was that he must work on now, whatever the risks.

'I am going out,' he announced to the boy's prostrate figure. 'In two hours I will be back.'

26

For Safia the most pressing problem after her release was where to live. A secret address, an assumed name and a niqab were minimum disguises for a woman reviled amongst Muslim ultras, not to speak of the far right. Militants saw her as a deserter to the cause, Islamophobes as a mass murderer who'd escaped justice. Both were prolific in their death threats.

After the publicity there could be no question of her returning to the camp, or to her parents' house. The police had finished trawling over it, but safety ruled it out. What they'd found there – or rather hadn't – made the question of her security more worrying. There'd been no sign of radioactivity in either house or garage, or the garden. Which suggested the bomb had been stored somewhere else. Additional evidence, the police felt, that there were more of them out there.

Nor could Safia do the most obvious thing: leave the country and hide out with her parents in rural Pakistan. The only time she'd seen them since the bomb was when they'd flown back to see her in jail: a painful occasion, with her father sunk deeper than ever in his furious silence, and her mother distraught. Potential targets themselves after the actions of their sons, following the trial they'd gone back to Pakistan, and showed no signs of coming back.

It came down to a choice. She could hide away on her own in the safe house the security service offered her, courtesy of Tony: a small, end-of-terrace cottage in a Bolton suburb. She went with him to see it, spent ten minutes inside, and that was enough. The thought of living there alone, knowing no-one, afraid even to answer the door, made her weep.

Tony stood next to her in the musty hall, wondering whether to put an arm round her. He did nothing. It wasn't just the harassment thing: in his eyes she was a not-so-innocent woman. So he stood there till the tears stopped, shifting from leg to leg, thinking this ought to have been a chore for a female officer.

The other option was to move in with the uncle she'd told Julie about. A recent widower, he had room in his house and had offered to take her in. Unsurprisingly, she chose the uncle. A former teacher whose premature stoop and sallow complexion were offset by lively eyes, Uncle Ishaq lived in Gorton, Manchester, where he'd taught maths at secondary schools before becoming a member of the local education committee, from which he was now retired.

It was some years since she'd seen him, but she had good memories of his visits. Especially the day he'd taken her mother's side against her father and Umair in a bitter row over her schooling, the row that got him banned from the house. Childless himself he was wonderful with children, and where religion was concerned the opposite of a bigot: he prayed with reasonable frequency, but he liked a glass of wine.

She moved in and a routine was quickly established. Part of it was the grey Vauxhall across the road that could be seen day and night through the new, permanently drawn net curtains. Sometimes it was directly opposite, sometimes diagonally, but almost always within sight. Today it was a hundred yards up the road, the only spot available after uncle Ishaq had taken the last place near his house after driving his niece back from a trip to a cinema at eleven in the evening, with the Vauxhall in attendance.

With no one around, and Safia safely in the house, Uncle Ishaq walked to the car and knocked at the window. The MI5 driver opened it an inch. Thanking him heartily for his help, Ishaq went on to suggest that his vehicle might be becoming a trifle conspicuous by its 24 hour presence. He'd be happy to recommend a friend in the garage business who could do them a re-spray and a change of number plate, cheap. Get you an up-to-date tax disk whilst he was about it, he added with a grin. The disk on the car, he'd noticed, was a week overdue.

'Thanks a bunch,' said the bald-headed Cockney at the wheel, and wound up the window. Either he'd been instructed to ignore his charges, or he didn't think it funny.

*

In taking Safia's side over her schooling Ishaq's arguments had been simple. The first lines of the Koran, he would point out tirelessly, called upon the people to read. Since the people included the female sex, illiterate drudges cannot have been the prophet's ideal women. Even assuming that a woman's duties were confined to the home – which he most certainly did not – what sort of a man would want an unschooled, blockheaded female running his household?

Now he was in charge of her education Uncle Ishaq had ambitions for his niece. First, complete her A-levels (English, mathematics, legal studies). Then a correspondence course in law. It wasn't his idea: Safia had been consulted, and Tony was proven right about the influence of the defence lawyer: she'd been in awe of the woman, couldn't stop talking about how brilliant she was and how surprised she'd been by the number of Indian and Pakistani female faces amongst the prison and court officials. So it was that she dropped her aspiration to be a doctor, and decided it would be the law.

Attending the local night-school being out of the question, Ishaq set up a regime for his niece at home. From nine to twelve it was English and mathematics conducted by himself, with a trusted friend and retired solicitor for the legal studies. Twelve to two-thirty was set aside for helping with the chores and the shopping, and for lunch. Two-thirty to six, private study. Evenings were at home, or with her uncle at the cinema.

Visitors were restricted: an aunt, an old girlfriend who could be relied on, and once in a while, Julie. From Sheringham to Manchester was an arduous drive, but that was no bad thing; the distance served both women as a pretext for the rarity of Julie's visits. The deception that had underlain their relationship was not easily forgotten, at least not on Julie's side. She did not take well to looking gullible, especially in Tony Underwood's eyes. For all the girl's insistence on how keen she was to see her, on the two trips she made to Gorton Julie never brought Jackie.

The regularity of her regime was at Uncle Ishaq's insistence. The girl was in a fragile state. Either she'd buckle down to an all-absorbing task, he felt, with the prospect of a new life at the end of it, or she would go under. The prison psychologist he'd talked to before her release shared his view.

'Her father and brothers made a mess of her all right. A classic example of how to foul up the lives of Muslim girls,' the woman had sighed. 'Only a kind of wily ingenuousness got her though.'

'Meaning?'

'In situations like hers clever people – and Safia isn't stupid, not stupid at all – learn to look after themselves in ways that are not always pretty.'

'So she needs to grow up fast, emotionally as well as intellectually?'

'That is most certainly what I'm saying. And given the security problem, and the difficulty she's going to have meeting people her age, that's not going to be easy.'

Unconvinced of the degree of Uncle Ishaq's enlightenment about women, the psychiatrist recommended a course the authorities ran for the guardians of newly released prisoners. Uncle Ishaq, who had overseen many such courses in his day, said that was kind, he would think about it, see how he went.

27

Since Safia's arrest Amer had fought off the temptation to visit Hani's café. Ruminating impotently about her, unable to pursue his plans, had been getting more frustrating by the day. Thoughts about ways she could be punished had begun forming in his mind. But before he could work them through there were things he had to know, things only the Internet could tell him.

There was another reason for a trip to Hani's. If his visits there stopped the very day the Safia story broke, and he never reappeared... Not that Hani himself would say anything. Though if one of the regulars were to remark on his sudden absence, and the word went round...

When he arrived that afternoon Hani emerged from the depths of the shop to greet him like a lost brother. What had become of him, he asked, with a slap to his shoulder, before teasing him as always about his missing beard. The beard Amer had told him he'd been advised to cut for dermatological reasons, and would be regrowing soon. Maybe he'd been ashamed to come without it, Hani joshed, his smile scarcely visible through his own luxuriant growth.

Then he went on about the trial, Safia's acquittal and the rest, asked what Amer thought.

'I'm out of touch. I've been away, visiting relations, a sick relation in Lebanon.'

Eager to get online he cut short the chatter and went to the machine he preferred, the one in an alcove, a little apart from the others, where no one could snoop on his screen. For over an hour he pored through everything he could find about Safia, and with each new item his fury rose. To judge by the bloggers and tweeters the reaction to her trial was more horrifying than he'd imagined. Nauseous, revolting, worse than the television! The wave of sympathy on her acquittal, her transformation from suspect to celebrity, criminal to victim, monster to national heroine, cut to his heart.

And it wasn't just infidels. 'A model for the Muslim young, a pearl of Muslim womanhood' an Islamic newspaper had written, in a plea for true believers to follow her example and assist the police. A website had been opened on her behalf, complete with missives from adolescent girls in praise of their idol. A veritable cult, Amer thought bitterly, a cult of the apostate.

Finally he found what he wanted. It turned up on a site he kept an eye on, a blog by a commentator said to be close to the security services. After speculating about the threats against her, the problems of her rehabilitation, what she would do and where she might be living, citing informed sources the blog went on:

> She is not thought to be close to her father, who in any case
> has returned to Pakistan. Nor, it is thought, has she gone
> abroad. Rumour has it that she is still in the country, staying
> with relatives in the Manchester area.

Manchester. A relative in Manchester. Amer dug into his memory – and there it was. What Umair had told him about the history of his family problems. The dispute over Safia's education, the argument with her uncle from Manchester, Gorton. Someone who'd been a teacher and tried to persuade her father to allow her to go to a Muslim sixth-form there, offering to take her in while she studied.

His father had sent him to look the place over, he remembered Umair telling him, make sure it was pious. And it wasn't, not remotely. Short skirts, scarves instead of hijabs, unseemly sports and music – how well he remembered the force of Umair's disgust! A milk-and-water Muslim Umair called his uncle – or rather wine-and-water. Yes, a drinker, with his own eyes Umair had seen it when they'd come back from the school to his uncle's house: a bottle of sherry, in a corner of the living room, on a silver tray, like something precious. And such a man was to be entrusted with his sister's education!

Safia, live with an alcoholic? The uncle was banned from the house and Safia not permitted to see him. Another drama followed, when her father discovered her writing her uncle a letter, and flogged her. After that the girl had come to heel, Umair had told him: returned to the ways of the faith and renounced her dreams of a decadent life with her Uncle Ishaq. Yes, that was his name, he was sure of it: Uncle Ishaq from Gorton, Manchester.

The Syrian sat before his screen, trembling. That's where she must be. He wanted to get up and go back to his basement, to be on his own, calm himself, think through his revenge. First he read on, feverishly, to see if there was more.

And there was. In his latest entry the blogger turned to the hunt for the bombers' friends:

The thinking following the trial is that the bombers' accomplices may not be Pakistanis at all. There have been ethnically mixed groups of terrorists before. There had been talk of Chechens, but this is now discounted, except perhaps as the source of the strontium-90. Security service contacts are suggesting that a Syrian may be involved. They refuse to say how they know, though common sense suggests it must have come from their debriefing of Safia.

Amer switched off the machine and strode to the counter. Edging his wife aside, Hani took over as he paid.

'So now that you're up-to-date,' he smiled, 'what's your hunch?'

'About what?'

'The trial! What else? You think she was guilty as charged? I'll tell you what I think.' He lowered his voice. 'She got off because they didn't have enough against her. And if she knows who the others are she can't have told them, can she?'

'How's that?'

'Because they haven't found them!' A throaty laugh issued from deep in his beard. 'Maybe someone's protecting them.'

'Who?' the Syrian found the strength to ask.

'Someone powerful.'

Looking mysterious he leant across the counter and, with something close to a smirk, whispered:

'Allah, perhaps.'

At other times the Syrian would have risked a smile. Now he shrugged and spread his hands, paid what he owed, said goodbye and stalked off.

His heart raced as he walked. Hani the Iraqi knew he was a Syrian, had guessed it the first time he'd come to the shop. And Hani, an indefatigable surfer, would be up to date with everything to do with the bombing. What if he'd read the blog? What if he was a spy, reporting to the security services? An agent provocateur cajoling his customers into offering opinions – then reporting. And his wife – was she part of it? Standing at the counter all day in her burka, doing nothing so far as he could see – except perhaps acting as a token of her husband's piety.

His walk back to the basement was troubled, yet there was also exhilaration, an urgency in his step. Bristol, Safia – finally things were coming together in his mind. He was glad he'd gone to Hani's.

*

'For the third time,' the woman on the enquiries desk at Manchester Education Department sighed, 'we can't give out people's telephone numbers.'

Jayson stood in a phone booth at the railway station. Before him, neatly arrayed, were a pound coin, a pencil, and a sheet of paper with three brief paragraphs in capital letters: a crib the Syrian had written.

'It's not his number I want, Miss,' Jayson read, slowly. 'It's only his address. I don't want to bother him on the telephone.'

A pause while he moved on to the second paragraph, then:

'You see he taught me years ago and he was a great teacher and I wanted to send him a card saying thank you, 'cos I got a job.'

'I see.'

Was this man or boy, the woman reflected? Either way he sounded simple. Disabled, maybe, in a wheelchair perhaps, and so grateful for his job, poor devil.

'Technically we're not allowed to give out addresses either.'

'Oh go on Miss,' Jayson implored, unscripted, in a whiny voice. 'It ain't gonna harm no-one.'

'Well it would help if you knew his full name.'

Jayson searched his crib. Yes, that was it, paragraph three:

'I don't know his surname 'cos he used to encourage us to call 'im by 'is first name when we was older. Ishaq is all I remember.'

A rustling.

'Well we do have an Ishaq. He's just retired from the education committee, I see here. But he used to teach.'

'Must be 'im.'

With several requests for a repeat, Jayson wrote down the address with his pencil and thanked the lady for her help, sincerely.

*

The house was a bungalow, one of a new development tucked away behind a main road and some council flats. After finding a cheap hotel, for several days Jayson hung round the area, doing what Amer said. Check if she's there. Watch for her coming out. See where she goes each day, whether there's a pattern. Keep an eye out for surveillance, make sure you take a variety of hats, and change your clothes. And so he did, daily: the coat bought in Kensington High Street the first day, a pullover the next, a T shirt and jacket the third. For hats he had a bobble and a flat cap, though as Amer had instructed, absolutely no hoodie.

The Syrian should never have worried about Jayson's abilities as a watcher. The clothes, the indeterminate complexion, the easy lope, all casual and sporty-looking – no one could have blended into the mixed neighbourhood better. A one-man distillation of his surroundings – the council flats housed every kind of ethnicity – he was a natural for the job. The head beating time to his Walkman and the mumbling lips were a last touch, perfecting the image of a genial, spaced-out guy.

The Walkman part was not an act. Remembering his dawn wait outside the Kensington store, to fill the empty hours as he strolled the streets he'd taken a couple of CDs with him: a collection of fiery sermons Amer had given him for his instruction, and excerpts from the holy books he was attempting to learn by heart. Hence the approvingly nodding head and mouthing lips.

Don't get too close to the house, the Syrian had insisted, and apart from walking the length of the street, once, to check out Uncle Ishaq's house number, he kept his distance. At the time he did it there seemed no signs of surveillance (watch out for men sitting in unmarked cars, Amer had warned), and for this there was a reason.

He didn't spot the Vauxhall with the bald Cockney and his mate, because as chance would have it the mate was away stocking up on coffee, and the Cockney, his head bent to a scrambled phone below the windscreen, was deep in discussion with the MI5 car pool about the delivery of a replacement vehicle. (Uncle Ishaq's joke had struck home).

That was day one. It was the second day, a Tuesday, when Jayson was accomplishing one of his lightning passes at the top of the street, that he spotted her leaving the house. He knew it was her despite the niqab, or rather because of it: at Umair's she'd been dressed like that, he remembered her tallish height and slim figure.

It was shortly before two o'clock and she was carrying a red shopping bag. No need to crowd her, he thought, taking a boyish delight in his task: women in veils were a minority in the area, and with the black and the red it would have been hard to lose her.

Coming out of the bungalow and walking briskly she made straight for the high street, for the shops he guessed. Joining her by another route and keeping well behind – far enough to change his bobble hat for the flat cap and his lope to a saunter – he ambled past the supermarket she went into. Minutes later she came out, bought something in a halal butcher's, walked back by the same route, and that was it. Forty-five minutes in all.

The next day, the same. Except this time Jayson began with the flat cap rather than the bobble hat. Also, he spotted the Vauxhall. Minutes after she disappeared into the supermarket it pulled up opposite. At the wheel what looked like a bald guy in a beret who stayed in the car: someone else got out, put money in the meter, then got back in. Had it been there on day one? If so Jayson hadn't noticed.

Instead of following her back – with the amount she was carrying today she could only go home – he stayed to watch the Vauxhall. It was them all right: three minutes and it turned round to cruise at a leisurely speed towards her road. Later he did a quick pass at the top of the street and there it was: parked half way down, opposite the house, pretty much.

Half-past one on Thursday and out she came again, with niqab and shopping bag, red. Though this time, no Vauxhall. He searched for it as she left the house but it wasn't there. Opposite the supermarket, not there either. Friday, she made the same trip. Still no Vauxhall.

When she'd finished her shopping and walked off back to the house he took a look in the supermarket: sauntered in and lingered at the back, out of sight of the till. There were magazines in this section and, his eye caught by its headline, he selected *The New Statesman*. The headline read *Is a Second Bomb a Fantasy*? Amer might like that.

There was no one else. Dawdling over the magazines till the owner was engrossed in stocking a shelf on the far side of the shop, on his way to the till he swung open a service door and peered out. It led into a backyard stacked with empty crates that gave onto an alley. The rear entrance to the shop.

After warding off attempts by the smiley fat man at the counter to chat to him about the magazine headline (We've got to hope they're right, don't we? What do you think about it all, Sir?... Dunno. Ain't for me, for my dad) he came out, collected his stuff from the hotel, caught a bus to the station and took the train back to London.

28

The evacuee camp was being wound up. Martin arrived the evening before Julie and Jackie were due to leave. After dinner at the Sheringham hotel – it was harder to get a table now the word had got around that the gangs were going – they came back to her flat and talked till late. Neither had mentioned where'd he'd sleep, and it was too late to find a hotel to stay in the town, as he had on previous visits.

'I'll doss down in the box room if you like,' he said, getting up.

It wasn't play-acting. There'd been little tenderness and no lovemaking since their separation. It was a discipline Julie had imposed on them both, rather than punishment for affairs. It was part of her confidence in herself that she had never suspected him of having other woman, and part of his dependence on her that he had never felt the need.

There were women who carried their imperiousness into bed, but then Julie was not imperious exactly, only a little too emotionally organised. Which made her readiness to forget herself with him the more delightful, and their lovemaking had been the most resilient part of their marriage. For her it was a respite from herself, for Martin the fantasist, a chance to be himself in her company.

So it was that the end of the evening resolved itself without embarrassment.

'You'll sleep with me,' she said, getting up from the sofa, in a voice halfway between a request and a command. 'I'm not infectious you know.'

That night, for the first time since the bomb, forebodings about the new precariousness of their lives were for an hour eclipsed.

*

'The trouble with this place,' Martin mused on the veranda next morning while Julie packed, 'is –'

'– never mind what it is. They're shutting it down. I met one of the owners, totting up the damage. I asked if he'd be re-opening it as a holiday camp and got a sarcastic reply. The gist was that a national slump isn't the best time to attract holidaymakers to a disused camp for dirty bomb evacuees from the slums of London. Especially now the media have crawled all over the place.'

'Shouldn't think anyone'll miss it,' Martin mused. 'There's something about the way it's perched up here that's'– he groped for the right word – 'against nature. An imposition on the landscape. Sort of over-cocky, inviting retribution.'

Martin sounded reflective. She wasn't used to him reflecting.

'I can't imagine what you mean.'

He thought before replying.

'It's nature getting its own back. There's erosion all along the coast, isn't there? How long will it be till the cliffs crumble away and the homes get genuinely mobile, and trundle into the sea?'

This was more like him: light-minded, sardonic.

'You know that picture,' he went on, '*The Last of England*, by Ford Madox Brown wasn't it? The one with the morose-looking couple emigrating to Australia or wherever, sitting at the stern of the ship looking out dolefully at the receding shore –'

'– I remember.'

'I wonder how many people will stick it out after what's happened? If they do they'll get as far as they can from the big cities. They'll cower in places like Norfolk, won't they? Right out on the edge. And now the bloody shoreline's crumbling away too.'

This was less amusing.

'That's enough heavy symbolism. Far as I'm concerned the place has served its purpose,' Julie said, adding after a silence, 'and I'll miss it in a way.'

'What way?'

'Well, the work, the people.'

'The work I understand.'

'Oh come on! The gangs were just a few dozen kids. There were good folk who showed incredible courage. There always are.'

'I'll take your word,' Martin murmured.

Julie was in the bathroom, packing Jackie's medicines. The girl had been sent off to say goodbye to Amel, her Pakistani friend. 'Why do I have to say goodbye?' she'd said, her tears forming. 'They're leaving as well, Amel said. Aren't they going to London? Won't they live in our street, like before?' The tears fell. 'Is Amel going to die?' It had taken a long time to soothe her.

The veranda where Martin stood looked down on the main road through the camp, where the last of the inmates were being loaded into coaches. A colourful queue had formed: turbans, veils, woolly hats, sedate Sikh and Muslim women, raucous Caribbeans and peeved white faces. Most were laden with suitcases, boxes, prams, bicycles and seaside gear they were hauling back to London, God knows why.

As the first coach came into view shouting and jostling erupted. Pushing forwards, a large black family was first to bustle aboard. Though muttering to one another in annoyance, the Muslim family they'd displaced made no attempt to follow. When one of their children tried to scramble on after the black kids her full-bearded father tugged her back.

Leaving the Muslims waiting in line, whites, blacks and Sikhs jostled to the front and piled in till the coach was full. It was done wordlessly, but everyone understood. When the next one arrived Pakistanis, Bangladeshis, Arabs and Somalis detached themselves from the queue and boarded, the others standing back to let them pass. And so on, in alternating fashion, till many hundreds of people were loaded swiftly and without trouble.

'Come and look at this,' Martin said as the last two buses were filling.

'What is it?' Julie called from inside the flat. 'Argy-bargy in that queue?'

'No, it's perfectly orderly. Something worse.'

Julie came, looked, shrugged, and said nothing.

'Do-it-yourself segregation,' Martin sighed. 'Not exactly the wartime spirit is it? I thought you said it was just the gangs?'

'I never expected a new humanity,' Julie called out a minute later. 'It was always a bit optimistic to expect the Sikhs and Caribbeans to open their arms to Muslims at a time like this.' She checked herself: wasn't that what Tony Underwood had said? 'It'll take time,' she went on, 'but you mustn't despair. Did I tell you about the nursery we set up?'

She hadn't – modesty about her good works was one of the things that humbled him – but now she did. Martin prepared to feel admiring and vaguely guilty.

Together with a Bangladeshi and an Indian woman she'd cobbled together the equipment: a second large tent from the army, with windows this one, desks and toys from the council. And she'd dug out a trainee teacher.

'First day we got half a dozen Muslim kids, and that was it. As far as the whites and Caribbeans were concerned it was a school for bombers. Then their kids kicked up hell till their parents let them come too.'

'Happy story.'

'Not entirely. At the end of each day the parents lined up, Muslims to the right, the rest to the left. Then snatched their kids as fast as they came out, even if they were chatting to the other side, which they often were.'

'Self-segregation. That's my point.'

'Not at all. The point is the kids wanted to socialise with each other, even if their parents didn't. If we're going to throw symbols around I prefer that one to your coach queue and your crumbling cliffs.'

*

The last coaches had gone, and only the bedridden were left in the camp. The medical unit was to stay open until enough hospital beds in London could be found for the sickest, and till recently Kingman had been among them.

It was months since his bone marrow transplant in Norwich. At first everything seemed to have gone miraculously well. After the painful preparation, then the transplant, his mood had been close to euphoric. He put on weight and was back in charge of the Bikeys, cock of the walk in his leather finery.

Weeks later he was back in bed. The worst had happened: GVHD – graft versus host disease – had set in, the transplant stubbornly failing to recognise the tissues in the rest of the body. He spent his days supine, his tall leather cap on permanently, not to hold his proud new locks in place but to camouflage his loss of hair.

'See why they made me sign up for the operation,' he said over his sheet to Julie. 'Red spots, blisters, fever and jaundice the doc said is what you get if it don't work, and I got it all. Lucky I not a white boy. If I wasn't so black you'd see I was red and yellow all over.'

A consultant was called in, and he wasn't hopeful: liver failure, he said gravely, could be next. 'Unless of course,' he added, seeing Julie's despondent face, 'he just shakes it off. Which people his age with a sound constitution have a better chance of doing. And the boy's got that all right.'

Sure enough Kingman pulled round. At which point the consultant began rowing back:

'He's doing fine, really fine – for the moment. The bitch with this disease is that you're never quite shut of it, even in the best of health. Couple of years, it could come back.'

'Have you told him?'

'No. Didn't want to confuse the boy. Best let him find out for himself, gradually. There's been a lot written about it.'

'Kingman isn't a great reader.'

'Well maybe you'd better break it to him – gently. I'd do it myself, but from me it might sound, you know, too official. Don't want him to lose heart just when he's feeling good.'

That was weeks ago, and she still hadn't said anything. That afternoon could be her last chance. One of the Bikeys had the loan of a car and was giving him a lift to London.

When he came to her flat to say goodbye Martin was careful to be out. It was Julie the boy needed. For Kingman – it was obvious to him now – she'd been a lifeline, in the moral and literal sense. Her hope for the boy, a little pious he suspected, was that the understanding she gave him of how different people could get along might sensitise him to what human ties could be.

'If you want my opinion the best thing you can do for him,' he told her before absenting himself, 'is give it to him straight. And I don't just mean the medical facts. The camp has got him into the gang mentality and if he takes that back to London he's a goner. He's playing at being the hard man but he's not. Even I can see that.'

'I told you, I don't moralise.'

Well you say that, Martin smiled to himself.

'There's another reason I don't want to nag at him,' she went on. 'When the consultant warned me about the ups and downs I had the feeling that what he was saying was that if he's already had one bad down, in the longer term he won't make it. So this is not the time for finger-wagging. There doesn't seem much future in lecturing a man who may be dying by degrees about the need to improve his ways, on the off-chance he might live.'

Martin left it there, and went. But his point had gone home. Julie resolved to combine a warning about the symptoms reappearing with a plea not to expose himself to unnecessary risks. In other words: stay out of trouble.

She couldn't do it. When the moment came, with Kingman sauntering into the flat, tough-looking as ever in all his gear, and her knowing of his fragility, all she said was:

'Kingman, you haven't forgotten about the graft-host business?'

''Course I ain't. Not the sort of thing you forget, is it?'

'Well just be sensible. Do what you can to avoid getting run-down, or wounds or infections of any kind. You've made a great recovery, but apparently it never quite goes away. The new cells and the old ones never give up the fight. They're sort of locked in struggle.'

'Like the crews,' Kingman laughed. 'Never goes away either.'

*

On the M11 to London they overtook a string of coaches that had left the camp before them and stopped for lunch. Antiquated models pressed into service, one of them had windows that opened, and a couple of the Bikeys were amusing themselves dropping beer cans onto the road.

Somebody must have recognised Julie as they drew level: smiling faces pressed to the glass, people waved and shouted, and Martin slowed to let her wave back. Then someone threw a can. It bounced off the bonnet, narrowly missing the windscreen. To avoid it Martin swerved, almost hitting the coach's side.

'Fucking idiots,' he shouted, then glanced over his shoulder, but Jackie was asleep. 'I know what you're thinking,' he grinned at Julie: 'It would never have happened to us if Kingman had been in there.'

'I was actually.'

Some other bastard would have copped it, he thought, but refrained from saying.

They were heading for a house they'd bought in south-west London. Their reconnoitre of the area had left Julie unenthusiastic. The twee houses and remnants of fashionable, pre-bomb Fulham – restaurants, delicatessens or antique dealers who hadn't gone to the wall – failed to appeal. It was only the closeness to Charing Cross Hospital that had swayed things. There were specialist doctors there for Jackie, whose health would need monitoring for years, and at a lesser level, Julie's too.

It had been a hard time persuading her to move from Aldgate. She'd miss the East End, she kept saying, but he'd marshalled an unanswerable case against returning. Judging by what he'd seen in the Midlands the damage the bomb had done would take years to heal. And after her year in the camp no one could say she hadn't done her bit. Just how many years of her life, he'd argued, did she want to devote to problems that might take a generation to resolve? Assuming they could be cured. All they could do was to leave things to time. Turning herself into a kind of nuclear Florence Nightingale wouldn't do much to help.

Too pessimistic, she felt, though at least he was being practical for a change. Maybe the bomb would be the making of him, the shock he'd never had in his culpably carefree life? The collision with reality he needed to jolt him from his fantasies, his indolence, his evasions.

29

The last of Safia's lessons that morning was English, and it had gone well. They were doing literature and a poem by John Donne captivated her. She'd got it by heart – learning passages from the Koran had given her a retentive memory – and liked it all the more when her uncle alluded to the erotic imagery. Her giggle when he explained the point was adolescent, but for Ishaq, cheering.

Two months into their regime he needed such moments. In recognition of her good work he was tempted to let her off early to do the shopping, though in the end he waited till the antique hall clock struck the end of the morning session. Routine was the key and she could do it, as always, after lunch.

At the usual time she went off to the shops. A minute or two later the surveillance car appeared and dawdled in her wake. Take no notice, they'd told her, and she didn't, chanting the Donne poem to herself sotto voce as she walked:

Are Sun, Moon and Stars by law forbidden
To smile where they list, or lend away their light?

Week by week the fear she'd felt in the streets – the first few days she sometimes ran home in panic – was decreasing. She was beginning to feel secure in her triple cocoon: Uncle Ishaq's house and curtains, the niqab, the surveillance car.

The supermarket where she shopped could be a problem. The owner, Babar Mohammed, a chatty fellow, appeared to have dedicated himself to rescuing poor veiled women from a life of silence by engaging them in conversation whether they wanted or not, and his fat man's garrulousness appeared to have focused on Safia.

The best avoidance techniques, she'd learned, were to wait till he was overwhelmed by customers before joining the check-out queue, so he had no time to launch into his questions. Or put on a show of being in a hurry, shaking her head in simulated nervousness in response to the most trivial enquiries, as if she was a hopeless invert and pathologically shy.

Today there were no customers. Convinced it helped attract them Babar had turned the piped Turkish music to top volume. Putting off his attempts at conversation as long as possible, she lingered amongst the books and magazines at the rear of the shop, out of sight.

She was glancing through a TV magazine (Uncle Ishaq was relaxed about evening television, after an hour and a half of reading) when a service door at the back of the shop swung open. Two men appeared carrying a crate of vegetables between them. At the sound of the crate being dropped a few feet from her she glanced up from her magazine. In that second two arms thrust under hers, lifting her off her feet. A hand clamping her veil to her mouth, and the din of Babar's music drowned her strangled call for help.

Outside the shop the bald Cockney and his mate were unhappy. The parking slot they'd found directly in front was less discreet than they would have liked. Normally it was somewhere across the street, preferably opposite the alley that led to the back of the shop. That way front and back were secure. But today road works had limited the choice.

Most of all the driver was unhappy about his car. Like most MI5 drivers the Cockney had put in for a new vehicle, without success; the Treasury had begun to suspect that emergency funding was being lavished on expensive or souped-up cars. The most they would do was to replace his ageing Vauxhall with a reconditioned Volvo, and it was giving him trouble. It was while he revved the stuttering motor, head down at the dials, that everything started. For the next few minutes nothing seemed to happen in logical order, though as an internal enquiry was later to establish, the sequence of events was roughly this.

Irritated by the exhaust wafting into his store Babar bawled out above his music a plea to the driver to 'Knock it off, can't you?' At the sound of his voice the driver and his mate looked up at Babar, then round the empty shop, then along the street.

The revving stopped, and Babar calmed down. Till two lithe-looking men in jeans vaulted from the car and lunged in his direction, one tugging a revolver from his back pocket. A lunatic overreaction to his complaint, it seemed, but they flew past him to the back of the shop, past a crate of lettuce lying unattended, and through the swinging service door. In the yard beyond the stink of rotting vegetables mingled with the exhaust of a recently departed vehicle.

Before parking their car (their evidence to the enquiry was emphatic on the point) the surveillance team had followed their routine to the letter: checked that she was in an enclosed space, and that the lane at the back, a cul de sac, was empty when Safia had gone into the shop. What they omitted to say was that, engrossed in their engine, they'd failed to keep an eye for anyone going in later.

The change of vehicle had been partly intended to confuse anyone keeping Safia under rival surveillance, and in that respect it seems to have succeeded. Whoever had been keeping watch on Babar's store had been confused all right – confused into believing that her surveillance had been called off. There was one stroke of luck. After a spate of burglaries as crime rocketed, Babar had installed a security camera in his back yard. So they got an indistinct image of Safia being bundled off the premises into a blue van, with no sign on the side and number plates that were bogus.

According to a woman who narrowly missed being mown down by it, the van had reversed out of the alley into the road wildly and roared off at speed. Followed some time later by an MI5 Volvo with a faulty engine, it was quickly lost.

In conclusion the enquiry recorded the woman as confirming that of the two men in the front seat of the van one was 'sort of black, but not really,' and the other 'sort of white, clean shaven with a long sharp nose, maybe from the Middle East.'

30

Had there been anyone on the back road north of Bristol curious enough to spare it a glance, the matt grey van creeping gingerly that morning from a rutted lay-by sheltered by a canopy of fir trees might have held their attention a second or two. For all the smears of dirt on its roof and sides it appeared to have been freshly painted, swiftly and by an amateur hand.

Then there were the two foreign-looking men in the front seat. In a poor state, by the look of them, crumpled and unkempt, as if they'd spent the night in the bushes. Which would be no surprise. With unemployment in the Bristol area at 21 per cent, there was no shortage of beggarly figures, immigrants often, sleeping rough. Whoever they were the men were not early risers: it was almost half-past ten when the van took to the road.

It was a smooth drive into town – traffic was still thin in this part of the country – and by eleven thirty they had reached the outskirts.

'Alright for time,' Jayson said. 'Got half an hour to get to the centre.'

The optimum moment, he'd reported after his visit to the shopping centre, was twelve.

They stopped at lights. Fixing his exhausted, over-bright eyes on the St George's flag he'd placed back onto the bonnet, he gave the nearest thing to a smile.

'An' look at that flag zappin'. Great, blowy day, brother. Help blow away the infidels.'

'And our traitor. Soon she too will mingle with the wind, Inshallah!'

'Careful, brother.' Jayson spoke softly, a thumb jerking at the partition. 'She can hear.'

'And so? Does it matter if she hears the words of a servant of Allah in her last minutes on this earth? She who has deserted Him? Through me she will hear the voice of Umair, her martyred brother, the brother she betrayed. It is good that she be reminded. There is yet time for her to repent.'

'Yeah brother, it's like you say, good she can hear. But no use her repentin' now, good as dead she is.'

They drove on, slower now through thickening traffic, towards the centre. At another set of lights Jayson leant back in the driving seat, an ear alert.

'Listen. She cryin'.'

Amer listened, and smiled.

'For an eternity she will wail. So many tears of shame to shed.'

Jayson craned back closer, an ear to the partition.

'An' shiftin' about. Cryin' and shiftin' about.'

'Shifting?'

'Yeah, you can hear. Shouldn't be, tied her well enough, and gagged her, hard. Showed no mercy, brother.' He drove on, then said. 'Don't want her movin' about, messin' with things. Maybe we should check?'

'We can't,' the Syrian snapped. 'We're too close. No stopping now.'

The line of traffic they had joined was sluggish, but moving. They were five minutes from the centre.

Amer pointed behind.

'I think there's a car following.'

'You're sure, brother?'

'No, not sure. But it could be. The grey one.'

Jayson stared into the rear mirror.

'I see it, brother. Four of 'em in it. So what we do?'

'Nothing.' The Syrian was determinedly calm. 'We drive on. If it's not them, it's not. If it is, perhaps they suspect, but what can they do? They'll be too afraid.'

'We're not afraid, brother. We don't fear death. Not on the Day of Glory!'

The Syrian didn't hear, had ceased listening. His eyes closed, he sat back in his seat. The switch on his lap was turned to the right, at three o'clock, his thumb, stiff and poised, an inch away.

He begun his incantations, in Arabic. Hearing him Jayson struck up his *La ilah illah Allah*. Then louder, again and again, as if to drown out the noise of the engine, of the traffic, of the car behind, closer now.

'We're 'is messenger now,' Jayson proclaimed. 'Messengers of Allah!'

The Syrian must have heard. He stopped chanting, opened his eyes.

'Messengers of Allah? You are comparing yourself to Mohamed?'

'I meant Mohamed's messengers, brother, not Allah's. No way, not Allah's.'

'I have told you, prophet is better than messenger. And you are not a prophet. You see how inexactitude can lead to error?'

The Syrian's eyes were about to close again, when Jayson said:

'Be big enough for my Ayan, right brother?'

'Ayan?' the Syrian said, in a lost voice.

'The hit, the numbers. Big enough for the baby. For Allah to make it healthy.'

'Not now, not now,' the Syrian moaned, as if interrupted in a dream, and closed his eyes.

The van jolted.

'Why do you have to brake so hard!'

'They cut in on me, didn't they? The grey car. It's them, brother, must be. Guy in the back gotta camera. Wanna photograph us from the front. An' look!'

A hand had thrust from the car's rear window holding a gadget like a TV zapper. It was pointing at them.

'They're monitoring us for radiation, is what they're doin''

'Let them monitor, let them photograph, do what they will. It is too late...' The Syrian glanced into the wing mirror and said in an abstracted voice, almost without interest. 'They have another one now, see? The green one. Perhaps there are more, but what does it matter? They don't dare stop us, because they are afraid. They see Allah's sword falling on them and they are afraid!'

His thumb flexed near the switch, simulating a pump motion.

More lights. They stopped. The grey car was still in front, the men on mobiles, staring back, talking energetically.

'We turn left, to the shopping centre,' Amer said. 'We are there, brother, almost there. I will meet Osama again, tell him what we have done…'

'I know it, brother, I know it. Oh brother, we are bound for Paradise…'

More incantations, then Jayson broke off:

'What's that?' Amidst the churning engines around them, a sound of sliding metal. 'Some bastard tryin' to open the door?'

To see into the near-side mirror, he craned forward.

'Never mind, drive!' the Syrian ordered. 'Do as I say and drive! Round the corner. We have to be closer! We have to turn the corner!'

The lights had gone green but the grey car wasn't moving, blocked them.

'Get it onto the pavement!' the Syrian screamed. 'Get round them!'

Jayson reversed, bumped the car behind, swung the wheel, measured the gap between the grey car and a traffic light post, took a run at it, mounted the pavement, tried to squeeze through. Too narrow. Jammed between the car and the post the van juddered, the engine revving. Then it stalled.

As the van came to rest the side door slid open. Safia almost fell as she touched the ground. Recovering, and holding her skirts in a curiously old-world gesture, like a crinoline, she ran. Leaping from his seat Jayson tore round the van and into the alley where Safia had disappeared, tugging at the back of his belt and shrieking 'Apostate bitch!'

From the grey car sprang two men in T-shirts and chinos. One levelled a pistol at the Syrian through the windscreen, bellowing at him not to move. The second, younger man followed Jayson. Seconds after he'd run into the alley came the sound of a shot. Then another.

The man covering Amer had stopped shouting. Talking so quietly the Syrian could scarcely have heard, in a kind of soft shoe shuffle he inched towards the van. He was within a foot of the door when, eyes closed, shrieking Allah is Great! in a high-pitched, reedy voice, the Syrian pushed his button.

31

Tony's luck was in. They'd said no to a holiday but he found himself on leave just the same: confined to his home in Norwich with a fractured ankle. It happened one night when he'd stumbled on the step of a pub, or restaurant as he'd told Jean.

'Just as well you did your ankle before they got her,' she said over breakfast the morning after the kidnap. 'Otherwise they'd have you in there day and night. Seems like the only way you get a bit of time off is to damage yourself, like those soldiers used to do in the war.'

More resolute than ever about protecting him from the office, when somebody rang later that day, rather than put them through she said he was sick, unavailable, convalescing.

'I'm a friend from work,' Chris Burnham assured her, 'and it's urgent.'

'Always is. It's the urgency that's made him ill. Always tearing about.'

'Please, Mrs Underwood, it's important.'

Tony was downstairs, his ankle on a chair, playing Scrabble with Heather. His red-haired granddaughter was staying the night. Coming up to nine now, she'd been six before he'd got to like her. A friendly, precocious girl, she was getting to like him too, though she had her complaints. One was the way he smelled. Why was it, she'd asked him that morning, that his clothes always stank of cigars, although she'd never seen him smoking?

Hearing his wife's exchange Tony shouted up:

'Who is it?'

'Chris Burnham. From the office.'

'Put him through.'

Sighing, Jean did. The phone at his side rang and Tony picked it up. A colleague from his Russian days the same age as himself, Chris had been put out to grass in Bristol around the time Tony had gone to Norwich.

'Chris! To what do I owe –'

'– there's been another bomb.'

'Jesus! Where?'

'Here. Bristol. Why I'm ringing. Thought I'd tell you first, given your involvement. Told me you were off sick so I'm ringing you at home. Keep a poor old boy up to date.'

Tony shouted up to his wife to take Heather out of the room and close the door. Looking affronted, she did. He went back to the phone:

'Chris, are you operational? Am I holding you up?'

'Not in the slightest. They've given me half an hour off after the stressful start to my day.'

'Tell me everything. In detail.'

'OK. Sit quietly, and listen. It's a long story.'

Tony settled his leg and lay back. If Chris was a rank above him it was partly because of the meticulous eyes behind the oblong glasses. Missing nothing, and with a versatile tongue in his head, with Chris everything turned into a long story.

'You heard about the van they used for Safia, right? Blue one. Turns out it had a record. Fingered it near one of those giant sales, this one in High Street Ken. Helicopter got lucky, found it was leaking radiation. Then our metropolitan friends manage to lose it because it gets itself under cover. And when it's used for the Safia job the Manchester boys send one up and lose it again. Technical malfunction they say. Amateur bastards, I say.

'Anyway there's people scudding about the skies all over the country and they pick it up in the Bristol outskirts this morning. Grey it is now, but the same vehicle, still emitting. Sounds nice, but what do you do? Funny thing, isn't it? Everyone's working their arses off on catching them before or mopping up after but no-one's given a thought to what you do if you come across them in mid-business.

'So there it is, weaving through the suburbs, cool as you like. We've got people behind it but what do they do? Jump it – and risk a dirty explosion in a residential street? Or wait and see?

'They wait because no one'll let them move a muscle. What we need is one of those 50 foot tent jobs the Yanks have dreamt up, full of foam to sort of smother the radiation. Turns out there's none in the UK – the not-invented-here syndrome – and it would take a day to fly one over. Not to speak of the reaction of the fellers in the van when we ask them to hang on while we build a marquee over their bomb.

'Meanwhile the boys clock a third person in the back. They ask permission to take the men out, from the side, so as not to hurt her, and guess what? With the memory of Jean Charles de Menezes fresh in everyone's minds there's dithering, following which permission is refused. I have views on that but I doubt you're aching to hear them.

'So on they go into Bristol. Low-profile target for them you might think, but there's been some nasty incidents. Plus it's a port, plus it's not where people expect, and best of all are the numbers. It's got this mammoth shopping centre, 300 stores and counting. So you go for it, don't you?

'It's making for the centre and the news goes up and up and the politicos – who never interfere in operational matters – realise a decision is needed. We're getting messages from our lads in the cars telling us that from a personal perspective they'd prefer to chance an assault, if the alternative is the certainty of nuclear immolation for all concerned.

'They're a minute from the shopping centre. The van stops at some lights. The girl must have worked her way free, opens the door and makes a run for it. One of the men follows, leaving the other one in the van. Our lads think that's it for them and what they're saying about the politicos I won't repeat. One of them goes after the girl and the bloke in the alley. The bloke catches up and kills her, gun to the head. Our lad picks up the bloke, bullet in the guy's thigh in the process.'

'And the other one?'

'Sitting in his van, chanting like a dervish and pumping away at his trigger. To no effect.'

'And the bomb?'

'Large, lethal and leaking furiously last I heard. The centre's been evacuated.'

'Chris, I can't tell you how grateful... I'd better let you get back.'

'No probs, I'm fine for a minute. Done my stint, the techno-freaks have taken over.'

'So what do you think happened?'

'Still working it out. The guess is the Safia woman we so carelessly mislaid was picked up and included in the party in revenge. Forcing her to do what she managed to avoid first time round. An involuntary suicide to placate the deity.'

'And the men?'

'Syrian and Caribbean. A haughty bugger and a holy idiot. The Syrian's not talking but the idiot is. Rabbiting on about how we mustn't tell his wife 'cos she's pregnant, poor darling, it might upset her.'

'Why didn't the bomb go off?'

'Faulty, probably, but we don't know. The loopy one says he was the technical man, trained in the usual places, and he's blaming it on the brothers who did the first. As if we cared. Or maybe the lady tampered with it, which would be nice to think.'

'So what's your guess? Was it her?'

'My guess is we'll never know. The contraption was unstable so they had to get the nuclear part out and blow up the detonator bit. Either way, she was a brave woman.'

'Assuming, that is,...' Tony swallowed his words. 'What else have they got about her? Is there any indication –'

'– Tony, they're paging me, some bloody drama, my tea-break's over.'

*

He put down the phone. After the relief, his next reaction was one of guilt and apprehension. Guilt because it looked like he'd got Safia wrong from the beginning. Wrong to the point where he'd mused on the phone to a colleague the night before about the possibility that the kidnapping was a set-up, that she'd been a jihadist through and through. And his fear was that sooner or later his misjudgement would be remembered, maybe surface in the media. *How Agent A Tried to Jail Muslim Heroine.*

'Grandad!' Heather tumbled into the room, Jean behind her. 'They caught them, grandad!'

'A news flash on the radio,' Jean explained. 'While you were on the phone.'

'I know. That's why they rang.'

'You could be more cheerful about it.'

'Can we go on with the game?' Heather dived to retrieve the board. 'I've thought of a word with –'

'– later.'

'Well now it's over at least you can get some rest. Come on Heather, grandad's tired. He wants to celebrate on his own.'

'I could do with a drink.'

Mechanically Jean looked at her watch.

'I know the time but I'd really like one.'

'I'll fetch a glass of wine.'

'Whisky please. And you don't have to go. Just switch on the TV, they'll be doing a special programme.'

And they were. Mobile phone shots, as usual. A van wedged against traffic lights. A dark figure lurching into the alley, drawing a gun. And in the van's passenger seat a sharp-faced man, his head down, eyes squeezed shut, mouth open in what looked like a shriek of pain. And finally paramedics carrying a stretcher, covered, from the alley.

It was all they'd got. To pad things out there were endless pictures of Safia. Safia on her way to the magistrate's court, with veiled face and frightened eyes. Safia during a break in the trial, frail and vulnerable, but alluring with her scarf and long lashes. Then speaking to the press after her release: bare-headed, confident, smiling, proud. Then her lawyer denouncing the monstrousness of the trial, followed by a newspaper headline welcoming her release: Firework Sceptics In The Dock.

'Looks like the press got it right for once,' Jean said when it was over. The glance she gave him was tight-lipped, as if there was something she could say if she chose. Then she said it all the same:

'I always thought the business about the fireworks had the ring of truth. I know it sounded fanciful, but it's the sort of low trick people like her brothers would pull. She turned out a heroine at the end all right. No two ways.'

Over dinner Heather pelted him with questions.

'It's so sad they killed her. She seemed very nice, and I like her name. Why did they arrest her, granddad, if she didn't do anything? Why did they think she murdered people? Is it because she was a Pakistan person?'

'It's complicated…When you're older…'

'Was it the police who killed her?'

'Heather, that's enough for today. Time you went to bed. Off you go…'

The girl lingered, pouting.

'I said now, Heather.'

'No need to snap,' said Jean, seeing the girl's wounded eyes.

*

Eleven fifteen. Jean was in bed, Tony downstairs with his bottle, when Chris Burnham rang again.

'Have I woken you up?'

'No.'

'Watching the news?'

'Seen it.'

'Just clocking off. Rang back 'cos I cut you off. You were asking something.'

'Was I?'

''Bout Safia.'

'Oh yes, forget it. Anything happening?'

'Not much more on the Syrian. Still staying schtum, evil bastard. Only authority he recognises is Allah, and so on. Asked him whether there's another one on the way and he says we'll find out when it happens. Got this prissy voice, like he's an elocution teacher or something. Plus a way of looking at you as if you're shit.

'The other guy's still banging on about his wife, and whether Allah will punish the child 'cos they fouled up on the job. Weird. They told him not to worry, he'd get a nice free check-up on his wife and kid by a Muslim lady doctor if he'd do them the favour of telling them everything he knows. She's getting it anyway, took her in this afternoon, though there's no suggestion she was involved. Baby's fine, apparently, so Allah can't be too upset its daddy's bomb didn't go off.'

'Has he said anything about Safia, and the first one?'

'Not to date. Claims they operated separately. Didn't know what the others planned for her, just that she was to reconnoitre. Seems to have been some sort of rivalry between them – which could account for the faulty bomb. Or not. All they knew about the Bank was when and where it was happening, so the pair of them could keep their heads down. Watched it on TV in a café, can you believe, like it was a football game.'

'So he didn't know Safia?'

'No. Just buried her tarty clothes when he was told to. Keeps telling us he didn't smell them, honest he didn't. Strange.'

'So he's got nothing on the firework story?'

'I told you, Tony, he's got nothing on the girl. Says all he knew was that his Syrian friend went ballistic when she said it was her brothers. Though nothing compared to his reaction when he found out she'd told us a Syrian was involved. Swore he'd wreak vengeance. Hence the kidnap and involuntary martyrdom. Looks like the kind of guy to do it.'

'So we'll never know whether she was in on the first bomb or not.'

'The courts have decided that, and I doubt there'll be much more to be said. Even if the evil one talks – which he won't – he'll probably know no more than the idiot, and they're not going to trust his evidence, are they?'

'Suppose not.'

'You sound disappointed. The girl's dead, martyred in a good cause. Let it go, Tony! What more is it you want?'

'And does the simpleton have any idea whether there's going to be another?'

'That's the best thing to come out so far. Says they only had enough gear for two bombs. They've had a look at the hideouts he gave us, garage in Scrubs lane and a sort of pill box, and there's no more there. So you can sleep easy. I will, I'm shagged.'

Tony too felt exhausted. Yet that night, three quarters of a bottle of whisky notwithstanding, he didn't sleep.

*

In the morning he rang Julie. Martin answered.

'She's at her surgery. Who shall I say rang?'

Tony gave his name.

'Ah yes, she told me about you. You must be feeling good this morning.'

'It's progress,' Tony said.

'Well I hope it's more than that. It's hard to contact her during the day but you can get her in the early evening. I'll tell her you called.'

Half the night gearing himself up to say it, and now a whole day's wait...

At six o' clock prompt he rang and got her.

'Tony Underwood. It's months since we talked. How have you been doing?'

'For the moment, fine.'

'Good. And Jackie?'

'Fine too.'

'Glad to hear it.'

'You're ringing about Safia, I imagine?'

'Well yes, I was. Nothing operational. I just wanted to make clear –'

'– to me it's clear already. An innocent girl has died in the foulest way imaginable. The press are saying she may have disarmed the bomb before –'

'– we don't know that. It may just not have worked. I'm not saying she didn't, just that we'll never know.'

'Well how about giving her the benefit of the doubt? If she did she saved God knows how many others. Is there anything more to be said?'

'For me there is, yes. You see the way things have turned out… I don't want to leave you with the idea I had it in for her. That I'm some sort of Islamophobe. I mean I just go where the evidence leads, and now that it looks less likely she was ever involved…'

'More than 'less likely,' I should have thought.'

'Well what I'm trying to say…'

'– Mr Underwood, I understand what you're saying and I appreciate your gesture in calling. I didn't enjoy having my judgement about the girl doubted, but my view was vindicated in the courts. Not to speak of her subsequent actions. Your feelings about her are for yourself. Personally I feel ashamed of only seeing her once or twice when she was with her uncle. I can't get it out of my mind that there's more I could have done. I don't know, something to get her out of the country, help her get on a course abroad.

'Now that it's over I suggest we simply put it to the back of our minds. I'm not going to go round telling everyone that you were wrong and I was right, and I won't be writing anything if that's what you're afraid of. People have been ringing, offering this and that, you know what it's like, but it's all too painful.'

'Well that's good of you.'

'I saw something in the press saying the Syrian's not talking. Does that mean there could be more bombs on the way?'

'It's early days, so don't quote me, but that's all garbled rubbish. According to the present state of our knowledge –'

'– you're sounding like a policeman again.'

'I'm sorry. I was going to say the Trinidadian's not a total loon and he's talking his head off. And the indications to date are, well, hopeful.'

'Thank God for that.'

'Talking about the press, I saw the pieces about you and Safia after the trial. How you nursed her into coming clean and so on. You came out of it well. As of course you should.'

It cost him something to say that.

'I did what seemed right.'

'On another subject, I'm sorry about what happened to your husband, though his career seems to be flourishing. I caught the first episode of his new investigative series on the box. Very good too. He's a great presenter. Quite the celebrity couple!'

'Celebrity is the last thing we're after.'

'A word of advice if I may – not that you'll need it. Don't let him go back to the place they killed the Muslim kid, will you? They don't forget, those people. The white guys I mean.'

'It had occurred to me that he shouldn't. At least the leaders are locked up.'

'I know. Though nine years doesn't seem much. And with remission… Seems a bit benevolent. Anyway, that's the system. Take care.'

'And you, Mr Underwood.' A gap, and she added: 'One more thing.'

'And what's that?'

'Where do you think we go from here?'

'With respect to?'

'Al Qaeda, the bombings.'

At least his opinion was being asked, though he hesitated before replying. She wouldn't want anything too downbeat…

'Well look at it this way. The bombings were revenge for Osama, because Osama's dead. They failed in New York, then Bristol, and – don't quote me – there's no evidence there's another cell here. Then there's the independent evidence that, gobally, Al Qaeda's on the wane.'

'So the Bank could be a last throw?'

'Let's hope so.'

'But do you think so?'

Another hesitation, then:

'I think I do.'

'Good to hear it.'

And that was all. A bit chilly, but never mind. At least he'd called, and it was worth the cringe. And with luck his retirement wouldn't be troubled by a programme in her husband's series about a blundering MI5 man hounding an innocent Muslim girl to a tragic death.

The way he saw it they'd come out in a draw. If Julie had had her way Safia would never have been properly questioned, let alone tried. And if he was an agnostic on the girl it was because that was his nature, and his job. Just as hers was the business of healing and compassion. And it wasn't sexism, he assured himself. Just the way the world worked.

32

It was Mrs Marusak's birthday. To celebrate, and toast the revival in their fortunes, Sergei was treating her to dinner at a restaurant in the City. A swanky joint complete with dark green awning, gold lettering and a top-hatted porter, the place had just reopened. Getting out of the taxi, before entering he took her arm, turned and threw a hand round the street.

'Beautiful, no?'

The area, close to the Bank, had suffered badly, but the sandblasting, pressure-washing and acid treatment had done their work. It wasn't only the pristine buildings: everything in the street looked uncannily new. To remove all trace of contamination roads had been resurfaced, pavements dug up and replaced, trees re-planted.

The flow of people coming back to the City was accelerating and Sergei and his lady had been amongst the first. There'd been no problem about visas: they'd come through with unusual speed. Nor had Sergei had any difficulty in getting back into his office. The building where it was located, a thirty-six floor steel and glass affair, had been badly hit, though one of the first to be pronounced clean.

For the owners – a Russian bank – it was a piece of luck, the kind of luck that was not entirely due to chance. Amongst the foreign firms allowed in to expedite the great clean-up was a Ukrainian company whose decontamination techniques had been developed, it claimed, during the Chernobyl disaster. Under pressure to get the job done fast, the authorities had overlooked the fact that Chernobyl had happened in 1986, a decade before the firm was established.

Its owner was Anatoli Stepanko, Mrs Marusak's old flame. The days of his girl-exporting scam were well behind him. His industrial cleaning business had prospered mightily, in tandem with his political career. By another non-coincidence, in which Mrs Marusak had played a hand, it was Anatoli who'd got the contract for sanitising the building where Sergei worked.

'I just stopped being jealous of him,' Sergei joked when the company issued the owners with a certificate of decontamination a good six months before other buildings in the area. The benefits to the pair were shared equally between them: Sergei earned a total of £250,000 in backhanders – £200,000 for his help securing the contract, plus £50,000 for expediting the certificate – and Mrs Marusak the renewed respect of her consort.

*

That evening he had a joke for everything. His line for the wine waiter over the two bottles – 'is not for me – is my wife who is drunkard'– was an old one, though it got him the usual slap on the hand. Then there was his crack about the cost of the handbag he'd given her for her birthday. *Soomka* meaning handbag in Russian, and *sooma* sum, the pun was not too abstruse.

Mrs Marusak laughed, briefly, as she always did at his jokes about her bags. Tonight was the first outing for the £2,400 Bottega Veneta drawstring leather number. Fit for a queen of business, as Sergei put it, in homage to her cleaning coup.

'Just watch what you do with the old one. Don't throw it away with stuff in it, make sure you clear out every scrap. It's not just the police. All sorts of people go through dustbins nowadays for information, like hungry wolves. Journalists, the tax people... And your bag *is* a dustbin.'

Again she slapped his hand, cheeky fellow.

'Don't worry, I did it this afternoon, my pigeon. Emptied it right out.'

It was as well she had. Sergei was right, you couldn't be too careful. The things she'd found in that bag. Screwed-up receipts for cash paid into banks in Wimbledon, Barnes, Lewisham. Cards advertising the one-room Camden Town beauty course, now replaced by something grander. Addresses for private VD clinics in the City, phone numbers for girls who'd come and gone over time, notes and letters from God knew whom that she'd carried about from bag to bag. Names she scarcely remembered, people she'd known only briefly and would never see again, from Moscow, the Donbass, London – into the shredder with them all.

Rummaging on, she'd felt something hard and fished it out: a bottle of nail varnish, the colour a deep purple, leaking. And what a mess it had made. A ten pound note, useless, a bill of some sort, illegible. And a postcard, all creased up and stained. Puzzled, she turned it over. Ah yes, the card she'd pinched from Safia's bag while she'd been in the shower, hoping it would have her address. But it wasn't to her, she saw now, it was from her: a picture of the Tower of London, no stamp, unposted.

She straightened it, read what remained of the small, neat hand:

Dear Uncle Ishaq, I am in London for the day. I can't say why – it is a mystery! I hope we –

And that was all. A great purple stain covered the rest. Another couple of lines were half visible through the blot, and she strained to read them before giving up.

What did she care about Uncle Ishaq? Classy-looking girl though, you couldn't deny, would have done well in Wimbledon or Barnes. Not much use to her now. With a shadow of regret she fed the card, sideways, into the machine. It wouldn't go through. Irritated, she turned it lengthways, forced it between the shredder's teeth and watched them chew it up.